HOLDING
ON TO
Forever

SIOBHAN DAVIS

S.B. ALEXANDER

NOTE FROM THE AUTHORS

1

ADAM

I tear my helmet off my head, shoving my fingers through my thick brown hair as hard as I can. I can't seem to throw the damn football to save my life.

Fuck!

I start a silent countdown, waiting for Coach Parker to scream his head off. Since the season began a week ago, the team hasn't been in sync. Hell, I'm not in sync. It seems my arm died a quick death during the off season.

Carter, Cypress University's best running back, jogs up to me. "We'll get in the groove before Saturday. We always do, hoss."

I chuckle at his nickname. He calls just about all the guys hoss. I'd learned when Mom, my sister, Phoebe, and I moved from New Jersey to South Carolina four years ago that hoss had a few different meanings. But here in the South, hoss is interchangeable with dude, at least from Carter's mouth.

Despite his Southern slang, the loss last weekend to Southern Coast University was gut-wrenching. I hate starting off the season losing to a team who has never won a game against Cypress University.

After blowing his whistle, Coach Parker shouts, "Get your asses off the field. Grab some water, and find a seat on the bench."

Yep, he's pissed. Hell, I am too. I don't know why we're playing like we don't know the game.

Some of us jog over to the sideline while others take their time, wiping the sweat off their faces.

Carter is still at my side cussing about coach under his breath. "He's been riding us hard since July when we started practicing."

I lift a brow at the blond surfer-looking dude. "This is your second year on the team. You know how he is."

"Sure," he says, biting his lip. "But he's especially ornery lately."

I clap him on the back. "Once we get a win under our belts, coach will take a breath."

Carter rolls his blue eyes, tucks his helmet underneath his arm, and saunters toward the team. As he does, he casually says over his shoulder, "You hanging around for the frat party this weekend?"

I shrug, trotting to the water cooler. I hardly do parties. They're mostly on weekends when I trek the thirty miles home to hang with Phoebe while Mom works double shifts. I hate Mom has to bust her ass while I play football and study. But she insisted, ordering me not to get a job.

"NFL is your future, Adam," she'd said. "I don't want to ruin that for you."

Neither do I, and only because the money will be great. Maybe, one day, I can buy Mom a house and have enough money where she doesn't have to worry about bills.

She was relieved when Cypress University offered me a full scholarship. We both celebrated the day I received the offer letter.

Despite that, I'm the only man in the family, and I should contribute. But since moving from New Jersey, our lives have been pretty okay. Mom's job at the hotel has kept food on the table and the bills paid. Still, if it ever comes down to football or my family, I'll choose my family in a heartbeat.

Carter hands me a cup of water before pouring his own. Downing the cool liquid, I use my jersey to wipe my face.

The hot afternoon sun is brutal to practice in, but the weather is always warm to hot in the South, depending on the time of year. It only starts to cool down in late October, and even then, it doesn't get that cold, not like the brutal winters of New Jersey.

At times, I miss living there only because Phoebe and I loved to play in the snow. We had to be careful though. The cold weather doesn't suit my sister with her cystic fibrosis, which is one reason we moved. Phoebe has less of a chance of getting sick here although the Southern climate isn't always a guarantee. We also made the move because the cost of living is cheaper in the South.

Carter and I find a seat on the bench when some chick in the stands calls his name. Odd that she's even in the stadium since our practices are closed.

Carter blows a kiss to the pretty brunette. "She can fuck like you wouldn't believe," he says in a low voice, smirking.

Whenever I'm around Carter, I roll my eyes repeatedly. I swear he has a different chick in his bed every night. I don't check out dudes, but one thing I'll say about my teammate is he's built to play football —broad in the chest, big in the arms, and the man can run like the wind on a stormy day. Aside from that, Phoebe thinks Carter is hot. So, I guess that's why he gets the chicks.

Soon enough, a security guard emerges to escort the brunette out of the stadium. She gives Carter one last wave.

We both chuckle at the sight until sounds of arguing tickle my eardrums. I whip my head around to investigate. Coach is in a heated discussion with Tom Price, one of our offensive line coaches. The man knows his football, and usually coach lets him do what he sees fit with the offensive line. For a moment, I wonder if their argument has anything to do with my poor performance today. Coach Price ran us through drills hard, and it isn't his fault I sucked.

I strain to hear what they're talking about, but out of the corner of my eye, I spot Sam running toward me like he's being chased by one of his enemies in *Call of Duty.*

What the fuck is my roomie doing here? Sam Spencer has never shown up to any of my football practices. I don't expect him to either for a couple of reasons. I would have to get approval, which Coach Parker doesn't usually consent to, and Sam isn't interested in football all that much. He's skinny, lanky, and a nerd who barely knows the first thing about sports. Everything he knows about football I taught him, and on occasion he attends a home game, when he isn't behind his computer.

Coach Parker storms away from Coach Price, narrowing his hazel eyes and glaring at me.

As I suspect, their tension was about me. But Coach Parker will have to wait to chew my ass out as my gaze is glued to Sam, my trepidation mounting as he nears. He's huffing and puffing as he practically skids to a halt on the track that edges the perimeter of the field. His blue eyes radiate with fear, and sweat drips down his temples. He lets out a shuddering breath. "Your mom called me." He gulps down more air.

My jaw hits the track I'm standing on. "What happened?" Mom would only call Sam in an emergency. I'd given her his number just in case she couldn't get ahold of me. She knows my phone is in my locker during practice and games.

"Phoebe was rushed to the children's hospital in town," Sam pants. "The guard let me double-park. Come on."

Motherfucker.

Panic grips me in my chest, and I feel like I'm having a heart attack.

"Go," Coach Parker says, having overheard the conversation. "We'll talk later."

I thrust my helmet at Carter and start jogging, not caring that I'm wearing shoulder pads and stink like a skunk has just sprayed me at close range.

Phoebe is the world to me, and I worry every fucking day about her. Hell, there are nights I can't sleep wondering how she's doing, and I hate that I'm stuck in my dorm room and unable to check on her.

At the age of four, she was diagnosed with cystic fibrosis, a disorder that damages several organs but mainly the lungs. Mom had noticed a salty taste to Phoebe whenever she kissed her. Then she developed a persistent cough that she couldn't shake. Multiple tests later, the doctor told Mom the bad news, and we've been living with it ever since, both of us trying to do everything we can to ensure she's well taken care of.

Sam is panting behind me as I all but sprint down the track toward the sports complex. Since Phoebe is at the children's hospital, which isn't that far from Cypress University, I briefly debate whether to run through the streets.

But a stitch grips my side before dizziness hits me like a damn brick.

Sam runs past me to his cherry-red Volkswagen bug.

Bending over, with my hands on my knees, I pray that the pain and sudden bout of dizziness subside.

"You're dehydrated," Sam suggests. "I got a bottle of water in the car."

I do my best to drag my butt inside, and it's challenging, because my body is way too big for the small interior.

It doesn't help you're wearing your shoulder pads, dude.

Sam starts the engine. "Don't you dare say a damn word about my car." His voice is light, but there's steel underneath it.

Usually, I rib him about his choice in cars, but he didn't get a say. When his sister trekked off to college on the West Coast, her cute little bug was handed down to Sam. Phoebe adores it, and that says it all.

It takes me a minute, but I manage to get my shoulder pads off. Once I do, I let out a breath, and the sharp pain in my side eases a little.

"Water bottle is in the back," Sam confirms, expertly navigating out of the parking lot like he's emerging from a race car pit on a NASCAR track.

I grab the bottle and guzzle it down.

As Sam flies through the city, dodging red lights, I ask, "Did my mom say anything else?"

He hands me his phone. "No. Call her."

I tap on her name, and within seconds, her voice filters through the phone. "Sam, did you find Adam?"

"It's me, Mom."

She emits a relieved sigh. "Are you on your way?"

Sam guns the gas before the yellow light turns red and keeps his foot pressed down on the pedal as he navigates one more light and two turns before the hospital comes into view.

"We're almost there, Mom."

"I'll meet you in the emergency room lobby," she says before she ends the call.

Less than five minutes later, Sam screeches to a stop in front of the emergency room entrance. Tossing his phone into the cup holder, I jump out of the car, almost stumbling.

"I'll meet you inside," he shouts before peeling away to park.

I sprint through the automatic doors of the hospital, my cleats clicking and clacking as I go. Cold air-conditioned air sweeps over me, and I inwardly moan at how great it feels on my heated skin as I search the large waiting room.

My gaze skims over a screaming baby being cradled in a woman's arms, a man pacing with a look of abject fear on his face, and various other people who are hanging around. Some are sitting, some are dozing, and others are engaged in whispered conversations, while some stare blankly at the TV, but I don't see my mom yet.

Fuck.

My pulse is all over the place. I should've kept Sam's phone.

When I run up to the information desk, I collide with a patient in a wheelchair, who seems to have come out of nowhere. I'm propelled forward as my face lands in her reddish-blonde hair.

The scent of coconuts invades my nostrils, and I inhale deeply. It takes me a second to right myself. "Sorry." I apologize to the man in tan scrubs pushing her.

The woman hangs her head, and her long, wavy hair falls around her face.

The assistant, who looks to be in his late twenties, narrows his dark eyes. "Watch where you're going."

"I'm very sorry, Miss. I didn't see you until it was too late," I say, deliberately ignoring the asshole and apologizing to the woman directly. She tilts her chin up, and our gazes meet.

I suck in a gasp, instantly forgetting how to breathe.

She's beautiful with these big blue eyes, pale skin, full lips, and a cute heart-shaped face. She's around my age, if I had to guess, and there's an aura of haunted vulnerability surrounding her that makes me want to wrap my arms around her and protect her.

I open my mouth to say something, but Mom calls my name. "Adam!" Her voice is frantic, and the girl is instantly forgotten as I remember why I'm here.

I rush over to her near a door that leads into the hub of the emergency room. "What happened? Where's Phoebe? Is she okay?"

Tears slide down Mom's cheeks. I brush strands of her brown hair from her face then hug her, my heart slamming against my ribs.

We don't talk for a long minute as she sobs into my chest, and I run my hand up and down her back in a soothing gesture as I try to get a handle on my fear.

I do everything I can not to lose my shit. We both know CF is a disease that gets worse with age, and as Phoebe grows into a teenager, her lung function is going to decline. But with routine care, there's hope she can live a long time.

Mom pulls away, placing a delicate hand on my cheek. "Phoebe's regular doctor is on vacation. Doctor Harmon is filling in for him. He's with her now. He thinks Phoebe has pneumonia."

I want to punch the white sterile wall until my knuckles bleed. It's a familiar sentiment. Every time we have a setback, frustration builds inside me until it feels like I'm going to explode. I hate my sister has to suffer like this. It's so unfair, and I curse genetics.

I want to do something to cure my sister, but I feel helpless, like I always have, and it makes me want to scream and tear through walls, anything to release the torment clawing at my insides.

Mom takes my hand, squeezing it for reassurance, and we walk through a set of double doors with *hospital personnel only* stenciled on the front.

Once inside, phones ring, nurses hurry around the hallways, and machines beep from the glass-encased rooms that patients are in.

Mom cranes her neck up at me as she stops at a water fountain. "There's something I need to tell you." Worry lines furrow her brow, and I instantly know I'm not going to like it.

A white-haired man wearing blue scrubs beneath a white lab coat emerges from a room, interrupting us before Mom can tell me her news. "Mrs. Miller." His name badge confirms he's Doctor Harmon, and he glances at me briefly before focusing on Mom. "We've sent Phoebe's blood down for analysis, and we've hooked her up to a breathing machine. We're going to get a chest X-ray, but I suspect she has pneumonia as we discussed earlier."

Pneumonia is a condition that is practically the norm for people with CF, and this isn't the first time she's succumbed.

"You mentioned she was playing outside with her friends when she collapsed?" he asks, and Mom nods. "How's her diet? Has she been keeping up with her vitamins and eating healthy? Also, her records indicate that she has a vest to clear her airways. Has she been doing her therapy?"

Phoebe hates to use her vest, a device that is essential in helping her expel all her built up mucus, and Mom regularly battles her over it.

Mom shakes her head. "It hasn't been working."

I rear back. "Since when?"

Doctor Harmon also startles. "The vest therapy is critical in her condition. I'm sure Doctor Johnson has told you." His tone permits no argument.

Mom hangs her head, talking quietly. "I know. We just don't have the money to buy another one." Embarrassment threads through her words.

I swallow thickly. Money has been a constant source of contention since my asshole old man left us for another woman when I was ten.

I clench my fists painfully, wishing the fucker were here so I could throttle him. He'd been mandated by the courts to pay child support that included extra for Phoebe's medical care. But after two payments, the asshole disappeared. Mom reached out to her lawyer, but lawyers want money she doesn't have. His advice was to hire a PI. Again, money was an issue. So, as a result, Mom was left to work two and three jobs to keep food on the table and the rent paid.

But life became much easier when we moved to South Carolina and she found a good job at a hotel.

However, money is an *ongoing* issue.

The price tag for one of those vests is at least twenty grand.

"Will your medical insurance pay for one?" I ask Mom. We're lucky she has medical insurance through her job.

She pins me with a cautionary look, urging me to drop it as she turns to the doctor. "Can we go in to see her?"

Doctor Harmon nods once. "I'll be back later to check on her. I'll have a nurse come in and talk to you about how you can get the vest repaired or at least looked at."

Mom starts for Phoebe's room when I catch her arm. "Wait. When were you going to tell me about the vest? And is that what you had to tell me before Doctor Harmon came out of Phoebe's room?"

She purses her lips into a thin line. "I'm trying to get the money, and I didn't want to worry you."

My muscles tense. "She needs that therapy. When was her last session?"

She puffs out her cheeks. "She used the vest three days ago. Since then, I've been doing it manually."

"Doesn't your insurance cover that?"

She stares at me with sad brown eyes that remind me so much of Phoebe when she's bidding me goodbye on weekends. They are so alike with brown hair and eyes and a cute button nose. Mom told me once the only attribute I inherited from her was my brown hair. My green eyes, strong jaw, and somewhat patrician nose, I, unfortunately, inherited from my asshole Dad's side.

Whatever.

I know one thing I'll never inherit from him, and that's his asshole cheating ways. I would never leave my family behind to fend for themselves. Especially if one of my kids was so sick.

She sighs heavily, her shoulders slumping in defeat. "I lost my job. That's what I was about to tell you."

A buzzing noise starts in my ears as I angle my head. "Lost your job?" I repeat her words in a bit of a horrified daze. "Why?"

Suddenly, the past is worming its way into my psyche, and I'm remembering the dark days when Mom didn't have a job. When she cried night after night trying to figure out how we were going to survive. How she was going to pay for Phoebe's medical expenses, rent, a car payment, food, and utilities.

Fuck.

We'd been forced to move out of our two-story middle-class house when my old man took off. We'd learned to survive on bread and butter and cans of soup, which was the only thing Mom could afford after she'd spent her entire savings on medical bills and trips to the hospital with Phoebe.

Mom's only sister couldn't help us, and most of her so-called friends gradually abandoned us. Aunt Irene has her own money issues, feeding the five kids she has as a single mom, but she provides moral support to Mom in many different ways.

Mom's soft voice cuts through the buzzing in my ears. "The hotel is closing down. So, they've started letting people go. I'm looking, but every hotel I've contacted, their administrative staff is full." She grips my arm. "Adam, not a word about this to Phoebe." I nod, and she drops my arm before disappearing into my sister's hospital room.

I don't follow her. I can't. My mind is a mess ,and I need to pull myself together before I go in there. *How the fuck are we going to survive this time? Or rather, how are Mom and Phoebe going to live?*

My dorm room is way too small for them to move in, and I don't have a job.

Mom pokes out her head. "Phoebe is asking for you."

I shake off the impending doom, which is going to be a fucking disaster if we can't support Phoebe's medical expenses. Right now, I need to see my sister.

I plaster on a smile and walk in.

Her brown eyes appear tired, and despite the contraption over her nose and mouth, she smiles when she sees me.

I pony up to one side of the bed while Mom is on the other. "Hey, love bug." I grasp her cold hand.

With her free one, she takes off the mask. "How's football? Find any girlfriends yet?"

I grin. "My only girl is you."

She rolls her eyes. "You need to have some fun, Adam."

Mom smiles. "He'll find a girl one day."

I lock eyes with Mom. "I only need you two in my life."

I date, but it's rare because I don't have time for girls. I'm also not like Carter who fucks every girl he meets. That's not me. The last steady girl I had was back in high school, and even then, I hadn't fallen in love. I liked Deb a lot, but she and I agreed our relationship would end when we went off to college, and I haven't regretted the decision.

She wanted to be free to experience college life and date without any ties. I didn't blame her, and I wanted the same too although football, family, and college have taken up all my time since I started last year.

Sam comes in, smiling at Phoebe. "Hey, girl. What's shakin'?"

Phoebe giggles, and my heart blooms. I love hearing her laugh, and in this moment, I know I'll do whatever it takes to make sure we have the money to support her treatments, medical equipment, and everything else we need to keep her healthy.

2

EMILY

Holding my shoes in one hand, I slowly turn my key in the lock and tiptoe into our house in my bare feet. All the lights are out, as I'd expect at this hour of night, but I've no idea if my parents are sleeping or still out. It's not unusual for Mom to work into the early hours of the morning, and Dad spends a lot of time socializing with his friends or watching game tapes during football season since he's head coach of the Cypress Bulldogs.

So, I'm usually home alone most nights.

It's the only way I can tolerate the fact I'm a college sophomore and still living with the rents.

Not that I had any choice.

When I left rehab, Mom made it very clear I was staying home so she could ensure I wouldn't embarrass her again.

I offer up silent thanks to HIPAA for deeming it unlawful for the hospital to call my parents without my consent. Otherwise, there'd have been hell to pay.

After what happened today, I'm not taking any chances. I creep up the stairs very slowly, and very quietly, like a sneaky thief prowling the hallways while everyone sleeps blissfully unaware. Light spills out from under Dad's bedroom, and my breath stutters in my chest when the floorboards creak as I move past his door.

"Is that you, princess?" he calls out, and I silently cuss. His door swings open before I've decided how to play it.

His brow puckers as he takes in the state of me.

And I know how bad it looks.

My strawberry-blonde hair hangs in limp, stringy waves down my back. My eyes are red-rimmed and bloodshot, and my pale skin is even paler than usual. My lips are cracked, and I smell like something dredged from the bottom of a cesspit. My clothes are creased, and dried vomit is visible on my top.

After the unexpected seizure, I puked all over myself, but there wasn't time to do anything about it because some do-gooder had seen me convulsing on the pavement and called an ambulance.

I brace myself for a lecture, preparing a slew of believable lies, hating that I'm back here again.

"What happened?" Dad asks. The fine lines at the corners of his eyes and around his mouth appear more noticeable as worry transforms his features, but I'm not sure if he's worried about me or his precious football team.

"I got food poisoning," I lie. "From this place downtown I went to for lunch. Scarlett brought me back to her dorm, and I passed out. Didn't realize it was late until I woke a while ago. Sorry if I worried you."

He peers deep into my eyes, and I silently pray for forgiveness. It's tempting to dismiss it, because what's one more lie when I've told an ocean full of lies in my nineteen years on this planet. Except, I think Dad genuinely cares, and I hate disappointing him. Hate proving my mother right.

Which is why they can't know I'm using again.

I won't give that bitch the satisfaction of throwing me out on my ass.

I hold my father's gaze confidently even though I've just blatantly lied to his face.

"Is that what really happened?"

"Yes, Daddy. I swear it's the truth." The devil on my shoulder chuckles gleefully. There's no angel to offer a balance because—if guardian angels exist—mine has long since given up on my pathetic ass and left me to my demons.

He cups my cheek. "You know I love you, princess, and you can tell me anything. I will never judge."

I gulp over the lump clogging my throat. "I know, Daddy," I whisper as a heavy weight presses down on my chest.

"I failed you once before and I won't do that again." He peers deep into my eyes, and I keep my mask in place, because I know what he's doing, and I can't go there. "So, if there's anything I need to know now is a great time to tell me."

"There isn't anything to tell," I lie, plastering a fake smile on my face. "Things are good. I'm working hard, and my grades are steady, and I have Scarlett, and we hang out with a great crowd on the weekends. Life is great." I'm smiling so wide I fear I'll end up with lockjaw.

"All I want is to see you happy." He kisses the top of my grungy head, and I inwardly cringe. I'm betting even my hair smells like puke. It's like I bathed in that shit. "But I'll settle for seeing you clean and healthy." His words are light, infused with humor, but concern is still there in the background.

I think it always will be.

After discovering me unconscious in the front yard during senior year of high school, lying in a pool of my own vomit, with a cold sheen of sweat on my brow, my father will never stop worrying about me. I know I almost gave him a coronary that night. My mother too. But for very different reasons.

"Grab a quick shower and then get into bed before your mother comes home."

"She's still out?" I shuck out of his embrace, glancing up at him.

His lips purse. "Working. Apparently." His tone is clipped, and I can tell he believes it about as much as I do.

My face drops, but I don't say anything, because what's there to say? My parent's marriage is a complete sham but we're the only three people who know the truth. Mom's high-powered job as president of Cypress University means appearances matter almost as much as her qualification for the role, so, on the outside, they look like the perfect couple, we look like the perfect family, but it's all lies.

It's no wonder I've turned out to be such a competent liar.

It's all I've ever known.

After I grab a quick shower, taking extra time washing my hair and brushing my teeth, I climb into bed with a loud yawn. My heart soars when I spot the glass of water and pills on my bedside table. Dad must have put them there while I was showering. At least one of my parents has made an effort to change their neglectful ways since my overdose, but it still doesn't eradicate the giant, gaping hole in my chest.

* * *

"How are you feeling today?" Scarlett whispers when we meet for coffee on campus the following morning.

"Like death warmed over," I truthfully admit. "At least, I slept. That's something." I have a ton of sleep issues, so getting five hours of uninterrupted sleep is heavenly. Not that it helps me feel any more energetic this morning.

Weekdays are hard, and it's becoming increasingly challenging to stay away from Molly during the week. I try to focus on my studies and my tutoring, Monday to Friday, and let loose on the weekends, but I've been depressed a lot these past few weeks, and the temptation is strong.

I only broke my self-made rules yesterday because Weston fucking Blakely drove me to despair.

"It's not like you to get high mid-week," Scarlett admits in a hushed tone, her green eyes appraising "What happened? You weren't very coherent when I collected you from the hospital."

"Weston was harassing me again, and I just needed to get away from campus and him. He has photographic evidence of me snorting coke from the last frat party, and he's threatening to send it to my parents."

"Fuck." Scarlett's eyes pop wide.

"I know. I freaked out and stormed off campus, stopping at Randaddy's for a drink, and I ended up buying some shit off a random dude. Worst mistake ever. I started convulsing almost straightaway, and the bouncer tossed me out onto the sidewalk. Some good Samaritan called an ambulance."

"Shit, Em." Scarlett rubs the spot between her brows. "You should've called me to go with. Then maybe it wouldn't have happened."

"I just wanted to be alone." I shrug, sipping on my soy latte. "To figure out what to do about that blackmailing bastard."

"We should hire a hitman," she jokes.

At least, I *think* it's a joke.

I snort. "Don't tempt me."

"That jerk isn't worth spending a life behind bars. We'll figure out a way to get him off your back." She punches out a message on her phone, speaking without looking up. "We need to find a reliable new supplier."

"Tell me about it." Our usual supplier, Loco, was arrested last month, and my supply is nonexistent at this point.

On a campus of this size, there are plenty of dealers, but you can't be sure what you're buying. Case in point—look what happened to me yesterday. I also need to find someone trustworthy who won't stab me in the back by reporting me to my mother. I can't take the risk of my parents discovering I fell off the wagon, because my miserable life definitely won't be worth living if they find out.

"Zach said he was chatting to a new guy. Ray something. He's a seriously legit operator with a network of dealers under his control. He's trying to hook us up with someone local who should be able to get us anything we want, so hopefully that'll be a runner."

"I hope he fixes it soon, because I never want to experience what I experienced yesterday." I shudder as the memory invades my mind.

My heart had been punching my ribs so hard and fast before I started seizing I legit thought I was dying at one point.

I'd like to say it scared me enough to make me stop.

But it didn't, and it hasn't.

Or maybe, it's just I place such little value on my life that the thought of it ending doesn't worry me in the way it should.

I know when I actively checked out of life, and it hasn't gotten any easier since.

"Either way, we'll head to the frat party Saturday night," Scarlett says, exiting the coffee shop with me hot on her heels. "We should at least be able to score some weed on the down low."

Except weed just doesn't cut it anymore. Last year, when I first relapsed, weed was my drug of choice, and it was a step up from the pills I was hooked on during high school. But it no longer satisfies my cravings. Not now I've experienced the euphoric high that ecstasy, a.k.a. Molly, supplies. When I truly want to get out of my head, and forget who I am, nothing beats it.

"It's not my first choice, but beggars can't be choosers," I admit, as we walk toward the main part of campus.

"Zach will fix us up with a new supplier." She drags her nails through her short, blonde pixie cut. "And if he's slacking, maybe a little threesome will incentivize him to try harder."

Scarlett and I are so alike in many ways but completely different in other regards. Like her casual reference to the wild monkey sex we all tend to indulge in when we're high. I love it in the moment, but the next day, I wallow in a pit of self-loathing, wishing I could turn back the clock and rewrite the scene.

"I'm making no promises," I say in between drinking the dregs of my latte.

She winks playfully. "Famous last words."

* * *

I MANAGE TO MAKE IT THROUGH THE DAY, BUT I'VE A BANGING

headache by the time my last class ends, and I'm grateful I don't have any tutoring sessions this evening so I can go home and crawl into bed.

"You look like shit," a voice I hate says, as I exit the auditorium into the hallway. My body immediately reverts to alert mode as Weston pushes off the wall with a smirk.

"What the hell are you doing here?" I hiss, casting troubled eyes around me as my fellow classmates trickle into the hallway. They usually ignore me, which suits me fine, but, of course, today, they are all up in my business, thanks to the asshole presently blocking my path.

Weston is a notorious player, and as president of the largest frat house, very well known on campus. With his six-feet-one-inch frame, jet-black hair, smoldering brown eyes, and ripped body, he attracts attention for all the wrong reasons.

He may look like sex on a stick, but he's an arrogant, obnoxious asshole who treats women like shit and thinks nothing of it.

Our parents are super close, and they've spent years trying to force us together, but Weston displayed zero interest in me, and that's exactly how I liked it. However, lately, he seems to have changed his mind and he's pursued me relentlessly.

His feelings may have altered, but mine haven't.

I want nothing to do with the conceited pig.

But I fear I've just lost my right to choose.

"Now, now, sweetheart," he says, sneering as he winds his hand around the nape of my neck and jerks me in flush against his body. "That's no way to treat your new boyfriend." His warm breath fans over my face, turning my stomach.

"Get fucked, Weston." I shove at him. "I'm not dating you."

A devilish glint appears in his eyes, and I immediately recognize my mistake. I've just played right into his hand although I'm not fully up to speed yet.

He shrugs, smiling. "Girlfriend. Fuck buddy. I don't care what label you put on it once you understand you're mine."

I'm struggling to release myself from his embrace when he tightens his grip on my neck, digging his nails into my hip as he prods my stomach with his obvious erection. Nausea churns in my gut, and it'd serve him right if I puked on him.

"Fighting me gets me horny," he admits, nipping my earlobe. "So, I could do this all day, but we have an audience to please. Act convincing, or I'll run straight to Carole's office and inform her that her precious daughter has turned back to her druggy slut ways. I'm pretty sure I overheard my mother telling my father she'll kick you out of the house and college if you start using again."

"I fucking hate you," I hiss as I force a smile on my face. He takes my book bag, slinging it over his shoulder as he grabs hold of my hand and smashes his lips against mine. It's more of an assault than a kiss, but I don't protest, because if I make a scene, it could get back to my mother.

"You can do better," he whispers against my mouth before probing the seam of my lips with his tongue. Reluctantly, I open for him, trying not to gag when his tongue invades all corners of my mouth.

"Good girl," he says when we break apart a minute later, and I want to tell his patronizing ass to fuck off, but I keep the fake smile on my face as I make my way outside the building with him.

We walk in silence toward the parking lot, and he keeps a firm grip on my hand. The entire time, I'm grappling for something I can use to halt this, but it's futile. He's got me in a bind, and I can't see any way out. Being beholden to someone like Weston Blakely is akin to swimming in a sea full of hangry sharks, blindfolded and naked, with blood smeared along my bare flesh.

I might as well just tell him to kill me now.

But a sliver of self-preservation still lingers in my tissues, and that stubbornness means I'll suffer through whatever humiliation he has lined up, until I find a way to extricate myself from this mess.

He roughly shoves me into the back seat of his blacked-out SUV, climbing in behind me. He locks the doors and unzips his pants while I try not to puke. Grabbing my neck, he pulls my face down to his bare cock. "Suck me off, bitch, and make it good, or I'll fuck your cunt instead."

I don't get the chance to reply as he rams his big cock into my mouth, shoving it all the way to the back of my throat. Tears spill out of my eyes, and I feel sick to the pit of my stomach as I start sucking him, but I cling to my resolve, more determined than ever to find a way to remove Weston Blakely from my life without everything blowing up in my face.

3

ADAM

On Friday night, I'm pacing outside a car repair shop in a seedy part of North Charleston, attempting to calm my nerves. The area has a reputation for drugs and violence. I guess the drug trade hasn't changed much. Donnie, my old supplier in New Jersey, ran his operation out of a car repair shop too. Only Donnie had a side business of stealing expensive cars of the rich and famous. That wasn't my gig. I'd been too young to drive for him anyway.

I check my watch.

Ray Diaz is late.

I'm half-tempted to call Donnie to make sure he gave me the correct address when headlights brighten the narrow alleyway.

The SUV is crawling toward me, and my nerves are jacked. I shouldn't be doing this. I should find a decent part-time job to pay for my sister's medical expenses, but I see no other way. We have to get her vest fixed or buy a new one. Selling drugs is the only way to make some quick cash. Besides, I'm good at it. I sold dope and pills for years, and I'd never been arrested. I always had my pulse on the neighborhoods, and I knew where cops loitered at night.

You've been out too long. Things might have changed, and you're in a new state.

I push my inner thoughts aside. None of that matters. I'm always alert. I always know what's around me, and as Mom tells me, I'm perceptive as hell. I have to be. Taking care of Mom and Phoebe—especially Phoebe—I have to be alert to her sounds, her breathing, and her emotions.

Thinking of my sister sends pain slicing through my chest. I can't let anything happen to her. She spent two days in the hospital, where the doctor pumped her with antibiotics, until she started feeling better.

The SUV pulls to a stop, and a short stocky guy gets out of the front passenger seat brandishing a gun. The driver, a taller man than his compadre, follows.

I lift my hands as if a cop is arresting me. "I'm unarmed."

Aiming the gun at my head, he stalks toward me. His dark eyes are hard, his mission resolute. "Move and you're dead." His deep voice is lethal.

An all too familiar wave washes over me, and I'm tempted to back out of this stupid idea to sell drugs and run before he pulls the trigger. I'm not any good dead to Mom and Phoebe. But I know his words are just a scare tactic while he frisks me.

I stand statue-still while the second dude, sporting a thin beard and no mustache, pats my sides, my lower back, down my legs, and straight down to my ankles. He sticks one finger in the air. "All clear."

The stocky dude lowers his gun, and, inwardly, I grin. The goon didn't find the blade in my boot. I'm not about to use it though. But I don't walk into situations like these unarmed. Still, I make a mental note of the type of men I'm dealing with.

A tall man climbs out of the back seat. He's sporting baggy jeans and a New York Yankees ball cap, and the gold bling around his neck probably weighs ten pounds as it glints off the dim light on the side of the car repair shop.

It's all I can do not to roll my eyes. Donnie doesn't show off like this dude. Donnie's motto is blend in with the crowd. Standing out only draws attention.

"You must be Wrangler. I'm Ray Diaz." Ray struts over to the metal garage door. "You understand I have to be careful." He punches a code in on the keypad tacked to the frame of the door. Within a second, it opens.

I tuck my hands in my jean pockets. "I'm well aware of the industry."

A deep chuckle erupts from Ray. "I heard. Donnie told me you were a cocky punk too."

It's my turn to laugh. "When I need to be."

Ray flicks a switch on the wall just inside the garage. Fluorescent lights illuminate the space, and sitting like a precious jewel in a museum is an Aston Martin Valkyrie. I can't help but lick my lips like I'm about to have sex with a hot babe.

This black as night car, glimmering before me, is worth at least two mil.

I wolf-whistle as I forget for the moment why I'm here. "The drug business must be booming in this area."

Green flashes like a beacon on a foggy night.

Green as in cash.

Maybe my future isn't the NFL.

Maybe my plans are all wrong. Maybe I should consider working full-time for Ray Diaz. I could pay Phoebe's medical expenses for a lifetime. I could also buy Mom a big house on the ocean that she dreams about.

Ray's thugs come in, and the one who frisked me hits a button. The garage door closes, the creaking sound snapping me out of my dream state.

"So, why should I hire you?" Ray asks, anchoring himself to an expensive chest of tools.

I circle the Aston Martin, my eyes big as basketballs. "Because I can make you money," I say, not taking my gaze off the pristine black jewel.

"Tell me how." Ray orders like he's already my boss.

His crass tone makes me jerk, and I pin him with a glare. "It doesn't matter how. All you need to know is I need the money."

Money *always* motivates people.

"For what?"

His two goons stand guard at the door like they're Secret Service.

"None of your business." Fuck if he needs to know my personal shit.

"You working for the cops?" Ray's tone is nonchalant like he's asking what kind of beer I prefer.

I fold my arms over my chest and widen my stance. "Donnie vouched for me. So, what's your problem?"

He pushes off the toolbox, pinching his thick dark eyebrows. "I like to know the person working for me. Tell me more."

I'm sure Donnie told him my real name. I'm also sure Ray has the network to find out where I live and my entire background. But I decide to throw him a bone. I do need the gig. And time is of the essence if I want to get Phoebe's vest fixed or acquire a new one. Plus, I know if I were in his shoes, I'd want to know the same thing.

I lift my chin defiantly. "I attend Cypress University. And before you even think to say anything about me selling on campus, that's not going to happen. I can't be your dealer there. If that's a deal breaker, I'll walk."

He scratches his unshaven jaw as he crosses the clean cement floor to a fridge behind the Aston Martin. He returns with two beers and hands me one. He twists his cap off the bottle, and I do the same. I could use something cold to coat the sandpaper feeling in the back of my throat.

He studies me. "Why don't you find a job on campus then? Or in town. The city is a tourist trap, I'm sure someone would hire you."

I grit my teeth. "What's your problem?" He's right that I could probably find a job, but at minimum wage and the limited time to work with school and football, Phoebe wouldn't get her vest or Mom wouldn't be able to pay the bills. I thought long and hard about my options, and drugs equals fast cash.

He takes a long pull of his beer. "My problem is I'm looking for someone with longevity, and you don't strike me as that type, college boy. I want someone my clients can depend on. You feel me?"

I don't know how long it will be before Mom finds a job. And if I'm being honest, I'm afraid to even go down this path. But desperation bleeds motivation, and I'm fucking motivated after seeing Phoebe in the hospital. I also don't want to see Mom working three jobs again like she had when we lived in New Jersey.

I chug a few gulps, inhaling the scent of motor oil. "Do you want me to sign a fucking contract?"

He points the tip of his bottle at me, his dark eyes stony.

A shiver creeps up the back of my neck at the way he's studying me. I make another mental note not to piss off Ray. I get this churning feeling in my gut that if I do he'll put a bullet in my skull.

He struts over to a round table with four chairs outside an office. "Desperation doesn't look good on anyone," he finally says as he waves me over. "But I like you." He slides into a chair, and I do the same.

"What about longevity?" I'm compelled to ask. "I can't promise you that I'll be selling for you next month." I want to be as honest as I can. He needs to know I'm not a lifer in this business.

He rubs his chin. "Let's just see where this relationship goes." He wags a finger between us. "Then we can talk about longevity."

I'm not sure I like the sound of that, but I will worry about my future later. "So, I'm in?"

"Let's talk specifics." He takes another swig of his beer. "My operation caters to the Molly market. I run the southern half of the state, but most of my money comes from a small area in and around Charleston. We cater mostly to college kids or anyone who can afford the two-hundred-and-forty-dollar bag of Molly pills. There's a dozen pills in a bag, and some of my dealers bring in about a grand a night after they pay me my cut."

I school my features as I'm doing some math in my head. "And my cut?" A grand a night doesn't sound bad, but it all depends on how many bags I have to sell, and since this will be a part-time gig, I need to get the biggest bang for my time.

"Ten percent." He eyes me with hesitation.

I sit back against the wooden chair. My mind is calculating. I would have to sell forty bags a night to bring in just shy of a grand. I'm not saying it's not possible, but with classes, homework, practice, and football, I would have to hustle hard or sell on campus, and the latter isn't going to happen. "I want fifty percent."

He takes off his ball cap, runs his gnarly fingers over his crew cut and chews on his lip ring before barking out a laugh. "No fucking way."

His arrogant smile contains amusement, and that rubs me the wrong way. I stiffen. He may throw me out on my ass, but Donnie taught me go big or go home. I stab a finger at the Aston Martin. "She yours?" I'm asking to prove a point.

His greasy forehead creases. "You want one?"

Fuck yeah. That sweet ride has a thousand horses underneath the hood. The thought of getting behind the wheel, starting the engine, and letting that beauty purr beneath my body makes my dick rock hard.

I temper my lust for the expensive ride. I'm here to do business not jack off over the car. "If you can afford a two-million-dollar car, you can pay me fifty percent of what I sell in a night." He's never going to agree to that, but I'm starting off high so I can negotiate the best deal. Twenty percent is the goal I have in mind. At that rate, I would have to sell twenty bags a night, which is more doable than forty. Even if I sold ten a night, that's close to five hundred, and in a week's time, I would be happy with two to three grand. That amount would certainly take care of Mom and Phoebe. Besides, I remember rich assholes in New Jersey who bought up the inventory Donnie gave me in one transaction.

Ray slaps his hand on the table, the sound exploding. "Who the fuck do you think you are?" His voice rises in pitch, as all trace of amusement evaporates.

I don't move or flinch or say a word. I know he wants a reaction out of me or to see if I'm scared.

His two goons at the door ready their Glocks at me.

Fuck if I care.

You should care. Think of your sister.

I stand. "I guess I'll find another gig." I don't take my eyes off him. I'm not one to waver or run away with my tail tucked in between my legs.

Another thing Donnie taught me. *As frightened as you are of the person you're making the deal with, don't ever let them see your fear.*

His chest inflates before he releases all the air through his nostrils. "I know Donnie didn't give you fifty percent. And you must be high if you think I'll agree to your demands. But if you're as good as Donnie says you are then I can offer fifteen percent."

"Twenty percent," I fire back. "And to put you at ease, I'll even commit to work for you for the next three months." The latter should satisfy his longevity bullshit. I can't say I blame him for that. After all, he is running a business, and he wants to keep his clients happy. But I just might've stuck my foot in my mouth, because in the drug business, there's no such thing as long-term employment when the risks are high for all sorts of shit to go wrong.

He's thinking hard until his lips curl at the edges. "I'll take your offer. But you need to do one thing before I hire you."

* * *

FUCKING RAY DIAZ WANTS ME TO SELL FIVE BAGS OF MOLLY TONIGHT to prove to him I can sell.

The task should be easy until he dumps me on a street corner of abandoned buildings with only two homeless people in sight.

The night air is humid, and the stench of piss is burning my nostrils.

"You have three hours. Show me what you got, Jersey boy," he says before leaving me.

The five bags of Molly in my jeans pocket feels like lead, and my gut is telling me the fucker set me up to fail.

I glance around to make sure I don't see a cop car or a slew of them anywhere.

He won't sic the cops on you, bro. He's got a business to run.

I cross the wide deserted road of neglected buildings that sit quietly beneath an overpass. Cars whiz by at top speeds, drowning out any noise below.

This is a perfect place to kill someone. I pluck the blade from my boot while keeping my eyes peeled. It's a small switchblade, so it easily fits into the front pocket of my jeans. I don't want to scare the homeless or have them pull a knife or a gun on me.

I saunter over to an old man who is sifting through a shopping cart. He looks up and snarls.

Taking a step back, I lift my hands. "Whoa! I'm not here to cause trouble. I just want to talk."

His neighbor, an oily-haired woman in her forties, perks up from her sleeping bag outside her tent. Both are glaring daggers at me for disturbing their peaceful night.

"Do you get much company around here?" I ask, keeping my hands in the air.

The old man cocks his head, his skin leathery and wrinkly. "Not sure of your question."

The lady sits up straight, sliding her tired eyes up and down my body like she wants to fuck me. "Are you a cop?"

A shudder works its way through me, and I need a shower.

"No, ma'am." My polite manners filter out. Mom taught me to respect my elders. "I'm wondering if you've seen drug deals go down around here?" No sense in sugar coating what I want. It's not like she's about to call the cops.

"All the time," the old man says. "Racing too." A glint of excitement is stamped in his cloudy green eyes.

I toss a look at the wide street. I picture myself behind Ray's Aston Martin as excitement bubbles inside me.

Oh, for fuck's sake. It's just a car.

"So, you've seen drug deals?" I'm not sure I believe him. The only sign of life is these two. "Any bars or clubs around here?"

The old man squints at me. "You're one of those party people who likes doing drugs and getting naked. Aren't you?"

I edge back at his odd question.

"You might want to check the building two blocks down." The lady points to my left. "Kids act like crazy folk at night in there around this time."

It's almost midnight, and I've heard scuttle around campus about big raves going down somewhere in the city. I'm guessing that's what the old guy is referring to.

Before I say thanks, I spot a weathered, worn ball cap in a carriage near the old man. "Sir, I'll buy that hat from you."

He grapples for it with shaky hands. "Twenty bucks."

I pay the crotchety old man his money and place the dirty gray cap on my head. I don't know if the hat will do its job, but I can't afford for anyone to notice me.

Making my way the two blocks, I keep scanning the street for any sign of life or Ray and his goons. I wouldn't put it past him to be lurking in one of the buildings. But I don't see anyone. And if what the homeless lady said is true about a party, I'm scratching my head as to why I don't see any cars parked on the street.

But as I get closer, the highway noise is overpowered by the thump of loud music, and a garage on my right is packed with expensive vehicles. None are an Aston Martin, that I can tell, but the Mercedes and the BMW are still worth a pretty penny.

A guy about my age stumbles out of a graffiti-strewn building in front of me as the bass of the music rattles the broken windows. Rushing to the curb, he bends over and pukes.

I hang back for a second in the shadows until he's done so I can ask him some questions. I'm still cautious that Ray set me up. With my luck, the cops are on their way to break up the party going on inside.

When he finishes, he spins on his expensive leather loafers. Rich kid, for sure. He probably drives the Lamborghini I spotted back there.

His glare finds mind. "What the fuck are you looking at? Haven't you seen someone lose their lunch?"

Plenty of times, sadly.

I flick my head at the door. "What's the party all about?" I ignore the jerk and his belligerent attitude.

A strawberry-blonde rushes out of the building, almost falling as she sways in her four-inch heels. "Zach, are you okay?" She stands in front of him, cupping his face.

That voice. Whoa! Her raspy Southern lilt sends heat straight to my groin.

I watch in quiet fascination as she dotes on her boyfriend. This also gives me time to sweep my gaze over her, and what a sight she is.

Her long, toned, and tanned legs go on forever underneath her black mini skirt. Her gorgeous hair falls in soft waves down her back. Her tits are visible from my side view, and I stifle a moan. They are perfectly round and big, poking through a clingy top that falls off one shoulder.

Thoughts of biting that shoulder and taking my time to explore those tits are causing my dick to grow. In an instant, I'm hard as the stone foundation of this dilapidated building. When she sets her ocean-blue eyes on me, I lose my breath.

"What are you staring at?" she snaps in her raspy, ball-squeezing voice as she turns to face me.

It takes a second to get air in my lungs. I'm thankful it's somewhat dark where I'm standing. Otherwise, she might catch a glimpse of my raging hard-on throbbing to get free.

What the fuck?

Zach wipes his mouth with the back of his hand, his amber gaze full of disgust. "Dude, are you mute? Drunk? High? Or just a fucking weirdo?"

His last question fractures my lust-filled thoughts. I'm here to sell drugs, not fuck anyone.

"Maybe, he's into threesomes," the babe says, sneering.

Annnddddd now my brain is picturing a threesome but not with Zach. Definitely with her though.

These two are quickly reminding me that I haven't been laid in months. The last girl I fucked was at Carter's big blowout party at the end of June. One of only two parties I went to and let loose.

"Come on, Em," Zach says, slurring his words a little. "Ignore him. We should call that new de…contact. What's his name?"

"Wrangler," she whispers, shooting me a suspicious look as she drags the back of her hand across the sheen of sweat on her brow.

My street name on her lips injects me with another dose of lust. But I shake off all sexual thoughts, put on my sales hat, and walk over to them. "Are you two looking for Molly?"

They stiffen, narrowing their eyes at me at the same time. The muted light spilling out of the building hits the girl's face, and her blue eyes up close are even more mesmerizing. Suddenly, she seems awfully familiar like I've seen her before.

Zach pulls the girl close to him as if I'm about to attack. I don't miss how she flinches either, so I take a step back. "I have Molly if you're interested. That's the only reason I'm here." It guts me to think any girl would be wary of a guy like me. But I can't exactly blame her. I'm a guy who walked out of the shadows, a stranger lurking and watching like some moron. Still, I get the feeling someone in her life hurt her. I would bet on that.

Em continues to eye me cautiously as she gives me the once-over, and I spot a brief flicker of interest before she shuts that shit down.

Her eyes have that manic, unfocused stare junkies have when they're high, and a lump forms in my throat.

Man, I've seen many strung-out people in my life, and I hate the thought of selling poison to this girl, because this shit fucks with your body and your mind.

For a split second, I question what the fuck I'm doing.

Until Phoebe flashes in my mind.

I can't afford to grow morals or start worrying about who I'm selling to. If they don't buy from me, they'll buy from someone else. It's a simple case of supply and demand.

I tug my ball cap down a little, allowing the bill to shroud my identity as much as the hat can.

"We're not interested," Em says, as though the shit I have in my pocket is made of dirt.

Dealers have been known to cut their Molly with other chemicals, and whether Ray does or not, I'm not one to question him. I'm out on the streets to sell the drugs, nothing more.

"What if I told you I'm Wrangler?" I say, knowing she won't believe me.

I don't give a crap if Zach believes me or not. He bares his teeth, his bloodshot eyes narrowing. "Fuck off, man."

I shoot him a cheeky grin when Em whispers, "Call Wrangler. Ray gave you his number earlier, right?"

I'm surprised Ray gave anyone my number if he's testing me. He hasn't exactly given me the thumbs-up as one of his dealers.

Still, my shit-eating grin only gets wider as I lean casually against a fire hydrant, waiting for the inevitable.

Zach gets out his phone, fumbles a tad, and then taps on his screen.

The burner phone that Ray gave me rings. I pull it out of my back pocket. "Hello."

Both of them stare at me, their jaws hitting the sidewalk.

"So," I say. "Ready to do business?"

4

EMILY

"You want a beer or vodka," Scarlett asks as we push our way through the heaving crowd to the makeshift bar at the back of the room. Alpha Sig is hosting an All-Greek party as they do every year, and they always draw a decent crowd.

I've come down from my high after the warehouse party last night, and I'm raring to go again, but Scar and I like to have a few drinks first, waiting until later in the night to avail of our drug of choice. Attending parties on campus makes me wary, so I try to keep most of my crazy for the warehouse parties in town where no one knows I'm the offspring of Coach Parker and President Parker.

"I'm in a vodka mood tonight," I say, smoothing a hand down the front of my fitted, black jersey dress. It's pretty plain, as dresses go, but most of the girls don't go overboard at these parties, and I don't like to stand out, preferring to blend into the shadows. I like how it hugs my curves without being obscene. It's off the shoulder, and it stops mid-thigh, showcasing my long legs. I'm wearing my black-and-white Vans, and my purple sweater is tied around my waist.

"Let's get fucking shit-faced!" Scar says, handing me a red cup filled with vodka cranberry as she drinks beer from her own cup.

"Amen to that, sister!"

We knock our drinks back in record time while we check out the room, and then I refill our cups.

"You and Zach looked cozy last night," she says, winking as she inhales her beer like it's liquid oxygen.

"Zach is fun, but it's nothing serious. You know he fucks around a lot."

"I know he's got a big cock, and he knows how to use it!" she hollers over the music, which has suddenly ramped up a few decibels.

I almost choke on my vodka. "Tell the room, why don'tcha?"

"Girl, you know these frat parties usually descend into orgies. No one gives a shit."

"Do you ever wonder what it's like to be normal?" I blurt, draining my drink and grabbing new refills for both of us before we make our way toward the main room.

"Normal is boring," she says, eye-fucking a guy with massive shoulders standing in the corner talking to two other guys.

"You really think that?"

She sighs. "No, but there's no point wishing for a different life. This is the one we have, and it's not too shabby."

"Do you ever think about the future and how much this shit could fuck us up?" In brief moments of vulnerability, I let the stuff I learned in rehab torment my mind.

They spent hours explaining the side effects and consequences of long-term drug use, but it was a scare tactic that only worked on me for a while. I don't really see any issue with my lifestyle. It's not like I'm using every day, and I know how to handle it. Life is stressful, and anything that helps take me out of my head for a while is a good thing.

"Sometimes." She pins me with serious eyes. "But I sure as fuck don't want to think about it tonight. And you shouldn't either." She pulls me into her side, talking in my ear. "We're here to have fun. To forget about reality. To find some sexy guys to fuck, and I think I've just spotted our prey." She turns me around by the shoulders, gesturing at the guys in the corner. "They're hot."

"How can you tell? Two of them have their backs to us."

"Their bodies are to die for. I want to climb both of them like a spider monkey. Preferably naked." She flashes me a cheeky grin, and heat crawls up my neck, onto my face, as I remember all the times we've indulged in group sex.

Both guys shirts are stretched tight across wide shoulders and glued to their toned backs and bulging biceps. She licks her lips, her eyes lowering. "And check out those fine asses."

My eyes drift to said asses, and I've got to admit both guys have drool-worthy buns, leading to muscular thighs squeezed into dark jeans. "They're football players," I surmise, shaking her hands off my shoulders, and turning toward the crowd jumping around the dance floor. "Which means they're off limits to me."

I used to attend all Dad's games when I was in high school, but I haven't gone to a single one since I started college, and he hasn't mentioned it. He doesn't want me there because I'm too much of an embarrassment, and I don't want to go because the last thing I need is to draw the attention of any jock.

Keeping my parents in the dark about my drug habit means I keep a low profile on campus. I don't date, and I only have sex with guys within our circle. I haven't even made any friends in classes, preferring to stick to myself. Scarlett is my sole friend, and I only know her through the drug scene. A lot of the girls in the circle are bitchy and unfriendly, but Scar and I clicked from the instant we met. Although our backgrounds growing up were vastly different, there are enough similarities to share a kindred spirit.

I love hanging out with her on weekends, and I sleep over at her place because her roomie goes home to see her boyfriend. My parents turn a blind eye because she lives in one of the dorms, and they think that means I'm sheltered, which is laughable.

One would think Mom, as college president, would be more clued in about the shit that goes on around campus, but I think she deliberately ignores it, because she doesn't want to deal with it.

It's bad enough dealing with her wayward drug-addicted daughter

—her words, not mine—so, knowing the drug culture is alive and thriving on *her* campus wouldn't go down well at all.

"Well, that fucking sucks." Scar pouts. "C'mon." She drains her drink, tugging on my elbow. "Let's dance." I knock the rest of my vodka back and let her drag me into the center of the mayhem. A happy buzz descends as alcohol mixes with the blood in my veins, and I sway my hips to the rhythmic beats pumping out of speakers dotted around the room, closing my eyes and losing myself to the lure of the music.

"Those football players are watching us," Scar murmurs, a few minutes later.

"They've probably recognized me," I reply without opening my eyes. Although I don't attend games, some of the football players know who I am.

Sucks to be me.

"Hey, sexy." Meaty hands land on my hips, and I instantly jerk my eyes open at the sound of *his* voice. He pushes my hair aside, running his tongue along the column of my neck, and I almost gag. "What a lovely surprise to see you here," Weston says, and bile floods my mouth as I recall the forced blowjob in his SUV during the week.

"Get fucked, Wes." Scar flips him the bird, as I shove him away, and I couldn't love my pint-sized friend anymore. Even though I tower over Scar, she doesn't let her five-foot-one-inch frame, or her petite figure, hold her back, and she's as fierce as they come. "She's not interested."

Wes cocks his head to the side, smirking. "That's not the impression she gave me last Wednesday."

Scar frowns, glancing up at me. As far as my bestie is concerned, Weston is blackmailing me into dating him. She doesn't know he's forcing me into the role of sex slave, and I didn't tell her what happened the other evening because I was too ashamed.

But Wes is insinuating it was something different, and I'm fucked if I'm hiding the truth from my friend anymore.

"Blackmailing me into blowing you is nothing to be proud of," I hiss at him, and Scar's claws emerge.

"Sexual assault is a crime. Something I'm sure you're aware of as a pre-law student," she snaps, glaring at him. "If you don't drop this blackmail bullshit, we may have to resort to a little blackmail of our own."

"Just try it, sweetheart." He puts his face right into hers, and an ugly sneer washes over his features. "And see where that gets you. You're Scarlett Morgan, right? A junkie whore from Bennettsville. I hear your uncle's getting out of prison soon. Maybe I'll pay him a visit."

"You fucking bastard." Scar's trembling, and I clutch her hand for moral support.

"Leave my friend alone." I jerk my chin up, piercing him with a warning look. "This is between you and me." I ignore the rapid pounding of my heart. "What do you want?"

"Good girl, Emily. I'm glad you can be reasonable." His patronizing tone grates on my nerves, and I grind my teeth hard. "You're coming with me." He grabs hold of my arm, cutting off my circulation.

"Don't do it, Em." Scar recovers her composure, pulling on my other arm, her eyes pleading with me.

"Hey, babe." A strong, muscular arm wraps around my waist from the side, extracting me from Scar's and Weston's grasp.

"Who the fuck are you?" Wes demands, glaring at the newcomer. I haven't risked glancing at him yet, curious to see how this plays out.

"I'm Adam. Emily's date."

I've no clue who this guy is or why he's ridden to the rescue, but I'm not stupid enough to turn help away.

"Yeah?" Wes steps up to him. "Well, I'm one of her oldest friends, and we've got plans, so screw off."

Tension radiates off Adam in waves as he places a gentle finger under my chin, forcing my gaze to his. I suck in a shocked gasp.

Adam is Wrangler.

Our new dealer.

The guy I haven't been able to stop thinking about since meeting him last night.

Adam is drop-dead gorgeous with his strong jaw, lush dark hair, beautiful emerald-green eyes, and a body honed to perfection. All I've thought about since last night is what it would feel like to roam my hands over those broad shoulders and trail my tongue along the grooves of those rock-hard abs while grabbing onto his bulging biceps. And how it would feel to have him thrusting inside me as he screwed me senseless.

My thoughts have shocked me.

Because it's been forever since I've lusted after any guy in this way.

His eyes penetrate mine, seeking permission, and I subtly nod. "You want to go with him?"

I've no clue how he's here, or what he thinks he's doing, and I don't know him to trust him, but I'd still rather stay with him than go with Wes.

I shake my head. "I want to stay here with you."

"That wouldn't be smart, Emily," Wes warns, and anger bubbles up my throat.

Fuck. Him.

He's not going to blackmail me into doing his bidding every time he feels like it. If I don't take a stand now, he'll trample all over me. Challenging him is risky, but I doubt he'll tell my parents.

At least not yet.

Not while there's something to gain. He enjoyed my lips on his cock, and I know he's banking on more.

If he turns me in, he's saying no to more sexual favors. That's not part of his playbook.

Although I could be wrong.

He *could* go straight to my parents and tell them everything.

Maybe it's *not* smart to antagonize him, but life is all about taking calculated risks. I don't want to look weak in front of Adam or Scarlett, *and* I don't want Wes thinking I'm his little puppet bitch.

Adam must sense something coming, because he pulls me in closer to his side, keeping a firmer hold on my waist. His spicy and citrusy scent wafts around me, reeling me in. He smells incredible, and, against my better judgment, I instinctively lean closer.

"Wes?" A stunning blonde with sultry brown eyes and a rocking body materializes at his side, looking at him with a frown on her face. "I thought you said you couldn't come tonight?"

Wes's jaw tenses, and he murmurs something under his breath. Plastering the fakest smile on his face, he turns to the girl, winding one hand into her hair. "Changed my mind, babe." He pecks her lips. "I was just asking if anyone had seen you." She notices us for the first time, blatantly eyeing Scar, and then me, from head to toe. A satisfied grin slips over her mouth as she instantly dismisses us as competition, and I release the breath I'd been holding.

Maybe I can get rid of the asshole without publicly challenging him. Blondie showing up like this has done me a huge favor.

Scar flinches, steam practically billowing out of her ears at Blondie's quick dismissal, and her claws reappear. I brace myself for it. "Aw, how cute," she deadpans, planting her hands on her hips. "Barbie's finally found her Ken."

Blondie narrows her eyes to slits. "And has the junkie slut found a loser boyfriend yet, or has every guy here already used your skank ass?"

Wes chuckles. "Play nice, darling. It's not Scarlett's fault she came out of the womb with her legs automatically open."

"Is that the excuse you use every time you open your mouth and shit spills out?" I snap, pissed on my friend's behalf.

"Wow, Emily. I wonder what your parents would think of your foul mouth?" It's a veiled threat, and it should force me to back down, but the alcohol in my system is making me recklessly brave.

I step up to him. "I wonder what yours would think of your black-mailing ways, asshole." I pin my eyes on the blonde clinging to his side. "Or maybe I should have a private conversation with your girlfriend."

Wes's fists clench at his sides, and his eyes flash with dark warning as he leans in close to my ear. "Careful, slut. I like your fire, but push me too hard, and I'll push back even harder. It won't be pretty."

Adam's body tenses, his intense green eyes shooting daggers at Wes, and I wonder how much of that he overheard. "It's time for you to leave. Both of you."

Wes snarls, ready to spit venom at Adam, because he doesn't like being told what to do. He pushes his face all up in Adam's personal space. They are not quite eye to eye, because Wes is a few inches shorter than Adam, something I'm sure pisses him off.

Scar is fuming, nostrils flaring, and she's got a familiar manic look in her eye. She obviously overheard him threatening me too, and she won't forget his insult on her character in a hurry either. She steps forward. "You fucking—"

Zach appears out of nowhere, clamping his hand over Scar's mouth. "Take your piece of ass and get lost, Wes."

Wes looks Zach up and down with obvious derision. "What the fuck happened to you McCartney? You might still dress the part, but you look like fucking shit, man."

"Think what you like. I've zero shits to give, Blakely." His sharp glare dares Wes to challenge him. "Just fuck off and leave the girls alone."

"You heard the guy," Adam says through gritted teeth.

Wes pins me with a menacing look, one that promises retribution. "We were just leaving." He slings his arm around Blondie's shoulder, keeping his gaze locked on mine, ensuring I understand there will be payback for this. A shiver works its way through me, and Adam wraps his other arm around my waist, repositioning me, so I'm encased in his protective embrace with my back to his front. I shouldn't allow him to hold me like this, but it's been a long time since anyone has made me feel safe in their arms, and I'm not immune.

Wes casts one final derogatory look our way before sauntering off with his girl. My entire body slumps in relief, and Adam's hold tightens.

"What the fuck was all that about?" Zach asks. "And what the hell are you doing here?" He eyeballs Adam.

Shifting his eyes around the room, Adam's strong jaw becomes stone. "Partying like you," he says in a low tone, conducting another sweep of the room.

Zach regards him cautiously, unsure what to make of him.

A tall muscular blond struts up, cautiously assessing the stare down between Adam and Zach. "Hey, hoss. Everything okay?" He directs his question at Adam.

Scarlett and I exchange a wide-eyed look, realizing he's one of the guys we were ogling from behind.

Adam nods once to his friend. "Zach and I are cool, right?" Adam is strung tight as a violin string as he drills a look at Zach.

Zach bobs his head, knowing it's in our best interest to keep Adam's identity secret.

The blond dude lets out a sigh. "Good, because Coach Parker would have our asses if we got into a brawl." With the threat of a potential fight gone, he regards Scarlett with interest. "Hi, I'm Carter." He flashes her a blinding smile, but she ignores him, because she's too busy watching me.

It takes me a second to register the name Coach Parker, and I glance up at Adam, catching my first proper look. He's the other guy who was standing next to the blond dude in the corner. These are the guys I'd correctly guessed are footballers.

I can usually spot them from a mile away.

Immediately, I wriggle out of his embrace, and he frowns as he lets me go.

A petite brunette sashays up with wide brown eyes only for Carter. "There you are."

Carter drapes his arm around her, and she snuggles into his embrace. "Don't leave without me, hoss." He dips his chin at Adam, and salutes Scar and me, before disappearing in the direction of the bar with the brunette on his arm.

"Emily, could we go somewhere quieter to talk?" Adam asks, in a husky voice that reaches hidden parts of me.

"We can talk here." We need to have a convo to ensure we're both on the same page, but I'm not keen on leaving with him.

I don't know him.

Don't know his agenda.

And while he seems like an okay guy, and he's on my dad's team, I've learned to be on my guard when it comes to strange men.

He addressed me by my first name, so one of his football buddies must've recognized me and told Adam before he made his approach. Or maybe he knew who I was last night but didn't say anything. Or he has no clue I'm the coach's daughter, and he just wants to ensure my discretion. Whatever the reason, we need to agree to keep the details of our dealings a secret.

"It's too open here," he replies. "I promise you're safe with me."

"Says the serial killer to his next victim." I fold my arms around my waist, thrusting my chest up in the process, noticing how his eyes automatically lower to my tits. "And ogling my tits doesn't help your case."

He has the decency to look ashamed. "I apologize." He clears his throat. "But you *are* safe with me. Zach has my number, and as Carter pointed out, I play for Coach Parker. Would I be so forthcoming if I meant you any harm?"

"Okay," I eventually concede, because he's made some good points, and we need to discuss how we're going to handle things going forward.

"Em." Zach's worried tone is clear in the extreme. "Are you sure you want to go off with him?"

"We need to talk." I pin him with a knowing look. "Besides, my dad is his coach." I mention that on purpose to gauge Adam's reaction. His wide-eyed shell-shocked look tells me he didn't know I was Coach's daughter. Carter didn't give me the vibe that he knew either, or if he does, he wears a great poker face. "I appreciate your concern, Zach, but I've got this."

Scar clutches onto Zach's arm. "You know I'm a good judge of character," she says, eyeing Adam circumspectly. "She'll be fine."

Zach levels Adam with a menacing glare. "Hurt her and you'll have me to deal with."

"Your boyfriend can come too," Adam coolly replies, looking directly at me.

"He's not my boyfriend. Just a friend," I admit although I'm unsure why. It might've been smarter to let him think that.

Zach's mouth tugs up at the corners, and I sense he's going to say something I won't like. I send pointed "shut up" vibes in his direction, and he chuckles. He kisses the top of my head, sneaking a cheeky feel of my ass. "Call me later, and we can hang out."

That's code for get high and fuck our brains out.

After the way Wes hijacked tonight, I desperately need both, so I give him a curt nod before I let Adam lead me outside, pretending I don't see the confused expression on his handsome face.

5

ADAM

My head is swimming as I usher Emily through the throng of bodies, packed in the frat house like sardines, with one hand on her lower back.

What the fuck is on repeat in my head as I replay the last ten minutes, trying to figure out what the hell is going on. First, I spotted Zach grabbing her ass. He was trying to be subtle, but I notice everything. He may not be her boyfriend, but they have something going on.

Second, I've just discovered Emily is Coach Parker's daughter.

Again, what the fuck?

Coach will have my balls skewered, grilled, and diced if he discovers I sold Molly to his little girl. And let's not mention the fact I haven't been able to get her out of my mind since I met her. Coach doesn't talk about his family much, but I knew he had a kid. But not one who attends Cypress, and sure as fuck, not one who is beautiful, sexy, and downright breathtaking.

Suddenly, I'm picturing her and me naked.

And my cock is straining against my zipper again.

I don't know what it is about this girl, but one look, one visual, and I'm hard as a brick for her.

The scent of rain lingers in the air as we step outside onto the massive porch of the plantation style frat house.

Emily purposely moves away from me, and my hand drops to my side, the loss of contact breaking me out of the spell she has me under.

"So, let's hear it." Her voice is sultry, lyrical, and it only intensifies the lust already flooding my body. Add that to the way she's standing with her hands on her hips, eyes narrowed, and chin up, oozing "don't mess with me" vibes, and I'm pretty much a lost cause.

"Coach's daughter, huh?" My tone is even as I study those ocean-blue eyes. Up close they're even more mesmerizing, and I could easily get lost in her gaze. She strikes me as the sort of girl who isn't aware of how captivating she is. Not like a lot of pretty girls on this campus who flaunt it excessively any chance they get. And don't get me started on the jersey chasers who make a beeline for athletes on this campus. I can usually spot them a mile away, and I always steer clear.

She casually lifts a bare shoulder, quietly assessing me. The way her black dress is clinging to her curves isn't helping me tame the beast raging to get free in my jeans.

"We both have a vested interest in keeping our dealings secret." She's ballsy. I like that.

I have my own concerns for sure. I flick my head at the street ahead. "Let's take a walk?" We don't need prying eyes or big ears.

And I need to do something to distract myself from what you're doing to me.

I can't afford to have someone discover I'm dealing drugs. Coach will kick me off the team, I'll lose my scholarship, and my chances to get drafted in the NFL will be shot to shit.

I'm sure she doesn't want anyone knowing she's into drugs. Especially not her parents, so we've a mutual interest in keeping it a secret.

She sashays her sweet hips down the porch steps, and I'm trapped in her snare again. My attention is riveted on her until I remember that fuckwad, Wes. It didn't seem like he wanted to take no for an answer. I subtly scan the area, because I wouldn't put it past that fucker to hide in the shadows.

It was Garrett—our wide receiver—who pointed out what was going down between Wes and Emily. As soon as I turned around and saw it was *her*, I wasted no time shoving my way through the crowd, ready to throttle the asshole. I usually don't get involved in other people's business, but one thing I can't stand is when guys think they can push around a girl. Fucking drives me insane. And Wes has a rep around campus that isn't pleasant. Can't understand how girls fall at his feet the way they do, knowing the rumors, but some girls will deliberately turn a blind eye for the enhanced social standing. Can't say I understand that mind-set, but it's the way the world works around here.

Emily doesn't have that mentality. She clearly didn't want to go with him, and my instincts are working overtime trying to figure out what's going on there.

I was semi-stoked when Zach stepped in. Not that I have a problem ramming my fist into Wes's nose, but I can't make a big scene. Coach would go ballistic if any of the guys on the team got into a fight, and at a frat party no less. But I wasn't about to let Emily or her friend get hurt, and I was prepared to suffer the consequences, if it came down to it. Surely, Coach would understand since Emily is his daughter.

Several partygoers are hanging around outside as we walk away from the house. Chatter pierces the night air. A couple making out is panting like they're two seconds away from stripping their clothes off and fucking right here on the front lawn, and two girls leaning against the far wall are giggling over something their guy friend is saying.

But none of them are Wes.

And I don't spot the blonde he left with either, so hopefully that means they're gone.

Emily is about ten feet ahead when she tosses a sexy smile over her shoulder. "You coming or what, big guy?"

I don't think she's being flirtatious on purpose, but I'm taking the wins where I can get them. Heat blossoms in my chest, and my legs kick into gear. I'm about to catch up to her when Carter shouts my name.

Shit. Emily has my brain on overdrive in more ways than one, because I forgot about Carter. I'm surprised he's looking for me when he's with the brunette. She's the same girl he eye-fucked at practice and the same one who got escorted out by security, but she's nowhere in sight now, so he obviously left her inside.

"You need a minute?" Emily asks.

"I won't be long."

"'Kay." She takes her phone out of her purse and ambles down to the sidewalk.

My gaze lingers on her for a long minute and then I do another quick sweep of the area, to ensure it's safe for her to stand by herself. We're surrounded by frat houses with another party going on across the street, and I don't spot any threats.

Carter settles in front of me. "I told you not to leave without me. What's going on, man?" He peeks around me, shaking his head. "Leaving with Coach's daughter is not a good idea."

No shit, Sherlock.

"Did you know who she was when we were inside?"

"Nah, man. Rachel told me when we went to the bar. That's one of the reasons I'm chasing your ass."

I shove my fingers through my hair. "Well, did you know he had a daughter at Cypress?"

Carter pushes out a shoulder. "Coach only talks about football. His private life is off-limits. You know that, but the gossip mill is alive and well, and I'd heard rumors he had a daughter here."

Private, I can understand. I still question why he doesn't have pictures of his family in his office, as it's usually the norm. I keep a picture of Mom and Phoebe on my desk in my dorm room.

"Interesting." I lift my head, checking on Emily. She's talking on her phone but looking up at me, and I can't help smiling.

Carter shakes his head again, groaning. "You hardly go to parties, and when you do, you capture the attention of the hottest chick south of the Mason-Dixon line."

I chuckle. "You're jealous."

He bites his lip. "Maybe. Or maybe I realize it's a shitshow in the making, and I'm glad I'm nowhere near it." He sends me a pointed look. "She's as off-limits as they come, dude. Besides, the night is still young, and we're celebrating our big win today."

It was a fan-fucking-tastic win. The score came down to the last second when Garrett caught the ball in the end zone. That put a smile on Coach's face and mine too. After that loss last weekend, we needed this win.

"I'm not feeling it. Sorry, dude."

"Aw, c'mon." He thumps me in the shoulder. "You can't fuck off now. Bring Emily with. I'll get Rachel, and Garrett is hooking up with a redhead."

I blow out a breath. My body is saying hell yeah, but my brain isn't. She and I need to talk. I don't think she will go for it either. She squirmed out of my hold so darn fast when she realized I played for her old man.

"Don't wait on me. Go and get laid."

He waggles his eyebrows. "I intend to. You have condoms?"

"This isn't my first rodeo, hoss." I level him with an amused grin. *Does he think I'm inexperienced because I don't screw every female with a pulse?* I know what I'm doing. I'm just a lot less vocal about my sexcapades than Carter is. "And we're only talking." I don't want him believing I'm about to fuck the coach's daughter. Rumors spread like wildfire on campus, and I need that rumor like a hole in the head.

He angles his head, and strands of his blond hair fall forward. "Talk? You can talk at the party."

Eh, no. But I'm not about to tell him Emily's a client of mine and this conversation has to happen in private.

"I'm sure Rachel is looking for you," I say as I start to walk away. "I'll text you in a bit."

Carter doesn't argue, grinning as he walks backward with a shit-eating grin on his face. Maybe the part about Rachel looking for him, or the fact Emily just called my name, is the reason he doesn't give me any more flak.

Or he thinks I'm full of shit, which is probably more like it.

I strut up to Emily as she drops her phone back in her purse.

"You up for an ice cream? I know this small shop that stays open late. My sister loves the place." Whenever Mom and Phoebe come down to see me, I take them to Charlie's Sprinkles and Cream. Phoebe loves the sprinkles, which consist of gummy bears and Swedish fish, which happen to be two of her favorites.

She shoots me a funny look. "This isn't a date."

My brow puckers. "I know that. I just thought…You know what, forget it." I rub a tense spot between my brows. *What the hell was I thinking offering to take her for ice cream?* I need to keep my distance from Emily, for a bunch of different reasons. She's right to keep a solid line between us.

Silence engulfs us as we walk, and I slide my hands into the back pockets of my jeans.

"You have a sister?" she asks, after a few beats, looking at me inquisitively as we head out of fraternity row toward the main campus. I've no idea where we're heading, but I'm following her lead.

"Phoebe. She's twelve. Although, at times, she thinks she's twenty." I chuckle. "You have any siblings?" I ask, not knowing much about Coach's family.

"No." That one word is laced with evident sadness. I want to uncover the reason for it, but I've got to remember who she is and the fact it's none of my business.

"Did you know who I was last night?" she asks, deliberately changing the subject.

The music from the frat houses begins to fade the farther we walk.

"I recognized you last night but not as Coach Parker's daughter. I accidently ran into you when you were in the emergency room."

Her gaze swings to me in confusion. Fine lines crease her brow as she thinks it over. "You ran into me," she says, after a few beats, her brow smoothing out as realization dawns. "That was you?" I nod. "You can't tell anyone you saw me," she blurts, panic obvious in her tone and her facial expression.

"I haven't told a soul, and I don't plan to." I reassure her, and she visibly relaxes.

"Thank you." Silence fills the gap between us again before she fills it. "Why were *you* there?" Curiosity threads through her question.

I debate whether to tell her more about my personal life. But I already mentioned Phoebe, and Emily understands the need for privacy. The crew I sell to are usually extremely guarded and private. They are also some of the most manipulative people I've ever met, and they'd literally kill to keep their habit a secret. Her old man knows about Phoebe too. So, no harm, no foul.

"My sister has cystic fibrosis. She was rushed to the hospital with pneumonia."

She sucks in a breath, her eyes widening as genuine emotion appears on her face. "Shit. I'm sorry."

I'm about to speak when she slams to a stop in front of Randolph Hall, the oldest building on campus. It's also where her mother's office is located. Coach might not openly discuss his family, but everyone knows he's married to the college president.

She stares at the building like it holds dark secrets. "My mom is probably up there working late as usual," she murmurs, and I detect more sadness from her. She locks eyes with me, her sadness instantly fading as she slants me with a steely look. "No one can know I buy Molly from you," she says in a low tone, casting a sharp look around.

"Trust me, I get it. Your father can't find out either. He'd have a heart attack if he knew his quarterback is selling drugs."

"Why do you?" she asks, appearing a little distracted. She's still looking at Randolph Hall, and a new frown mars her beautiful face.

I follow her gaze. Maybe she sees her mom. But upon close inspection, all I see is a light spilling out of the second-floor window.

"I have my reasons." None of them she needs to know, because I've already been forthcoming enough when she's been cagey as shit.

"Look, I sold to you and Zach last night before I knew who you were, but I'm not selling anything else to you." I'm all about taking risks, but this one is too fucking close to home, and I can't jeopardize it. Besides, those two bags I gave them contain twenty-four pills. That amount should last a while.

Her entire demeanor changes faster than I can blink. "I don't think so." She plants her hands on her hips, leveling me with a dark stare. "The last people I will tell are my parents, so you've nothing to worry about."

I study her as her blue eyes battle with me. Desperation shimmers in her gaze, sucker punching me. I feel her anguish for a very different reason. Hers is to get high. Mine is to make money. It's a win-win for both of us. *But how can I trust her?*

Suddenly, a list of questions bombard me. *Why does the thought of losing her supplier terrify her so much?*

What or who is driving this girl to drugs?

How badly is she addicted?

Does she just use it recreationally, or is it more serious than that?

A smart, beautiful girl from a good family shouldn't need drugs. But I've been around this culture long enough to know people from all walks of life come to rely on narcotics, for a whole heap of reasons.

Still, she seems together, and I can tell from her eyes that she isn't high right now, which should calm me down, but I've known addicts who appeared to be fully functioning members of society, and no one knew what was going on, before they spiraled. I've also known addicts who lie, cheat, steal, and manipulate to get cash for the next hit.

I don't want to believe that of Emily, but I don't know her well enough to form an educated opinion.

Now, I'm as worried about her as I am about my own little secret.

Phoebe, man. Money, bills, Mom, medical expenses.

That's my priority. Not some girl I don't know and can't know. I need to steer clear of Emily, because getting any more involved with her is risky on so many different levels.

"I don't sell on campus for a reason."

"Like I don't buy on campus for a reason."

"You're better off finding someone else. It's less risky," I continue arguing.

She steps in closer to me. "Think about it." She runs the tip of her finger down my chest, batting her eyelashes at me, and I know what she's doing. I step back, disappointed in her. She shrugs, smiling coyly at me, not willing to let this go. "This is the perfect arrangement for us. We both have a legit reason to keep our secrets. I trust you not to tell and you can trust me to do the same."

Her logic is sound, but it leaves a sour taste in my mouth. Yet, if I don't sell to her, she'll find someone else who will. It would make life easier if I had a few trustworthy clients on campus I can get rid of my gear to. And she knows what I do already. There's nothing to stop her from telling her father, unless she continues to buy from me, and then she has as much to lose as I have.

I hate this fucked-up scenario, but there isn't much I can do about it now. "You're right. We both have reasons to keep this quiet." I harden my jaw. "But if you double-cross me, my sister is the one who will pay the ultimate price." I play on her emotions, because her reaction to Phoebe's illness was genuine, and it might be the only thing to keep her lips permanently sealed.

She opens her mouth, to pry, no doubt, when a rustling sound claims our attention. Emily tenses, shuffling closer to me. I look around, but I don't see anyone. "You worried about Wes? He's a dick-wad, and you should stay away from him."

"Believe me, I'm trying." Her gaze darts up and down the street. "He's a family friend. Well, a friend of my parents'." She visibly shivers.

I take that opening to untie the sweater around her waist. I suspect she's not cold, but every fiber in me wants to touch her even as my head is screaming at me to step away. I drape the soft fabric around her shoulders, and she arches a brow, regarding me curiously. "Why are you being nice to me?"

"Why wouldn't I be?" I scrub a hand along my jaw. She shrugs, not offering me anything else. "What was that about with Wes back there?" I add, not letting her deflect. I've given her plenty to ponder, and she's told me next to nothing. "Is he hassling you? I mean, it sure seemed like it tonight."

"He wants me to date him although I've no idea why if he's with the beautiful blonde." I can't tell if she's hurt by that or it genuinely doesn't bother her.

I gingerly grip her chin, guiding her to look up at me. Big blue eyes meet mine, and I'm drowning. "You're a million times more beautiful than that blonde."

She blinks long lashes as she stares deep into my eyes. An electrical charge crackles in the space between us, and her lips curl into a soft, sweet, pure smile that does strange things to me. Her hands slide slowly, hesitantly, up my chest, and she bites down on her lip, making me groan. "Are you hitting on me?" she whispers, her gaze settling on my mouth.

"Maybe," I admit, because I've no idea what the fuck I'm doing.

Her hands curl around the nape of my neck, and her tits press against my chest, radiating warmth in everyplace we're connected. My body demands I claim her, and I slide my arms around her waist, holding her even closer.

Her eyes continue to draw me in until it feels like I've lost all self-control. My dick throbs, urging me to take what she's offering, while the voice in my head says I shouldn't kiss her, shouldn't get in any deeper, but my head is lowering on autopilot until our lips are almost touching.

Fuck. My heart is racing as my stomach flips like an out of control gymnast the moment my lips brush against hers.

She jerks back, as if electrocuted, snapping both of us out of whatever the hell that just was. "I need to go." She wraps her arms around herself, avoiding eye contact. "We have a deal, right."

"Yeah." I reluctantly nod, even though she can't see because she still won't look at me.

"Good." She walks backward. "I'll be in touch."

Then she takes off running, and confused and horny as shit, I watch her until she's out of sight.

I take a shower the instant I get back to the dorm, coming hard against the wall as I imagine it's Emily pumping my cock to release.

6

EMILY

"You're not coming to the fundraiser dressed like that," Mom says, frowning as she examines me from head to toe.

I narrow my eyes, wanting to tell her she doesn't look good in red or she should've worn a pantsuit like she usually does to university functions, anything to get on her nerves, but I know my criticism of her will only fall on deaf ears.

"What is wrong with this dress?" I gesture at the elegant, black floor-length gown she bought me for the annual university ball last year.

She swipes a hand up the back of her head, making sure not a strand of her blonde hair is out of place in her tight chignon. "You wore it last year, and a lot of the same guests will be in attendance, for one."

"So what?" I flap my hands around. "It's not like anyone's going to remember what I was wearing." True fact. Most people don't give a rat's ass who I am.

"They remember." She gives me a tight smile. "You might as well just prop your naked breasts on the table for all the coverage it offers."

It's true it plunges straight down to my navel, and I can't wear a bra, so it showcases some boob but not to the extent she's implying. Mom is a B-cup, at most, and I'm a generous D-cup. It's always bugged her, and the fact it does bugs me.

If she's that envious, she can always get a boob job.

It's not like she can't afford it. Both my parents have high-paying jobs, and Mom comes from a wealthy family. When her father died three years ago, he left his entire estate to her. Mom could easily retire now and enjoy a comfortable life until she dies.

I admire the fact she wants to keep working, and I'm proud of her career. But she has achieved it at the expense of everything else in her life, and I don't admire her for that.

When I needed her most, she wasn't there for me.

And I won't ever forget that.

It's a pity my grandfather placed a stipulation on the trust fund he bequeathed me, ensuring I can't get my hands on the money until I'm thirty. Or maybe he knew what he was doing. Because if I had access to that cash now, I'd be long gone.

"If that's how you feel, why did you buy it for me in the first place?" I ask.

She rubs at her chest in obvious annoyance. "I didn't realize it was so revealing." Her blue gaze drifts to the clock on the wall in the living room. "I don't want to be late, and we need to leave in five minutes. Go change into the green dress I bought you for tonight, and hurry."

I'm cursing her under my breath as I stomp up the stairs, returning a few minutes later in said aforementioned dress. This one isn't half as pretty, but I have zero fucks to give.

"That's much more appropriate," she says, nodding her head in agreement.

The dark-green dress has a tight-fitting bodice with a heavy lace overlay across the chest, which adequately squeezes and conceals my boobs, and the hem rests midway between my knee and calf. It's like something you'd put on an older woman, but I don't complain because I just want this night to be over.

I hate going to these things, because they're usually boring as fuck, and I'm forced to make small talk with a bunch of overweight middle-aged men and their mute wives, who sip their wine while sitting dutifully by their husband's sides even as they ogle my breasts and flirt with me outrageously.

But I'm especially dreading tonight because I'm pretty sure Wes is going to be there. It's why I've just drained a quarter bottle of vodka for liquid courage. I'm going to need it to help me survive this night.

* * *

"STOP FIDGETING," MOM HISSES IN MY EAR AS SHE SMILES AND NODS at a few new arrivals from our position at the bar.

The ballroom is humming from the clinking of glasses to the soft music spilling out of the speakers overhead.

"The dress is scratchy and hot," I complain, fighting the urge to pull at the coarse fabric again.

"Stop whining," Mom says as Dad gestures to the barman for another round.

Mom sends him a sly look. "You need to slow down," she hisses, under her breath, all the while keeping that fake smile plastered on her mouth.

"And you need to stop telling me and Em what to do," Dad hisses back.

I'm ready to say "Thanks, Dad" when we're interrupted.

"Coach. Good to see you." A large man with gray hair and a matching mustache slaps Dad on the back, dragging him into a private conversation. This happens all the time when I'm out with both of my parents. There is always someone claiming their attention, and I'm left to the sidelines.

"I have to talk to a few people. Behave while I'm gone, and don't do anything to embarrass me," Mom warns, shooting daggers at me before she wanders in the direction of a dark-haired man with his arm around a red-haired woman.

The moment she's gone I feel like I can breathe again.

I lean against the bar as I scan the busy ballroom, silently promising myself that once I graduate and leave this place behind I am never stepping foot into one of these stuffy events again.

The fundraiser is being held in a ritzy hotel in town, and it's crammed full of the usual blue bloods—distinguished families with old money who've kept their traditions and names intact.

Obnoxious assholes in my opinion.

It's the same ole, same ole, and I honestly can't fathom how anyone finds these nights entertaining.

I spot a broad-chested guy with thick brown hair from behind, listening to an elderly lady, and immediately, my mind drifts to the frat party and Adam. I've thought about him a lot since our encounter in front of Randolph Hall. Like how my body ignited on contact at the unspoken intimacy we shared.

I can't remember the last time I had that butterfly feeling, but I sure felt it with Adam that night. Thoughts of that almost kiss, and the way his hard body felt pressed up against mine, sends shivers coursing through me. I moan quietly, biting down on my lip and squeezing my thighs together, as an intense need overwhelms me.

But it's short-lived when the guy turns around, and I discover it's not Adam.

Part of me is disappointed.

The other part is relieved.

Getting involved with my drug dealer is a mistake, and he's a football player too, which is a double no.

The broad-chested guy saunters away, and my gaze follows him until I spot Wes's smug head. My face contorts, and a low growl escapes my mouth. He's in a huddle by one of the tables with his parents, and he's got Blondie on his arm.

Good.

All I have to do is ensure I'm not left alone with him, and I should be safe.

I eye the bar with longing, and I would literally kill for a drink, but

I'm not legal, so I'm stuck with soda. The vodka I ingested prior to coming here has worn off. I don't even have any Molly on me.

Not with Mom around.

She checked my purse before we left, like she always does. She loves any opportunity to remind me of my failure. But even if she didn't check, it's too dangerous anyway, especially knowing Wes is in attendance. I need my wits about me, which is unfortunate, because if there was ever an occasion where I need to get high or drunk, this is it.

"Hey, beautiful." An arm drapes around my shoulder from behind. "I didn't know you'd be here."

I spin around, grinning at Zach. It's the first time I've seen him in a suit, and his blue tie brings out the color in his amber eyes. "Nor I you." I fling my arms around him, genuinely delighted to see him. "Did you bring a date?" I ask, looking over his shoulder.

He snorts, taking a sip of his drink. "As if. I'm flying solo with my parents."

"Please say you'll sit at my table and pretend to be my date?" At least, if I have Zach there, it'll be bearable. And I'll have a buffer against Wes.

Zach places his hands on my lower back, steering me over into the corner where it's more private. He toys with a strand of my hair, smiling mischievously at me. "I'll sit at your table but only if there's no pretending going on."

I jerk back, eyeing his face to see if he's joking, but he looks deadly serious. "You want to be my date? For real?"

He brushes his thumb across my cheek. "Why is that such a surprise? We're hot together."

"That's because we're usually stoned and drunk when we screw."

He slaps a hand over his chest. "The lady doth wound me."

I grin. "If we were dating, you'd have to be exclusive."

"Ah, yes, the damn exclusivity clause." He tweaks my nose, and I swat his hand away. "That would be a problem." He flashes me a wicked grin.

I roll my eyes. "Yes, your propensity for group sex would be an issue, which is why we're better off maintaining the current status of our relationship."

He sets his drink down on a tray next to a collection of half-empty glasses. "Except in front of your parents," he adds in a low tone, slipping his arm around my waist. "Follow my lead."

"Mrs. Parker. Mr. Parker." Zach extends his hand as my parents approach us. Dad gives Zach a not-so-subtle once-over, while Mom beams at him, as they take turns shaking his hand. I've got to admit Zach cleans up well in his designer suit, shiny shoes, and perfectly groomed hair. He's even shaved, and there's no way an unpracticed eye would guess he's doped up.

"You're Sylvia's boy, aren't you?" Mom says.

"Yes, ma'am."

"Are your parents here?" she inquires, glancing around the room.

"They are. They're seated at a table at the back of the room."

"I must stop by to say hello before the night is over."

"I'm sure they'd like that," Zach coolly replies.

"How do you know my daughter?" Dad asks, pinning him with keen eyes.

"Zach's a friend from college," I rush to answer, looping my arm through his. "And he's my date for tonight."

"How wonderful," Mom says, actually looking like she means it. "Let me have a word with Georgia and ask her to set another place setting at our table." She shoots me a brief, sharp look when Zach isn't looking. "Emily neglected to mention you were joining us or I would've already ensured there was a seat for you."

"It was a last-minute arrangement," Zach says, loyally coming to my defense. "And it's not a problem. We have room at our table if Emily wants to sit with us."

I could happily plant one on him right now.

Mom waves her hands about. "Nonsense. I'll get it fixed." She wanders off with urgency in her step.

Ten minutes later, we're all seated around the table as the waiters serve the first course. Zach is on my left and, as might be expected, that asshole Wes had to maneuver it so he's sitting on my right. Blondie is on his other side, sucking up to Mr. and Mrs. Blakely as she engages them in mindless chatter, which suits the jerk to a T.

Wes clamps a hand on my thigh, under the table, digging his nails into my flesh as he leans into my ear, talking in a low voice. "In five minutes, I'm going to excuse myself to go to the bathroom, and you're going to wait a couple minutes and then follow me. I'll be in the men's restroom on the lower level. Don't keep me waiting."

"You're clearly delusional if you think I'm going to blow you at this event with my parents close by," I whisper back, keeping a pleasant smile on my face even though my stomach has just lurched to my toes, and I'm on the verge of throwing up what little food I've eaten.

He digs his nails in harder, and I wince a little. Zach jerks his head around, trying to continue his conversation with my father while checking out what's going down with me.

"I'm not asking you to blow me," Wes says, his eyes shimmering with barely disguised lust. "I'm going to fuck that pretty cunt of yours, and then blow my load all over your ass."

A shudder works its way through me as bile coats my mouth. "Not happening!" I hiss, gulping back panic as a cold, hard mask washes over his face.

He leans across me to my father, raising his voice so he's heard over the conversation at the table. "I'm surprised you approve of your daughter's choice of date this evening, Coach Parker," he says, as if butter wouldn't melt in his mouth.

Dad's brow furrows as he looks between Zach and Wes. "You boys know one another?"

"McCartney used to attend my high school," Wes confirms, pausing for a split second, as Zach stiffens beside me. "Before he was expelled," he adds, popping a piece of smoked salmon in his mouth.

I know nothing of Zach's background. Hell, I know very little about his life now except he's from a wealthy family, is a junior studying business in CU, he knows how to party hard, and he's an excellent fuck.

I don't need to be a genius to work out his expulsion has something to do with his predilection for Class A drugs.

"Don't you know it's rude to tell tales," I chastise Wes, laughing lightly to offset the brewing tension. "And I thought you said you needed to use the bathroom?"

A slimy grin graces his ugly mouth as he pushes his chair back. He slaps Zach on the back. "Sorry if I embarrassed you, man. Was just making conversation."

Dad watches Wes walk away with narrowed eyes. "I'm sorry," I whisper to Zach.

"Don't apologize for that asshole," he says his hands still balled into fists under the table. "And whatever you've just agreed to, don't do it." His eyes drill into mine, and a flush creeps up my neck as I realize he knows a lot more than I thought.

"I can handle Wes," I lie, setting my napkin down on the table. I glance briefly at Blondie, but's she's still in ass-licking mode, and she hasn't even noticed her boyfriend has left the table. "I need to powder my nose," I say, grabbing my purse and standing. "I'll be back soon."

Zach goes to open his mouth, but I use my eyes to send him a silent message, and he shuts up.

I hurry out of the room and down the stairs to the lower level bathrooms, wiping my clammy hands down the front of my dress and wishing I'd brought my pepper spray with me. I don't want to do this, but I can't let Wes spout any more shit. He's already planted the seeds of suspicion, and I wouldn't be surprised if Dad wasn't, at this very minute, talking to Wes's parents to see what they know about Zach. If it's as I suspect, and he discovers he was expelled because of a drug habit, it won't take him long to put two and two together.

As soon as I walk into the empty men's room, a hand snakes out, and I'm yanked sideways into the handicap stall. I react on instinct, kneeing Wes in the groin before he has time to lock the door. "What the fuck do you think you're doing!" I bark, as he drops to his knees, cradling his crotch. "If my father discovers Zach was expelled for drugs, it'll take him a hot minute to figure things out."

"He ... wasn't ... expelled ... for ... that," he pants out, glaring at me. "Got kicked out ... for screwing the principal's underage daughter."

Air whooshes out of my mouth, and my shoulders slump in relief. Thank fuck for that. But my relief is short-lived.

"You fucking bitch," he rasps, staggering to his feet as he recovers.

"It's your fault for scaring the shit out of me," I snap, turning on my heel to leave when he grabs me around the throat from behind and pins me to the wall, pressing my cheek up against the cool tile.

"Where the fuck do you think you're going," he demands, shoving my dress up to my waist and tucking it into my panties. "You're going to pay for that."

"No!" I scream, but he covers my mouth, muffling my cries, as his other hand pins my wrists behind my back.

"Get your fucking hands off her!" Zach roars, grabbing Wes by the back of his jacket and ripping him away from me. He shoves him into the other wall, and they go at it, swinging fists and throwing punches. I fix my dress, silently cheering Zach on as I watch them beat the shit out of one another.

Zach has the upper hand until Wes kicks his knee, and Zach cries out, tumbling forward, falling face-first to the floor. Wes is on him instantly, rolling him over and pummeling his fists into his face and his ribs. The look of rage etched in Wes's eyes sends tremors of fear racing through me.

He's going to kill him! That's my only thought as I jump on Wes's back, clawing my nails down his face.

He rears back, emitting a guttural roar, as he shoves me off, sending me skittering across the small space. My back slams into the wall with a loud thud, and pain rattles my tailbone, skittering up my spine. Adrenaline courses through me, and I ignore the pain, pushing off my elbows and charging at Wes again.

Zach is on his feet, but he's clearly struggling to stay upright. He's clutching his torso and swiping at the blood gushing from a cut over his eyebrow. I slam into Wes's side, and the punch meant for Zach lands squarely on my nose, sending me reeling. Blood pumps from my nose as I lose my balance, falling to the floor again, my shoes flying off in opposite directions. My dress bunches up, exposing my lace panties, and I'm flat on the floor, moaning and pinching my nose as the oldies burst into the bathroom.

"What the hell is going on here?" Dad yells, his gaze bouncing around the space.

My mother takes in the state of me with a look of abject horror on her face.

"They ambushed me, sir," Wes lies, swiping at a trickle of blood oozing from his split lip. "Apparently, I wasn't supposed to mention anything about Zach's expulsion. It seems he's finally realized that having sex with an underage girl was disgusting and immoral, and he didn't want you to know."

"Weston?" Mr. Blakely pushes his way into the room as Zach helps me to my feet.

"That is not what happened," Zach says through gritted teeth, and I clutch his arm tight in warning. We can't tell them the truth, because then it'll all come out, and it's not like my mother would actually believe it of Wes anyway.

"It's okay, Zach," I say, seeing triple of him. Pain ricochets through my skull. "You don't have to protect me."

I face my parents, or at least, I think I do. "It's my fault. I followed Wes here to tell him to keep his big mouth shut, and we got into an argument. Zach came to my defense, and then it got physical."

"I'm very sorry, Mrs. Parker, but we'll have to ask your daughter and her date to leave," Georgia, the organizer, says, shaking her head in disgust as she looks between me and Zach.

This is the best news I've heard all night.

"I understand," my mother says, shooting her an apologetic look. "And I'm very sorry for any embarrassment or inconvenience. If there's been any damage, I'll cover the costs. Just send the bill to my office."

Mom takes hold of my arm, making an effort to be gentle, only because we have an audience.

"I'll call you," Zach mouths at me.

"Hopefully, I'll still be alive," I mouth back before I'm ushered out of the room to await my fate.

7

ADAM

S am and I are on our way to see Mom and Phoebe when my burner phone pings in my back pocket.

Sam's gaze darts to my normal phone sitting in the cup holder of my truck. "Since when do you have two phones?"

Oh, since I became a drug dealer.

"It's not mine." That isn't a lie either. The phone technically belongs to Ray. "Garrett left it behind when I dropped him off last night from playing pool." Now that's a lie, but I have to improvise, to keep the secret. I hate that I'm concealing shit from my roomie, but that's par for the course with this gig.

"How was the frat party last weekend?" Sam asks, propping his booted feet up on the dash.

The burner phone quits ringing. Thank fuck.

"Decent." But only because a certain, enigmatic strawberry-blonde with gorgeous blue eyes was there. "When are you going to get your ass out with us?" I've been trying to coax Sam to leave his dorm room, and join us. While I don't go to parties much, I do hang out with the guys after training. Either grabbing food in the diner, or shooting pool at the local pool hall. Sam is a bit of a recluse, and I'm worried about him. In his spare time, all he ever does is play Xbox or hack into who knows what.

"My schedule is busy. You know I tutor in the student center most nights after classes. I barely have time to do anything else."

I roll my eyes. "What are you at level one thousand in some game?" I ask to make a point.

Cars speed by us in the left lane as I ease up on the gas pedal and maneuver the car onto the off ramp.

"I'm out with you now," he volleys back.

"I mean to a party."

He belts out a laugh. "Like you party. You're not Carter Banks."

Carter? That dude probed me like the FBI after class on Monday, wanting to hear all about Emily. I gave up nothing except for telling him, over and over, that we didn't fuck. Didn't matter though. He doesn't believe we just talked, and in the end, I gave up. He'll believe what he wants to believe.

"What do you know about Emily Parker?" I ask. Sam might be a recluse, but he knows everything there is to know about this campus. Dude definitely has too much time on his hands.

He whips his head around, and I'm sure it's about to fall off his neck. "Coach's daughter? Please tell me you didn't hook up with her."

I brake at the red light at the bottom of the ramp. "Are you jealous or scared? And what do you know?"

"That coach will cut off your nuts if you lay a finger on his daughter. I like you, Adam, and I'd hate to lose you as a roomie or friend." He smirks, and I sense he's concealing something.

I squirm in the driver's seat. "Spill, man." When the light flashes green, I turn left.

"She tutors sometimes in the student center." His cheeks flush a little, and it's clear he's got a bit of a thing for her. "She's one hot chick. That's it."

I'm surprised she tutors. I assumed she was strung out on Molly most nights, but everyone knows what they say about making assumptions. She wasn't high at the party, so maybe she only uses it occasionally. That thought sits easier in my gut, than the thought she might have a serious problem.

The burner phone goes off again just as I'm pulling into Mom's driveway.

"Someone must really want to get in touch with Garrett," Sam says.

"Why don't you go in," I suggest, cutting the engine. "I'm going to call Carter so he can tell Garrett I have his phone." The lies keep coming, and I'm quickly reminded of how I lied constantly when I worked for Donnie. "Tell my mom I'll be five minutes."

Sam knows Carter and Garrett are roommates, so this doesn't raise his antenna. He nods once and climbs out.

I wait until he's inside, then remove the burner phone, cussing under my breath when I spot the recent missed calls from Ray. I haven't spoken to him since our initial meeting last week. He had one of his lackeys call me to see if I'd sold the five bags he gave me, and I've been expecting his call. Typical he'd phone when I couldn't answer. I press redial and call him back.

The line rings once. "Fucker. I've been calling your ass. Don't ever ignore me."

The last thing I want is to get angry. It's Sunday, a day I usually kick back and hang with Mom and Phoebe. I don't want to raise any red flags with them. Mom is as perceptive as me, and Phoebe is pretty alert too, but I'm fucked if he's going to speak to me like that.

"Nice game yesterday," Ray says, losing his punk attitude. "You've got one hell of an arm, boy." I wonder if he means that, or he's just letting me know he checked me out.

The second win of the season is a high I'm still riding today. Carter, Garrett, and I celebrated last night at the pool hall along with other teammates. Sadly, the frat houses didn't throw any parties this weekend. I was hoping one did, and maybe I could've run into Emily again.

"I'm not your boy." I grit my teeth.

"You are whatever I fucking tell you you are, at least for the next three months," Ray announces like he's a proud father. "You did well last week."

Suddenly, regret worms its way through me. I probably shouldn't have put a timeline on our deal. "Why the fuck did you drop me off like a piece of trash?"

He belts out a laugh. "I wanted to see what you were made of."

I squint as the sun filters in through my window. "A warehouse party was going down that night. Surely, you knew that."

"Maybe, but strung-out junkies don't buy when they're stoned. They're too busy enjoying the high. I wanted to see what you would do. Besides, you need a glimpse of what you're in for. You might've sold drugs for Donnie years ago, but the world is much different now, and you don't seem like the type to get your hands dirty."

Fuck off is on the tip of my tongue, but I refrain from telling him that. "I'll bring your money by tonight."

"Good. I've given you a week to consider it, so, tell me, do you still want in?" His tone grates on my nerves, but I shove my annoyance aside. Ray is a necessary evil. One I'll just have to get used to. I briefly debate whether to renegotiate my employment time frame, but I could make decent bank in three months' time.

Phoebe comes out of the house, her brown ponytail swishing behind her. "Adam." She beams at me, and my heart melts.

"I'm in. I'll be by later." I end the call, not giving a shit about Ray.

I hop out of the car as Phoebe jumps into my arms. "You shouldn't be outside," I chastise.

She hugs me. "I'm fine. You worry too much."

"And you don't worry enough." I swallow thickly as I hug the bravest girl I know. "Too many germs out here." I set her on two feet. "You should've waited inside."

"It's cool. I'm on antibiotics still." She runs ahead of me, and I can't stay mad at her. Some days, I love that she's laid-back about it. She doesn't get a chance to be a normal kid, and on those days, I think it's good she can be carefree. Other days, I get frustrated at how flippant she is, because this shit is serious, and I want her to treat it as such. *But what do I really know?* She's the one with the illness. I don't get to dictate how she is.

When we're inside, Mom greets me with a smile. Her brown eyes appear tired and so much despair is oozing off her.

My heart splinters into tiny pieces, and I hate she's going through all this stress again.

After I unloaded the bags of Molly, and my encounter with Emily, I contemplated whether to continue. But one look at Mom, and the answer is a big fat yes.

I need to do this.

At least until she can find a new job. Even then, her job won't pay the outstanding hospital bill. Phoebe had X-rays and drugs and a two-day stay. That adds up to thousands of dollars, for sure, and someone's got to pay it.

Phoebe kneels next to Sam, grinning at him like he hung the moon. Her jewelry kit is strewn across the coffee table, bringing a smile to my face. The TV is on, but the sound is muted.

"Come on, Adam," Phoebe urges, waving me forward. "I've been waiting for you to make these cool beaded bracelets. I got some new colors. Maybe you can make one for a girl," she teases, her eyes sparking with hope.

I strut over to Phoebe and kiss her on the head. "Love bug, how many times do I have to tell you you're my only girl."

Sam says, "Mine too."

He and I didn't finish talking about Emily although the blue-eyed beauty has taken up a permanent home in my head. I jerked off in the shower again this morning envisioning me inside her. It's becoming a problem. One I'm not sure how to fix.

I playfully mess up Phoebe's hair. "I want to talk to Mom for a bit. Then I'll join you. Okay?"

Sam is threading a string with beads, and it's comforting how he fits in with my family and how much he adores Phoebe.

I leave them as Phoebe starts singing a Shawn Mendes song.

Mom's in the kitchen stirring a pot of meat sauce. On Sundays, she either makes spaghetti or chicken pot pie. Both are favorites of mine, and I eagerly look forward to my visit every week.

I settle at the counter near the sliding glass door that flows into the backyard. The house is a modest one-story with three bedrooms and one bathroom, which Mom has transformed into a homey family space. When we moved from New Jersey, we lived in an apartment for a year before Mom got her job at the hotel. Then she found this house in a decent neighborhood with a good school system.

I take out my wallet and count out three hundred dollars.

"Where did you get that money?" Mom's tone rises as she visibly gulps.

I can't lie to her. I thought about it. But she knows my tells. When I lie, I chew on my lip and I subconsciously avoid direct eye contact. I'm only aware because she once shared that tidbit with me.

"Don't ask, please." I slide the money across the counter. "It's not much, but I'll get more." My twenty-percent cut doesn't add up to three hundred bucks. I'm not telling Ray I overcharged for the bags.

I'm well aware if he finds out he'll have my hand on his workbench ready to slice it off with one of those expensive tools he owns. But he didn't say I couldn't charge more. The deal is to give him his standard cut, and I plan on doing that.

Tears cascade down Mom's face. "Adam, please tell me this isn't drug money?" She keeps her voice low.

I glance through the archway leading into where Phoebe and Sam are. Phoebe is still belting out a song, and Sam is singing along with her. He's completely off key, but it's the thought that counts.

I sigh heavily. "Phoebe needs her vest, and we have a hospital bill to pay. It's only until you find a job." The last part is somewhat of a lie. I have three months with Ray, and if I try to quit before then, I'm sure he'll string me up by the balls.

Or put a bullet in my skull.

She shakes her head in quick succession, crying softly.

I wrap my arms around her. "Please let me handle the money situation."

She sniffles. "What about football? And school? You can't risk that."

"Mom, I can't risk anything happening to you and Phoebe."

She sobs quietly.

My heart is breaking and breaking and breaking. I know she's disappointed. I know she's scared. But there is no other quick solution for fast cash, and a job paying minimum wage just won't cut it.

"I'll be careful." And I will. Emily isn't going to rat on me. The stakes for her are just as high.

Or at least I pray they are.

8

EMILY

Prison is the only way I can describe my weekend. I swear my bedroom walls closed in on me minute by excruciating minute. Mom grounded my ass, and it's ridiculous how much power my parents have over me although it was Mom who went ballistic.

Friday night, when we returned to the house after the disastrous fundraiser, Mom launched into a hissy fit. Rage poured out of her as she flung an expensive vase against the stone fireplace. Her precious antique shattered into tiny pieces.

Dad watched on in disgust.

I feared for my life with the way she glared at me like I was an intruder and not her kin. Mom is downright scary when she wants to be.

When she was done cleansing the rage from her system, she turned her temper to me, but Dad stepped in. I knew he was livid with me too, but that didn't mean he'd let her harm me. When he tried to calm her down, a fight ensued between them. After an hour of shouting at one another and throwing my name around like I wasn't even in the room, Mom stormed out of the house.

It pains me that I'm the crux of their problems. But if Mom had the decency to treat me like a daughter, and not one of her employees or students, we might be a close family, and I sure as shit wouldn't have to resort to drugs to numb my pain.

She didn't return until the following morning, and wherever she went to cool off must've been a place that sucked out all her fury, because she calmly laid out the terms of my punishment.

I'm grounded for the next two weekends.

I'm forbidden from seeing Zach.

And she's reached out to Wes to find out how I can make it up to him.

I almost lost my breakfast when she admitted that last one because I'm pretty sure rape and sodomy are high on his list of punishments, and that's only for starters.

If I refuse to cooperate, she's throwing me out.

Dad wasn't any help, and his disappointment in me felt like he drove a dagger into my heart.

He's been a little confusing to figure out recently. In one breath, he's on my side, and in the next, he's siding with Mom.

Still, didn't he know I was a gnat's ass away from relapsing?

I realize I'm on my own again, and watch out world, because Molly, here I come. Scar's my best friend, but Molly just might take her spot.

When Monday rolls around, I'm like an eager puppy at the front door waiting to be walked.

"You will attend classes, and your tutor sessions, and then it's straight home," Mom reminds me as I'm halfway out the door.

Fuck. You.

I think it, but I don't say it. Because she has me in a bind, and she knows it.

Anytime I step out of line, she threatens to disown me. I've thought of calling her bluff, but she's a heartless bitch, and I cannot afford to be out on my ass with no roof over my head or money in my pocket. I need money. I need Molly. And I need to stay in college and get my degree, because it's my ticket out of here. And frankly, I don't want to give her the satisfaction of seeing me grovel because, honestly, I think she'd enjoy that.

So, I keep my insults to myself and walk out of the house without uttering a word.

"I can't believe your parents grounded you," Zach says, stealing a fry off my plate as we sit with Scar at lunchtime in the dingy diner. We chose a place off campus, rather than eating in the cafeteria, in case we bump into Mom or one of her many spies.

I look outside, through a layer of grime coating the window, absently watching a clerk sweeping the sidewalk outside the convenience store across the street. I swivel in my seat, my gaze skimming over the room. This place could use a facelift, as I doubt the décor has been upgraded since it first opened if the peeling wallpaper, stains on the ceiling, and worn tables are any indication.

But it's clean inside, and the food is good. And, most importantly, it offers us privacy.

"It's like being fifteen all over again," I admit, stabbing a piece of lettuce with my fork.

"She's such a bitch," Scar seethes, opening her mouth wide and biting into her burger. "I wish I'd been there. I would've loved to rip off Wes's balls with my bare hands."

Zach and I chuckle. It took both of us to try to put the hurt on Wes, but the fucker is strong. Not to mention, he'd probably enjoy Scar's rough hands on him.

"I'm used to it." I shrug.

Zach touches the cut over his eye that's crusted into a scab. "Why does she treat you like that?"

"She's always hated me," I admit, taking a sip of my water. My mind wanders back in time. "There was this one occasion, when I was seven, when I fell down the stairs during one of her dinner parties. She'd put me to bed, but I'd snuck into her room because I loved trying on her shoes and wearing her makeup. I'd thought it was a good idea to come downstairs to show her me in a pair of her highest heels, but I tripped on the carpet at the top of the landing and tumbled down to the bottom of the stairs." I drag my lip between my teeth as I stare off into space. "She was furious when she found me, plastered in her makeup, with the heel on her favorite shoe broken, crying in a ball as she loomed over me, giving me one of her special stink-eye stares."

I swipe at a stray tear. "Oh, she acted the doting mother in front of her friends, but as soon as I was upstairs in my room, she slapped me across the face and told me I was a disgrace and an embarrassment." I rub at the ache slicing across my chest. "Then she told me something I've never been able to forget."

"What did the bitch say?" Scar asks, pausing with her glass halfway to her mouth.

"She said she wished I'd never been born. That I was a mistake and I'd ruined her life because she'd never intended to have kids." Every time I replay that conversation, my chest constricts and the need to wash away the pain is stronger than ever.

"Fuck." Zach leans across the table, taking my hand. "That's rough. She's a complete cow and not worthy of your love, anyway."

I shrug, because I'm not sure what I believe anymore. "I can't ever do right by her. I'm a complete fuckup in her eyes, and she loves taunting me with that."

Scar visibly swallows as she sets her glass down. "Why does your dad stay with her?" She rests her elbows on the table.

"They stay together for appearance's sake." I tear a napkin to shreds, piece by piece, wishing for a better life. Wishing my parents loved me. But everyone knows what they say about wishful thinking.

Molly is the one who loves me. Molly is the one who shows me how good life can be.

I'm tempted to ask Zach if he has any more pills, but the waitress comes over, slapping the check down on the faded tabletop.

"That's fucking ridiculous," Zach says, snorting.

"I know. But that's my life."

"This should help ease the boredom at home," Zach says, sliding a plastic bag filled with pills into my book bag, as we wait outside the diner for Scar to return from the bathroom.

He's a mind reader. "How much do I owe you?" I sigh contentedly, knowing I have Molly. Now, the nights at home will be bearable. But I have to be careful. Mom might not notice, but Dad's more suspicious.

"It's on the house, babe." He hugs me to him. "You know I always look after my two favorite girls." Zach has more than enough cash, and he rarely takes payment from Scar or me. I'm lucky he's my friend, as finding money to feed my habit is challenging at the best of times. I discovered the code to my parents' safe a few months ago, and I dip into their cash stash when I'm desperate, but I'm careful not to take too much, and, so far, they don't appear to have noticed.

"You got something special for me too?" Scar inquires, joining the conversation.

Zach grabs hold of his junk. "I've always got something special for you, Scarlett lady."

She flips him the bird. "I meant something of the hallucinogenic kind."

He leans over to kiss her, slipping a baggie into her pocket.

"You're my favorite friend," Scar says, batting her eyelashes at him. "Because you have the best drugs and the biggest cock," she adds, deliberately feeding his ego. "Want to come over later?" She waggles her brows suggestively.

"Is the pope Catholic?" he jokes. "I'll see you later." He turns puppy-dog eyes on me. "I hate that you can't join us. We'll miss you."

I'll probably miss them later too when I'm horny as fuck and only have porn and my little electric friend for company.

Scar pulls me into a hug. "Keep fighting, babe. Don't let the bitch grind you down."

We wave her off as she heads in one direction and we move in the other.

"I'm glad I caught you alone," Zach says, slinging his arm casually over my shoulder as we walk. "We need to discuss your Wes problem." I arch a brow in silent question. "Scar told me."

Air whooshes out of my mouth. I can't fault Scar for telling Zach. I know they both worry about me. Besides, Zach practically caught Wes in the act, and he did get hurt on my behalf. But I don't need him to continue where he left off with Wes. Any action Zach dishes out will only infuriate Wes, causing more pain for me.

"Hey." He tilts my chin up. "She was worried, and we want to help." His jaw tenses. "I'd like to say I'm surprised he blackmailed you into blowing him, but that's his usual M.O."

My spirits perk up. "It is?" He nods. "You know anyone else he did this shit to?"

"He did it to a bunch of girls at our high school, and I sincerely doubt you're the first girl he's tried it with at Cypress."

My pulse ticks higher with a newfound determination. Maybe once and for all, I can show my parents who Wes really is.

The scum of the earth.

A bottom dweller who eats dirt and shits cockroaches.

Maybe then, Mom will look at me differently. And Dad. Well, I'll enjoy seeing Dad unleash that fierceness I know he has.

To think he worries about me dating his precious footballers.

I roll my eyes.

They are the least of his worries.

Sure, they party and fuck. Some more than others, but Wes is in a whole different league—one that if Dad knew he would feed him to sharks off the coast of South Carolina.

"Can I get their names?" I ask, removing a notepad and pen from my bag.

"Why?" He stops walking, angling his head like I lost my mind.

"Because I have a plan. Of sorts." The one good thing about being bored out of my tree all weekend at home alone is I had plenty of time to conjure up some potential solutions.

"I'm all ears," he says, tugging on my hand, and we resume walking.

For the first time in forever, I feel a sense of purpose. "I know this guy, another tutor, and he's got mad computer skills. I've heard rumors he's into hacking. Mainly targeting big corporations and trying to uncover fraud and evidence of corporate greed. I thought I'd offer to pay him if he'd dig some shit up on Wes. Everyone's got secrets, and I just need to find *one* thing I can use to hold over his head, and then I can make him go away. This could be exactly what I need." Giddiness threads through my words.

Oh, the look on Wes's face if I can pull this off will be priceless.

Zach starts walking again. "How trustworthy is this guy?"

"He's a good guy and about as trustworthy as they come."

He scrubs a hand over his jaw. "I can email you a list of names later. But you need to be careful. If Wes finds out what you're up to, you know there'll be hell to pay. Besides, the names probably won't do much good. He terrified all of them into keeping their mouths shut." A pained look washes over his face. "I tried to out him, but he turned it around on me and got me expelled."

"What?" I splutter, slamming to a halt again.

"I wasn't fucking the principal's underage daughter. *He* was." A muscle pops in his jaw. "Only I call it rape. She agreed to come forward and fess up, but he got to her somehow. She fessed up all right, but she pointed the finger of blame at me. I guess I should be glad she said it was consensual, but in the eyes of the law, it was rape. I only avoided criminal prosecution because my father made a hefty donation to the school and my parents agreed not to contest the expulsion."

A dark cloud blocks the sun as I seethe. "I fucking hate that bastard," I snap. "And now I'm even more determined to bring him down."

* * *

ONE WEEK ROLLS INTO TWO, AND MOM HAS BEEN ON THE WARPATH. The minute she walks in the door, she's telling me what a disappointment I am, stating I'll amount to nothing, telling me how I'm the talk of the campus after what went down at the fundraiser. After she lets loose on me, she turns her madness to Dad, and a fight match always ensues.

The tension, the fighting, her voice, the screaming, it's all too much. I'm jonesing to get the fuck out of the house, and staring at the same four walls is driving me insane. Molly is my only savior. My only release from the tsunami brewing in my head.

The only time I get to see my friends is at lunchtime, and it's always over way too fast.

I've missed a ton of parties, and it feels like I'm being left behind.

And Sam turned me down flat when I asked him if he'd do some investigative work for me, failing to conceal his shock and his disgust when I suggested it.

My life is on a spin cycle, and I'm spiraling so fast I'm not sure how much more I can take.

The depression is real, painful, maddening, and the only consolation is the bag of goodies Zach supplied. I've resorted to taking one pill every night, because it's the only way I'm getting through this hell. But now, my stash is running low, and I'm on edge.

I pop my second-to-last pill Thursday morning before my first class, ignoring the queasy feeling in the pit of my stomach that says this is a bad idea. It was either do this or slit my wrists, because my mood is the blackest of black today, and I need a hit.

I clench my teeth, as sweat beads on my forehead, attempting to focus. The professor is rambling on about something, and from where I'm sitting in the back of the room, I can barely make out what he's writing on the board.

Being buzzed in class is…different. I burst out laughing at the most inappropriate times, hum songs that are playing full volume in my head while swaying in my chair, and I'm struggling to keep my butt in my seat. Other times, I'm paranoid people can tell I'm high, and I slink in my chair, tucking my chin into my chest, slyly checking the room to see if anyone's watching me.

The chick next to me says, "Shh, I'm trying to listen."

I smile sweetly at her. "Oops, sorry." My voice is loud, my giggle obvious, causing the professor to stop talking.

All heads turn my way.

I couldn't give a shit what they think. I'm in my happy place, and nothing or no one can touch me. My mind floats, higher and higher, and I slink lower and lower in my seat, grinning widely as liquid bliss replaces the blood flowing through my veins.

The professor clears his throat. "Ms. Parker, you're disrupting this class. It's time for you to leave."

I waste no time in gathering my things, but when I do, I sway on my feet. The chick next to me offers to help, but I swat her hand away.

Luckily, I'm close to the door, and I manage to walk out without tripping.

I'm sure my not-so-student-like behavior will get back to Mom. But, right now, I don't care.

I've no clue how I make it to the diner, but I'm humming to myself, slurping through my third soda at a table in the back, when Zach and Scar arrive.

"Are you high right now?" Scar whispers, giving me the once-over as she scoots into the booth alongside me.

"As a fucking kite," I joke.

She frowns. "That's pretty fucking reckless, Em."

"I'm in a pretty fucking reckless mood, Scar."

"Did something happen?" Zach asks.

"Nothing happened. That's the issue." I giggle, swiping my hand across my clammy brow. My eyes dart wildly around the diner, and I chase the dust particles floating through the air with my gaze. "They're like the brightest stars," I mutter.

"What are?" Zach asks.

"Dust stars. That's what I'm going to call them." I reach up, swiping at the air, curling my fingers around a handful. "I wonder what they taste like," I say before slapping my palm against my mouth.

"Fuck, are we usually like this?" I hear Zach question Scar.

"You're usually running around naked, slapping chicks with your big cock," Scar tells him, and they laugh.

"Fuck. We can't let her go back to class like that."

"She has no choice. Bitchface checks her attendance reports. Hope-fully, she'll have come down by the time classes resume." Scar stares at me, and I grin back at her. "Babe." She grips my chin. "How long ago did you take it?"

I shrug. "It was before my first class." A goofy smile spreads across my mouth. "I love you, chica. You know that, right?" Scar's lips tug up at the corners. "And I love you too, Zach."

"Love you too, babe," he says with a knowing grin.

Briefly, I consider asking him to come to the bathroom and fuck my brains out, but it's not Zach I want to fuck.

Adam's handsome face appears in my mind's eye, and I squirm as a host of fantasies involving him, me, a bed, and zero clothing lay siege to my body. A wave of euphoria ghosts over me, and I lean back against the booth, closing my eyes and murmuring contentedly.

The rest of lunch passes in a blur. I don't even remember if I ate anything. Scar has a firm grip on my elbow as she guides me back to campus. I'm starting to come down from my buzz, and I shiver as cold chills tiptoe up my spine.

"You got any more Molly?" I ask, squinting, as we round the next corner. The sun or light is too fucking bright, and my head wants to explode.

"Shush." She glances anxiously around her. "You've got to keep your voice down. And I've got nothing with me here."

The farther we walk toward campus, the more reality sinks in. "Fuck." I bury my head in my hands, feeling hot one second and cold the next. A line of sweat glides down my back, sticking my top to my spine. "I feel like shit."

"Maybe it wasn't such a good idea to break your own rules," Scar says.

"You don't say!" I snap, rubbing my temples. "I need another high, not a lecture, Scar."

Scar growls under her breath. "If you're going to be a grumpy bitch, you're on your own from here."

"I don't need a fucking babysitter anyway."

"You know where you're going?"

I glare at her. "Do I look like a fucking imbecile?" I throw my hands in the air. "Of course, I know where I'm going," I lie, because I'm experiencing sudden brain freeze, and I can't recall what class I have next.

"You're lucky I love you and I understand." She kisses me on the cheek, holding my shoulders and turning me around. "Go that way and call me later."

"Scar!" I holler, turning around a couple beats later. "I'm sorry!" Butterflies flutter in my chest, comingling with the tight slicing pain cutting across me.

"I know, babe." She blows me a kiss. "Hurry to class before you're late!" I watch her disappear before pivoting on my heel, slamming face-first into a solid obstacle blocking my path.

"Look who it is, boys." His voice radiates with smug superiority, and bile shoots up hot and fast to settle in my throat.

I don't want to look, but I have no choice. I'm plastered to his body, and as he grasps my upper arms, digging his fingers into my sensitive skin, I lift my chin.

Wes's malevolent gaze meets mine.

"Get the fuck away from me," I bark, shoving his chest.

He squeezes me even tighter. "You never learn, do you, bitch?"

A few chuckles ring out behind him, and he glances over his shoulder, still keeping a firm hold on me. "Come say hi to our Saturday night entertainment."

Four guys step forward, eyeing me like I'm their next meal.

I have a horrific feeling I might be.

The short, stocky guy with black eyes to match his black hair checks me out from head to toe. "Sweet body," he admits with a crooked grin.

"Nice ass," another guy says from behind. He must have moved around while I was watching the stocky dude. I shriek as two hands grab hold of my ass, squeezing.

"Get your fucking hands off me!" I attempt to wriggle out of Wes's hold, but the guy at my rear presses into me, shoving me right into Wes's chest.

A hand brushes the sides of my breasts, and I scream, but the sound is muffled as someone shoves my head in tighter to Wes's upper body

"Enough." Wes releases me, suddenly, wrapping his arms around me as if he's hugging me. "Don't say a word unless you want me to cut your tits off and feed them to my wolfhound.

"Sup," he says, as a crowd of guys and girls pass by us. He runs his hand up and down my back in an affectionate gesture, as his friends send surreptitious warning looks my way. A couple of girls narrow their eyes at me while the guys just look amused.

"Fuck," Wes says, when they're out of earshot. "If they mention this to Cassandra, she'll string me up by my balls."

I'm sure Blondie is well aware of his rep and she turns a blind eye because she wants his ring on her finger and his last name on her passport. She made it clear the way she fawned all over him and his parents at the hotel.

"If she hasn't found out about all the other sluts, I think you're safe," a tall guy with massive biceps says, reaching out and fondling my boob.

"Hands off," Wes snaps. "It's too risky out here." He cups my face, forcing my gaze to his. "But Saturday night, she's all ours, and you can do what the fuck you want to her."

"In your dreams, asshole," I say, hating how my voice quakes.

They all laugh, and someone pinches my ass. Tears prick my eyes, and I push at Wes's chest. "Let me go, or I'll scream."

He grips my face even further, and my lips scrunch up. "Your mom is tripping over herself to make up for the fundraiser. What a naughty little bitch you are, Emily." He tut-tuts, shaking his head. "She thinks you're coming over to help me study, Saturday night."

Another round of chuckles breaks out.

"She's helping us study, all right," a lanky guy with dirty-blond hair says.

"Study our cocks," another idiot says.

"And we'll be studying every fucking inch of your body," Wes says, his eyes glinting with dark promise. "And filling every fucking hole," he adds, grabbing me against him as he thrusts his cock into my stomach.

My stomach lurches violently, and I struggle against his hold.

He pushes me away, and I lose my balance, dropping to my butt on the ground.

The five guys loom over me like a menacing thunderstorm. "See you Saturday, slut." He spits on the ground by my side. "Don't bother wearing underwear." His evil eyes bore into my skull. "You won't be wearing it long enough to matter."

9

ADAM

The last few weeks have been balls to the wall with practice, games, studying, and working to the early morning hours. The drug business is booming, and Ray has been singing my praises, telling me how his clients don't want to buy from anyone but me. I should be happy that I'm his best dealer, but selling drugs isn't something I'm proud of.

It's also sucking the life out of me. I can barely keep my eyes open in class, and running my ass through drills and workouts hasn't been easy.

I'm gearing up to throw the football when Coach blows his whistle. "That's it for today. Five laps around the track before you hit the showers. Miller, a word."

Everyone scatters—some of the team pounding out their laps and others grabbing water before they do.

I remove my helmet as I trot up to Coach who's standing on the sideline, reading something on his phone.

For a second, my stomach forms a knot. I can't tell if Coach is mad or he just wants to talk strategy. He's been pleased with my performance although he's been quite moody for the last couple of weeks, which makes me scratch my head.

The fact I'm selling drugs to his daughter is something that weighs on me anytime he calls my name. I'm fucking terrified he's going to find out, and it keeps me awake some nights. I'm risking a lot. But I can't stop. Not as long as Mom and Phoebe need the money.

Speaking of Emily, I haven't spotted her at any of the frat parties. I attended one last weekend solely in the hopes of seeing her. Zach seems to be deliberately keeping her away from me. Showing up alone when he needs to replenish supplies. And I swear he's doing it to keep us apart.

Coach lowers his phone and squints at me. Practice was good, so I've no clue what he wants. But the way he's staring at me leads me to believe he knows, and that knot I have gets tighter.

I'm not one to blurt out shit. So, I wait.

All the guys are jogging, and our assistant coaches are packing up.

Coach shoves a hand through his reddish-brown hair. "How's Phoebe?"

I flinch only because I'm expecting something quite different. "Her pneumonia is gone, and she's doing better." I've made enough money recently to pay for the repairs to Phoebe's vest.

"Good," he says, shooting a brief glance at Coach Price who keeps looking over at us, for some reason. They stare at one another, and Carter runs by, his blue eyes wide. I lift a shoulder. I've no idea what's going on. The tension between Coach Parker and Coach Price seems thick. They've been arguing about plays for the last week.

"Is there something else?" I ask Coach Parker. "I need to get my run in." I have a full night ahead with an English paper to write and then several clients to see.

Mom still hasn't found a job, and as much as she wants to, I want her to stay home. She needs to take care of Phoebe. But she doesn't want me to ruin my future. I can't say I blame her. I worry constantly that I'll get caught or, worse, Ray will discover I charge a little over the asking price for a bag of Molly. It's not much, and I don't do it all the time, but it's risky. The guy will sever my head if he finds out. While I like my head, I can't give two fucks about Ray. My family comes first.

Coach Parker breaks his weird face-off with Coach Price, giving me his sole focus. The lines around his eyes deepen. "I got a call from an NFL scout about you."

My jaw comes unhinged. "What?" I splutter, attempting to shake the shock from my brain.

Coach grins, clamping a hand on my shoulder. "You're good, son. Don't shortchange yourself."

It's not that I don't think I'm good. It's just I wasn't expecting to hear from any scout so soon in my college career. While I'm fucking stoked as shit, my gut is telling me the timing isn't good.

Fuck timing.

Coach folds his arms over his chest. "I sent the scout some tapes of the last couple of games."

"What team?" My brain is clearing of the shock, and I'm eager to know if it's the Carolina Panthers. If I could play for them, Phoebe and Mom could attend games since the stadium is one state over. I can also stay close to home in the event my family needs me.

"The Chicago Bears," he confirms, as his phone rings. "I'll let you know more when I do. For now, he's just inquiring. I have to take this call." He struts away, leaving me pumping my fist in the air. It's not the Panthers, but so the fuck what.

It's the NFL.

Coach Price follows on Coach Parker's heels as they cross the field toward the sports complex.

I start into a slow jog. *The Bears are interested in me!* I can't wait to tell Mom. But the moment I think how happy she'll be, I decide it's not a good idea to say a word. She'll tell me to stop selling drugs.

Fuck. Drugs.

I pick up my pace, running like I'm sprinting in an Olympic fifty-yard dash. The team has left the track, and I don't even see Carter. I forgo the rest of the run, getting in only a lap. I've got too much to do, and I can at least share the good news with my teammates.

I head into the locker room amid laughter and chatter. The guys are buzzed from the great practice. We're all still flying high with our record this season, and the feeling is better than any buzz I get from alcohol.

I shrug out of my T-shirt when Carter lifts his head from untying his cleats. "What's going on, hoss?"

I open my locker, which is right next to his. "The Bears want to see my tapes."

His mouth drops open. "Fucking A. That's awesome."

The locker room chatter dies.

Carter stands up on the bench. "A round of applause for hoss, our illustrious QB is being scouted by the Bears."

The room explodes with guys banging on the lockers and hooting and hollering and throwing out compliments. I barely hear my phone ringing on top of my wallet in my locker.

I want to join in on the celebration, but I need to make sure it isn't Mom calling about Phoebe. I know it's not my burner phone. I tuck that baby away in a secret compartment under the back seat in my truck where not even Sam would find it. I don't keep Ray's phone on until I'm getting ready to hit the streets. He insists I check in with him before I unload my supply. I usually drop by the car repair shop on most nights to pick up my inventory anyway. I try not to keep that shit on me if I can help it.

Seeing Sam's name on the screen, I immediately answer. The panic coursing through me makes my hands shake. *He never calls me.* He's usually tutoring, at the library, or immersed in *Mortal Kombat*, at this time of day, which only means something happened to my sister.

My heart splinters as I say, "What's up?"

The guys are loud, causing me to stick my head in my locker to hear Sam.

"You better get back to the dorm." His tone is laced with worry. "Emily, man. She's here."

I check on the guys around me, making sure no one is listening. My gaze is bouncing around the room like a ball that got away from a basketball player. The last thing I need is for Coach Parker lurking in the shadows. He's been known to listen in on our convos as we talk after practices.

"Adam," Sam practically shouts through the phone.

With the coast clear, I stick my head back in my locker. "Are you telling me..."

"Yes, Emily Parker," Sam confirms. "Please, get over here now. She's...she's strung out on something and stinks of alcohol."

Fuuuck!

I hang up, making quick work to shower and dress. As I do, the guys are giving me high-fives for the scout news and saying congrats. But all I hear is Emily Parker is strung out, and my gut twists and churns. I don't have time to think.

Coach Parker is so going to have my balls staked in the end zone for sure if he finds out about this.

I'm hurrying the fuck out when Carter catches up to me. "You look like you lost your lunch, hoss." His blue eyes are swimming with concern. "Everything okay?"

Fuck no.

I'm about to puke up the big bowl of chicken pasta I ate earlier.

"I need to call my mom. She left me a message, and I want to be sure my sister is okay," I lie.

Fucking drugs. I don't take them, but my actions in some ways sure reflect that of a stoner as the lies keep coming.

"We'll talk later," I holler as I'm hoofing it to my truck.

Thankfully, Carter is cool and knows my family is important. "We'll celebrate this weekend," he shouts at my retreating form.

It's too soon to get excited about the Bears. Sure, I'm fucking over the moon that a team is biting, but that's just it—they're only biting.

But the Bears, football, school, and everything else vanish as I rush into my dorm room ten minutes later. The room reeks of booze as I inhale second-hand alcohol fumes.

I take in the sight of Emily, and my fucking heart disintegrates, knowing I'm the one who has helped do this to her.

She's curled up on my bed, wiggling her arms and legs about, as if she's dancing horizontally. Her gorgeous strawberry blond waves are a mess around her face. Her bare legs are tanned and toned beneath her tiny white shorts. I can't help but let my gaze roam wild and free until my eyes land on her tits poking out of a clingy top.

Sam vaults off his desk chair. "It took you long enough." He's whispering.

Emily is in her own little world, half in and half out of reality, until the door click shuts.

She sits up, looks our way and waves. Then, as if she looked right through us, she flops down on the bed, smiling to herself while gazing at the ceiling, as if it's the most fascinating thing.

Her voice is pretty as she softly starts singing "Somewhere Over the Rainbow."

Sam and I exchange a sad look.

What the fuck happened to her to cause her to turn to drugs and booze? Who would willingly do this? And how often does she indulge? Zach is one of my best clients, and he buys regularly. I've long suspected he's supplying the girls, because Scar and Emily rarely buy directly from me, and this confirms it.

"She's been singing that over and over again," Sam says. "She's also asking for Wrangler. Who's that? And what is going on?"

My blood turns to ice at the mention of my street name. Sam can't know what I've been doing every night coming in late. He's a cool guy and leaves my business to me. But I'm not sure how long I can keep lying to him.

My body is frozen solid until Emily levels me with those big blue eyes that always suck me in. Now, my legs are moving until I'm kneeling in front of her.

Tears cascade down her cheeks as she reaches out to touch me. The minute her clammy fingers land on my face, my heart falls out of my chest.

Sam comes closer. "We need to do something."

The only thing we can do is let her come down off her high, and no fucking way she's leaving until then, especially with the guys in the dorm. The last thing the three of us need is for anyone to know she's here. Sam can't afford to get in the middle of my shit or Emily's. He's got his future all mapped out with his plans to start his own tech company. He's dead set on moving to Silicon Valley and becoming the next Steve Jobs.

"Did anyone see you come in?" The question is aimed at Emily, but it's Sam who answers.

"The whole dorm probably did."

No doubt. The guys would notice a beautiful girl walking the halls. I suspect some of them know who Emily is too, and that makes my pulse stop for a beat.

Emily giggles then cries. "Wes didn't see me. He doesn't live..." Her angelic voice trails off.

I grit my teeth. "Did Wes do something to you?" I emit a low growl. The need to find the fuckwad and beat him to a pulp is strong.

I steal a glance at Sam. He's sweating, and his blue eyes are drenched in fear.

"T-the Molly is gone." Emily slurs her words, and it's clear she's drunk. If she's mixed it with drugs, she's in a bad way, but I doubt I'll get anything coherent out of her in this state. "I need more."

"Sam, can you get a wet washcloth?" I ask in a calm voice even though I'm trying like hell to keep my shit together.

She's worse off than I thought, and panic swirls in my gut. I can't see straight. I'm not sure I can even breathe. I've seen addicts strung out on street corners and in dark alleys, but to see someone I know go down this path is heart-wrenching.

And I'm pissed at myself.

Ray is right.

The world of drugs is different now.

Maybe it's because I'm older, wiser, and an adult. But I care what I'm putting into people.

When I worked for Donnie, I was a novice and too young to care.

"She's on Molly?" Sam's voice rises in pitch as he threads shaky fingers through his blond hair.

I shrug, because I honestly don't know. She said the Molly was gone, but there's no way of knowing when she last took it. Sam's been a great friend, and he doesn't deserve to be treated like he means nothing to me. But I can't bring myself to tell him the truth. Not yet anyway, and Emily is my first priority right now.

"Washcloth, Sam," I repeat, more harshly than I meant to.

He nods as he rushes out of the room.

I climb up on my bed, leaning my back against the wall. As if we've done this a thousand times, Emily snuggles up to me. I drape my arm around her, rubbing my hand up and down her arm. Her skin is piping hot, and her hair is sticky with sweat as I rest my chin on her head. Alcohol fumes cling to her clothes and her sweat-slickened skin, and I wonder what could've happened to send her into such a dark pit.

"Talk to me," I say softly. I want to know how much Molly she took and when. How much booze she drank. I want to know if Wes touched her. I want to know why my heart is all over the fucking place and my cock is growing in my jeans. I want to take away her demons, but I know I'm partly to blame for her state of mind. Guilt jumps up and bites me, and I'm so fucking conflicted.

I think of calling Zach, but he'll only enable her more.

Emily buries her face in my chest. "You feel nice," she says rubbing her hands up and down my sides. "And you smell nice," she adds, inhaling deeply.

Oh, man. If she was sober, and I believed she was telling the truth, she'd be under me with my mouth molded to hers right now.

But she's not, and I don't.

You feel like somewhere over that rainbow where I imagine it's a blissful place devoid of drugs, and parties, and sickness.

She starts running her fingers across my abs, and my stomach is doing cartwheels. Meanwhile, my cock is painfully hard, and straining noticeably against the zipper of my jeans. When her hand lands on my belt, I suck in a sharp breath.

She lifts her head, and her eyes are dilated as she searches my face.

The need to kiss her, to touch her, is so fucking strong, but I'm not one of those guys who takes advantage of a girl when she's down.

I kiss her on the forehead as I remove her hand to her side. "Rest, babe. You need to sleep." I'm not letting her leave until she's more coherent. I can't let anyone see her leaving either.

It's not because I don't want her to leave.

Or because I want to hold her in my arms and take care of her.

The best thing is for her to stay put I convince myself. But fuck it. I'm working tonight, and Ray will hunt me down if I don't show.

Emily sighs one last time as her body deflates against mine.

Sam returns with a washcloth, handing it to me. "She's going to be okay, right?"

I have no fucking idea. But I'm going to make it my mission to ensure she is.

Emily starts to breathe deeply.

"She's sleeping," Sam confirms, sinking into his desk chair, his blue eyes appraising.

Silence fills the room.

I could stay like this all night, but I need to make a phone call. Carefully, I lift her off me, setting her down flat on the bed and adjusting her head so it's on my pillow, before covering her with a light sheet. A sheen of sweat still clings to her brow, and she's hot to the touch, so I don't want to tuck her under the covers even if my nurturing instinct is screaming at me to do just that.

I climb off the bed, and Emily lets out a soft mewl.

"She can't stay," Sam murmurs. "Her mother runs this campus." Panic is evident on Sam's face.

I pace the room. He's right. But until the entire building is sound asleep and Emily is in a better state of mind, she isn't leaving.

"She came here thinking a guy by the name of Wrangler lived in this room." Sam leans his elbow on his knees. "Something about needing to buy Molly from the guy."

I shut my eyes briefly, staving off the nausea in my stomach. I can't tell Sam. He'd be so disappointed to know Wrangler is me. That I'm the one who did this to Emily.

"I need to make a call." I start for the door. Fresh outside air is necessary to quench the burn from the acid in my throat.

Sam pops up. "Wait. You can't leave." His voice is low.

"I'm not, man. I'll be back in five minutes. I don't want to wake her."

I want to crawl into bed with her. I want to fuck her until the sun comes up, but I mentally slap myself out of my lustful thoughts, because she needs something different from me tonight.

Sam meets me at the door. "I need to tell you something. Emily came to me last week and asked for my help."

I jump back a step. "What the fuck? What kind of help?" Worry floods my veins.

And why Sam? Why not me? I'm not jealous. I'm curious. Usually when an addict wants help, they want drugs.

"She asked me to do some investigative work on Weston Blakely. I turned her down." He glances at Emily who is sound asleep. "What's that all about? She mentioned him earlier. Do you think he's supplying her with drugs?"

I claw my hands through my hair, yanking it in the process, and the stinging pain quells the urge to put my fist through the wall. "No idea, man. No idea. But I intend to find out." I intend to erase Weston Blakely from Emily's life until he's nothing more than a bad memory.

10

EMILY

A familiar dark cloud hovers over my head as I slowly come to. My tongue is glued to the roof of my mouth, and it tastes like something died in there. I search through my mind trying to remember what happened last night.

The bed dips behind me, and an arm tightens around my waist. I stiffen, opening my eyes more fully, and take in my surroundings. I'm on the outside of a stranger's bed, looking at another twin bed across the way. The covers are neatly made, and I can't tell if anyone slept there. Posters hanging over the bed confirm whoever lives here is into computer games.

"Hey." A gruff voice says at my back, and bile travels up my throat. I wrack my brain for some clue as to where I am, but it's a complete blank. It's not surprising. Most times after partying hard, I can't remember a fucking thing about where I was, who I was with, what I took, or who I screwed.

The usual self-loathing washes over me, and I wriggle against the hard, warm body at my back, trying to get free. "Let me go."

The arm is gone almost instantly, and I stumble out of the bed, falling flat on my ass. I tilt my chin up, gulping nervously, until my gaze locks on emerald-green eyes I'm familiar with.

"Adam?" I glance around me, noticing the layout. "Fuck." I rub a hand across my chest. "Please tell me I'm not in one of the male dorms."

"Yeah. About that." His shirt is wrinkled as he sits up, yawning while dragging a hand through his dark hair. It's sticking up in all directions, and with the five o'clock shadow lining his chin and cheeks and the adorable lopsided smile on his face, he looks utterly delectable.

And completely fuckable.

Thank hell, I've come down from my high, or I'd probably have tackled him by now. A worrisome thought flits through my mind. "Oh my God." I clamp a hand over my mouth, my eyes popping wide. "Please tell me we didn't fuck."

His brows knit together. "We didn't. Because I'd never take advantage of any girl in your condition, but it's not good that you don't remember." His frown deepens. "And I'm kind of hurt you think that'd be such a terrible thing."

"I… It… I." I stop babbling, taking a moment to collect myself. "I have zero recollection of what happened last night, but that's not uncommon." I drag my lower lip between my teeth, fighting a blush. "And I don't think that. Only that it might've happened and I hadn't remembered."

His lips curl into a smile, almost fading straightaway. "Does that happen a lot? That you wake up and can't remember anything?"

I shrug, accepting his hand and letting him pull me to my feet. He pats the spot on the edge of the bed beside him and I sit down, noticing my attire for the first time. "What the hell am I wearing?" I tug at the hem of the unfamiliar T-shirt, which barely covers my ass.

"You puked all over the place last night. I snuck you into the showers while Sam replaced the bedcovers." He waves his hand at the shirt I'm wearing. "That's all I had to give you."

"Ugh." I bury my head in my hands. "I'm sorry," I whisper.

"It's okay." He takes my hands away, and delicious tingles zip up and down my arms at the contact. "Neither of us will say anything."

"Where is Sam?" I only discovered they were roomies when I stole onto Mom's home computer to find out which dorm Adam lived in.

"He went to class."

"Shit. I've missed class?" Mom is going to flip out. Not coming home and skipping class is a big no-no.

"We both have, but don't worry. Sam said he'd cover our asses."

"How?"

"He'll hack into the school system and amend our attendance records so no one is any the wiser."

"Wow. I knew he had mad skills, but that's insane."

"He doesn't normally do stuff like that," Adam admits, and his voice is strained. "I might've had to bribe him to do it."

"I bet he thinks I'm a bad influence, and he already thinks I'm a weirdo."

"Because you asked him to spy on Wes or some other reason I don't know about?"

"If you mean have I pulled a stunt like this on Sam before, the answer is no. I try not to get high during the week."

"So, what happened last night?" His soft tone matches the look on his face.

"Since the fiasco at the fundraiser, my parents have had me on lockdown."

Understanding dawns on him. "I heard you and Zach got into trouble, but what do you mean by lockdown?"

"I'm forbidden from hanging out with Zach, and I've been grounded from partying for a while."

His eyes splay wide. "Aren't you a sophomore?" I nod. "Then how the hell can your parents demand that of you?"

"I still live with them. Unfortunately." I sit on my hands to disguise the slight tremors taking hold of me.

"Coach is strict with us, but I never imagined he'd be that strict on his own daughter." He leans back on his hands.

"To be fair, it's more my mom. I embarrassed her."

He bolts upright. "The way I heard it, Wes was out of line, and Zach was only coming to your defense."

My jaw drops. "Who told you that?" I don't think Zach would've shared what happened with Adam. Certainly not Wes. And the only reason I'm surprised is because Adam heard correctly, which is unusual, because the rumor mill never gets the story straight.

He bites down on his plump lip and it's sexy as fuck. "I told you I didn't want you anywhere near that asshole and I said it for a reason. Asshole's got a rep around campus among the guys. I've heard rumors. He's not a good guy." His tone is reserved, but worry and irritation sit idly underneath.

I want to tell Adam he doesn't own me and he can't tell me what to do. My parents think they have that right too.

But I like he's worried about me.

That he seems to want to protect me.

It's been far too long since I've had that warm feeling of someone caring about me. Dad is still all over the place. One minute, he's sticking up for me, and the next, he's siding with Mother Dearest.

And Mom?

Well, she's consistent in how she feels about me.

I snort. "Yeah, tell me about it."

His eyes narrow, and he reaches out, taking my hand. I lower my gaze, marveling at how swamped my hand looks in his large one. Thanks to my height, I've always felt gangly and awkward around guys, but Adam makes me feel small and feminine, and I like that feeling a lot.

"Are you going to explain that?"

I yank my hand back, wrapping my arms around my torso, trying to hide the bruises compliments of Wes and his disgusting crew. The movement causes the shirt to lift a little, flashing the edge of my panties. His eyes dart to my crotch for a split second before he jerks his head up. Thank fuck he didn't remove those last night. I'd die of mortification if I'd just flashed him my bare pussy.

I drop my hands to my sides. "I already explained. Wes is trying to date me, and he won't take no for an answer."

"It's that last part I'm afraid of." He cups my face, forcing my gaze to his. "You can tell me. I'm trustworthy. I promise."

"Why?" I whisper.

"Why am I trustworthy?" His face creases in confusion.

I shake my head, and warmth floods my cheek from his large palm. "Why do you want me to tell you?" I don't find it easy opening up, and I don't allow many people to get close. Even when my therapist in rehab tried to peel my layers back, I fought her tooth and nail. But Adam isn't my therapist. He's a sexy as fuck guy, staring at me like he wants to take away all the bad in my life.

I wish he could. But no one holds that much power.

I can't help but get lost in his beautiful green eyes framed by the longest lashes. They are thick, and jet-black, and I've a mad case of lash envy. With his strong nose, chiseled jawline, thick dark hair, and tan skin, he can definitely rock the cover of GQ. And that's before I mention his lick-worthy abs and the impressive snake in his pants. A snake that is growing in size the longer we stare at one another.

My mouth is parched, and I lick my lips subconsciously while my libido sluggishly wakes up. My nipples stand to attention, and I'm sure they're trying to poke their way out of his shirt. He may have left my panties on, but I'm one hundred percent *not* wearing a bra. The thought he might have caught a sneaky look at the girls sends warmth flooding to my core.

His eyes drift to my mouth before lowering farther, and my nipples could cut glass, they're so sharp.

Slowly, he drags his gaze back up to my face. I struggle to keep my eyes locked on his when I notice the giant erection tenting his pants. I love that he's as turned on as me. That he feels the spark too.

"Why wouldn't I want to know?" he says, finally breaking whatever spell we were both under.

I blink for a few seconds while I try to remember what we were talking about. "Because you don't know me, so it doesn't make sense for you to care."

"I know enough." He moves his hand from my face, winding his fingers in my hair. "And if Wes is bothering you, I want to help."

Tears pool in my eyes, and I wish he could help me, but it's looking more and more inevitable.

I managed to deflect Wes's plans the last two weekends, playing innocent while telling Dad it wasn't a good idea for me to help Wes study at his frat house. Not with all the guys and partying that goes on there. I knew that was all it would take to switch the venue, and it worked like a treat. Wes was practically frothing at the mouth that he had to study at our place. Especially when he realized my father was in attendance and he couldn't lay a fucking finger on me. I'd made all of Dad's favorite foods and suggested he invite his buddies to our house to watch the NFL game instead of going out, and he loved the idea so much he did it two weeks in a row.

But I know I'm on borrowed time.

Wes keeps loitering around outside my classes, so I've taken to leaving in a big group of people so he can't accost me.

And I ignore all the obnoxious messages he's sending me from an anonymous account. He's smart enough to know I'm saving them, so he's going to great lengths to cover his tracks.

Which sickens me. Because it means he has nefarious plans in mind, and I know it's only a matter of time before him and his buddies get their hands on me.

Zach gave me the list of girls from their old high school, and I've been doing some investigative work of my own, but it's slow progress, and I'll admit I've dropped the ball recently in favor of Molly. But thoughts of what he has planned for me have me so on edge I need the high to just get through each day.

"Emily." Adam clicks his fingers, peering into my face with concern in his eyes. "You still with me?"

"Sorry. My mind wandered." I clench my hands in my lap, swallowing back bile as my body trembles all over.

"You're shaking." He pulls me to his chest, and I rest my cheek against his shoulder, allowing him to comfort me. He smooths a hand up and down my back, and it's such a tender gesture it brings tears to my eyes again.

Adam is one of the good guys. Last night and this morning have proven that. If I was a normal girl, I'd be ass over tits crazy for him.

But I'm not, and I can't afford to be.

I shuck out of his hold. "Thanks for looking after me last night." I stand. "I should go."

"Emily, wait." He stands, threading his fingers in mine. "I know you're scared. I can see it in your eyes. And I want to help."

"Why me?" I tip my chin up, peering deep into his eyes.

He takes a big breath. "Because I like you and I don't want to see you hurt."

"Is that the only reason?"

He blows air out of his mouth, looking undecided for a few minutes. "I know all the reasons why you and I shouldn't hang out," he says, and my heart splutters in my chest. "But there are more reasons why we should." My heart grows wings and soars.

"You want to hang out with me?" I blurt.

He rests his forehead on mine. "I want to do so much with you, Emily," he whispers, and his warm breath fans across my face, igniting new flames. "But why don't we start with being friends?"

"I don't have many friends," I admit in a hushed voice.

"Then it's settled." He hugs me to him, and I don't protest this time, wrapping my arms around his solid body, and clinging to him like he's my only lifeline. He tilts my chin up with the tip of one finger. "Now, tell me what's really going on with Wes."

* * *

IT'S RELATIVELY EASY TO SNEAK OUT OF ADAM'S DORM AS MOST students are in class by now. But it was still supremely stupid to come here last night. I'm not sure if Adam fully bought my explanation about Wes, but I did my best. I told him he has a photo of me snorting coke, and he's threatening to show it to my parents, but I didn't tell him the rest. I wanted to, but I just can't. I can't drag anyone else into this mess, and he's already severely pissed at Wes. Imagine how pissed he'd be if he knew the full truth.

Adam is one of my dad's guys, and he can't get involved. Especially now the Chicago Bears are showing interest in him. Adam's eyes lit up like a Christmas tree when he was telling me about it as he walked me outside. Having a scout take an interest is a big deal, so there's no way he can get dragged into my shit.

Besides, there's nothing anyone can do to help me.

I didn't remember when I first woke up, but I remember now.

I know exactly why I was banging on Sam and Adam's door last night. Why I got so completely trashed I was beyond the point of caring. Maybe a part of me wanted someone to find me. To report to my mom. Because if I'm kicked off campus, and thrown out of the house, I'll be forced to leave, and then Wes won't find me.

Intense pain presses down on my chest, and my thoughts turn dark. I lean against a tree across campus, trying to stifle my sobs as pain climbs up my throat.

Images of the video Wes sent me yesterday return to haunt me.

I don't know when it was taken, or how he got his hands on it, but someone in the room clearly recorded it. It's obvious that the majority of people engaged in the orgy, myself included, were out of their fucking minds on alcohol or drugs or, in my case, most likely a mix of both.

I threw up watching myself being fucked, simultaneously, by Zach and another guy in our circle.

The thoughts of my parents watching that or, worse, the entire campus—if he uploads it to the college app like he threatened—has me practically convulsing, as I squeeze my eyes shut, hugging the tree, silently crying out for someone to tell me what to do.

I don't know how to make him go away this time.

If I don't show up at the hotel room he's rented on Saturday night, he says he's uploading it.

Reality is like a stake through my heart as I realize there's only one thing I can do.

I need to let him, and his friends, do what they want to me.

Even if I already know this is one rape I'll never ever recover from.

11

ADAM

Practice was a blur for so many reasons. My mind has been on overdrive since Emily slept in my bed. I can't shake that night. I can't concentrate on my classes. I even fucked up a sale, charging less than Ray's asking price.

Then there's Ray.

He reamed my ass for not showing up for work. He almost took my cut away, but I shut that shit down. He loses me. He loses clients.

My phone rings as I'm getting out of my truck outside my dorm. Mom's name comes across the screen.

"Mom," I answer as panic sucks the air out of my lungs. "Everything okay?"

"Yes. Yes. Phoebe and I are fine."

I wipe the sweat from my brow, releasing a relieved breath.

"I wanted to tell you the good news. I have an interview on Monday at a bed and breakfast in town. It's an eight-hour shift while Phoebe is in school, and no weekends. So, if I get the job, then you can stop...you know."

I suspect Phoebe is in the room with her or close by where she doesn't want her to hear.

"That's great news, Mom." It is. But her minimum-wage job isn't going to erase all our debt or support her and Phoebe, particularly Phoebe's medical bills.

"If I get the job, you'll quit. Right?" she asks.

If I know my mom, she's holding her breath.

I can't bring myself to confirm I won't sell drugs anymore. I'm digging myself into a situation I might not have a way out of, but it's one that keeps food on the table for them. Besides, my commitment of three months isn't up yet.

A group of guys exit the dorm as I'm walking in. They nod at me, and one holds the door open.

"Mom, can we talk later?" I take the stairs two at a time to the fourth floor.

"Adam." Her motherly tone stops me in my tracks. "I love you, and I know why you're doing it. But please think carefully about it. You're messing with your future, and I'm not okay with that."

I pop my head against the wall in the stairwell, feeling like I've disappointed her. In part I have. Drug dealing isn't going to win me a spot on an NFL team. It's going to land me in jail if things go south. And that's what she's worried about. Not a day goes by that I don't think the same fucking thing.

"Remember," she says softly. "You're no good to us in jail."

My heart sinks to my feet. "I know, Mom. I love you, too. I'll see you on Sunday."

She tells me she loves me again before she hangs up.

Sam flinches when I walk in, shutting his computer screen down like he's hiding something—which he is.

A crease forms between my brows. "What's going on?" I ask, eyeing his computer.

He spins around in his desk chair. "Sit down." He waves to my bed without looking at me.

Hesitantly, I do as he says only because I'm afraid of what he's about to tell me. It's been par for the course since Emily shared what Wes has on her. And it's one of the main reasons I've been a bear to live with or be around. I'm surprised none of the guys on the team, or Coach, has noticed. Coach is the only one who snaps at us, but I took a play out of his book today. I lost my shit on Garrett for not following the play we were trying to perfect before the game tomorrow.

I chew on the inside of my cheek. "You found something on Wes?" Sam and I fought about him looking into the fuckwad. I know Sam doesn't want his name anywhere close to this, since President Parker could put a hurt on us.

But Sam saw how strung out Emily was the other night, and he can't sit idly by and not help. Like me, he's afraid Wes will do something drastic, and as vulnerable as Emily is, he doesn't want that on his conscience, and fuck, neither do I.

But it's more than that for me. I want to protect her. To shield her from Wes and anyone who would try to manipulate her. It's been a long time since I've felt so strongly about any girl. Especially one I haven't even kissed yet. But Emily Parker has gotten under my skin, and I like feeling her there.

Most of us on campus know Weston Blakely is a dick and treats girls like shit. I've witnessed it a couple of times at parties even before I saw how he treated Emily at the frat house.

Sam purses his lips. "I know you have a thing for Emily even though you won't admit that. Are you sure she's worth the potential trouble you could get into? Think NFL, dude. The Bears. Your future."

I close my eyes briefly. "I could say the same to you, man. Your future is bright." I scrub a hand down my face. "She's worth it, Sam." Sure, I'm attracted to her. I want to feel her naked body against mine, want to taste her, tease her, and devour her. It was so fucking hard not to do any of those things when she slept in my arms.

Changing her out of her clothes and into my T-shirt was hell; I'm not going to lie. I looked, but I didn't touch, because I'd never do that to any girl who was so out of it. Right now, this thing with Emily is not about our obvious attraction. I won't let any guy blackmail a woman into dating him.

Sam snaps his fingers. "Earth to Adam."

I blink. "Sorry. Look, no girl should be subjected to a guy like Wes. He's vile, and he has zero respect for women. I'd kill any guy who'd dare to treat Phoebe like that."

His face darkens. He adores Phoebe, and I know, even after we graduate, Sam will always be a part of our lives.

I pop to my feet and pace. "We need to stop him."

He grabs the back of his neck. "I agree, but you don't need to be punching walls or anyone. You have a game tomorrow."

I crack my knuckles, the sound exploding in the silence between us. "What did you find?"

Sam shakes his head. "I'm not sure you want to see this."

I cross my arms over my chest, leveling him with a 'get real' look. "Sam, I'm a big boy."

"Wes has upped the blackmailing stakes." He gnaws on his lip, and my heart stutters in my chest. "He sent her a video, anonymously, but it wreaks of that asshole." His nostrils flare, and fire flashes in his eyes. I don't think I've ever seen Sam so mad. "It's not pleasant viewing. You've got to keep your shit together. Promise me." His tone drops a notch.

I settle behind him, my pulse jumping erratically, as he opens his computer screen. "I promise." I want to believe what Sam's about to show me can't be worse than what Emily already shared with me, but his reaction is scaring me.

He taps a key and video begins to play.

It takes me a second to register what's going on—naked bodies, group sex, strung-out junkies, and what the fuck...

I spin around, clutching my head, trying to erase the picture of Emily being fucked by Zach and some other dude I don't recognize from my mind. Rage pours through me, constricting my airways. She's stoned, amped up on some shit, and letting these guys screw her every which way to Sunday.

She doesn't know what she's doing, dude. The drugs are controlling her.

My fury wanes for the moment until the image of two guys fucking her flashes like a beacon before me.

Drugs or not, the need to strangle Zach overpowers me, because he isn't Emily's friend if he's allowing her to do shit like this.

He's an addict, man. Come on, you know that. He's an enabler.

Fuck, I am too. I'm the one selling Zach the shit. Regardless, Emily isn't safe around him—that much I'm certain of.

I'm about to bolt out of the room and find the jerk when Sam blocks the door. "You're not going anywhere until you calm down."

I angle my head and pierce him with a scathing look. "I can move you out of the way, you know." I could lift Sam with my little finger and not break a sweat.

He nods. "But as mad as I am, I might give you a run for your money."

I chuckle, allowing myself a minute to regroup.

"You don't know the worst of it," he says, torment sweeping across his features.

Everything locks up inside me, and I feel ill. "Spit it out."

"Wes is demanding she meet him in a hotel in town Saturday night. If she doesn't show, he says he's going to send it to her parents and upload it to the college social app."

I push out all the air in my lungs. "I'm going to take a walk."

"Then I'm coming with."

"No. Stay here. You've done your part, and I thank you."

"Too bad. I'm not letting you do this alone," he says with a shitload of bravado. "And we need to have each other's backs. You're family."

That last part hits me right in the chest. When he finds out I'm a drug dealer—Emily's, in fact—he won't consider us family.

The humid air outside is as thick as the tension in the dorm room. I have no idea where I'm going, but I find I'm walking in the direction of my truck.

Sam grabs my arm to stop me. "Adam. You can't confront Wes. He's got President Parker on his side. I've seen emails exchanged between Wes's parents and her. He'll run straight to her and land Emily in the shitter."

I growl so loud that a couple walking by stops in their tracks.

Sam waves them off. "He's having a bad day."

The couple resumes their nightly stroll like their lives are a bed of roses without the thorns. Maybe so. Perhaps it's only ours that are a clusterfuck of epic proportions.

As much as I hate it, Sam is right. I can't confront Wes. Especially if he's covered his tracks. We've got to outsmart him to defeat him. But even the thought of Emily meeting him in a hotel room makes me want to rip his balls off and feed them to him and his disgusting posse of fratholes. We need a plan, and we need help. "I'm thinking of paying Zach a visit."

"Who's Zach?" Sam asks.

"One of the guys fucking her in the video."

"You know him?"

"I se..." I catch myself before spilling to Sam that Zach is a client. "I met him at the frat party that night I saw Wes and Emily get into it." I shared some of the details with Sam previously.

"For real?" Sam's blue eyes are huge. "Is he the one selling drugs to her then?"

"This is why I don't want you involved." I shake my head. "You're going to rule the world one day. Stick to that plan, and let me handle it."

Sam tucks his hands in his pants pockets. "You need my help, because Emily hasn't exactly been one hundred percent truthful."

I hate that he's right. "I fucking knew she was leaving some shit out." On one level, I can't blame her. I do play for her old man. But I hate that she doesn't trust me enough to fully confide in me. I thought we'd made some progress the other morning. We fucking agreed to be friends, and friends lean on one another. A pang of hurt clutches at my chest like a vise, but this isn't about me. I've got to push my feelings away. She agreed to let me help her, and that's exactly what I'm going to do

* * *

I COULDN'T SLEEP LAST NIGHT. AFTER SAM TOLD ME ABOUT THE video and the email, I tossed and turned all night. Images of Zack and that other asshole fucking Emily tormented me for hours. I wish I'd never seen it, and it'll take colossal effort on my part to forget about it. But the fact is, it's before I knew her. I might be mad that she's totally wasted, but it was still consensual. No one was forcing her into it. And we've all got history. I need to put it out of my mind. Especially when the more pressing concern is Wes's imminent plans for Emily.

I was itching to ask Ray if I could borrow one of his guns and kill the fucker. The only reason I didn't was Sam. He wants to find as much evidence as he can to put Wes away for a long time. I have to agree. Killing the fucker would be too easy, and a guy like Wes needs to rot in some hellhole for the rest of his life. But first, I need to stop Emily from meeting him tonight.

Sam, Carter, and I are waiting on Zach one block from the hotel where Emily is shortly due to meet Wes. The plan is to confront him before Emily arrives. We have one hour before the big meet, and it needs to go smoothly.

I enlisted Carter because he's got the muscle, and I trust him. He was on board the minute I told him I wanted to screw over Weston Blakely. He didn't ask what it was about, and I didn't offer more than the bare minimum. Emily is clearly terrified of her parents finding out about her lifestyle, and it's not my secret to share.

I brought Zach into the fold since he's Emily's friend and he's already tried to defend her from Wes, so I figured he'd want to help. As much as I want to beat the ever-loving shit out of him for fucking the girl I'm into, I've shelved my personal feelings. There is safety in numbers, and we need him.

It's as simple as that.

But after tonight, I'm not selling to him anymore. I can't have him feeding Emily's habit, and I want to be a true friend to her and help her kick the habit before she ends up in a dark place she can't come back from.

He'll be pissed, but I don't give a fuck.

Ray will be too. Again, I don't give a fuck.

After this is all over, I need to quit the drug-dealing business. I can't ask Emily to stop taking the shit when I'm selling Molly to Zach who feeds it to her. I know they can find drugs elsewhere, but it won't be from me.

And I'm determined to do everything I can to help Emily clean up her act.

"How many times did you call Emily?" I ask Sam as I scan the busy street of people window-shopping in a touristy part of the city.

"I left her several messages to call you or me," Sam says.

My cell was off during the game, but I'd checked it the second I hit the locker room, disappointed there was no missed call from her. She's avoiding me, and that makes me uneasy.

The game was a complete blowout. We lost big.

I played like shit. I got sacked three times because I hesitated, which is unlike me. I had two interceptions. If the Bears were watching, I'm sure they aren't interested in signing me anymore.

I couldn't look Coach Parker in the eye when he yelled his head off at me after the game. I apologized, but he didn't want to hear it. If he knew where my mind was at, he'd probably be hugging the shit out of me and giving me a fucking medal.

But after Emily told me about her parents believing Wes more than her with that incident at the fundraiser, I didn't see a point in telling Coach. Anyway, I can't. Not unless I want to lose her from my life permanently.

My pulse is on overdrive as I keep checking the time. "Where the fuck is Zach?"

Carter slaps me on the arm and flicks his head at the traffic light at the corner.

I spot Zach strutting up, hands in his pockets, hair styled perfectly, clothes neatly pressed as if he's headed to one of the many clubs in the city. "Did you get ahold of Emily? Because I didn't."

Instead of answering him, I ram my fist into his nose. Can't help it. Just looking at his face sets me off, knowing what I know. "What the fuck, man?" He holds his nose as blood oozes out.

"Hoss," Carter warns. "Save it for that asshole."

"This is a bad idea," Sam mutters, regarding me with concern.

I rub my stinging knuckles, leveling Zach with a glare. "That's for not looking out for Emily." Zach wasn't aware of the video, until we spoke over the phone, and I filled him in. Although, he did know Wes was blackmailing her, courtesy of Scarlett. Zach shared news of Wes's past. Something which made me almost hurl up my lunch. Wes is far more evil than I've given him credit for. I shudder to think what would've happened to Emily if Sam hadn't discovered that email, and hadn't uncovered the evidence proving how much of a lowlife Blakely is.

"I'm doing my fucking best," Zach snaps. "And I'm here, aren't I?"

I want to confront him about the things I know, but this isn't the time or the place. I walk a few paces to blow off some steam. "Did you go by her house?" I ask Zach.

He looks at me like I have five heads. "Her mother hates me, and I'm not supposed to be around Emily. Even if I did, her mother wouldn't let me see her."

We don't need to draw suspicion anyway.

Sam waves his iPad at me. "Let's go. I need to hack into the hotel's system if we want to find out what room he's in. Our luck, Wes is already there."

Sam tried hacking into Wes's phone to track him, but he couldn't access it, so this is our Plan B.

The lobby of the hotel is bright, busy, and loud. A bar sits off to one side. The concierge desk and check-in counter are on the other. People are coming in and out, going about their usual business.

Sam locates a suitable spot near the business center while the three of us linger near the bar.

"I can't wait to see Wes's face when he finds us in his room," Zach says, grinning.

That's one thing we agree on.

Carter leans against a pillar. "And if he walks in now?"

"Then we approach him." I say. "He won't make a scene." He's the type of guy who worries about his reputation. That's why, when we're done with him, the only reputation he'll have is being someone's bitch in prison. Prisoners don't like rapists. A truth Wes will learn quickly.

Carter grins. "Fuck yeah. I'm ready to put the hurt on the asshole."

Zach looks pensive, but I don't get a chance to ask what he's thinking when Sam rushes over.

"Got it. But bad news. He checked in an hour ago."

"What the fuck?" I pull on my hair, immediately racing to the elevators with the guys on my heels.

"Room six zero five," Sam blurts.

I stab the button for the elevator. "Sam, stay in the lobby."

He arches a brow. "Sorry, man. I might not be buff like you three, but I can help."

I don't have time to argue when the elevator doors open, and we all rush in.

I'm primed to explode. Terrified of finding Emily in that room in a vulnerable position. If he's laid one finger on her, he's a dead man. I'm fidgeting, bouncing on my heels, cracking my knuckles, and virtually swinging off the walls as the elevator ride seems like a slow boat to China.

As soon as the doors open, I'm sprinting down the long corridor, dodging a man coming out of room, almost tripping.

When I reach the room, I turn the handle, but it's locked.

I pound on the door. "Maintenance." I shout.

The heavy beat of music thumps inside, and bile swims up my throat.

I motion to Carter to get on the other side of the door. Sam and

Zach hang back by Carter. I don't want Wes looking through the peephole and spotting us.

I bang again. "Maintenance. If you don't open up, I'm coming in." Mom explained to me once that maintenance has a right to walk in after announcing themselves.

I wait a beat, praying like a motherfucker it's not too late, but my gut is spinning like an F-5 tornado.

No movement.

I jiggle the handle as Carter beats his fist on the door. "Maintenance!"

Fear drips off Sam, and Zach has a look I can't quite figure out.

The handle moves, the door opens a crack, and I barrel in like I'm the linebacker and not the quarterback. The guy falls back on his ass, and I freeze as my eyes quickly search the room.

Sex toys litter a coffee table, surrounded by empty beer bottles and lines of coke. Four big guys are lounging on the couch. Most of them are stripped to their boxers, making the intent clear. A camera is set up in the corner, trained on the spot where Emily is semi-naked on the floor with Wes's hand around her throat.

The need to puke is strong, but the need to draw blood is even stronger. I'm seeing stars as fury propels me into action. I emit a loud roar as I race toward Wes. He scrambles off Emily, trying to cover his dick.

She coughs repeatedly, and a strangled sound rips from her throat. Judging by the way her eyes are rolling back in her head, and the drug paraphernalia in the room, I'm guessing they doped her up to make her more compliant so it looked consensual if anyone ever found the tape.

Rage pummels my insides from all angles, and I launch myself at Wes, throwing him flat on his back before he can get away. I straddle him, ramming my fist into his face.

"Sam," I shout, looking up briefly. "Find Emily's clothes."

The other guys in the room start throwing punches at Zach and Carter, but they're stoned and drunk and no match for the guys who are lashing out in anger, same way I am.

Intense pain shuttles through my skull, and I yell out, clutching the side of my head as Wes shoves me off him. He drops the vase he used to hit me, backing up toward the sliding door that's open to the street below. His jaw is tight, and he's holding his nuts as if I'm going to cut them off.

Not a bad idea.

I climb to my feet, pain forgotten, and stalk toward him with my fists clenched and teeth bared. "You'll pay for this, motherfucker."

He chooses that moment to grin like he won this battle.

No, fucker. You're about to splatter to the sidewalk six stories below.

The sound of engines trickle by as Wes keeps inching backward.

"You're not going to hurt me," he says, shaking his head, displaying his usual level of smug arrogance. "You don't want to go to jail." He stumbles as his bare feet catch on the sliding door rail.

I push him into the railing.

He lets go of his nut sack, grabbing onto the iron rail. He sticks out his chin, defying me, daring me to try to throw him over.

My brain is clear as the night sky, and I debate whether to hang him over the railing by his now limp dick. Maybe that will scare him into not gang-raping a woman.

He grins, sending me over the edge.

My fists are flying and connecting with his nose, his jaw, and the side of his head.

He laughs. The fucker laughs. Even as blood sprays from his nose and trickles from a cut in his lip.

I zone out, consumed with black rage as I go at him, uncaring whether he lives or dies. This piece of shit doesn't deserve to live. I'm pounding my fists into his face and upper torso like I'm working out with the punching bag in the gym.

His head flies right then left. Bones crack. Blood splatters.

I'm so into my zone that I don't hear Sam's voice until he touches my back, grabbing hold of my shirt and yanking me back.

"Adam, enough. Emily is safe now."

I stop mid-punch, glaring at Wes's bloody face. "Touch her, go near her, call her, or even say her name, and I get wind of it, and you're fucking dead." I nod to his groin. "I'll cut off your small dick and force-feed it to your buddies."

I release a breath, letting Sam drag me back inside the room, as Blakely slumps to the floor of the balcony, groaning and hugging his ribs. Emily's cries reach my ears the instant the screaming dies down in my head. I rush out into the hallway, dropping to my knees in front of her. Her legs are pulled into her chest as she sobs, and the sound is breaking my heart.

I lift her in my arms. "Shhh. I got you, baby. No one will hurt you again."

I'll kill anyone who dares to.

12

EMILY

"Where are we?" I ask Adam, as he lays me down gently on a large, black leather couch after I've showered and freshened up in some stranger's bathroom. All I know is we're in someone's apartment, off campus.

"This is my buddy Carter's place," he confirms, kneeling in front of me. "His roomie went home for the weekend, and Carter is staying with his girl. He said we can stay as long as we like."

I touch my fingers to the large Band-Aid covering his left temple as a fresh bout of shivers whips through my body. I haven't stopped shaking since we left the hotel, tortured over thoughts of what would've happened if the guys hadn't shown up to rescue me. "Does it hurt?" I whisper.

"Nope." He grasps my wrist gently while shaking his head. "I have a hard head and it's only a few surface scratches." He smiles, and his entire face lights up in a way that does funny things to my insides. "I'll live."

"You can come sleep at my place," Zach blurts, pushing off the doorway. I don't miss the scowl he directs at Adam.

I turn onto my side, sliding my hands under my head. "I can't. I'm still banned from seeing you."

"I don't like you with *him*." He spits out the word, sending daggers at Adam.

"It's my choice, and I'm not going anywhere." I need to talk to Adam. To find out how they knew where I was. And I need to think. And time to process all that's happened tonight. I might look like I've got my shit together, but the truth is, I'm barely holding on. Another shiver tiptoes up my spine, and I swallow back bile. I was almost gang-raped tonight. My stomach lurches violently, and I move my palm to my tummy, rubbing gently as if that will make the awful churning go away.

I spent a half hour at their mercy, and even though I was drugged, it felt like a hell of a lot longer. I clamp my lips shut, forcing the panic bubbling up my throat to recede. Humiliation and shame compete with anger and frustration inside me as I remember how they toyed with me.

"Are you sure, babe?" Zach kneels beside Adam, reaching out and taking my hand. "He doesn't know you like I do. I can take care of you. We can check into a hotel."

"Because she really wants to go back to a hotel," Adam sneers, doing little to hide his contempt for Zach.

"What the fuck is your problem with me?" Zach demands to know.

Adam's nostrils flare. "The list is too long to get into right now." He whips his head around to mine, gently cupping my face. "My priority is looking after Emily."

Zach scoffs, but I tune him out, focusing on the tender way Adam is looking at me. His touch is soft and soothing, the complete opposite of the rough way Wes and his friends manhandled me earlier.

I squeeze my eyes shut, in a feeble attempt to ward off the images replaying in my mind, and an errant sobs flies from my mouth. I quake all over, and I'm so cold. I wrap my arms around myself, tucking my knees into my chest.

Adam climbs onto the couch, hauling me into his arms, as a fresh bout of tears takes hold of me. I cling to his shirt, siphoning his warmth and his comfort, needing it to remind me not every guy is a monster. The dam breaks, as restrained terror breaks free, and I fall apart in his arms. If Wes and his crew had had their way tonight, I would be broken beyond repair. *What the fuck was I thinking going over there?* A fresh layer of shame sweeps over me, and I've never felt more weak or more stupid.

When I finally stop sobbing, I look up, realizing we're alone. "Where did Sam and Zach go to?"

"They left to give you privacy, but I can call them back if you like."

I shake my head, sniffling. "I'm not in the mood for company."

"I'm not leaving you alone, but I can go in the other room if you want privacy." He rubs a hand through my hair, and it's amazingly comforting.

"Don't go," I whisper, fisting a hand in his damp shirt. It's soaked from my tears. I peer up at him. "Thank you for rescuing me."

His jaw tenses. "I'm sorry we got there late. We thought we were early."

"He brought the time forward because he had a date with Cassandra later tonight," I say through gritted teeth as my fear transforms to anger.

He brushes his thumbs under my eyes. "You want to talk about it?" he quietly asks.

"Not really." I gulp over the messy ball of emotion lodged in my throat.

"They didn't... Did he..." His body is balling into a knot as he tries to get the words out.

"They didn't rape me." A shudder works its way through me again, and he wraps his strong arms more firmly around me. "They hadn't gotten that far, but they cut my bra off with a knife and took turns groping me," I admit in a shaky voice. "They enjoyed humiliating me, poking fun at my body, and taunting me with all the ways they were going to fuck me." Tears prick my eyes again, and my lower lip wobbles. "If you hadn't arrived when you did..."

He pushes the air out of his lungs. "We didn't arrive soon enough," he says, and I can tell he's working hard to keep a level tone. "And now I'm regretting not throwing that fucker off the balcony. That animal doesn't deserve to live."

I don't disclose that Wes rubbed coke on his fingers before shoving them inside me. He wanted me docile but not too high that I didn't know what was happening, but he underestimates how often I use, and the dose he gave me wasn't near enough to get me out of my head.

Pain slices through me, ripping my insides into shreds, and I cry out before darkness swoops in to claim me.

"Em?" Are you okay?" Adam's voice worms its way through my subconscious. "What just happened?"

"Nothing. I'm okay." I offer him a weak smile.

"You're not okay." His eyes penetrate mine. "But you will be." Electricity crackles in the air as we stare at one another. His expression is a mix of concern and desire, and it's doing funny things to my insides. Which is weird. Because after what happened this evening, sex should be the last thing on my mind.

"How did you know where I was?" I ask, needing to understand how much he knows.

His tongue snakes out to wet his lips, and I greedily follow the motion. "Please don't be mad."

I narrow my eyes to slits. "That's not terribly reassuring."

"I knew there was more to this Wes shit, and I was worried. I convinced Sam to do some digging." He lowers his voice. "He found the email and the video."

My stomach roils, and I want the ground to open up and swallow me. I avert my eyes, looking at the floor as I knot my hands in my lap. "I didn't want anyone to see that." Shame washes over me. "What must you think of me?" I whisper. "I'm so ashamed."

"Don't be." He gently cups my face. "You take all these hits and keep getting back up. I think you have more inner strength than you know."

A solitary tear leaks out of the corner of one eye. "I wish I was that person, Adam. But the truth is, I'm weak."

"Maybe you've just reached your breaking point. It happens to everyone at some point when the stress gets too much."

I nod slowly. "Perhaps you're right. After he sent that video to me, I just fell apart. I accepted the inevitable and downed an alcohol and Molly cocktail that lasted all week. And then I walked my stupid ass to that hotel, knowing what lay in wait for me." Except I didn't think they'd drug me and record me.

"Why do you do it, Em? Why do you resort to drugs? What happened that you have to numb your pain?" His hand drops away from my face.

"Why do you sell them?!" I retort.

He averts his gaze, dragging a hand across his unshaven jaw. "Fair enough." He blinks, and when he does, his green eyes are penetrating mine. "I told you my sister is sick. My mom lost her job, and we have a shit-ton of medical bills. There's not a minute that goes by that I don't want to quit. I hate seeing what drugs do to people." He bites his lips. "I haven't sold shit for years, but circumstances forced me down this path again."

I'm instantly remorseful. I'd just assumed he was in it for the money. But the guy I've come to know isn't that guy.

"I'm sorry." I sigh. "I should've known there was some noble cause behind it."

A look of disgust crosses his face. "There is nothing noble about selling or taking drugs. And I'm getting out of the game." He sits up a little straighter, repositioning me so I'm sitting across his lap, with my legs dangling over the side of the couch. "I have a proposal for you."

I eye him warily.

"I'll give up dealing drugs if you stop taking them."

I arch a brow. "Why would I agree to that?"

"Because you're better than this, Em." He threads his fingers through my hair. "I know there's a story behind it, and I promise I won't go digging. But I want you to share it with me someday."

A heavy weight presses down on my chest. "I want to tell you," I truthfully admit. "But I can't do this now. Not after what's happened. I just want to try and forget that my life is a shit show, and with every passing day, it descends into even further chaos."

"Then let me help you." His eyes are sincere as they pin me in place. "Even the strongest people need support sometimes."

I trail my fingers across his jawline. "I'd like that, and I like being here with you. You make me feel safe."

"I will keep you safe, Em, and you can trust me with the truth."

I brush my lips across his cheek. "I will, but right now, I need something else."

Fire dances in his eyes, and his gaze flicks to my mouth as I straddle him, my core pulsing as I feel him hardening underneath my ass.

"What do you need?" His voice is deep and heavy with desire.

"I need your hands on me. I need your tender touch to erase the memory of rough hands. I need you to kiss me like I'm the only girl in the world and you'll die without my kisses."

A rare smile graces his gorgeous mouth, lighting up his whole face. "That's not far from the truth." He runs his thumb along my lower lip, and a rush of tingles races through me. His smile fades. "But are you sure that's what you need. I don't want you to feel like I'm taking advantage of you."

"You're not." I peck his lips briefly, and that feather-soft touch unravels some of the knots in my gut. "I asked you, and I'm not talking about sex. I just mean kissing and touching and you holding me."

For once, I want to do things right with a guy. Let things happen the way they're supposed to happen.

"Unless you're not into me, and then that's fine."

He pins me with an incredulous look. "I think you know exactly how I feel about you, beautiful." He winds his large hand around the nape of my neck. "I told you a few days ago I wanted to be friends, but every time I see you, I want to be more than friends."

"I want to be more than friends too," I admit, both to himself and myself.

"But we should take it slow," he suggests, drawing me in closer until there is only a millimeter between our faces.

"Agreed." I close my eyes as his warm breath fans over my face.

"And we need to discuss a lot of stuff, but not right now."

I open my eyes, and the loving look in his eyes almost has me sobbing again. But for all the right reasons this time.

"Because right now, I want to demonstrate how much I like you, and I want to take care of you, because you should only ever be worshiped and cherished."

Our lips collide in a searing-hot kiss, and as he cradles me to his chest, running his hands up and down my spine, sending beautiful warmth flooding through my veins, I wonder how it's possible to experience abject terror and blissful joy in the same day.

13

ADAM

My right arm is numb, and it's the only limb that fell asleep last night. Every other body part was alive and throbbing. The moment Emily and I crawled into bed, she curled up against me like we were a normal couple and dropped into a deep sleep. It surprised me she could sleep after what happened, but I'm guessing it was the drugs and adrenaline leaving her system that wore her out. I stared at the ceiling most of the night, listening to her soft snores, thinking of life, her, me, and that mind-blowing kiss, her tongue on me, our lips fused. It was so fucking hard not to take advantage of her.

As much as I want to roll her over and shove inside her, she doesn't need that right now. I'm not sure I need that right now either. I know without a doubt that when we have sex it's not going to be a one-night stand. At least not for me. She's everything I'm looking for in a woman —beautiful inside and out despite her addiction to drugs.

Honestly, as fucked up as this sounds, her drug habit doesn't bother me. I can see past that. I can see a vibrant and strong woman underneath the demons she's carrying on her shoulders. Mom has told Phoebe she's a flower waiting to bloom, and when she does, watch out world. I see the same in Emily. I know CF is vastly different than drug addiction. There's no cure for Phoebe. But she's a fighter, and I catch glimpses of the same determination within Emily. She just needs someone to love her unconditionally, to fight with her, for someone to be there to pick her up when she falls.

Emily stirs, her soft hand mindlessly wandering over my abs as she hooks her silky leg in between mine.

I clench my teeth, my dick throbbing, my balls blue as fuck. I have a ton of willpower, but the beautiful goddess tangled around me is tearing at my resolve.

She lifts her head as her hand dances down to my granite erection. Her big blues are begging for permission. One I would love to give her, if I knew I wouldn't fall hard. But my body has a mind of its own before my brain kicks into gear.

I roll her over and straddle her, careful not to put my weight on her as I pin her hands above her head.

She giggles, a sound that sends hellfire straight to my balls. My body is sweating. My chest rises and falls, and when her tongue darts out to lick her lips, I lose all self-control.

In lightning speed, I'm hovering over her, my cock straining to get out of my boxers. I pepper kisses along her neck, chest, and tits, trying to devour every bit of her.

She squirms beneath me, arching her back, pressing her big tits into me. Every one of my nerve endings is on fire, and if I don't get any relief, I might self-combust.

I thrust my dick against her core, and inwardly, I'm frowning that her panties are in the way.

She moans, and that breathy sound is enough for me to go fucking wild. My hands are shaping her hips. My lips are all over her tits, chest, and neck, and just when I'm about to unsnap her bra, my fucking phone rings.

"Ignore it," she says, raspy and breathy, her seductive tone sending electrical charges to grip my cock.

I slide my body down, dying to taste her. She's spewing soft moans as she wiggles her body upward so that my mouth meets her pussy.

The ringing dies only to ring again.

Panic jolts me up. "Fuck." I have to answer it. Something must've happened to Phoebe. My heart constricts when I climb out of bed and see Mom's name on the screen.

"Phoebe okay?" I rush out, answering the phone while shoving my fingers through my hair.

Emily tenses as she watches me.

"Yes. Yes. Son, you can't panic every time I call you."

I release a huge breath, and Emily seems to relax too.

"Can you stop by the grocery store and pick up a few things before you come home today?" Mom asks. "I'll text the list to you."

Emily crawls out of bed, and I frown even though I know we need to take things slow.

"Sure." The one word out of my mouth is painful as I watch Emily comb her fingers through her long hair. I want to be those fingers. I want to touch every part of her slowly, deliberately, and worship her like she deserves.

You're talking to your mother, Adam. Get your fucking mind out of the gutter.

"Adam, are you there?" Mom's voice penetrates through my lust-filled mind, and my erection is gone.

"Yes, ma'am. I'll..." I forgot what Mom wants me to do. "I'll be there around one."

"Do you have money to buy the groceries?"

Emily mouths, "Bathroom, then coffee." I nod, and she sashays her hips out of the room.

"Adam." Mom raises her voice. "Are you still sleeping? Did I wake you?"

I shake my head vigorously. "Sorry, I'm here."

"Are you with a woman?" She asks so innocently, but I swear she sees through the phone.

It's too soon to tell her about Emily. I don't want to answer her hundred questions either about who the girl is. Mom has a tendency to grill me about the girls I date. Sadly, I haven't had a steady girl in quite some time, and I don't share my rare one-night stands with her. But I'm not going to lie to her either.

"Just having breakfast with a friend."

"Well, you can tell me all about her later. See you soon." She hangs up.

For a beat, I stand in Carter's black-and-white room dumbfounded that Mom is so sure I'm with a woman. But I shrug it off and slide into my jeans and go in search of Emily.

It's not hard to find her. Carter's pad is small, but it's Emily's lyrical voice pulling me to her.

She's singing "Somewhere Over the Rainbow." This time she's not strung out, and her voice is even prettier than when I heard her sing in my dorm room.

She doesn't hear me as I approach. I prop a shoulder on the wall and watch her as she makes coffee like she's the one who lives here.

"Dreams really do come true," she sings.

I hope they do because my dreams are beginning to include her.

I don't want to startle her, but my legs are moving before I can think. "You know you have a pretty voice?" My hands curl around her waist.

She jumps a little before she leans her head back into my chest. "Thank you."

I flatten my large palms on her stomach, and I plant a kiss just below her ear. "I'm sorry about the phone call."

She spins around, looking up at me with doe-like eyes. "Don't be. She's your mom." A hint of sadness threads through her last sentence.

I drag my fingers along her cheek, sweeping her hair behind her ear. We stare at each other for a long minute.

Her hands slide up my chest. "Adam." She worries her bottom lip. "I'm concerned that Wes is going to have you arrested."

I lift her up easily and set her on the counter, rubbing my hands up her bare legs.

The coffee pot is gurgling as the aroma of caffeine floats in the air.

Heat spreads through my chest. "You're worried about me." I grin, searching her face.

She's still holding her bottom lip hostage as she bats her long lashes.

My heart races as my lips crash to hers, my tongue wasting no time snaking in. Her hands fly into my hair. Mine dive into her silky strands. The kiss is dominant, wild, wet, and my body is on fire, burning with the need to take all of her—mind, body, and soul.

My phone rings again.

Fuuuck.

I debate whether to answer the damn thing, but if I don't, I'll have Emily splayed on the kitchen table. And I have to dig deep to stick to my gentlemanly ways, but fuck, a man can only take so much before he breaks, and Emily is chipping away at more than my need to fuck her.

She giggles as she pulls my lips between her teeth. "It's not meant to be today."

The coffeemaker beeps as if to agree.

It seems the universe is trying to tell us something.

I edge back as I answer. "Sam, what's up?"

Emily hooks a finger in the waist of my jeans with a flirty smile.

I growl, holding my phone to my ear with my shoulder, as I help Emily down.

"Everything okay?" Sam asks.

Not at all. My cock is begging for attention. "Perfect," I respond as Emily's hands roam freely up and down my chest.

"I've found something. Is Emily still with you?"

"Yeah." My voice is strained as I lock eyes with Emily.

"Put me on speaker," he says.

Once I do, Sam says, "Hi, Emily. Are you feeling better?"

I set the phone on the table and plant my ass in a chair.

Emily loses her playful look as she sits in the other, eyeing the phone with anticipation. "I'm feeling much better, thanks to you."

"What did you find?" I ask.

On the way to Carter's last night, Sam said he would continue to search until he found something concrete that we could use on Wes.

I want to bury that bastard.

To put him behind bars where he can't hurt Emily or any other girl. Ever again.

"That Weston Blakely isn't as smart as he thinks," Sam says smugly. "I found a video of Weston and his crew with another girl. Only this time, they each took turns raping her."

Motherfucker.

Emily gasps and pops to her feet, gnawing on a nail. "And my mother thinks he's the perfect catch. He can't do anything wrong in her eyes." Her jaw tenses, and rage bubbles beneath the surface as that strength of hers blooms.

I'm ready to find the fucker and finish what I started last night.

Emily's pacing, her bare feet slapping on the tile floor. "So, where's the video of me in that orgy or the film of what went down in the hotel room?"

I look at the phone because I'm not sure what Sam has done with it either.

"The video of the orgy is wiped clean from your email and his hard drive," Sam says.

Emily swings her gaze to the phone. "He could've saved it on a thumb drive or to a cloud account. He's smart, guys. He knows how to cover his tracks."

I reach out and gently grasp her hand. "Hey, Sam is the best there is with computers. He'll find every copy and make sure that video never sees the light of day."

Sam mutters something that I can't make out.

"Where's the camera from last night, Sam?" Emily was my only focus when shit went down.

"I have it," Sam says. "It's in a safe place in the event that we can use it. Emily, you should consider pressing charges."

She pinches her eyebrows, shrugging out of my hold. "No! Wes will find a way to make it look like you two are in that video and not him or his asshole friends. Besides, if I make waves, Wes will retaliate, and both of you would get into trouble for assault."

I'm on my feet. "Wes won't do anything of the sort." I pull her to me, holding her as she shakes. "I told you. I got you, baby. You don't need to worry about me either."

"I *am* worried about you. This isn't your fight."

I guide her chin up, grinning that she finally admitted she cares. "It is *our* fight."

"Adam." She melts in my arms. "If my mother finds out, she'll think I asked for it. And I can guarantee you she'll have my head on one of her gold-plated platters. She hates negative publicity. She'll brush all this under the table and make it go away. Somehow, Wes will come out smelling like a rose."

"Not if she saw this video," Sam says.

Emily's face turns snow white, and she shakes her head. "We can't use it, so that's not an option."

"Not now," Sam agrees. "But maybe later."

"What if we can find this other girl to make the case stronger?" I suggest.

She presses her small hand on my cheek, sadness dripping from her. "You shouldn't get involved. You've got football and your family to think about. I want to graduate so I can get the fuck out of Dodge. None of that will happen if we make waves."

I temper my anger because she's scared. She feels she's alone. But I want to bust up some heads. I want to make Wes suffer. Last night was only a taste of what I can do, but Emily is right; I have my family to think about. But Mom will understand my motives of protecting a friend.

"Adam," Sam's voice breaks the brief silence. "Do you want me to send what I found to Wes?"

Emily stiffens in my arms, a sign she's hesitant to do anything to upset Wes.

"Baby, Wes needs to be taken down a notch. He needs a taste of his own medicine. I'm in this with you all the way." I glue my gaze to hers, hoping she sees that she can trust me, feels that I have her back. I'm not letting her go through this alone. "He won't know that you are involved."

Sam clears his throat. "Adam is right. We have to stop Wes. We need to protect other women." Anger weaves through his tone.

Emily leaves my arms and heaves a sigh. "You're right. We can't let him do that to any other woman. He's been getting away with it for far too long." She massages her temples, looking a little perplexed. "Sam, you didn't want to help me when I asked you. What's changed?"

"Adam asked me to help. He's like a brother to me, and he adores you. Family sticks together. Besides, now I know what that rat bastard has been up to, I no longer have any crisis of conscience. I'm happy to help, especially if it'll put that creep away." He pauses for a beat. "I'll send Wes an email from an anonymous account that he'll never be able to trace."

She rolls her pretty blues. "He'll know it's from Adam."

"You let me worry about that," I say, drilling her with a serious look.

She drags her lip between her teeth as fine lines furrow her brow. Silence engulfs us for a few seconds. Air whooshes out of her mouth and her shoulders slump in defeat. "Okay."

"Good. I'll work on it. Talk soon." Then Sam is gone.

Emily wrings her hands together. Suddenly, I'm not sure if it's nerves or she needs a fix or both.

I close the distance between us. "We'll get through this. But promise me one thing."

She's biting her lip, fear evident on her face.

"As bad as things might get, no drugs." I'm asking her to stay away from something that is impossible to drop cold turkey, but she's got to try.

"I only do drugs on weekends. It's no issue, Adam."

I lift a brow, wanting to remind her she was strung out in my dorm room and that was a weekday. But I don't want to argue. "I want to be your drug. That sounds corny, I know. If you feel the need to use, come to me, and I don't mean for drugs." I grin in the hopes I can break through to her. That she'll let me take care of her.

She smiles, wiggling her hips as she sashays over to me. Her gaze roams my bare chest. "I think I might like you being my addiction." She lifts up on her toes and kisses me.

And just like that, nothing matters but her and me.

14

EMILY

When Monday morning rolls around, I peer at my reflection in the mirror, reminding myself I can do this. I've been on edge since Sam sent the anonymous email to Wes threatening to expose the recording he found. So far, there's been no response, but it hasn't even been twenty-four hours yet.

I know Wes won't take this lying down. I know he'll find some way of attacking. And I know I'll be caught in the crossfire.

But I'm done being the victim.

And I'm done denying the truth.

I'm spiraling down the rabbit hole, and I alone have the power to claw my way back to the top. It's easy to blame my parents, blame what happened when I was fifteen, for the mess I've made of my life, when the reality is I am responsible for my own actions.

In a weird, sick way, Wes did me a favor.

What happened Saturday night—what *could've* happened that night —was the wake-up call I needed. I walked over there like a lamb to the slaughter. Believing I had no choice. *And how fucked up is that? To willingly walk into a gang rape?* To think it would resolve things when it clearly would've only made things worse.

I'm disgusted with myself for being so weak. For going on a bender all week and being incapable of making any sound decisions. I'm smarter than that. And it's about time I started acting like it.

A smile slips over my mouth as I grab my book bag and leave the house. That I can even smile after the weekend I've endured speaks volumes. But I find myself smiling every time I think of Adam. His handsome face flashes before me, and I almost trip on the sidewalk.

Everything about him draws me in.

His gorgeous face and drool-worthy body.

His deep, sultry voice that kick-starts my hormones every time I'm around him.

How protected I feel in his big, bulky arms.

The tender look in his eyes when he promises he'll keep me safe.

The way my body tingles all over when he touches me, warming me from the inside out.

And that's before I've considered how hot it is that he's so devoted to his mom and sister.

It's clear money is an issue, but real wealth resides in the strength of that all-important family bond.

When it comes down to it, Adam is the wealthy one in our partnership because he has something I've never had—a true family unit.

Something about Adam gives me hope.

Hope for something I've never dared to dream for—a guy who makes me the center of his world. A love that exists before now only in the romance novels I read. A love so encompassing that my shitty family situation doesn't matter. A prospect of something real that gives me the strength to kick my dependence on drugs and find a new high to live my life by.

Maybe I'm delusional, because I don't even know him all that well. And being with him is complicated. But Adam has instilled a new fire inside me, and I'm going to embrace that with both hands.

* * *

"WHAT'S HIS AGENDA?" ZACH ASKS WHEN WE'RE SEATED IN THE DINER at lunchtime waiting for our food to arrive.

"Why does he have to have an agenda?" I inquire, sipping on my water.

"Every guy has an agenda when it comes to women, babe," he replies, sitting up straighter and propping his elbows on the worn table-top. "Especially football players."

"He's not like most football players," I say, rushing to defend Adam. "And I've been around enough to know."

"I still don't trust him." Zach leans back, slumping in the booth with a sulky expression on his face.

"Don't trust him or don't like the fact he's clearly interested in Em?" Scar inquires, arching a slim brow.

A muscle ticks in his jaw as he glares at Scar for daring to call him on it.

"I don't know if anything will happen with Adam," I say, "but if it does, it doesn't change who you are to me." I reach across the table and take Zach's hand. "You're still one of my best friends."

He links his fingers in mine, staring at me through a troubled lens. "But for how long?" His eyes penetrate mine. "How long before he asks you to give up your lifestyle and the friends who go along with it?" I avert my gaze, and Zach cusses. "Fuck. He's already demanded that of you?"

"He hasn't demanded anything of me. That's not who he is." I yank my hand back. "He proposed that we both make changes."

"And you're seriously considering it?" Disbelief drips from Scar-let's tone.

"Yeah." I nod. "Yes, I am." I tuck my hair behind my ears. "I'm sick of feeling like shit all the time, Scar. I'm sick of feeling alone and lost and afraid. And I'm sick of being a victim. If the guys hadn't rescued me Saturday night, I'd be in a new hell of my own making. Something has got to change, and maybe, just maybe, Adam is right. Maybe there is another way."

Two sets of incredulous eyes meet mine, and my temper flares. "If you were true friends, you'd support this." I stand, grabbing my bag and pulling a five-dollar bill out from my wallet. "But it's clear I'm on my own with this."

"Sit your whiny ass down, and shut the fuck up and listen." Scar glares at me, jabbing her finger in the air.

I'm tempted to storm out of there, but I owe my friends the courtesy of listening to them, so I sit back down.

"If you've found a guy worth getting clean for, good for you."

"That's not it," I interrupt. "If I do this, I'm doing it for me."

"Even better," she admits, leaning across the table. "But you've got to realize those worlds don't coexist. How can you continue to hang with us if we're high and you're not? Can you honestly say you could resist the temptation when it's right there in your face?" Sadness washes over her features. "If you do this, our friendship will come to an end whether you want it to or not."

* * *

SCAR'S WORDS ARE STILL LINGERING ON MY MIND AS I MAKE MY WAY home after my tutoring session. *I know we're usually high or recovering when we're together, but could we not hang out when we're sober? Does she mean our lunch dates are over too? Do I mean that little to both of them that they only want to associate with me if I'm still adopting the same party lifestyle?* Her words have done little for my self-confidence, and I've been on a downer since our conversation in the diner, and it's only getting worse.

Now, I'm rethinking my plan. I mean, I had it all worked out fine. Keeping on the straight and narrow Monday to Friday and letting loose on the weekends. There wasn't any harm in it. If I stick to my guns and limit my partying to weekends, then I'm fine.

Except Adam throws a wrench in the works. But, honestly, his proposal was never going to work. He needs to deal to earn cash for his sister's medical bills, so suggesting he go cold turkey with me wouldn't have lasted.

But I don't want to cut ties with him.

I like him. *A lot.*

More than Molly? My inner demon taunts me again, but I push that devil off my shoulder.

I want to spend more time with him. I want to see if this connection between us could go further. Maybe, he'll accept a negotiation of the terms. We could both cut back and still call it progress.

My spirits are slightly lifted as I step foot into my house. My brow puckers as the sound of voices trickles out to greet me. "Hello?" I call out.

"In here, honey!" Mom hollers from the sound of the living room. She only uses terms of endearment in front of others, so that means we have company.

Great. Just what I'm in the mood for.

I tack a fake smile on my face as I walk into the living room. Instantly, the walls spin, and I sway on my feet, clutching onto the door frame to steady myself as I blink successively, sure my eyes must be deceiving me.

"I know," Mom says, walking toward me. "I got a dreadful fright when I saw him too," she adds, mistaking my horror for shocked sympathy. She attempts to drape her arm around my shoulder, but I duck out of her embrace, shaking myself out of my terrified stupor.

"Get out!" I snap at Wes, rage pummeling my insides. The absolute nerve of him to show up here. But I guess I shouldn't be surprised.

"Emily!" Mom instantly chastises me. "That is no way to speak to Weston! Especially when he came here to ask for your help."

"Help with what?" Barely holding onto the contents of my stom-ach, I step into the room but keep my distance from the asshole as he stands.

"I know you're angry because I stood you up Saturday night," he smoothly lies. "But I can explain. I was jumped by a bunch of football players in an alley on my way to meet you. Ended up in the hospital with a concussion and a few broken ribs."

His face is a smorgasbord of mottled bruises and cuts, and he's hunched over in obvious pain. I make a mental note to properly thank Adam the next time I see him for working him over so thoroughly. Although, there's a part of me now wishing he had pushed him over the balcony in the hotel room. And I feel zero remorse for having such thoughts.

I snort. "Unbelievable."

"Emily!" Mom interjects, moving over to Wes's side. "You're being rude."

"I don't care."

"Are you pissed because you're worried it might be that football player you've been seeing?" Wes says, acting all wide-eyed and innocent.

"What?" Dad's bark has me jumping a couple feet in the air. He stalks into the room, sucking up all the oxygen with each heavy stride. "What football player?"

"There is no football player." I cross my arms, and glare at Wes. "Wes is just trying to cause trouble. As usual." I narrow my eyes at him. "And if he persists, he'll find out it won't work to his advantage either." He seems to have forgotten we have the tape of him and his friends drugging and assaulting me. If he turns on Adam, or me, he will also be exposing himself because then there is nothing stopping us from releasing that tape.

"I don't know what's going on here, but this is no way to treat a guest in our house." Mom is purple in the face, and I know there'll be hell to pay for this later. But I don't care. I'm not letting Wes blackmail me anymore. I would rather live on the streets than put up with this until I graduate. Or worse, be forced into marrying the asshole.

"Just so we're clear, Mother." I level her with a solemn look. "I hate him. He is nothing like you think, and he is no friend of mine. I won't be coerced into helping him or dating him or having anything to do with him. You won't believe me. I already know that. Throw me out of the house and off campus if you want, but I am done with Wes."

I step right up to her, fists clenching and adrenaline pumping through my veins. "If he shows up here again and you let him in, I will have no choice but to do something that will ruin your reputation forever. We both know you don't want that, so for once. *Can you at least be on my side*!!" I scream that last statement.

"How dare you speak to me like that!" Stinging pain lances across my cheek as she slaps me. Wes chuckles, and I lunge at him, but strong arms haul me back.

"I think it's time for you to leave," Dad says to Wes, keeping me locked firmly in his embrace.

"I think your daughter will regret speaking to me like this." Menace filters through Wes's tone as he slyly threatens me.

"That sounds like a threat," Dad replies, his voice cold as ice. "For your sake, I hope it's not."

Wes clears his throat and smooths his features into a neutral line. "I apologize, sir. I let my emotions get the better of me. I would never hurt Emily." He pins me with a look loaded with intent. "All I've ever tried to do is love her, but she continuously knocks me back."

"I'm sure your girlfriend would love to hear that," I hiss. "And I've heard enough of your bullshit. Get the hell out of my house."

"This is *my* house." Mom positions herself in between Dad and me and Wes. "And I'll determine who stays and who goes." She levels me with a warning look.

"Last I checked, my name is on the lease too," Dad says. "And if we want to be technical, it's the university's house." He lowers his tone. "I won't ask you again, Weston. You need to leave."

"I'm going." He lifts his palms in a conciliatory gesture. "I only came to ask for your and Emily's help in identifying my assailants."

His meaning is obvious. Dad drops his arms, shoving me behind him as he steps up to Wes. "I don't take kindly to unsubstantiated claims against my players or veiled threats so be very careful what you say next, son."

"If I was you, Coach"—Wes puts his face all up in Dad's, not disguising the smug arrogance ghosting over his features—"I'd take a long, hard look at the guys you seem willing to go to war for." He shoots me a sly look. "I think you'll find not all of them are worthy of your loyalty."

He pushes past us, leveling a lethal look in my direction before exiting the room. I flop down onto the couch in grateful relief when the door slams, signaling Satan has left the building.

"How dare you!" Mom seethes, prodding her finger in Dad's chest. "How dare you embarrass me like that in front of Veronica and Anthony Blakely's son!! You know they are one of the university's biggest benefactors!"

"You think I give a shit about that!" Dad shouts, swiveling around and pointing at me. "Open your eyes, woman! Your daughter was shaking at the sight of him!" It's only as he says it that I realize my entire body is trembling.

The couch dips as Dad sits down. "Princess." He cups my face. "You need to tell me what's going on."

"Oh, puh-lease." Mom throws her arms into the air. "Don't tell me you're buying into this act."

"Enough, Carole!" Dad hisses. "I've had all I can take of this, and I can't handle much more."

She huffs. "Say what you really mean, Grayson."

Dad stands. "I've had enough of the way you treat your daughter and me. And I'm sick to death of hearing you threaten her if she doesn't comply with your outrageous demands. It ends here."

She laughs. "What makes you think you have any power in this situation." She shoves at his shoulders. "I'm the fucking *president*. I can fire your ass like that!" She clicks her fingers in his face.

An ugly sneer appears on Dad's face. "And I can ruin you in a heartbeat, darling. If you try to take me down, you're going down with me."

The bickering cranks up a few notches, descending into familiar territory, and I slip out of the room without either of them noticing.

I grab my bag and close the front door quietly behind me, checking the area to ensure Wes isn't lingering anywhere. Not wanting to take a chance, I call an Uber to take me to Zach's.

I need to get high.

To forget that the last hour exists.

To force the internal screaming to stop.

I'm proud of myself for standing up to Wes, but I'm terrified too. Afraid all I've done is ruffle the hornet's nest. He won't take this lying down, and he'll come back ten times stronger.

I bend over the bush at the end of the driveway and expel the contents of my stomach. I've just finished rinsing out my mouth with water when the Uber arrives. Climbing in the back, I give him Zach's address while my mind continues to churn.

Wes mentioned football players on purpose. He was sending me a deliberate message. Like I thought, he's going to go after Adam. And possibly drag Carter into this too. I can't let him draw a spotlight on Adam, because it's far too risky. He has so much to lose. And I won't let anything happen to him because he's trying to help me. I remember how he asked me to come to him in this very scenario, and right now, I need him.

I pop my head between the two front seats. "Actually, I've changed my mind. Can you take me to the Fleming Residence Hall instead?"

15

ADAM

My eyes are heavy as I walk into my dorm room. Practice was hell. Coach ran us through the wringer in preparation for our big game coming up. But I don't have time to sleep. I have a Western civilization test tomorrow, and I still have a couple of deals I need to take care of later tonight.

Sam spins around in his computer chair. Dark circles color the underside of his blue eyes, and his blond hair is matted to his head. Poor guy has been behind his computer since Saturday night, trying to drum up more dirt on Wes and find the chick in the video. He's tracking all incoming and outgoing emails to and from the frat house, hoping he catches something. He's distraught and determined to get the goods on Wes, especially after watching him and his crew gang-raping that girl.

I couldn't blame him. The video made me want to go ballistic on Wes or someone or something. Regardless, we're at a standstill at the moment. Sam has been trying to locate an address for the girl in the video. Even then, we're not sure she'll want to cooperate. But it's our only play unless Wes fucks up again, and I don't see that happening now he knows we're onto him. He'll be looking over his shoulder every minute of the day.

"Well, you look like crap," Sam says.

I arch a brow. "Right back atcha. Anything yet on the girl?"

He runs his long fingers through his hair. "Nothing. I wish I had access to face recognition software." He lets out a frustrated sigh. "I really want to take down Wes. It's been eating at me."

I throw my bag on my bed. "A bullet will take care of him."

Sam's mouth falls open. "For real, Adam. Prison will be hell on a rich bastard like him. To me, that's worse than a bullet."

I drop down on my bed, rubbing my temples. "Man, you're right."

He kicks out his legs. "Have you heard from Emily?"

I climb on my bed, resting my back against the wall, sleep a minute away. "With classes and practice, I haven't had time to check in with her today. I'm sure if Wes tried to contact her, she would let us know." And if she was jonesing to get high, she would reach out to me too although a part of me isn't so sure. It's hard to kick a vice cold turkey, especially ones like alcohol and drugs. Still, I'm hopeful she would keep to our agreement and come to me if she feels the urge to get high.

"Do you think Wes will out you to Coach?" Sam asks. "I mean, have you thought about that?"

Wes can do many things to me, but Coach would be the last person he would go to since Coach is Emily's old man. "I can see him going to President Parker but not Coach. He would demand evidence, and Wes has none." Coach Parker isn't the type to believe everything he hears. I couldn't say for sure about President Parker though, but Emily did say he can do no wrong in her mother's eyes.

"Let's talk about President Parker," Sam's eyes shift back and forth as he thinks. "If Wes goes to her, she could do more damage to you than Coach."

I shake my head. "Coach won't let that happen. Look, man." I pound a fist to my chest. "I love ya for worrying about me. But Emily is the one we need to protect. Not me." Sure, I'm not going to lie. I don't want to get kicked off the team or lose my scholarship or even get thrown out of school. And if I had to choose, I would give up football only because I could do more with a college degree. The NFL is a fucking dream and it's still in my sights, but so many things have changed in such a short time that I need to be realistic about where I'm headed.

He pops forward, elbows on his knees. "Admirable, dude, and I want to protect her too, but someone needs to watch your back too."

Suddenly, I feel like someone is driving a knife into my gut as guilt swirls into a violent storm inside me. I should fess up, right now, about selling drugs. The longer I wait, the harder it will be to tell him. He'll be devastated, but he needs to know.

A knock sounds on the door, and I breathe a sigh of relief for the interruption.

I'm such a coward.

Sam answers the door, and the moment I lay eyes on Emily, I fly off the bed.

Her face is pale and her blue eyes are brimming with fear.

"What's wrong? What happened? Did Wes confront you?" My pulse quickens. I'll kill the bastard this time. Fuck sending him to prison.

Automatically, I pull her to me, and the minute her body is flush with mine, I let out a contented sigh.

Sam clears his throat. "What's wrong, Emily?"

She buries her face in my chest as her arms wind around my waist.

Fuck, if this isn't what I needed—to feel her against me, to breathe in her scent, and to know she came to me with whatever has her freaked out. Progress.

My heart settles as I kiss her head. "Talk to me."

She pulls away and sits on my bed. "Wes came to my house. He's not backing down." Her tone cracks. "I can't do this. I need..." Her hands begin to shake violently.

I ease down next to her, taking her hands in mine. "You're safe, baby."

She moves her head back and forth. "Adam, I need." She peeks at Sam through her lashes.

I kiss her hands. "You don't need that."

I'm sure Sam is putting the pieces together that Emily needs to get high.

So, to distract her, I say, "Tell us what happened."

Sam returns to his chair.

Withdrawing her hands from mine, she picks at the hem of her shorts. It's only then I take in her long, tanned legs and pink painted toenails. Phoebe would love to have her toes painted pink.

A vision of Emily painting my sister's nails pops into my head out of nowhere, scaring the shit out of me.

Because I like the visual a hell of a lot.

And that thought frightens me as much as it excites me.

"Wes told my parents some football players jumped him. He's going to make sure you pay, Adam. He's not letting up." Tears coat her eyes. "He's going to come after you."

Pure joy floods my chest that she's worried about me. That's the only reason I'm not punching my fist through the window to expel my rage that the fucker had the nerve to go to Emily's house when we clearly threatened him to stay away from her.

Sam shakes his head. "He's just trying to scare us."

I chuckle at my dear friend at how calm he is when I'm seriously considering putting a bullet into Wes's skull because that seems to be the only way we can get rid of the asshole.

As if Sam knows what I'm thinking, he says, "Save the aggression for the football field."

Emily's tongue snakes out to lick her lips.

Woman, do that again, and I'll have you splayed out on my bed regardless if Sam's in the room or not.

My dick is in agreement too as blood pools in my groin. Now, instead of coming up with our next move or trying to clear the anger away, I'm conjuring up images of when I had Emily under me in Carter's bed. She felt fucking amazing as I licked my way down her neck, tits, and stomach. Fuck. I can still hear her seductive moans.

"Adam," Sam barks. "Did you hear a word I said?"

I blink and find Emily and Sam with eyes wide and heads angled.

"Where did you go?" Emily asks so sweetly and softly.

I notice then she isn't trembling anymore. Instead, she appears concerned for me. Warmth spreads through my chest, and the need to kiss her is strong, but this isn't the time or place.

I blink. "Sorry, I was thinking." Of you and me naked. "What were you saying, Sam?"

"That maybe Emily knows the girl in the video," he says.

I round my gaze to the gorgeous woman on my bed. "Are you sure you want to see it?" I watched it last night, and Sam and I were both disgusted at what we saw. Although if she sees the video, it might make her realize how close she came to being seriously hurt, and that might make her think twice before she pops the next pill.

She nods. "If it helps, yeah. We need to find that girl... To see if she'll press charges now we have proof of what they did to her."

Emily is right. We've got nothing except empty threats. Wes has nothing too. He can go to Coach all he wants, but he can't prove a thing. Sam has the camera that was in the hotel room. So, all the evidence of what went down that night is in our hands. He can't turn me in without incriminating himself. If he'd found a way, the police would've already showed up at my door.

Sam swivels in his chair, tapping a few keys on his computer. "I'm watching all the frat house's email traffic and Wes's text messages, but things on his end have been quiet since we sent him the threat."

Emily and I stand behind Sam. While he's pulling up the video, I grab Emily's hand.

She flashes her big blues at me, and I swear I just fell one step closer in love. But the moment is severed when Wes's voice blares out of the speakers.

Emily abandons my hand, her jaw locks up, and she grips the back of Sam's chair, her knuckles white as fresh fallen snow.

The video shows a similar scene to the one Emily played a part in the other night. Wes's crew sits back and watches while Wes straddles the girl who appears to be drugged with no fight in her to protect herself.

Sick fucking bastard!

Emily clamps a hand over her mouth, tears ready to spill.

I drape an arm over her. "Sam, cut the video. She's seen enough."

Emily turns into me, devastation evident on her pretty face. "Oh my God! That could've been me." Her voice trembles. "I want to kill him."

No truer feeling has been felt. I tug her to me. "He'll pay."

Without turning around, Sam asks, "Do you recognize her?"

"No," Emily says.

A ping resonates on Sam's computer.

"Oh, what's this?" Sam says to no one. He flicks a key, then another, and an email pops up on the screen.

The email is addressed to a Kim Roberts. It's sent from a generic email address with no identifying components.

Silence fills the room as the three of us read the two sentences. *Remember our deal. If you talk, you're dead.*

"Who sent that?" Emily asks, frowning.

I shrug, waiting on Sam to confirm.

He slides out of his chair and stands, stretching his arms above his head. "Wes sent it from an anonymous profile."

My brows lift. "How do you know?"

"Same IP address he uses at his frat house."

"But anyone at the frat house could've sent that email," I say.

Sam bites his lip. "True. But come on. Wes goes to Emily's parents, trying to what? Feel her out to see if—"

"He could break me," Emily finishes Sam's sentence. "Since he couldn't. He's scared. So, he needs to cover his bases."

"And even if this sender is one of his cronies," Sam adds, "all of them just implicated themselves." He waggles his brows. "I think Kim Roberts could be our mystery girl."

"We need to talk to her as soon as possible," I say. "Wes is a nasty, unpredictable prick, and who knows what he's capable of. I don't want Wes to keep terrorizing Emily or any other girl."

All the stress melts off Sam. "I'll have her address in a flash." He jumps back in his chair, fingers flying over the keyboard.

Emily beams, and it's the first time I've seen such a radiant smile on her face. In that moment, I just fell in love with her.

"We should talk to her tonight," Emily says, holding her bottom lip hostage.

Man, I would give anything to be that lip.

The tick, tick, tick of the keys is the only sound in the room as Emily and I lock eyes. Electricity crackles in the air, and I pray she's feeling this thing between us too. I hold her tighter, and there are so many things I want to do to her. So many positions I'm desperate to try with her.

My gaze drifts to her lips, the bottom one sticking out a little farther than the top. The urge to kiss her is so fucking strong. If I do though, we'll be naked in next to no time. So, I rub my thumb over her soft lips, and an inferno zips straight to my balls. I'm thinking about how she tastes, when she captures my thumb in her mouth.

I suck in a sharp breath.

"You two okay?" Sam asks, typing away and not looking up.

"Yep." Reluctantly, I step back as Emily gives me a ball-busting smile.

"Tease," I mouth to her.

She gives me another flirty look as Sam spins around.

"Good news is, Kim was a student here, and that email addy is bogus. She must've changed it. So, she won't see Wes's email. I also found a picture of her in student records, and that girl in the video is definitely her. Bad news is, she lives in Charlotte, North Carolina."

Emily's smile gets even bigger. "Road trip." She says it like she's never been out of this town before. Of course, I know she's excited to see if Kim Roberts will take down Weston Blakely.

Hell, I'm stoked too, but my schedule sucks, and I can't drive three hours and back this week.

As if Emily can see the war going on in my head. "Football. Right. You have a game too on Saturday."

I nod.

"Let's go after your game. I need to get out of this town even for a night," she admits.

How could I say no to her? Not only that, I'm already thinking of her and me alone for a couple of days.

Hell yeah!

16

EMILY

"I love your truck," I say, glancing around the old beat-up Chevy pickup. It's late Saturday night as we head out on the road to Charlotte. I thought Adam might've changed his mind after their amazing win today. I wouldn't have held it against him if he'd wanted to stay to party with his teammates, but he was resolute that we go ahead with our plans.

And I fell a little more in love with him for it.

"It's not much, but I love old Bertha." Adam lovingly pats the dash, and my grin grows. "Took me years to save for her. Although she's old, she's never let me down."

"Why Bertha?"

"The old dude who sold her to me made me promise I'd continue to call her by the name he'd christened her."

I roll my eyes even though I love the story. "Men and their trucks."

"You want to listen to the radio?" he asks, his fingers reaching for the old-fashioned stereo.

I shake my head. "I'd rather talk. We haven't had much time to get to know one another." I bite down on my lip as I glance at him. "And

I'd like to know you better." Butterflies scatter in my chest, reminding me I haven't been this excited about anything in ages.

"In the biblical sense?" he throws out, a grin spreading across his mouth.

I slap his arm. "You know what I mean."

"I'm only teasing. What do you want to know?"

"Have you always wanted to play football?" I angle my body so I'm looking at his beautiful profile. There's a thin layer of scruff on his chin and cheeks that I'm itching to touch.

"From the time I was little." He drums his fingers off the steering wheel. "Mom jokes I came out of the womb with a ball in my hand."

"I can tell you're close to your mom and your sister. But what about your dad?" I tentatively inquire.

"He's not on the scene anymore. Abandoned us when I was ten."

"I'm sorry."

"I'm not." A muscle clenches in his jaw. "He was a worthless piece of shit, and we're better off without him."

"Some people aren't suited to parenthood," I truthfully admit, tucking my hair behind my ears.

He glances at me briefly. "It sounds like you're speaking from personal experience."

I shrug. "Mom admitted as much to me when I was a little girl. She never wanted me, and it shows." I'm usually guarded around people, and I would never admit that to just anyone, but I feel myself around Adam. Like I could share anything with him, and I just know he'd keep my confidence.

Or perhaps it's because we both have secrets we're guarding for one another that leads me to trust him when I don't trust most others.

"She said that to you?" Disbelief drips from his tone.

"Yes. And she continually points out all the ways in which I'm a failure and an embarrassment."

"That is so wrong. I'm sorry you have to deal with that."

"It's all I've ever known," I admit, tugging on a loose thread at the end of my blouse. "She's never been much of a mother to me. Her career is her real baby, and I'm an inconvenience. She has never been there for me. Especially when I've needed her the most." Tears prick my eyes, and a tightness spreads across my chest as my mind meanders into the past.

"Did something happen?" His voice is low, his face etched with concern as he looks across at me.

I gulp over the sudden lump in my throat. "It's not really something I like talking about," I whisper. I haven't told anyone about what went down that night, and I've successfully banished all thoughts of it from my mind. Lately, though, with everything that's happened, the memory has been trying to resurface. But I refuse to go there, instantly shutting that shit down anytime a thought rears its ugly head.

"If you ever change your mind, I'm here for you." He reaches across the console, squeezing my thigh.

"You really mean that." It's not a question, because I already see the truth in his eyes.

"I do." He removes his hand, replacing it on the wheel. "I'm sensing you haven't had many people in your corner, Emily, and I want you to know I'm firmly on your side."

"Why?" I'm genuinely curious. "Why would a guy like you want anything to do with a girl like me?"

He arches a brow. "A guy like me?"

"You're a star athlete and all-round good guy. Why would you want to get mixed up with me?"

"Maybe because you're smart, kind, beautiful, and you intrigue me like no woman has ever before?"

My heart soars. "That's one of the nicest things anyone has ever said to me."

"Please tell me that's not true? Please tell me someone in your life has told you how incredible you are before now?"

An urge to fling myself across the console and wrap myself around him rides me hard. "Keep talking like that and I'll turn into a level-five clinger," I joke.

"Cling on tight, babe. I'll never let you go." He flashes me a huge grin.

This time, I give into my urges, stretching across the console and pressing a kiss to his cheek. His spicy, citrusy cologne wafts around me like a comfort blanket. "Thank you." I reluctantly pull back, because it's getting dark and he needs to concentrate on the road. "I don't think I've said that enough. Thank you so much for everything you've done for me so far. It's embarrassing to admit you've done more for me, and treated me with more kindness, than my own family." My eyes burn with rejection. "All I ever hear from my mother is how much of a disappointment I am. No matter how much I devote myself to my studies, and how good my grades are, it's never quite good enough. And I never wear the right clothes or say the right things. To her, I find creative ways of humiliating her. In fact"—I bite down hard on the inside of my mouth—"I can't actually remember a time when she has ever told me she loves me."

Red-hot pain slices across my chest.

"And your father lets her get away with that?" Fire blazes in his eyes, and he grips the steering wheel tighter.

"She bullies him too."

His eyes widen in shock. "I cannot imagine anyone bullying Coach Parker. He's fierce. It's one of the reasons we all respect him so much."

"I guess you never know what someone is dealing with behind closed doors." I shrug. "And he tries to defend me, but he's not always consistent." I stare out the front window, watching cars fly by on the other side of the highway. "He's distracted a lot lately, and I don't really know what's going on with him."

Silence engulfs us for a few beats. "I presume he doesn't know you're taking this trip with me?"

I jerk my head back around to him. "Hell no! I value breathing. As I'm sure you do."

He chuckles. "Has he specifically warned you off me?"

"No, but he has told me his football players are off-limits. He knows what you guys get up to in your spare time and, that's not who he wants for me."

"Hey. Don't paint us all with the same brush." He pins me with serious eyes. "I don't play the field, and my last serious girlfriend was in high school."

"I know that's not who you are." He doesn't have a manwhore rep like a lot of the guys on his team do. All the gossip I've ever heard about him is how he likes to keep to himself and he's a gentleman. Nothing I have seen since our paths crossed has proven otherwise. "But even if you were, your sexual history doesn't define who you are as a person."

I hope he shares that sentiment, because my own background is hardly saint-like.

His features soften as he glances at me again. His green eyes radiate sincerity. "Agreed. And there is far too much emphasis on that shit these days. People should be free to screw who they want if they are respectful and make their intentions clear."

I pull my jean-clad knees up to my chest, smiling at him. "You're definitely one of the good guys, Adam Miller."

"Shush." He places one long finger against his delectable lips. "Don't tell anyone."

"Your secret is safe with me."

"Speaking of secrets." He shifts in his seat. "Why were you in the hospital that first time I met you?"

I decide to come clean. "I bought some bad shit in a bar and had a seizure."

"Fucking hell, Em." My nickname rolls easily off his lips, and I like it a lot.

"I know." I sigh. "It was a poor judgment call, but I'd had a bad day. Wes had pulled some shit, and I wasn't thinking clearly."

A dark cloud passes over his face at the mention of Wes. "I fucking hate that prick, and I hope this Kim ponies up, because she's all that's standing between Wes and an early grave."

* * *

"WILL THIS DO?" ADAM ASKS, PULLING THE TRUCK TO A STOP IN THE half-empty motel parking lot. We're only a half hour from Charlotte, but it's late, and we've both agreed it makes more sense to approach Kim in daylight. So, we're going to stay here for the night and head to her house after breakfast.

A fresh wave of butterflies scatter in my chest. "It's perfect." The motel looks like your typical motel, which means the Ritz it ain't, but the walls are newly-painted and it looks clean and tidy, and that's all that matters.

He turns to face me, a hint of uncertainty briefly appearing on his face. "Is one room okay, or you want me to book separate rooms?"

"One room is fine." I'm pleased my voice doesn't betray my nervous excitement.

He unbuckles his seat belt, cupping my face. "I would love to hold you in my arms all night, but I expect nothing more."

"What if I do?" I blurt.

His lips curve up at the corners. "I don't expect anything, but I never said I didn't want you." He leans in, brushing his lips once against my mouth. "Just so we're crystal clear, I've been dreaming about fucking you. More than is normal." He kisses me again, and my entire body relaxes.

"I've been imagining that too," I whisper over his lips. "I really like you Adam."

He winds his big hands into my hair. "I really like you too, Emily."

I'm grinning like a crazy person as I watch him walk across the parking lot to the reception desk. His Cypress Bulldogs T-shirt is stretched tight across his broad shoulders, and the muscles in his back flex and roll as he walks. My eyes lower to his toned ass, and intense heat floods my pussy as I imagine grabbing handfuls of his butt as he fucks me. His muscular thighs mold to his dark jeans, and there is no denying Adam Miller is one damn fine specimen of masculine hotness.

I slink out of the truck, grabbing our overnight bags from the back.

Dumping them on the ground by my feet, I lean against the hood of the truck and stare up at the smattering of stars in the nighttime sky. Adrenaline floods my system, and my core aches with anticipation.

I've never spent the full night with a guy before, and this is the third time I'm spending the night with Adam. First where I'm clean and sober. Shock skitters across my face as I realize I haven't thought about getting high once today. Ordinarily, I'd be at the warehouse or some frat party, wasted by now.

And now, I'm thinking about Molly and craving a high.

Way to go, doofus.

"You okay?" Adam asks, startling me.

I jump a little. "Yeah." It's not like I'm itching for a hit or anything.

He peers deep into my eyes, rubbing his thumb along my bottom lip. "I don't want to make you uncomfortable. I can get a second room."

I place my hands on his waist. "I'm not uncomfortable." Well, not for the reasons he thinks. "Truth be told, I'm a little nervous, but I want to share a room with you."

His mouth presses against mine in a tender kiss. "You call the shots, gorgeous. We can do as much or as little as you want."

I circle my arms around his neck and stare into the depths of his emerald-green eyes. Adam is my new drug of choice, and if I focus on him, I'll forget all about needing an illegal high. "Now, it's my turn to be clear. I want everything you're offering, Adam."

Adam slams the door closed with his foot, dropping our bags on the ground and stalking toward me like a man on a mission. My lady parts explode as he pins his heated stare on me. Instinctively, I back up until my legs hit the edge of the bed, and I let myself fall. I flop onto the bed, and he crawls over me, his eyes burning with lust.

"The things I've dreamed of doing to you," he rasps, lowering his head and brushing his hot mouth along my collarbone.

A trail of shivers skates across my flesh as I dig my fingers into his thick, dark hair. "How about we turn those dreams into reality?" I yank his head to mine, slamming my lips into his. We devour one another in a frenzy of lips, tongue, and teeth while he hovers over me, propped up on his elbows. Heat rolls off his powerful body in waves, doing funny things to me. I pull him down on top of me and then roll us over until I'm straddling him. I tug at the hem of his shirt. "I need this off."

"Do what you want to me, baby. My body is yours to worship."

I snort out a laugh as I peel his shirt away. "That was so cheesy."

He grins as his fingers wander to the buttons on my shirt and he starts unbuttoning them. "I think you'll find, when it comes to you, I'm a walking cliché."

I press a kiss to his toned stomach. "I don't mind in the slightest." I peek up at him. "As long as I get to have my wicked way with your sexy body."

He rears up, lifting his shirt over his head one-handed, and his abs tighten with the motion. My eyes are glued to his six-pack. Or is that an eight-pack? My eyes almost bug out of their sockets.

His soft chuckle snaps me out of my daze. His thumb swipes at my mouth. "You had some drool there."

I swat his hand away before moving to the buckle on his jeans. He unbuttons the last button on my blouse, pushing the silky material off my shoulders. It flutters to the floor, joining his shirt.

He stares at me with hooded eyes as lust mixes with something else I can't figure out.

I press my hand to his chest. "What is it?" He seems to be struggling with something.

His chest heaves as he pins me with a serious expression. "I need to know that you're clean."

I hate that he has to ask, but I get it. I nod. "I get tested regularly, and I'm good."

I can almost see the stress lift from his shoulders. In a lightning-fast move, he flips me flat on me back. Looming over me, he buries his head between my bra-covered breasts, and when he drags his tongue over both swells, goose bumps sprout on my flesh.

"Oh my God." A breathy moan escapes my lips as he tweaks my nipples through the thin lace while his tongue does laps of my breasts. Before I know it, he has my bra unclasped and he's sucking one taut nipple into his hot mouth. I drag my fingernails down his back, slipping my hand into the loosened band of his jeans, surprised when my fingers meet warm flesh. "No boxers?" I inquire.

He lifts his head from my chest, grinning. "I was in such a hurry to meet you I forgot to put them on."

My heart melts. *This guy can't be real, can he?*

He slides down my body, and I pout at the loss of his hot flesh under my touch. He laughs. "I need to get you naked, baby, and then it's your turn." He shoots me a devilish wink, and I lie back and close my eyes, happy to let him undress me. He makes quick work of my jeans and undies until I'm laid out before him in all my naked glory.

"Fuck, Emily." He sits back on his heels. "You are so beautiful." He takes a slow, lazy perusal of my body, and his gaze is like a sensual caress that I feel all the way to my toes.

I'm usually high or drunk when I have sex, and most guys don't waste time admiring my body before screwing the shit out of me. This entire experience is completely different, and it's only now I realize I've been craving this kind of connection with someone. "I need to taste you." His eyes take on a hungry look as he lowers his head to my pussy.

I automatically spread my legs wide, groaning as he licks along my slit before plunging inside me. My hips jerk up, and his large palm holds me in place as he eats me up. I'm squirming and writhing on the bed as a whole host of incredible sensations swarm my body. My skin feels electric. Like I'm hotwired and primed to explode in a frenzy of pent-up energy.

Adam pushes two fingers inside me, frantically pumping them in and out as his lips close over my clit. He sucks on the little bundle of nerves for a few minutes, and my orgasm detonates without warning. I scream out his name as I ride the euphoric train, my body sinking into the mattress when I finally come down from my climax.

I push damp strands of hair off my face as I hear the telltale rip of a condom wrapper. I prop up on my elbows, coming face to face with his impressive erection. His cock stands long, proud, and thick, and I lick my lips as I crawl toward him, swiping my tongue over his crown before he can roll the rubber on.

"Fuck, Emily." He grabs the back of my head, stalling me.

"As much as I love the feel of your lips on me, it's been a while, and I need to be inside you. Right now." His eager eyes plead with me.

Who am I to deny the man after he gave me the most earth-shattering orgasm of my life? I straighten up on my knees, leaning into him. I press my lips to his, shoving my tongue into his mouth, and we kiss passionately as he rolls the condom over his rock-hard dick. "Fuck me, Adam."

He caresses my cheek as he stares into my eyes. "You sure?"

"I've never been more sure of anything in my life."

"Thank fuck." He lays me down gently on the bed and spreads my legs, positioning himself at my entrance. "Because I've never wanted anyone as much as I want you."

"Adam." Happy tears sting my eyes. "You say the most amazing things."

"I'm only speaking the truth," he says, pushing inside me a little. I wrap my legs around his back, allowing him to go deeper.

I gasp at the sensation of him filling me up, completing me with every inch he advances. He keeps his eyes trained on mine the whole time, and it's the most intimate moment of my life. His face conveys so much, and my heart is beating superfast behind my rib cage. I feel every movement, every careful thrust, my nerve endings firing on all cylinders as he moves slowly inside me.

It's not like he's making love to my body.

It's as if he's making love to my soul.

When he's fully seated, I stare at him in wonder, my heart full to a bursting point.

I wonder if this is what it feels like to find that one person who completes you mind, body, and soul.

Because, right now, in this moment, with superstar quarterback Adam Miller buried balls deep inside me, he feels like the other half of me.

17

ADAM

I stare at the woman who blew my fucking mind last night—not once but four times. I seriously don't think we slept but an hour. I replay several moments as my jeans grow tight. Holy hell, shower sex with the blue-eyed goddess this morning topped my list of things I want to do again and again. Fuck. I'm ready to blow breakfast and screw her again in the shower. Something about the feel of water cascading down our bodies while I pump inside her makes me as hard as the steel tabletop separating us.

She peeks over her menu, her eyes alight with pleasure. "Stop staring." I can't see her mouth, but I know she's smiling, and it's a beautiful picture. I love seeing her sober, happy, laughing, and being herself. I worry though that her new lease on life will be pulled out from underneath her.

It's only been a week since I rescued her from that creep who I'm praying like a motherfucker we can take down. Still, not a minute goes by when I'm not thinking about her, hoping she's dealing with her shit without the need to indulge in Molly or any other drugs.

She places the menu on the table, her cheeks a rosy pink.

Man, how did I get so lucky?

"Are you blushing?" I tease.

Not tearing her gaze away from me, she slides down in the booth just a tad before dragging her foot up my leg.

My brows lift. "Be careful, Em. I'm not opposed to taking you right here." I'm not one to do something as brazen as sex in a hotel diner, but this girl is doing things to me that send delicious shock waves throughout my body and she's shredding my self-control.

I swear, if my body wasn't so big, I would get under the table and taste her for breakfast until she was screaming my name.

Fuck. That thought makes my dick harder than it already is.

She searches the empty diner slyly, holding her bottom lip hostage between her teeth.

Except for two waitresses who have been watching us since we walked in, only a handful of patrons are paying us any attention. Most are just enjoying their food.

As soon as her cute foot finds my cock, I'm holding in a groan that would shake the damn windows. My breathing ramps up as I grab her foot, tilting my head, wondering if she's ticklish. She tenses, and I have my answer.

Before I can follow through, the brunette waitress shows up, snapping her gum, studying Emily then me.

Emily doesn't move but giggles. Her laugh is infectious, and suddenly, I'm laughing with her. The act is freeing, and for the first time in what feels like forever, I'm not worrying about money or football or even Mom and my sister.

"Are you two lovebirds ready to order?" the waitress asks without batting an eye. I'm sure she's seen all kinds of things working at a hotel diner.

Emily sits up, regarding the waitress, casually moving her strawberry-blonde locks over one shoulder. "I'll have two eggs over easy and bacon."

Chewing that gum like a cow gnawing on cud, the waitress turns her attention to me. "Sir." Her eyes roam down my chest.

I want to laugh because the woman—who I would guess is in her thirties—is trying to gauge the package in my jeans. Thankfully, my boner is now gone. "Three eggs cooked hard, bacon, sausage, and pancakes. Oh, and a tall orange juice."

The waitress snags the menus. "Coming right up."

"You're going to eat all that?" Emily asks, shock leaping off her.

I sit back. "I worked out *a lot* last night." I give her a cheeky grin. "Growing boy too."

A wicked glint appears in her eye. "We could work out again." Her tone is seductive.

I swear I'm in puberty again. I can't seem to control my fucking erections since she got into my truck to come up to Charlotte. *Hell, who am I kidding?* I've had a constant hard-on since I met her outside the warehouse at that rave.

I lean forward, reaching over to take her hand. "Not to sour the mood, but how are you doing? Any cravings since you showed up at my dorm last week?"

She blows out a breath as if she's trying not to think of getting high. "I'm not going to lie. It's been hard. But I've managed to keep busy with the English paper I had due and my tutoring job. Not to mention, my mom hasn't been home all that much."

I relax against the vinyl booth, seething inside with hatred for the way her mother treats her. When she told me her mother didn't want her, my heart broke into a million pieces. No wonder Emily turned to drugs. I would too if Mom didn't want me. I knew my old man didn't want Phoebe or me, but he took off, and I didn't have to hear him berate or shatter my self-esteem every day. Yet people handle problems differently. For me, anger always lies under the surface when I think of my old man, and thank God for football. The field is a safe haven for releasing my rage.

She sips on her coffee. "You told me at Carter's that you hadn't sold drugs in years. How old were you when you started?"

I glance out the window, thinking back to the first time I'd met Donnie, which seems like a thousand years ago. I swing my attention from a hotel guest loading up his car to Emily, who is eager to hear my story. "I was in the ninth grade. I met Donnie outside my new school. We'd just moved from a big two-story house to a one-bedroom apartment. We were on our last ten dollars." I suck in a breath.

The waitress brings our food to the table. "Anything else?" she asks.

"No, ma'am," Emily says, not looking at her.

Once the waitress is gone, I continue. "My mom must've had five job interviews, and not one would hire her because she didn't have any experience. Staying at home to take care of us was her job. But after my old man split, life took a drastic turn. Donnie was kind and showed me the ropes. At first, he didn't want me selling anything. He would pay me to clean up around his garage. But it wasn't enough, and when I saw the money he counted in the evenings from the drug sales, I wanted in. High school kids love prescription drugs, especially the rich ones. And one thing led to another, and I was selling and making some good money."

"Did your mom know?"

I frown. "Sadly, she found out when I brought home a wad of cash. She tried everything to get me to stop, but with Phoebe's medical expenses, it was a no-brainer for me. And before you ask, she does know I'm selling again. Believe me, she hates I'm doing this. But Em, her and Phoebe are my world, and I would die for them or anyone I love." I'd never spoken truer words as I pin her with a serious look, hoping she understands I'm here for her too.

She picks up a slice of bacon. "Do you keep bags of Molly on you?"

I do a double-take. "Em?" I say her name in warning.

She bites into the bacon. "I'm not... I'm... Never mind." Her gaze drifts out the window.

Suddenly, I'm not hungry. "Emily. Look at me." My tone brokers no argument.

She drops her bacon into the plate and sits back. Her chest rises. "It's hard, Adam. I'm not going to lie. Just talking about it makes me want to get high, and knowing you could have some on you, I'm not sure I have the willpower."

I leave my spot and circle the table to sit next to her. "You're strong, Em." I guide her chin so I'm looking into those big blue eyes that do crazy fucking things to my body. "I know it's hard as a mother-fucker. But you've done so well this past week."

"You really believe that?"

I move silky strands of her hair behind her ear. "I do. I see what drugs do to people, and I hate that I'm supplying them, but when something happens to Phoebe, and we need money, I have to purposely forget how much I fuck up people's lives. Because in the end, I want to save my sister so fucking bad it hurts right here." I pound on my chest.

Her eyes fill with tears.

"I want to save you too, Em." I don't give a shit how corny that sounds. Emily needs someone, and I want that someone to be me. I want to help. Maybe in a fucked-up way, helping her makes me realize my own flaws need fixing.

She presses her lips to mine, softly, tentatively. "My knight in shining armor."

I give her a weak grin. "I wish I could agree. But you need to be your own knight. You need to save yourself. I'm just here to catch you if you fall."

"Promise?" she whispers.

My hand hooks around her neck, and I kiss that pouty bottom lip. "As sure as it's raining outside."

Her expression is a mix of hope and disbelief, and it guts me that she's unsure. Guess I'll just have to prove myself through my actions. "We should probably get moving," she says, after a couple beats of silence, and the bubble we were in bursts.

* * *

EXCEPT FOR THE NAVIGATION APP ON MY PHONE TELLING ME WHEN TO turn, the ride over to Kim Roberts' house is quiet as a mouse. Emily stares out the window, lost in her own thoughts.

I know she's thinking of our conversation just before we paid the bill at the hotel diner. That's all I've been thinking about too. I'm worried she's going to go on a binge, but there's nothing I can do other than to be there for her.

I comb my fingers through my hair as the navigation tells me to make a right up ahead.

Emily's phone pings in her lap, breaking her concentration. She reads the screen, then taps out a text. I'm dying to know who it is and not out of jealousy if it's Zach. I know they are friends even if I don't believe he's a good friend to have. Not when he enables her. But I'm not about to start telling her how to live her life. It sounds like she's had enough of that with her mom. But Wes is still out there, and for all we know, he could be stirring up trouble on his end.

I make the right onto a street lined with one-and two-story modest homes. Most cars are parked in the driveways.

"Zach wants to know where you are," Emily says, keeping her gaze out the windshield. "He needs some Molly." She says Molly as though she's jonesing for a pill. "He's been calling you."

Zach only has the number to my burner phone, and it's wrapped in a towel in a lockbox underneath my seat. If he wants any Molly, he'll have to hold his horses until I return. Even if I were home, I sold all of my supply on Friday, which worked out well since I knew Emily and I would be away this weekend.

"What did you tell him?" I didn't even ask her if she told Zach what we were doing this weekend. But I'm guessing she told him something because he knows she's with me.

I slow the truck, searching for the address Sam gave me.

Emily is scanning the homes. "We're busy, and he'll have to wait until we get back into town."

"So, he knows what we're doing?"

"I didn't give him all the details. Just told him and Scar that you and I were hanging out this weekend. The less people know what we're up to, the less of a chance Wes gets wind of it. Not that either of them would rat on us."

I agree with her about Zach. He wants in her pants so badly he won't put her in jeopardy and not after how we found her in that hotel room about to get gang-raped. Scarlett, though, I couldn't say. I don't know her at all.

Emily stabs a pink-painted nail at the house on the left. "There."

I drive past the one-story stone structure with a well-manicured lawn so I can make a U-turn and park in the empty spot in front of the house. It also gives me a chance to scope out the area. I don't believe Wes will pay Kim a visit, but I don't trust the asshole.

Sam says Wes isn't that smart, but I think we need to treat him as if he were. Just to be on the safe side.

I cut the engine, not seeing any signs of Wes lurking or anyone in the car parked across the street. "You ready?"

Emily bites on her nail. "I pray she wants to cooperate. It will make my life easier."

It will also take away one problem that causes her to turn to drugs and bring her one step closer to sobriety.

We both get out of the car at the same time. After I round the front of my truck, I hold out my hand.

Once my large paw swallows her small hand, she lets out a contented sigh. "I'm needing that hit, Adam. Right now."

I stop halfway up the driveway. "You're beautiful, strong, and have the world at your feet. Repeat that every time you feel the urge to get high." Honestly, I don't know if it'll work, but Mom has a similar mantra when things get tough.

She nods. "You think it'll help?"

I kiss her forehead. "When my mom has to dig deep for strength, she says, 'I'm a good person, I'm tough, and nothing can get in my way."

She pokes out her chest, seemingly satisfied. I'm about to kiss her for good luck when I spot someone looking at us through the bay window.

I tug on Emily's hand. "Someone is watching us."

Before we ring the bell, the door opens. An older lady in her fifties with gray hair and soft brown eyes, greets us. "Can I help you?" Her gaze swings between Emily and me, suspicion mounting. "If you're selling something, turn around and leave." Her tone is rather harsh.

Emily tenses. But I press on. "We're not here to sell anything, ma'am." I give her my sugary voice, the one I use with Mom. "We're looking for Kim Roberts."

Her gaze hardens before she scans her neighborhood. "Who's asking?"

"We're students from Cypress University," Emily says. "We were hoping to talk to Kim."

"Are you friends with her?" the lady asks, looking ready to shut the door on us.

I'm not excited about giving out too much information. More to protect Emily from her mother. If President Parker gets wind that we're responsible for bringing down Weston Blakely, I'm not sure what she'll do. She might commend us once she finds out what Wes has done not only to her daughter but to the students she's supposed to protect on campus. Or maybe not.

"Mom, who is it?" A young woman about our age saunters up, studying me with her brown gaze and startled smile. "I know you."

Emily and I exchange a surprised look.

The girl nudges in beside the woman. "Mom, I got this."

"Kim, honey," her mom says, mashing her lips into a thin line as unease drips from her tone.

Clearly, someone has a done a number on her psyche, and I'm guessing it's Wes.

"Mom. This is Adam Miller, the quarterback of Cypress University. I can handle this. Why don't you finish making coffee?"

Her mom pivots on her heel, not looking happy.

Kim glances over her shoulder, watching her mom until she's out of sight. Then, as if she switches masks, her dark eyes narrow on us. "What's this about?"

"Weston Blakely," I say in a low voice. It was clear Kim didn't want to upset her mom. So, I want to be respectful.

Kim pales and sways on her feet.

I reach out to steady her, but Emily beats me to it, gently taking hold of her hand. "I'm one of Wes's victims too, Kim."

Kim's chest heaves before she blows out a shuddering breath.

Emily lets go of her. "The last thing we want to do is bring up what happened to you." Emily seeks me out as though she wants permission to continue. I nod even though she doesn't need my approval. Emily regards Kim. "We have a way to stop him, but we need your help. Can we come in?"

Lifting her chin, she contemplates Em's request for a few beats before she nods. She steps aside to let us in.

"How do you know Adam?" Emily asks in a soft voice as she crosses the threshold.

A pinch of color returns to Kim's face as she eyes me. "Adam is a god in the eyes of my younger brother. We used to go to a few games during the season."

Emily tosses a proud look over her shoulder at me, and I find myself grinning at my girl before my gaze drifts around the spacious floor plan that combines the kitchen and living area. The room gives a comfy vibe, and I wouldn't mind hanging here on a Sunday afternoon with a sixty-five-inch TV hanging over the fireplace. Nothing better than a football game on a big-screen TV.

"Please, have a seat," Kim says, walking into the living room, pointing to the tan L-shaped sofa.

The sound of water running filters out from the kitchen as Emily and I sit down together on the couch.

Kim folds her petite body in an oversized chair adjacent to us. "I wish my brother were home. He spent the night at his friend's house. He's going to be disappointed he didn't get to meet you, Adam."

It would've been nice to meet a fan. I always enjoy when little boys are waiting after games for the team to sign their stuff. "If he has a football or jersey hanging around, I'd be happy to sign it for him."

"Oh," Kim says. "He'd love that. I'll see what I can find in his room before you leave."

Silence dangles for a beat.

Emily straightens, sitting on the edge of a cushion. "Kim, I know talking about Wes is going to be hard."

Kim twirls her thumb ring as the color drains from her tan complexion.

I motion to stand. This is a bad idea. The woman looks like she's going to pass out.

Kim holds up her hand. "Please. Give me a second." Her nostrils flare as she blinks successively. "I've worked hard to remove his name from my mind," she whispers.

"I'm sorry to bring something so traumatic up," Emily says. "But we wouldn't have come if it wasn't important. I know your pain and what you're going through."

Kim shudders, blinking away tears.

Fucking asshole has that type of effect, and he isn't even here.

"Maybe it'd be better if I left you two to talk alone." I need some air, but I'm also thinking that Emily will get more info out of Kim woman to woman and all. Plus, I want to call Zach and find out how much Molly he needs and when we can meet.

I lean in so my lips are brushing Emily's ear. "I'll be right outside." I kiss her quickly, before standing and heading out to my truck.

18

EMILY

"They raped you too?" Kim asks with tears streaming down her face.

I move to the other side of the couch closer to her. "They tried to. Would've succeeded if Adam and a couple of other guys hadn't busted into the hotel room and saved me." I wet my dry lips.

Everything rests on me convincing her to report the rape.

Because without her we have nothing.

We can't use that video without her permission because there's no way I'd expose any woman if she didn't want to press charges. "But they drugged, stripped, and groped me, and I know they would've gang-raped me if the guys hadn't shown up."

"Oh my God." She joins me on the couch, pulling me into a hug, sobbing. "I'm so sorry. I was afraid of this."

"It's not your fault," I rush to reassure her.

She sniffs, easing back, her eyes drying with firm resolve. "He's an evil bastard. They all are. And I wish I'd been strong enough to do something about it, but I had no proof. It would be my word against theirs. They have money and contacts on their side, and I knew I couldn't win."

"What if I told you we discovered proof?"

"What do you mean?" she stammers, her lower lip wobbling.

I take her chilly hands in mine. "Do you remember a camera in the room when they assaulted you?"

She shakes her head. "I don't remember, because I was completely wasted from the drugs and booze they'd pumped into me. But Wes told me he had it. He used it to blackmail me into silence. He said if I breathed a word to anyone he would show them the tape and, according to him, it would exonerate them." A muscle ticks in her jaw. "He said I was begging for it and willingly fucked all of them." She glances over her shoulder, lowering her voice. I look behind me too, spotting Adam talking in hushed tones with Kim's mother as they both nurse cups of coffee.

I return my attention to Kim. "He lied. We've seen it, and that is not the way it looks." More tears spill out of her eyes, rolling down her cheeks, and she hangs her head. I squeeze her hands. "We didn't watch it all. It was too distressing, but it was clear you were barely conscious, and it was not consensual."

"Who has seen it?" she whispers.

"Just me and Adam and a friend of ours who is the tech genius who found it. I promise you no one else will see it." I slip the thumb drive out of my purse and hand it to her. "It is your decision what you choose to do with the evidence." I curl her fingers around the device. "But we are hoping you will help us to put him away." I peer into her eyes. "To stop him from doing this to any other woman. And, I have a feeling if you come forward that others will too. I can't make a statement because Adam beat the shit out of him, and we're afraid he'll end up facing charges if it comes to light."

"Remind me to thank Adam for that before you leave." She swipes at the hot tears coursing down her face, clutching the device firmly in her hand. "I don't need to think about it." Steely determination glimmers in her eyes. "They are monsters, and they need to pay for what they did to me. I had to drop out of college and move away because they destroyed me. There was a time when I didn't get out of bed for a month, and I spent weeks crying for hours every day. My nights were consumed with flashbacks and nightmares. I was in hell. Barely existing. Barely holding on."

I gulp over the aching lump lodged at the back of my throat. My heart picks up speed, thumping painfully behind my rib cage, as a night I've fought so hard to forget prods at the edges of my mind.

"It's only therapy and the love of my family that pulled me through," Kim continues, and a pang of envy jumps up and bites me.

No one supported me because no one knows.

If my parents hadn't been at one another's throats all the time, maybe they would have noticed the drastic change in me. If they cared enough, maybe, they would have asked why I turned to drugs. But their answer was to pretend the problem didn't exist. To shove me into rehab and have someone else whip their wayward daughter into shape.

"Hey." Kim's tone is soft as she peers into my eyes. She glances over her shoulder again, leaning in close to my ear. "Is that all that really happened with Wes? Because I'm sensing—"

"I was raped when I was fifteen," I whisper. The most intense pain settles on my chest as I reveal the secret I've been hiding for four long years. "You're the first person I've admitted it to." Quite frankly, I'm shocked I just blurted it out like that. It certainly hadn't been my intention coming here.

Shock splays across her face. "You haven't even told your parents or your boyfriend?"

I shake my head. "I don't have a supportive family like you, and I've only recently met Adam."

"You should tell him." She drapes her arm around my shoulder. "And you need to talk to someone. I speak from experience when I say keeping it locked up will eat you from the inside out. There is no way to survive if you continually avoid confronting it. I'm going to put that bastard Wes away. For you and me, and the countless other women he has probably done this to. I give you my word. But I need you to give me your word too."

I force my gaze to her.

"You need to promise me you will go and speak to someone about it. A professional. That you will put yourself first and deal with it before it destroys you completely."

* * *

"ARE YOU SURE YOU'RE OKAY?" ADAM ASKS ME FOR THE THIRD TIME as we drive toward home.

"I'm fine," I lie. Since we left Kim's house, I've been in a weird funk. Memories I've struggled to bury are taunting me, and I wish I had half of Kim's strength.

She's amazing.

To battle on like she did after that horrific assault and to instantly decide to seek justice. She didn't even need to think about it. She immediately knew taking the evidence and reporting the gang rape to the cops was the right thing to do. She sent me a message ten minutes ago confirming she was on her way to the local station with her mom.

"Did Kim say something to upset you?"

"It's just brought it all back," I admit, and that's not a full lie. I also just promised her I'd seek help, and that's also weighing on my mind. I don't know that I'm strong enough to open up about this.

He rests his hand on top of my thigh. "I'm such an idiot. Of course, it would."

Now, I feel bad. I wish I could tell him. I want to. But I've spent so long keeping it buried inside me that I'm afraid of letting it out. In a way, it was easy to tell Kim. Because she's a stranger and she's been through it. Telling those I'm close to is another matter entirely. It's so much harder to confide in my loved ones, for a whole heap of reasons. But the pain of it is something I carry with me every day like a phantom limb. I don't have to think about it to feel it. It's just there. Always pressing down on me. Forcing me to run to my best friend Molly to help forget my emotions.

I bring his hand to my lips, pressing a kiss to his knuckles. "You're not an idiot. I had no idea I'd react like that. She's so brave. I'm in awe of her."

"I can't believe she agreed so readily and that she's already taking action."

"I wonder how long it'll take them to arrest him."

"Considering Sam sent that fake, anonymous email from Wes's IP address with the video and confession, I'm guessing next to no time."

"What if they find out it wasn't Wes who sent it?" I ask, only thinking of this for the first time. "I don't want Sam to get in trouble. Or Wes to get off."

Adam returns his hand to the wheel. "Sam is a freaking genius, and he's got what I refer to as tech OCD. He's meticulous, and there's no way they'll link it back to him." He shoots me a happy smile. "And even if they did, there's no way Wes will get off. The evidence is there whether he sent it or not. And Kim is making a full statement, and it's still within the statute of limitations so it's rock solid."

"I wonder if more girls will come forward?" I muse, lifting my bare feet to the dash.

The truck rumbles as Adam speeds up, moving into the left lane. "I think that's a given. If he was pulling this shit since high school, there are more victims."

I briefly think of the man who raped me. Wondering if he has more victims. If I'm at fault for not reporting it. A pang of guilt slaps me in the face.

"Hey, how would you feel about an impromptu visit to my house? I'd told Phoebe I couldn't visit today, but I'd love to introduce you to my mom and sister. They are dying to meet you."

My eyes pop wide. "You told your family about me?"

He grins. "I fessed up this week. You should've heard them screaming on the phone. It's kind of embarrassing to admit."

I lean across the console and kiss his cheek. "It's not embarrassing at all. I love that you told them about me." My heart is careening around my chest, jumping for joy. He must be serious if he's told his family, and that has me doing a silent happy dance.

Adam has lifted me out of my head, and I want to pepper his gorgeous face with kisses.

But he's driving.

So, it'll have to be a rain check.

"I'd love to meet them."

"Yeah?" Pleasure seeps into his tone and his facial expression.

"Yep." My smile is genuine as I grin at him. "I could think of no better way to spend the day than spending Sunday with you and your family."

* * *

"Mom. Phoebe." Adam tucks me under his shoulder. "This is Emily." He beams at me, and I melt under his adoring gaze.

"Oh, my. Look how beautiful you are." Adam's mom holds out her arms, and I willingly fall into them. Her hug is warm and gentle. She holds me at arm's length. "Now, I can see why my boy has been so distracted lately!"

"Thank you." I laugh. "And I can't believe you're Adam's mom. You don't look old enough." It's true. Although I know she's had a tough life, you couldn't tell by looking at her. Her brown hair is thick and long with no hints of gray, and her skin is remarkably unlined for a woman of her age.

"I'm Phoebe." Adam's sister is the spitting image of their mom with her voluminous, long dark hair, big brown eyes, and heart-shaped face.

I extend my hand. "I have heard so much about you from your brother, and I'm so happy to meet you."

She squeezes my hand, her eyes twinkling mischievously as she casts a quick glance at her brother. "I'd like to say the same, but Adam's been holding out." She tugs me forward. "I'm kidnapping Emily," she says with supreme confidence. "You can go drink coffee with Mom in the kitchen," she tosses over her shoulder at her brother.

He chuckles. "I should've warned you, Em. Prepare for the Spanish Inquisition."

"Should I be afraid?" I quip.

"Very," all three of the Millers say in unison, and I burst out laughing.

"I made you something," Phoebe says, pulling me into a homey living room cluttered with family pictures on every wall and surface. She sits cross-legged on the floor in front of a coffee table littered with glitter, string, and beads. "I didn't know I would be meeting you today, but I was going to work on Adam until he brought you to see me."

"I suspect you have your brother wrapped around your little finger, Phoebe," I tease, dropping down alongside her on the carpeted floor.

She winks. "I do! Him and Sam." She giggles. "I bet you have him wrapped around your finger too."

"Not yet. But it's early days." I waggle my brows, and she giggles again. "Got any pointers for me?"

She taps a finger off her chin as she considers it. "Let me work on a list for you."

"Sounds like a plan."

She rummages around on the table, plucking a green, white, and yellow bracelet from the pile in the center. "I hope you like the colors. Adam told me you had beautiful strawberry-blonde hair, so I picked colors I thought would work." She chews on her bottom lip, and it's adorably cute.

"You made this?" My eyes are out on stilts. It's as good as any I'd buy at a market.

She puffs out her chest. "Been making my own jewelry since I was ten. Sam helps me. Adam too, when he has time."

"It's beautiful," I say, slipping it on my wrist and holding it out to inspect it. "And it fits perfectly." I smile at the bright, beautiful girl as I slide my arm around her shoulders, giving her a soft hug. "Thank you so much. This is the nicest gift anyone has ever made for me."

She dazzles me with a glorious smile, and it's only the faint shadows under her eyes and her off-white pallor that remind me she's ill. "I feel so bad I brought nothing for you. This was a spur-of-the-moment decision." I wrack my brain to see if I have anything with me I can give her.

A light bulb goes off in my head, and I glance at her bare hands. "Would you like your nails painted?" I wiggle my fingers at her. "I have this color polish in my purse."

She claps, bouncing around on her heels. "Yes, please! I would love that." Leaning into me, she squeezes me tight. "I just knew I was going to love you. If you've managed to catch my brother's eye, I knew you would be someone special."

Tears sting the back of my eyes, and I'm bowled over by her effervescent enthusiasm, her openness, and her warm welcome. "I think you got that mixed up, honey." I playfully tweak her cute button nose. "You are most definitely the special one."

19

ADAM

I step into the shower as most of the guys have already left the locker room and gone home.

"Hey, hoss." Carter's voice bounces off the tiled walls. "Are you in here?"

I turn on the water, and the cold spray jolts me for a second before the hot water kicks in. "What's up?"

"We haven't had a chance to talk," he says, leaning against the sinks across from me, fully dressed. He'd done his required laps and come in before me.

I decided to run several more laps than the allotted number Coach dishes out after practice. Since I dropped Emily off last night, I've had this pent-up energy just waiting to explode. It's a combination of missing her already and being on edge, wondering when Wes will get his ass thrown in jail.

Kim went to the police, and everything Sam set up is in play, but I haven't heard a damn word, and I've been texting Sam every minute today. He's keeping tabs on Wes, but so far, nothing.

It's driving me insane.

Well, not as much as wanting to get my arms around Emily.

Ever since we had sex, I want more of her. And it's not just sex. I loved hearing her laugh and seeing her let her hair down. Don't get me started on her hair. Having my hand wrapped around the silken strands while I had my way with her was...

Just that image and I'm hard as the tile around me. My dick pops to attention, and I seriously need to get a grip.

This girl has me in a tailspin.

What's most surprising is how much I love that she does.

Carter snaps his fingers. "Dude."

I blink, wiping hot water out of my eyes as I zero in on the blond ladies' man, sporting a grin, as he points to my dick. "You need to jack off? I can leave."

"Then get the fuck out. I'm trying to shower anyway. What guy watches another rub soap on his dick? Don't answer that." Not that he's gay. For all I know, he might swing both ways.

I'm ready to launch the bar at him when he holds up his hands. "Rachel wants to know if you and Em want to grab a bite this week."

I peer around to be sure no one else is in here. The last thing Emily and I need is someone eavesdropping and running to Coach or spreading rumors.

"Don't worry," Carter says. "The room is empty."

"I don't know. Her old man doesn't know about us, and I'm not sure we should be seen around town, especially with her mother too." President Parker has her eyes and ears everywhere. I couldn't give a shit about her mother, but her old man, my coach, he'll go ape shit if he finds out I'm dating his daughter.

"Well, let me know. If not this week, maybe another time. I'm out of here." His footsteps echo in the empty room, and when I hear the door click shut, I groan in frustration. I really want to jack off, but with my luck, someone else will walk in. Like Coach. I can picture that now.

Oh, I'm sorry, Coach. I was jacking off to images of your daughter.

Then I wouldn't have a dick anymore.

I'm heading to my truck fifteen minutes later when my phone rings. I snag it from the front pocket of my jeans to find Mom calling.

"Hey, everything all right?" My usual question when I answer a call from her.

Ignoring me, she says, "Phoebe can't stop talking about Emily. Do you think you two can come home for dinner later in the week? I know you have practice, but maybe one night would work?"

I lazily scan the parking lot. The sports complex is empty except for my truck and Coach's car.

"Coach has something to do on Wednesday. So, he's canceled practice. I'll see if Emily can make it first before I say yes. How's Phoebe?"

She'd been so disappointed when we left last night. She attached herself to Emily so quickly Mom and I had our jaws open the whole time. I lost my breath when Emily told Phoebe she was the special one. Then when Emily painted Phoebe's toes and nails pink and Phoebe beamed like she'd found a new best friend, my world was complete.

Mom shed tears as we listened and watched Phoebe and Emily bond. Fuck. If I knew Emily was serious about me, I would've proposed right then and there.

"Your sister's health is okay. If that's what you're asking?"

Suddenly, all the euphoria vanishes. "What do you mean *okay*, Mom?" Something in her tone makes the hair on my neck stand up.

I stop feet from my truck.

"She has a cough. Nothing to worry about," Mom admits in a weak tone.

Odd. Phoebe didn't show any signs of a cold or even a cough when she was bonding with Emily last night. "Did it just start this morning?"

"Adam, you know I'll call you if it's anything serious."

I sigh heavily, trying to expunge the panic coursing through me. "I know. Are you sure she's okay?"

"Adam, I love you. Give Emily a hug for us."

Shit. Mom is falling faster than me. And Phoebe already fell head over heels for Emily too.

"Kiss Phoebe for me, and I'll check with Em. Love you."

I pocket my phone, fishing my keys from my jeans.

Ten to one, she isn't telling me everything about Phoebe. But I can't let that worry me right now. If I do, my mind will be a complete mess this week, and with our upcoming game and all the other shit I have going, I need all my wits about me.

I run my hand through my wet hair as I climb in my truck.

Before I even start the engine, I tap on Emily's name on my cell. I'm dying to hear her voice since our parting kiss last night. It was fucking explosive, and neither of us could get enough of each other.

"Hey," her breathy and sexy as fuck voice comes through, causing every muscle in me to relax.

I pop my head against the seat. "How's my girl?"

She yawns or it sounds like she does. "Sleepy. I've been listening for my mom to come home, hoping she has news of Wes getting arrested, but the house is quiet."

"Your dad is still here at the sports complex. We just got done with practice." Coach always stays late watching last season tapes of games between Cypress and our opponents, particularly the team we're scheduled to play on Saturday. "Do you want me to come over?" Please say yes. Although, sneaking into the president and coach's house to fuck his daughter isn't the smartest move on my part. But I'm up for the adrenaline rush. Nothing heightens the senses more than doing something risky and forbidden.

She sucks in a breath, or maybe, she moans as though she's remembering our hot and steamy weekend. "I would say yes, but we can't chance it. You've got too much to lose."

"Are you worried about me?" Warmth blooms in my chest.

"Maybe," she coyly whispers.

"Em," I say, watching the trees fronting the sports complex sway in the light breeze.

"Yeah." She sounds like she's about to fall asleep.

"I really need to see you." I grab my throbbing cock.

"I've got a jam-packed week with tutoring," she says. "But I'll call you tomorrow and we can make plans. I really want to see you too."

"My mom invited us to dinner this week," I say, listening to her breathy noises. My dick is now straining against my zipper, and she's driving me crazy. Jerking off later is a definite. Otherwise, my hard-on isn't going away.

"Aw, I so want to go, but it isn't a good week. Can we reschedule for next week?"

I chuckle. "Phoebe might hunt you down before then."

She giggles. "She's amazing. I adore her."

And I think I'm falling in love with you.

I dare not voice that out loud. Not yet anyway. Besides, I don't think Emily is ready to hear how I feel.

"Get some sleep, beautiful. We'll talk tomorrow unless you hear anything about Wes."

"Okay. Night, Adam."

Neither of us hangs up, and a grin spreads across my mouth. "Why aren't you hanging up?"

"Why aren't you?" she retorts.

My grin widens. "I'm not ready to say goodbye."

"Neither am I." I can almost see her matching grin. "What are you doing to me, Adam Miller?"

I pop my head back against the seat. "I could ask you the same thing."

"Has it been like this for you before?"

"Never," I truthfully admit. "I can't get you out of my head. I'm going crazy."

Her tinkling laugh filters down the line. "You're not alone in it. You are all I'm thinking about."

I close my eyes, picturing her with Phoebe again. "That makes me happy."

"*You* make me happy."

"I think I might die of blue balls before the week is out."

Loud peals of laughter tickle my eardrums. "You have two working hands. You'll survive."

I pout. "If I have to."

"Look, let's talk tomorrow. We'll find a way to get together. I don't think I'd last all week without seeing you either."

"I'm going to hold you to that."

"See that you do." Another yawn slips out of her mouth. "Let's hang up on the count of three."

My belly rumbles with laughter. "One."

"Two."

"Three."

She hangs up, and the flat line of the ringtone reverberates in my ear for several seconds before I end the call and switch off my cell.

Hearing her voice and her words was just what the doctor ordered. Starting my truck, I grin as I turn on the radio. I can't remember the last time I felt this happy. We may not have admitted it to one another yet, but I'd bet my life Emily is falling for me in the same way I'm falling for her.

* * *

TWO NIGHTS LATER, I'M STILL FEELING THOSE WORDS WHILE I HAVE Emily pinned under me in my bed in my dorm room. She's giggling uncontrollably. "Please don't. I can't take anymore, Adam." Sam won't be back until later, and Emily's tutoring client canceled, so we seized the opportunity to grab a couple hours together. My cock thanks me for my quick thinking.

I squeeze her side again as my erection grazes her thigh. "Say it. Or else I'll tickle you senseless." I'm hiding a grin, trying to be serious, but it isn't working.

Seeing her laughing and squirming beneath me is by far the best picture I've ever seen.

She grabs my cock. "Fuck me, please."

"Now was that so hard?" I quip.

She shakes her head, holding in laughter, flashing her blue eyes at me. "But come on. It was funny."

"Calling my cock Mr. Willy isn't something any guy wants to hear." I tease her more than anything. She can call my dick anything she wants, and I'd drop to my knees and worship at the altar of Emily. "I usually refer to him as the pleasure machine." She busts out laughing, and I grin. I position my cock at her entrance. "Are you ready to meet the pleasure machine?"

Her lids fall closed as she lifts her hips, digging her nails into my triceps. "I've been ready from the instant I stepped foot in the door." She runs the tip of her finger down my chest, eliciting a trail of shivers in her wake.

"I don't like to keep any lady waiting." In one move, I thrust inside her drenched pussy, and she cries out in a loud moan.

We're on round two, and I'm thankful Sam is tutoring. Since our lust-filled weekend, all I've thought about is how to get Emily alone. Yesterday, we made out in my truck on a dark street off campus. While I'll take whatever stolen moments I can with Emily, my truck isn't big enough for the things I want to do to her. Regardless, we're trying to be careful not to be seen in public, and finding a place to have sex is monumental. Sam tutors late every Wednesday, so we might be able to make this a regular thing. For about five seconds, I debated taking her to Mom's for dinner, but it's late, and Phoebe goes to bed early on school nights.

Lowering my head, I capture one of her nipples between my teeth and bite down.

"Harder," she moans.

I swirl my tongue around, licking then nipping, teasing her. I love seeing her squirm when I don't give her what she wants.

She digs her nails in me. "Harder and start moving."

She's such a bossy little thing, but I wouldn't have her any other way. I pull out, and she shoots up almost to a sitting position. "Where are you going?" she protests, scowling.

I grin as I adjust my body, lifting her legs over my shoulders and burying my face in her pussy.

She flops back, and the minute I flatten my tongue on her clit, she moans so loud the guys next door can probably hear her.

But I've zero fucks to give.

I've got a good rhythm going, alternating between sucking her clit and plunging my tongue into her wet heat, when the sound of a key turning in the door makes me fly off the bed. I throw a sheet over Emily and hunt for my clothes.

Her blue eyes are huge as she clutches the sheet to her chest.

I grab a pair of sweats off the floor, but it's too late.

Sam barrels in, completely out of breath. When he takes in the scene, his mouth falls open. He quickly averts his eyes, looking at the side of the room. "Have you heard?"

I manage to pull my sweats on.

Emily tugs the sheet up to her neck, remaining calm and attentive as she asks, "What happened? Did Wes get arrested?"

Sam flicks on his computer, taps a few keys, and a video brightens the screen. "Wes is in jail."

Hallelujah.

Emily squeals, dropping the sheet in her excitement, exposing her perfect tits. "For real?" She jumps up and into my arms buck-ass naked. "Oh my God. Did you hear that, Adam?"

"You need to put some clothes on," I whisper in her ear.

"I agree," Sam says, not turning around yet, being the perfect gentleman. He clearly has supersonic hearing.

I can't say for sure the last time Sam has gotten laid. We don't talk about sex much, and he hasn't dated any girl since he came to CU. I pray one day he finds a girl who will rock his world like Emily has rocked mine.

Emily slides down my body, taking her sweet time and cupping my junk along the way.

"Tease," I mouth at her as blood rushes to my cock.

Emily dresses as fast as she can before rushing over to Sam to read what's on the screen. "This says he was arrested yesterday. What the fuck? How come we're just getting wind of this now? I even eavesdropped on my mom's conversation last night, hoping I'd hear something."

I want to know too. Sam was supposed to have tabs on Wes.

Sam pops to his feet, his face beet red. "Sit, Em."

She takes his seat and starts reading the page he brought up from a local news station. "Weston Blakely, a pre-law student at Cypress University, was arrested last night on multiple charges of gang rape and sexual assault." She goes quiet for a minute. "Holy crap. Two girls aside from Kim came forward. I have to call Kim." Just then her phone goes off.

Then my phone pings.

It's Carter. "Did you see the news?"

Emily is talking at the same time, and Sam's blue eyes are bouncing between Emily and me with a look I can't quite figure out.

"Yeah, man. It's fucking fantastic, but can I call you later?"

"Sure," Carter says and hangs up.

I pocket my phone and walk to Sam. "You okay? You seem a little out of sorts."

"I'm cool," he says. "Glad this Wes shit is over."

"How come you didn't know when it happened?" I ask.

"Wes's old man kept the whole thing from going public. And since the police confiscated Wes's computers and phone, I couldn't do a thing. But I found out Wes's crew got tagged too."

Emily is listening to her caller, smiling and bouncing her knee up and down. "I know. Best news ever. I feel like I'm walking on air."

Shit. I feel like I can breathe again too.

"So," Sam says. "Did anyone see Emily come in?"

Bingo. That's what he's freaking out over.

"Nah. I snuck her in the back way."

Emily hangs up her phone, beaming from ear to ear. "That was Kim. She's so relieved. I bet my mom is pissed." She says the last sentence with some giddiness, and Sam and I laugh.

Sam stabs a thumb at the door. "I'm going to get something to drink. I'll be back."

When the door snicks shut, Em walks right into my arms. "He doesn't seem excited."

I thread my fingers through her silky strands. "He's worried about you getting caught in here."

She wiggles her hips against my crotch. "I can't blame him. I actually hate us sneaking in here. I worry about you and Sam. My mom would freak out for sure. Maybe we should tell my dad."

I rear back. "Say what?"

She pokes my chest. "You heard me."

I shake my head. Fuck no. Coach will string me up by my balls for dating his daughter and then cut off my dick for fucking his daughter. Not ready to go down that road.

She crosses her arms over her tits. "If he knows you rescued me, he'll change his tune."

I tug her to me. "I don't share your confidence."

She snorts. "I get it. You're not ready."

She's not ready either. "Does your dad know about what Wes did to you?"

Fear freezes her in place. "No, but I'm going to tell him." Determination washes over her features. "I'm not looking forward to that convo, but it has to happen."

I agree.

She slides her hands up my abs and over my chest. "I want to resume playing with the pleasure machine." She slants me a flirty look as her tongue darts out, wetting her lips.

As much as I want to slide my cock into her and finish what we started, Sam will walk through that door any minute. "We'll have to take a rain check. Sam will be back any second."

"Can't blame a girl for trying." She stretches up, planting a passionate kiss on my lips. She sighs dreamily as she pulls back. "I better get going," she says, as a smile lights up her face. "I can't wait to tell Scar and Zach. I'm sure they already heard though."

"Most likely, it's all over campus by now." Serves the douche right. I fucking love karma. I lace my fingers with hers. "Come on, beautiful. I can maul you in the stairwell on our way out." I know the perfect place to finish what we started.

She slaps a hand over her chest. "You say the most romantic things." A giggle escapes her lips, and it's becoming my most favorite sound in the whole world.

"Anything to please my girl," I say, brushing my lips against hers as I pull her out of the room.

20

EMILY

The sound of glass breaking greets my ears the second I enter my house. Frowning, I drop my bag and keys on the hall table, walking in the direction of the kitchen. Dad pokes his head out of the living room. "Princess, do you have a minute?"

"Sure." I smooth my hair back, tucking it behind my ears, hoping Dad can't spot the freshly fucked aura I'm sporting. "What's going on?"

"I'm not quite sure." He paces the polished hardwood floor, running a hand through his reddish-brown hair. "And I was hoping you might be able to help me out."

All the tiny hairs stand to attention on the back of my neck as I sense where he's leading. I sink onto the couch, sitting ramrod straight.

"Your mother has been locked in her study since she arrived home early today. All I know is she's dealing with the fallout of Weston Blakely's arrest, but she's been throwing things around the room the last ten minutes, so whatever is going down isn't good."

"I suppose it's too much to expect an apology from her." I purse my lips, swallowing back bile.

Dad stops pacing, sitting down alongside me. "I never liked that guy, and I couldn't understand why Carole was so keen to push you together when it was obvious you couldn't stand him."

"Then why did you allow it?"

He has the decency to look ashamed. "For an easier life." His shoulders hunch forward. "I need to ask you about him, Emily, but first, *I* want to apologize to you."

My eyes pop wide.

He takes my hands in his big, meaty ones. They are warm and comforting. "I haven't been much of a father to you—"

I open my mouth to speak, but he places a finger over my lips.

"Don't attempt to refute that. We both know it's the truth. And I need to say this. It's long overdue."

I nod, urging him to continue with my eyes.

"I haven't been in a good place for a long time, Emily. That's no excuse for not taking proper care of you, for allowing your mother to push both of us around, but I've been meeting a therapist, and I'm seeing things more clearly now."

"Like what?"

He shakes his head. "I don't want to get into that now. Just know that things are going to change. Starting with this ridiculous threat your mother is holding over your head. I don't want to see you sliding back into a dark place again, but threatening you with eviction is not the answer. We failed you two years ago. *I* failed you. And that's not going to happen again. All I want is for you to be healthy and happy." He presses his lips to my cheek. "And I want you to know you always have a home with me. I would never let her take home or college away from you."

"You really mean that, Dad?" I can scarcely believe it.

"I do, honey." He presses a kiss to the top of my head this time. "But you need to be honest with me too." He pins me with a serious look. "Are you taking drugs again?"

I vigorously shake my head, and it's not really a lie, because I haven't been high in almost two weeks. "I'm clean and sober, Dad."

His shoulders relax a little. "That's great, princess. I was a little worried there for a while."

He's more observant than I've given him credit for.

"And maybe you should consider going for a few therapy sessions. It's really helped me."

"I'll think about it," I lie, because there's no way I'm ready to delve into all the shit stored in my head.

"I want you to know you can come to me about anything. I mean it. I know we haven't had that kind of relationship since you were a little girl, but I am here for you. No judgment. Just support."

Tears sting the back of my eyes as I launch myself at him, hugging him tight. I hate that I can't remember the last time we hugged it out. His arms go around me without hesitation, and I cling to him, squeezing my eyes shut and committing this moment to memory.

"How touching." Mom's words are laced with venom, and she's not attempting to disguise it.

We pull apart.

"If you don't have anything nice to say, how about saying nothing at all," Dad calmly replies.

"Did you have anything to do with this?" she snaps at me, as if Dad hasn't even spoken.

"To do with what?" I feign innocence, frowning in confusion.

Her eyes narrow to slits and she plants her hands on her slim hips, slanting me with a look of cool disdain.

I think my mother hates me.

Like legit can't stand me.

And I hate how that affects me. Because she's a cold-hearted bitch, and I shouldn't care.

At least I'm not like her. At least I can still feel. Even if the overriding emotion is hurt at her continuous rejection. I stand, and Dad rises too.

"Don't play dumb. You know I'm referring to this mix-up with Weston."

"Mix-up?" My voice oozes disbelief. "It's no mix-up, Mother. He is everything those reports say he is." She stares blankly at me, and I'm disgusted. *I know she's an unfeeling bitch, but she's the fucking president of the college! And she's a woman! Where is her empathy?* I didn't think it was possible to hate my mother any more than I already do, but I guess I'm learning something new today. Because her reaction sickens me.

"I've told you what he's like, but you refused to listen to your own daughter," I hiss, on a roll. "You've had a monster preying on women on this campus. Monsters, actually, as in plural, because his buddies are every bit as perverted as he is, and yet you did nothing." My gaze challenges her as much as my words.

"It's just a misunderstanding." She continues to deny the truth.

I fist my hands at my side as red coats my vision. "You're kidding, right? Three girls have come forward, Mom. *Three. Victims.* And I'm betting more will make statements in the coming days. He is a predator, Mom. A sick, disgusting, vile, pathetic excuse of a human being."

She glares daggers at me. "Just because you've never liked him doesn't mean you get to throw stones. He will be exonerated."

"Don't you even care about how this will impact CU? How it will impact your job?" Because the fact she hasn't considered that angle is really odd. *Mom lives and breathes her job, so why isn't she more concerned?* This case is already garnering international attention and there's no denying enrollment will drop. *She's going to come under severe pressure from the board, so why isn't she worried? What the hell is going on with her?*

A low growl erupts from Dad. "Open your ears, Carole. Listen to what your daughter is saying. And if you won't do it for Emily, I know you'll do the right thing for your position." Dad's thinking is in line with mine. "After all, that is all you care about." Usually, Dad would bark those words at Mom, but his voice is even-keeled, and it doesn't appear he's trying to cause an argument.

"Don't talk about stuff you know nothing about," she fumes, wringing her hands. "Ensuring Weston avoids prosecution is what's best for my position," she murmurs, more to herself than us.

Dad and I exchange suspicious expressions.

"What exactly do you mean by that?" Dad asks, taking a step toward her.

"Nothing that concerns you." She turns on her heel.

"Where are you going?" he asks.

"Back to my office for an emergency meeting. We need to do damage control and come up with some new policies and procedures that will keep everyone happy until this is resolved."

"That can wait." Dad folds his arms across his toned chest. "We need to listen to what Emily has to say."

She lingers in the doorway for a split second with her back to us. "Don't wait up." Then she stalks off, the tap-tap of her stiletto heels echoing along the hallway until she slams the front door shut and we're met with dead silence.

"I want to know what happened, honey." Dad circles his arm around my shoulder.

"And I want to tell you." I will have to be circumspect. To hide Adam and Sam's part in all this because Adam isn't ready to admit our relationship to him, and Sam is virtually afraid of his own shadow. "We need to be sitting," I explain, dropping onto the couch again. "And you need to prepare yourself because some of this will be hard to hear."

A COUPLE OF BLISSFUL WEEKS PASS, AND IT'S INCREDIBLE HOW MUCH my mood has improved now Wes is no longer lurking around campus, waiting to pounce. Of course, I also feel considerably lighter after unburdening to Dad. He doesn't know all of it, and I haven't plucked up the courage to tell either him or Adam what happened that awful night when I was fifteen, but it's one step at a time.

Right now, I'm celebrating the positive turn my life has taken lately. Dad's newfound support has done wonders to ease the constant ache in my chest. Being sober and drug-free for one month is something I never thought I'd achieve or feel proud of, but I have and I am.

And having an incredible guy by my side is the icing on the cake. While Adam and I continue to sneak around behind Dad's back, something I'm growing increasingly unhappy about, I can't deny how deliriously happy he makes me.

"Penny for your thoughts, babe." Adam tucks me in tighter under his arm as we walk away from the restaurant, waving one last time at Rachel and Carter as they head in the opposite direction.

We'd settled on a hole in the wall Mexican place miles from campus just to ensure we wouldn't be seen.

"I'm just reflecting on how great my life is right now." It's not perfect. Not by a long shot, but I've made great strides, and it feels good. Feels epic. The only downside is that I'm drifting apart from Zach and Scar. Just like she predicted. But I'm not strong enough to go out with them when Molly is around. And I don't want to test my limits just yet.

"Ditto, babe." He stops, pushing me up against the nearest wall, caging me in with his big arms. Leaning down, he presses his hot lips to that sensitive spot just under my ear, and delicious shivers ripple along my skin. "And that's all thanks to you." He captures my lips in a feather-soft kiss, and I melt against him.

I caress his cheek. "You make me very happy, Adam." I peer into his beautiful emerald eyes. "More than I ever thought it was possible to feel with a guy."

He lowers his hands to my hips, tugging me in close. "I love how in sync we are with everything, because I feel the same way, Em." He worries his lower lip between his teeth for a second before adding, "And I think it's time we told your father about us."

I smother a gasp. "Really?"

He bundles me into his arms. "I'm serious about you, Emily. More serious than I've ever been with any girl." He presses his chin to the top of my head as I rest my face on his broad chest. His arms tighten around me. "I want to hold on to you forever, Emily. I'm in this for the long haul, and I can't promise you that and keep expecting you to lie to your father." He tips my chin up with one finger. "It's time to man up and fess up. Even though I'm fucking terrified of his reaction."

I press my body closer to his, smiling at him. "He'll probably throw a hissy fit at first. Say you're not good enough for his little girl, blah, blah." His face leaches of color, and I giggle. "But he'll be cool with it because he's making a huge effort to repair our relationship and he's already told me he wants me healthy and happy. I'm both of those things, thanks to you."

I stretch up and kiss his gorgeous mouth. "And I'm in this for the long run too, Adam." My cheeks heat as I prepare to open myself up to him. "I've never considered too far into the future, because I never truly believed I had one worth daydreaming over. But then I met you, and now I see endless possibilities."

His lips slam onto mine, and his kisses are fiercely passionate and brimming with emotion. My heart swells to bursting point, and I know what I'm feeling is true love. I know we're still in the honeymoon stage, and all this creeping around adds a layer of excitement, but I know what's in my heart.

I'm in love with Adam Miller.

I love him with every part of me.

Enough to want to be a better version of myself because he deserves the absolute best.

"I want so many things with you, Em," he rasps over my mouth. "And I see endless possibilities too." He places his forehead to mine, peering deep into my eyes. His gaze burns a hole in mine. "The road ahead may be rocky, but I feel like I can achieve anything as long as I have you by my side."

Intense emotion lands on my chest, and I'm so happy I could scream.

"I love you, Emily Parker," he adds, admitting it in words for the first time. "And I want the whole world to know."

I peck his lips, swiping at a few errant tears creeping out of the corners of my eyes. "I love you too, Adam. But I think we should start with my dad first."

His mouth curves up at the corners. "Sounds like a plan." He tucks me under his arm again, steering me toward the parking lot, dusting my face with kisses the whole time, and I'm floating on cloud nine.

* * *

I'VE STILL GOT A MASSIVE GRIN ON MY FACE THE FOLLOWING NIGHT AS I leave the library after a tutoring session. I'm practically skipping along the sidewalk, high on the wings of love. I snicker to myself. My inner thoughts have been corny as fuck all day, but I couldn't give two shits. I'm in love, and it's the best feeling in the world.

Even the fact I won't see Adam this weekend doesn't dampen my mood too much. Because I know we're having dinner with Dad Monday night to tell him about our relationship, and after that, I will be stuck to Adam like glue. I didn't bother extending the dinner invite to Mom because she wouldn't come and she wouldn't approve of Adam. He's not a rich prick from an asshole family, so she won't want to know him.

Mom's like a bear with a sore head since Wes got arrested. Girls are coming out of the woodwork in droves, and it's clear Wes and his crew won't be buying their way out of this mess anytime soon.

I love it when karma delivers by the bucketload.

Although, I'm not happy so many girls suffered at his hands.

At least he's been stopped now.

While the university has come under attack, it still doesn't fully explain Mom's mood. We have barely seen her, and anytime she is home, she's snapping and snarking and lashing out.

Dad and I are like our own little island, distancing ourselves from Carole and her drama, a little bit more by the day.

I'm lost in my own little bubble as I walk, and before I know it, I'm at our house. A strange sleek, black sedan is parked at the curb. An ominous sense of foreboding sweeps across my skin, and I'm instantly on alert as I walk up the four steps toward the front door, noticing it's slightly ajar.

"You shouldn't have come here," Mom hisses. "It's too dangerous!"

I rush to flatten my body against the brick siding in between the tall window and door, hoping to hide myself from sight. I check the window and release a quiet sigh that the blinds are closed.

"You wouldn't answer my calls, so you left me no choice!" A deep, baritone voice says.

All the fine hairs lift on my arms, and butterflies scatter in my chest.

"For good reason, Richard! Are you that desperate to get laid you couldn't wait until the weekend?"

"I miss you, sweetheart." He pronounces it like swee-heart, and panic swells in my throat. My legs buckle, and I clutch onto the wall for support.

"That's not a good enough excuse. We need to stick to the plan. Now go before Grayson or Emily make an appearance."

My heart is stuttering behind my rib cage, and I've lost the ability to breathe. Acute fear has a vise grip on my internal organs, and I can't suck enough oxygen into my lungs. Heavy footsteps come toward me. I dart around the house and behind the manicured hedges along the side, wishing I had Harry Potter's invisibility cloak to hide myself.

I peek up just as the hulking form stops under the portico, and he turns ever so slightly. "This isn't like last time, Carole. I love you, and I'm going nowhere this time."

"Just go you...you fucking idiot!" Mom hisses as she scans the property. "Anyone could see you, and my reputation is already in shreds. I will see you over the weekend like we arranged. Grayson will be gone until Sunday night."

The clunky watch on his wrist glints under the moonlight, and I shake all over. A little whimper escapes my lips, and I clamp a hand over my mouth, crouching even lower behind the bush, praying that he didn't hear.

But he's too angry over the confrontation with Mom to notice, and he stomps off down the driveway, gets into the sedan, and peels away from the curb with screeching tires.

My legs give out, and I sink to the ground, shaking and sobbing silently. My entire body trembles as memories I've tried so hard to deny breach the final wall, surging to the forefront of my mind. I pull my legs up to my chest, wrap my arms around myself, and squeeze my eyes shut.

No. no. no. It can't be.

Does she know, or is this just a coincidence?

A strangled sound rips from my throat as I struggle to get air into my lungs. The worst pain imaginable presses down on my chest, like someone has placed a concrete block on top of it, constricting my ability to breathe.

The onslaught in my head continues, and I cradle my head in my knees, begging someone, anyone, to make it stop.

No. I can't. I just can't.

I scramble to my feet, gripping the side of my head, as tears cascade down my cheeks.

I need it to stop. I need to forget it all. To make it go away.

There's only one choice.

I need to call on my old friend Molly.

21

ADAM

I haven't been able to breathe for the last few days. My schedule is crazy, and with our away game coming up this weekend, Coach is keeping us late every night. I haven't seen Emily since our double date with Carter and Rachel, which is driving me fucking crazy. She's on my mind every minute when I'm not throwing the ball or getting pummeled in practice. Hell, even when I'm sitting in class, I find myself doodling her name in my notebook instead of taking notes or listening to the professor. Yeah, I have it bad. I've never experienced butterflies in my stomach this intensely about any girl.

If I'm not thinking of Emily, Phoebe's been consuming the other part of my brain. That minor cough she had a couple of weeks ago hasn't gone away. Mom and I know that recurring chest colds are part of Phoebe's condition, but we don't want it to turn into pneumonia again. Her doctor put her on meds, and she's been using her vest frequently to clear the mucus.

I know the way I've been making money isn't on the up and up. But knowing Phoebe has a working vest to help her CF is the only thing that matters. Ray can hurt me, the cops can arrest me, and I still won't regret choosing to sell drugs. But it's time I call it quits. Emily has cleaned up her act, and I need to do the same.

Besides, I have plenty of money saved and Mom's bills are paid. On top of that, Mom's new job is going well. The only thing that scares me is the money I've saved isn't going to last long if something happens to Phoebe again. Maybe I should stick it out for a while longer. After all, I did commit three months of my life to Ray. And I could make a boatload more to put away for a rainy day.

Greedy bastard, aren't you? What about Emily?

I throw my truck in park and climb out, growling to myself as I snatch my gym bag. My girl. The love of my life. Man, do I miss the heck out of her. I never thought I would fall in love. Not that I'm not capable, but Mom, Phoebe, and football have been my world. Mom is going to be ecstatic, and Phoebe. Well, my little love bug will be over the moon when she finds out Emily will be a permanent figure in my life. That's why I have to stop selling. I need to stick to my guns and not get tempted by the prospect of banking more cash. Emily is making a huge effort, and it's time I do the same. Ray isn't going to like it, but I don't give a fuck.

Hiking my bag over my shoulder, I head into the dorm, grinning like a schoolboy as I pull my phone out of my pocket. All I want is to hear Emily's voice and tell her I love her. *Who am I kidding?* I want to hear more than her voice. I want her beautiful body tangled around mine as I devour her. The only problem with the latter is we have no place of our own.

I remove my phone from my pocket, when a familiar voice calls my name. I come to an abrupt halt halfway down the path that leads to the dorm. A chill skates up my spine as I pivot on my heel and find Ray Diaz getting out of his black SUV. He never goes out of his way to find me. And he's never stepped foot on campus, at least not that I know of.

Something is up, and I have no clue, but whatever it is, that scowl on his face tells me it's not good.

Just what I need—another fucking problem.

I march up to him, glancing around the area. I can only see as far as the streetlight will allow, but I don't spot anyone close by. The last thing I need is for Sam to see me talking to Ray. Then it will be the Spanish Inquisition, and I'm not ready to tell Sam yet.

Ray closes his door, then leans against it, adjusting the bling around his neck.

I angle my head. "What are you doing here?" I look up and down the sidewalk just to be sure I don't see Sam. He's working late tonight, but he's due back shortly.

Ray crosses his tattooed arms over his chest. "You haven't returned my calls."

"I'm busy." I clutch onto the strap of my gym bag like it's my lifeline.

"I've called you at least ten times," Ray says, narrowing his eyes.

I shrug. "So. I'm not on the clock yet." Not that I punch a time-card. But I am consistent in the hours I work, which are way past bedtime. I'm surprised Sam hasn't questioned me before now since I tend to tiptoe into the dorm room around two a.m. on nights I'm working the streets. "And I don't carry my burner phone with me. You know that. Just cut to the chase." I nervously look around for a third time.

"It's come to my attention that you're charging my clients more than my going rate." His tone is calm on the surface, but that muscle jumping along his angular jaw says he's ready to put his fist through my nose.

My blood gels. "If I recall, you told me what your cut was and what mine was. You never said I couldn't charge more."

The passenger window slides down and beady eyes glue to mine. It's the same guy who frisked me that first night I met Ray. "Problem, boss?"

Ray scrubs his fingers along his hardened jaw. "Not yet," he says, his gaze never wavering from mine. "So, you admit you've been skimming off me?"

My nostrils flare, anger bubbling to the surface. "Five or ten bucks here and there, but I don't do it all the time." I've been careful not to get too greedy.

He sucks in his lip ring, his hazel eyes glinting dangerously. "That could add up to a lot of money."

I haven't kept count. "Look, man. I'll give you what I made so far this week, and we can call it even. In fact, I'm done. I'm not working for you anymore."

He gives me a lethal sneer as he pops off the car, grinning like I said something funny. The mask falls over his face, and I swear I see fire burning in his eyes. "The fuck you are. You're mine. And let's not forget your three months isn't up."

Stupid me for coming up with that agreement.

I get in his face. "Are you threatening me?"

The short stocky guy always with him flies out of the car ready to pull his gun on me.

Ray holds up his hand to his bodyguard, glaring at me. "If you don't want me to out you to your coach, you'll do as I say. Or better yet, I can let the president of the college know what you've been doing. I'm sure she'll love to hear how her husband's star QB has been selling drugs to their daughter."

I clench my fists at my side and step into him. "Like fuck you will." Clearly, Ray has done his homework on Cypress University. Then again, Zach is a client. So, he could've told Ray about me. Not sure why Zach would do that unless he's pissed that I'm dating Emily. Or maybe, he went to Ray directly to get his supply when Emily and I went to Charlotte.

"Do you want to test me," Ray says calmly. "Because I have no problem heading over to see your coach now."

Fuuuck!

I know he'll do it. Drug dealers like Ray don't take shit from anyone. I'm kidding myself if I think I can stand up to someone who wouldn't think twice about shooting me. More importantly, Coach cannot know I'm a drug dealer. I mean, telling Coach Parker I'm dating his daughter is nothing compared to what he'll do if he finds out I'm selling drugs.

I turn my head slightly, shoving my hand through my hair when I see Sam jogging toward me.

Double Fuuuck! Can this night get any worse?

Ray follows my line of sight and must see the panic on my face because he adds, "Do you want him to know too?"

I whip my head back at Ray. "What?"

"He's your roommate, right? And he doesn't know what you do."

Asshole. He's done his due diligence on me all right, which means he knows all about Mom and Phoebe too. A line of sweat glides down my back, and I gulp over the panic swimming up my throat.

Sam is fast approaching. I have no choice but to agree to Ray's demands. I can't tell Sam. I want to, but even if I did, it wouldn't change the fact I skimmed money off Ray. And he's going to make me pay in more ways than one. That's what my gut is telling me.

I'm so fucking stupid. I shouldn't have gotten money hungry.

Sam slows to a walk. His blond hair is windblown, and his blue eyes take in Ray and Ray's thug. "What's going on?" he asks, frowning.

Ray extends his hand to Sam before I can say a word. "Hi, I'm Ray Diaz, a friend of his." Ray flicks his chin at me.

Sam shakes Ray's hand. "Sam Spencer."

"Got to run," Ray says. "We'll be in touch. Remember what I said."

As soon as the SUV pulls away from the curb, my blood thaws a tiny bit.

Now to face Sam and his thousand questions. I don't want to lie to him. But I don't want to have this conversation right now either.

"How do you know a guy like that?" Sam asks, suspicion threading through his tone. "He's shady as fuck. Are you in trouble, Adam?"

I can't look him in the face, and I won't lie to him. I'm not sure I can stay in the dorm room tonight.

I start for the building when Sam grabs my arm. "Dude, answer me."

"I don't want to get you in the middle of this." That's the truth. The last thing I need is to worry about my roomie, someone I consider a brother. "Can we talk about this later?" I give one of my pleading looks that usually work on Mom and might work on Sam. "I promise I'll tell you, but I'm beat, my head is throbbing, and I want to talk to Emily."

He scans my face, studying me like he can read right through me. "I'll give you some space, but I'm here for you. You know that."

I clutch his shoulder. "And that's why I love ya, dude." There's a door to hell with my name on it. A huge fucking knot forms in my stomach, and I just pray that when I finally tell Sam he'll understand.

Right now, I need to hear my girl's voice. I need her to calm me down because I'm finding she's the only one who can.

* * *

WHERE THE FUCK IS SHE? I CAN'T GET AHOLD OF EMILY, AND IT'S driving me fucking insane. I want to pull out every hair on my head. I'm standing in the locker room at Greenville College, staring at my phone, feeling an almost uncontrollable urge to throw it at the wall.

This week sucked balls. Ray's watching my every move. When I visited some clients, one of Ray's goons shadowed me. Clearly, Ray doesn't trust me now. And that makes me nervous. Fucker.

Coach rode the team hard, keeping us late at practice every night. This game with Greenville is huge. If we win, we could get an invitation to a bowl game.

Gnawing on the inside of my cheek, I lace up my cleats while the team gets dressed. I need to get my fucked-up head in the game. If I only knew Emily was okay, I might be able to think clearly.

Carter slaps me on the back. "Hoss, what's wrong. Is Phoebe okay? Were you able to talk to your mom?"

On the bus ride up, I filled Carter in about Phoebe. I wanted to tell him I haven't been able to get a hold of Emily and it was driving me bonkers, but it was too risky with Coach sitting only seats in front of us and the guys all around us.

Maybe she has cold feet. Maybe she changed her mind about coming out about us to her dad. Maybe she's feeling like she told me she loved me too soon. Or... Nah, I don't want to think that she fell off the wagon. My heart sputters at that thought. But I shake it off. Wes is securely in jail and not around to mess with her.

Wes isn't the only one to drive Emily to drugs, dude.

Ah, fuck. Maybe she got into a fight with her mother.

Then something hits me. I should call Zach. He might have heard from Emily. That thought drives a knife into my chest only because when I think of Zach I think of him fucking my girl in that video, and I want to spill his blood.

Carter snaps his fingers in my ear. "Adam. Your phone is ringing."

I shoot up and fumble with the locker door.

Carter mumbles something under his breath that I can't make out. Right now, I really don't give a shit anyway. But I know I need to focus. I can't let the guys down. I can't let Coach down. If I do, he probably won't let me date Emily.

I finally have my phone in hand, and Sam's name appears on the screen. Déjà vu blankets me. Something is wrong. Sam knows I'm about to play. He wouldn't call unless it was an emergency. Suddenly, I'm taking a road trip back to early September when he came running down the track to tell me Phoebe was in the hospital.

"Everything okay, man? I have maybe five minutes at most," I rush out in a huff. "My sister okay?" I went home mid-week to see Phoebe for a quick visit. As sick as she's feeling, she still had a smile on her face, especially when she asked about Emily.

"Sorry," Sam says in a dire tone. "I thought you wouldn't pick up. I was going to leave you a voicemail. Look, we need to have a serious talk when you get back."

He knows about Ray.

I should've known Sam would do some digging on Ray. After all, Ray introduced himself to Sam.

I bang my head against the locker door. "Sure thing." I have no other words, and I don't want to talk about it now or rather I can't, not with Carter listening and the rest of the team in proximity. Plus, I need to tell Sam to his face. It's not a conversation to have over the phone. Nausea sits heavy in my stomach. "As soon as I return tomorrow." Or maybe not the minute I return, because if I don't hear from Emily, I will hunt her down even if I have to storm her house to find her.

I had every intention of waiting for Emily outside the tutoring center one night this week, but that didn't happen. The only reason I haven't scoured campus is because Sam told me he saw Emily briefly and she was fine. Honestly, hearing that on Thursday kept me calm, but when Friday rolled around and she still hadn't responded to my text or phone call, I was beside myself. I almost didn't get on the bus to come here.

I hang up and return my phone to the locker.

Carter is eyeing me. "Well?"

"Just Sam. He's pissed about something." I lie.

"Hoss, we need your head in this game."

Some of the other guys around us stop talking.

I take in a deep breath, and when I release it, I pin a look on each of the players. All of us have busted our asses in preparation for this game. "I'm good, guys." I assure them, lying through my teeth. Hopefully, when my cleats hit the field, the roar of the crowd will pull me out of my head and into the moment.

College football games are off the hook with the fans and the band, and the stadium is always electric. I love the adrenaline rush I get the second I hit the field.

The locker room door squeaks open. "Miller," Coach barks. "I need a word."

What the fuck now? I hardly get drunk, but I'm going to after this game. I'm beginning to understand why people drink or take drugs. Because my nerves are fried.

My mind is racing in time with my pulse as I meet Coach out in the hall. He's probably about to give me a pep talk, but maybe not. He seems like he's struggling to tell me something as he grips the back of his neck. "I'm not sure how to tell you this."

Nausea continues to swirl in my gut as several curse words fly through my head. My breathing ramps up. *What can he possibly tell me that's making him nervous?* If Ray had paid him a visit, I wouldn't be here. Unless something happened to Emily. But if that were true, he wouldn't tell me. He never talks about his family. Or maybe Emily told him about us already. Maybe she didn't want to wait until our arranged dinner. That must be it, and he doesn't want me seeing her. Man, I wish she was here so badly. My mood would be fantastic walking out onto the field knowing she was in the stands. I'll be pissed if Coach *does* know about us, because that's the only reason I didn't beg her to attend today. Well, that and the fact I haven't been able to get a hold of her.

"Give it to me straight," I say, preparing myself for a verbal tongue lashing.

He grips my shoulder. "Son, I'm so proud of you. I can't tell you how much I've enjoyed seeing you grow into the quarterback position."

Oookay. I so wasn't expecting that. Some of my muscles loosen, and I release the breath I was holding.

"The scout from the Chicago Bears will be in the stands. He's here specifically to watch you." Coach grins like a proud father. "I was reluctant to tell you out of fear you would be too nervous. But I want you to kick ass out there. Be yourself. Be the QB I'm proud of and the university is proud of."

My jaw slams on my cleats. "For real?" Excitement bubbles up my throat.

"And if we win," he says. "We'll get that invitation to the bowl game."

No pressure whatsoever!

I'm fucked.

22

EMILY

"You have no idea how freaking awesome it is to have you back, chica," Scarlett says, circling her arm around my shoulders and smacking a loud kiss off my cheek.

"We missed you," Zach adds, yanking me away from Scar. He wraps his arms around me from behind, grinning as he blatantly looks down the front of my low-cut little black dress.

I shake him off. "It's good to be back." Truth. Because since Molly and I became reacquainted last night, I've spent the hours in between in a blissful state of ecstasy. It helps that both the rents are gone this weekend, so Dad isn't there to witness my fall from grace. "But I'm still with Adam." I pin Zach with a look, reminding him some things *have* changed.

"But for how long?" Scar inquires. "He won't be happy if he knows you're back on the party scene."

"He's my boyfriend, not my jailer," I retort, even if she makes a good point. *And isn't that one reason why I've been avoiding him?*

"I don't want to argue. Just saying what I said before. Your lifestyle and his don't gel."

"We'll make it work. I love him, and he loves me, and that's all that matters."

Scar and Zach trade similar expressions, and I see red. "If you're going to be assholes, I'm going home." I'm not, because I don't have any more pills on me, and I'm relying on Zach's usual generosity until Adam returns.

"Don't be such a drama queen." Scar loops her arm in mine. "You're not going home." She makes a zipping motion with her finger against her lips. "And I won't say another word."

Zach slides his hand on my lower back. "Now, enough of the heavy. Let's go party."

* * *

I'M SPREAD-EAGLED ACROSS A LUMPY COUCH OVER IN THE QUIETER corner of the warehouse, reveling in the hazy euphoria clouding my troubled mind. Right now, I can't even recall what it is I was worried about, just that I know I need this high to last so I don't remember.

"There you are." Zach flops down beside me. "I've been looking all over for you."

I slap his thigh. "Was right here the whole time."

A familiar song thumps from the loudspeakers, and I jump up, bouncing on my feet and swaying my hips to the electric beat. I yank Zach up. "Let's dance!"

Without warning, he flings me over his shoulders, and I giggle as he shoves his way through the crowd, slapping my ass every few seconds. He slides me slowly down his body, keeping me close while we start moving. I fling my arms into the air, screaming the lyrics to the song as Zach grips my hips, swiveling his pelvis against mine in time to the music. His hard-on digs into my lower stomach, awakening my libido.

Adam.

He's the one coherent thought in my mind, and I shove at Zach's shoulders, pushing him back. "I can't dance with you like that anymore. I'm taken," I say, wiping my arm across my sweat-soaked brow.

Ignoring me, he reels me into his arms. "Not for long," he murmurs, burying his head in my neck. He licks a line along the column of my neck, and a moan slips out of my mouth unbidden.

Sultry green eyes appear in my mind's eye, and I push Zach away again. "Stop."

"Come on, Em." He steps into me. "I know you're horny as hell. Let's fuck. Hard. Just the way you like it."

I shake my head even though my body is down with that plan. "I love Adam."

"He's not here, babe." He runs his hands down either side of my body, brushing my breasts on purpose. His caress is like a shot of liquid lust to my pussy, and I ache between my thighs. "And what he doesn't know won't hurt him."

I fight an inner battle. The horny party animal side of me wants to take all Zach's offering, and it's so fucking tempting, but there's some sliver of sanity still residing in my brain.

I'm a lot of things.

But I'm not a cheater.

"No." I take several steps back, bumping into someone, as my teeth clench involuntarily.

"Watch it!" Some asshole shoves me, thrusting me straight back into Zach's arms.

"Look. It's fate that you were meant to be in my arms and writhing underneath me tonight." Zach shoots me a familiar cocky grin, and my resolve is wavering, my hands wandering up and down his chest of their own accord.

I pull my hands back, wriggling out of his hold. "I need to get out of here." I push past people, stumbling on my high heels in my haste to get away, before I do something I'll later regret.

"Em. Wait." Zach grabs my elbow. "C'mon, babe. You know you want to."

"Stop!" I yank my arm away, almost losing my balance. "I said no!"

"There's no need to be such a bitch." He crosses his arms, leveling a harsh glare at me. "And when your square of a boyfriend kicks you to the curb, don't come looking for me."

"Don't worry, I won't." My lower lip juts out as I stomp toward the exit fuming. A cold chill tiptoes up my spine, and I slam to a halt as I suddenly remember I have no stash. I race after Zach's retreating form, ready to eat crow. "Zach, wait."

He spins around, a slow grin curving the corners of his mouth. "Knew you'd come to your senses." He gropes my boob, and I slap his hand away.

"I need a couple of pills. I'm out."

The smile slips off his mouth, and his eyes narrow. "You've some nerve." A mischievous glint appears in his eye. "I'll trade you. A fuck for a pill. Two fucks for two pills." He waggles his brows, making a grab for my boob again. "I think you get the idea."

"I'm not fucking you. I'm in a relationship, and I don't cheat."

"Then it's no deal." He shrugs.

"Zach, please." I'm not above begging, because I can't let this high fade. I can't let reality come crashing back in, because I might not survive the night if it does.

"Get lost, Emily. I'm done supplying you. Get your boyfriend to throw you a few pills. We both know he's good for it."

With those parting words, he disappears into the crowd, leaving me standing there with my mouth open.

* * *

I STAGGER TOWARD THE TAXI PULLING UP TO THE CURB. "CYPRESS U campus, please." I scramble into the back seat, pulling the door shut behind me. The car glides out onto the road.

Fuck. *What the hell am I going to do now?* I kick off my heels, swinging my legs up onto the seat and stretching them out. The driver eyes me through the mirror, but he can fuck off if he thinks I'm taking them down. My veins are buzzing, and my body is jittery, and I tap out a rhythm with a foot against the seat. I'm not done partying, but I have a free house so I can blare the music and dance around the living room to my heart's content.

Except I'm going to come down from the high soon, and I need to find a solution.

I grapple with my fuzzy mind until an idea comes to me. Adam is at an away game, but I bet he has some pills stashed at his dorm. Sam will be there, and he'll let me in.

Fifteen minutes later, I'm pounding my fists against their door, but Sam either sleeps like the dead or he isn't inside.

"You shouldn't be here." I spin around, glaring at the guy with the glasses across the hall. "Leave or I'll report you to the RA."

I flip him the bird as I leave, holding my shoes and walking in my bare feet.

Desperation jumps up and bites me as I make the journey across campus to my house. Sweat clings to my brow, and strands of hair plaster to the sticky skin. I barely feel the asphalt under my feet as I walk, my heart thump-thumping behind my rib cage as panic sets in.

They say desperation makes people do stupid things, and my next action proves that.

I slump to the ground in the hallway the second I step foot in my house, slamming the door shut with the palm of my hand. Rummaging in my purse, I extract my cell, not stopping to second-guess myself, punching in Adam's number.

He'll answer.

I'm sure of it.

Because I've been ignoring his calls and texts.

"Emily?" His breathless voice filters down the line. "Are you okay? I've been worried sick—"

"I need some pills," I admit, cutting across him. "I went to your place, but Sam isn't there. Can you call the RA and get permission for me to gain access to your room?"

Dead silence greets me.

"Adam! Did you hear me? I need Molly, and I need her now."

"You're high."

"Well, duh." I roll my eyes even though he can't see me.

"You promised," he says in a clipped tone, disappointment underscoring his words.

"So did you," I snap. "And you're still dealing, so quit with the martyr routine."

Silence descends again.

"What happened?" he asks.

"Nothing. I just needed to let loose."

"Don't fucking lie to me, Emily." He's tempering his rage.

"I didn't call you to be interrogated! Just tell me where you keep your supply."

He lets out a disgusted laugh. "Absolutely not. Are you crazy?"

"Adam, please." I use a softer tone, begging.

He growls. "No, Emily. I won't enable you."

Anger jumps up and bites me. "Fuck you, Adam. If you won't, I'll find someone who will."

I end the call, screaming from the pit of my lungs, flinging my phone away. It skitters across the floor. My knee jerks as panic travels up my throat.

His voice reverberates in my ears, and tears roll down my cheeks.

No!

My skin crawls as the memory of his callused hands on my soft skin surges to the forefront of my mind.

A whimper escapes my mouth as I climb awkwardly to my feet, almost slipping on the polished hardwood floors as I bend down to retrieve my phone. There's a new crack along the screen, but it's still working. I race through the house toward the formal dining room. Dropping to the ground in front of the liquor cabinet, I almost yank the door off its hinges in my haste to get at the contents.

I can't get my hands on any Molly, so alcohol is the next best thing.

I grab an unopened bottle of vodka and push off the floor, wobbling on unsteady legs as I make my way up the stairs.

The door to my bedroom slams off the wall as I stagger inside, swigging straight from the bottle. I drink it like it's water, needing to consume as much of it as possible so I conk out before my high completely fades and the nightmare returns. Stripping out of my dress, I crawl under the covers in my underwear, placing my cell on my bedside table before bringing the bottle to my lips and drinking until I pass out.

I've the mother of all headaches when I wake sometime the next day. My hand shoots out from under the covers, my fingers skimming the table for my cell. I blink my eyes open, attempting to ignore the pounding in my skull as I glance at the time. Holy shit. It's after lunch.

At least one part of my mission succeeded.

A headline on my feed jumps out at me, and I skim the article with a heavy heart. The guys lost the game last night, and the reporter is slamming Adam for a less than stellar performance. Dad will be pissed, and Adam will be disappointed in himself. An intense longing to feel his arms around me hits me out of nowhere. I wonder when they'll get back, because I really need to see him.

For that hug.

And some pills.

My stomach sinks as I vaguely remember calling him last night. Flashes of our conversation return, along with images I'm trying so hard to forget. A shiver works its way through me, and nausea churns in my gut. Leaning over the side of the bed, I heave into the trash can repeatedly until there is nothing left to expel. I stagger to the bathroom, clean out my mouth and the trashcan, and then crawl back into bed.

Without overthinking it, I call Adam again.

He answers on the fifth ring.

"I'm sorry about the game," I blurt, knowing I need to make amends. "And I'm sorry for last night."

"I haven't slept a wink all night worrying about you. I would've come back early if it was possible."

"I'm sorry I worried you, but there's no need. I'm fine." Thank fuck, he isn't here to see the state of me. "When are you back? I need to see you."

The sound of keys jangles. "I've just arrived at my dorm." A few beats of silence trickle down the line. "You need to see me for me or for Molly?"

"Can't it be both?"

A frustrated sigh leaves his lips. "Emily. I don't understand. You were doing so great."

"Come on, Adam. Don't make such a big deal out of it. You had no issue selling Molly to me before. How is this any different?"

"It's different because I'm in love with you and I care about what you're putting into your body. That shit is not good."

I grip my phone hard. "You are such a fucking hypocrite!" I yell. "You sell to all kinds of people, but you won't sell to me, and I'm your girlfriend, or have you changed your mind about that too?"

"Of course, I haven't. But I wouldn't be much of a boyfriend if I didn't try to talk you out of this."

"You're my boyfriend, not my dad, Adam."

He growls loudly. "Don't pull that shit with me, Em. I'm not in the mood for it."

"Don't fucking take it out on me because you played like shit and lost the game."

A gasp echoes down the line, and I know I've gone too far. "Shit, I'm sorry, Adam. I didn't mean it. I take it back."

"It's too late. Look, I'm tired. We'll talk later."

"Adam, please. Let me come over, and I'll make it up to you."

"Not today, Emily." He sounds defeated and hurt. "I think we'll only end up in an argument, and that's the last thing I need."

That familiar panicked feeling settles on my chest. "At least let me come over to grab some Molly."

A bitter laugh filters down the line. "Seriously?"

Silence stretches as I look up at my ceiling wishing upon a star that he'll give in.

I know he's still there because I can hear him breathing heavily. "Adam, please, baby."

"Tell you what. I'll hand you some pills if you tell me what happened that caused you to undo all your progress."

He just had to go there.

And now, there's no stopping this train wreck from happening.

An imaginary hand tightens around my throat, and I'm struggling to breathe as vivid images of that night assault my mind.

Ending the call without uttering a word, I curl into a fetal position, wrapping my arms around myself as I rock back and forth, with silent tears tracing a path down my face, praying for someone to take the pain away.

23

ADAM

I gawk at my phone. Un-fucking-believable. I take in several deep breaths, but each one does nothing to repair the hole Emily seared right through my heart a minute ago.

What the fuck happened to make her use again? I squeeze my eyes shut, tugging on my hair. My head is throbbing like someone took a sledgehammer to it, and I can't even think. My brain shut down the minute I walked off the field yesterday. The disappointed look on Coach's face was enough to send me over the edge.

The team tried to cheer me up, telling me it wasn't my fault, but it was. My nerves over the Bears' scout in the stands and worrying about Emily, Sam, and Phoebe all got to me, and it showed in my performance. I growl, throwing my phone at the wall.

I need a release—something to take the edge off. Otherwise, Sam's computer will join my phone on the floor next to his desk.

As for Sam? I have no clue where he is, but I'm relieved he isn't here. I can't deal with him right now even if I wanted to. For all I know, he moved out. I wouldn't blame him. I lied to him.

A sharp pain pierces my chest, and I bury my head in my hands. I hate myself for issuing Emily an ultimatum. I hate myself that I let the team down. I hate that I let Coach, Mom, and Sam down. This isn't me. I'm not an asshole.

I fucking love the shit out of Emily, but I can't give her Molly.

I won't do it.

It's bad enough I sell to Zach who gives her the shit.

Which is an interesting thought. *Why is she asking me for it when he's her usual enabler?*

She had a point though. I said I'd quit. I didn't. Even when Ray showed up on campus, I had no previous plans to quit. I only tried to because it felt like the perfect time to tell Ray to take his drugs and shove them up his ass.

The four walls close in, and suddenly, I feel dizzy. Everything is unraveling at once, and I need fresh air. I change into my workout clothes, and I'm tying my sneakers when someone bangs on the door.

I look around for something to use as a weapon because I have a feeling Ray Diaz is here to collect his money. After my runs the other night, I told his bodyguard to fuck off when he demanded I give him the money. No way was I trusting him to hand over the cash I made to the boss. So, he called Ray. Ray laughed but relented, allowing me to pay him in person. But I didn't have time before I left for the game. He probably thought I took off with his money.

I grab one of the ten-pound free weights I keep next to my desk, not that a weight trumps a gun. But it will slow down Ray's thug before he can fire off a shot.

I barely open the door when the person barges in, pushing me backward. I stumble, and the weight falls out of my hand as Coach launches his fist into my nose before I can do anything to protect myself. Blood spurts out. I blink several times, trying to orient myself, but it's no use. Coach lunges for me, grabbing me by the shirt.

I'm seeing stars, shaking off the blurry vision and the pain lancing my face.

"You were like a son to me," he says. "You were going places."

I lift up my hands as blood drips down into my mouth, the metallic taste waking me the fuck up. Coach's face is redder than a ripe tomato, and he's spitting fire. If I clear my vision some more, I know I'll find steam coming out of his nose.

He pushes me against a wall, pressing his forearm into my throat, cutting off my airways. "Why, Miller? Why?"

I can't think. I can't breathe, and I'm struggling to get Coach off me. He's using his body weight to keep me pinned in place. So, it's a losing battle as I force myself forward to pry his arm away.

"I'm sorry about the game." I say the words, but all that comes out is a garbled mess of nothing.

Apparently, Coach understands parts of what I said because he snarls like an angry bear. "You think I'm here to kill you because of a game?"

The word kill sends shards of fear through me.

Fuck.

He knows about Emily and me.

I make a gurgling sound as the room spins violently.

"Get off him!" Sam shouts, materializing from somewhere as the door slams shut.

Coach doesn't move, and I'm struggling like a motherfucker to breathe.

Sam wrenches Coach's arm away from my throat, but he's no match for him. Where Sam is lean in the chest, Coach is broader and hence stronger.

"Coach Parker, you're cutting off his oxygen," Sam says. "I'm pissed at him too, but this isn't the way to handle it."

Coach slowly lowers his arm, standing his ground, ready to use me as a punching bag if I make one false move.

Sam steps in between us, facing Coach. "Sir, sit in that chair over there." Sam points to his high-tech computer chair.

I clutch my throat, coughing and gagging, sucking in as much air as I possibly can.

Sam guides me to sit on the bed.

Coach drops his tense body into the chair.

Sam's blue eyes are rife with anger, disgust, disappointment, and hurt as he regards me before crossing his arms over his chest.

Silence fills every corner of the dorm room as Coach shakes his head. I'm still coughing and rubbing my throat.

"Well," Sam says. "Who's going to talk first?"

I want to laugh at how Sam is playing the moderator when I know he wants to scream at me.

I swish around some saliva to coat the sandpaper feeling in my throat. Then I start. "I'm sorry." I swing my gaze from Sam to Coach. "To both of you."

Coach scrubs his hands down his face. "Sorry isn't going to cut it, Adam." His hazel eyes drill a hole right through my brain.

"Emily and I were planning on telling you," I say.

Sam rests against the door, no longer strung tight. But I'm certain I'll feel his wrath after Coach is done with me.

Coach rears back. "What were you planning on telling me?"

I keep my gaze on Coach, but I catch a glimpse of Sam out of the corner of my eye, and he's listening intently.

"That Emily and I are dating," I admit. Fuck if I'm going to apologize for dating his daughter. Sure, I understand he's protective, and I don't blame him. I'm going to have Sam do background checks on guys when Phoebe is old enough to date.

Coach doesn't even blink. "I'm not really pissed at that." He pushes to his feet, clenching his fists at his side. "Do you know what I've been through with my daughter? Do you know how hard it was to get her to stop doing drugs? And now I find out she's back on drugs again." He takes in a gulp of air. "And you're her fucking supplier? *My QB is selling drugs.*" His fists ball up at his sides. "You're done, Adam Miller. You'll never be drafted. You'll never see the inside of an NFL stadium as a quarterback or any player. Not if I have any say in it."

The room spins again. My blood freezes. And something vile and insidious eats at my gut.

Emily told him I sold drugs.

All because I wouldn't give her Molly.

Fuck me sideways. It's clear to me she loves Molly more than she loves me.

I'm so fucking stupid.

I believed she changed.

I truly did.

Now, I wonder if I was ever anything more than the means to an end.

I whip my head at Sam, more to quiet the pain that's pressing on my chest as though an eighteen-wheeler just ran over me.

"Don't look at me," he says. "You and I have some talking to do, but I didn't tell him."

Coach turns to Sam. "If you had—"

I shoot to my feet just in case Coach has any ideas of taking his anger out on him. "He didn't know I was selling drugs. Don't bring him into this."

"You're done, Miller. Clean out your locker. You won't finish the season." Rising, he stabs a finger at me. "My daughter is off-limits. If I see you anywhere near her, I will have you arrested. Are we clear?" His voice booms in the room.

All I can do is nod. I have no words. It's my own fucking fault.

Hey, asshole. You did what you had to do for Phoebe.

Coach might understand that if I didn't supply Emily with drugs.

He storms out of the room, slamming the door in his wake.

Sam rubs his hands down his jeans as he folds his body into the chair Coach just vacated. He looks calm, and I'm not surprised. Sam isn't one to throw things or blow up when he's mad.

"Do your worst," I say, sitting back down on my bed.

"Drugs? Why?" he asks.

I lower my gaze to the floor. "Phoebe. We needed the money."

He sucks in air. "Dude, if you needed money, why didn't you come to me?"

"Do you want to support my mom and sister? Do you want to pay all our expenses, including Phoebe's medical bills?" Sam will be rich one day when he's CEO of some high-tech firm he owns. But right now, he gets money from his parents and from his tutoring job, and he's hardly flush.

"What about a legal job?"

I laugh, rolling my eyes, only because he's smart. He knows that a legal job wouldn't put a dent into paying Phoebe's medical bills. And that I don't have time for one.

Or at least I didn't before Coach booted me off the team.

"Phoebe needed her vest repaired. End of story."

He leans forward, elbows on his knees. "I get it, okay. I love your sister like she's my own, but what if you got caught by the cops, man? I'm fucking pissed at you, and not because of your motives. You put Phoebe and your mom in harm's way! Think about that, Adam. That dude, Ray Diaz. I did some checking on him. Did you know he was arrested for murder two years ago?"

I shut my eyes, counting to three. I was so blinded by taking care of my family that I didn't even think of all the consequences other than me going to jail.

I throw my head in my hands. "I fucked up. I'm sorry."

"I talked to your mom," he says.

My head lifts so fast I'll probably have whiplash. "You did what?"

He sits back, running a hand through his blond hair. "I went to see her while you were away. We talked for a long time. In fact, I spent the night. Phoebe is doing okay, by the way."

I want to catapult across the room and hug him for nothing more than telling me Phoebe is okay.

"She told me you sold drugs in the ninth grade and if you hadn't the three of you would've been homeless. I don't agree with you selling drugs, but a part of me understands. However, there are other options. There are jobs out there and friends who would help you. Hell, man. If you went to Coach and asked him for financial support, I bet he would've helped. And selling to Emily? What the fuck? Is that how you two met?"

I nod as guilt steals the air from my lungs. I could tell him I didn't sell to her. But that wouldn't matter. I'm one of her enablers. I sell to

Zach and he supplies her. I have every mind to pay Zach a visit, but I can't put all the blame on him. Emily is the one in charge of her actions. She's at fault in this too.

I knit my brows together. "Wait. Why did you ask me if I sold drugs when you talked to my mom?

He pushes out his shoulders. "I wanted to hear you say it. I'm still pissed. But." He briefly closes his eyes. "I've never had to live on the streets or worry about being evicted. Your mom told me the horror stories of when your father left you guys. I knew things were rough, man, but not that rough." Air expels from his mouth in a loud rush. "But next time, talk to me. Let me help you."

I'm choking up at Sam's reaction. I know he's got a heart of gold, but I expected a different reaction, like him moving out or telling me to leave. I push to my feet and cross the room in two strides until I'm holding out my hand to him. He takes it, but instead of exchanging a handshake, I pull him up and give him a hug. "Thank you, man. I promise you there won't be a next time. I'm going to tell Ray I quit." No sense in worrying about his threat to out me to Coach anymore. The cat is out of the bag.

* * *

RUN-DOWN AND BOARDED-UP BUSINESSES LINE BOTH SIDES OF THE streets as we pass by in my truck.

"I've never been in this part of town," Sam says, keeping his eyes peeled out the window.

"I grew up in a neighborhood similar to this in New Jersey," I say as I brake at the stop sign.

Sam shakes his head. "Sorry, man."

He and I have been talking for hours since Coach almost strangled me. I came clean about Donnie and what I did for him. I came clean that I was Wrangler. I told him about bumping into Emily in the hospital and then again the first night Ray threw me out on to the streets. By the time we got in my truck, Sam knew every sordid detail of the things I've done that I'm not proud of. He didn't judge. He listened, shook his head and nodded in spots, and in the end, he became my true brother, which is why he's with me now. He doesn't want me to face Ray alone.

I laugh out loud, as I turn the corner down the narrow road leading to Ray's shop. Streetlights blink on and off. Maybe that's a sign I should turn around and get the hell out of Dodge.

"What's funny?" Sam asks, still keeping watch like a soldier on patrol.

"You realize we both can get our asses beat to a pulp."

I didn't intend to pay Ray a visit tonight, but what the hell. I might as well get the bad shit over with, because come Monday, I need to decide what's next now that I don't have football. And then there's Emily. Just the thought of her gives me butterflies despite her betrayal. I'm so fucking livid she told her old man I sold drugs. But I shove her down a deep dark hole for now as I park outside Ray's shop.

I'll deal with one problem at a time.

A light spills out from a small square window, and a shadow is visible behind the glass.

"He's here," Sam mumbles with a hint of nerves.

I cut the engine. "Stay in the car. If I'm not out in ten minutes, take off and call the cops."

Sam's features twist. "Hell no. Where you go, I go." He climbs out before I can stop him.

I dig that he's got my back, but he doesn't need to get in the middle of this. "Sam." My tone is abrupt.

"Look, I've set up a safeguard before we left. If we're not back in the dorm room in three hours, then the file I've compiled on Ray so far will be sent to the cops. Besides, Ray already knows me. So, let's go." He puffs out his chest.

I should've known Sam would have our backs covered.

I chuckle. "Since when did you become all badass?"

"Since you got me into this shit."

We barely reach the door when it opens. The short stocky thug comes out. No doubt he saw us on the camera tacked to the garage above the door.

Stocky thug doesn't say a word. Just flicks his head, gesturing for us to come inside.

Sam tucks his hands in his pockets, and anxiety rolls off him in waves.

I strut in like I own the joint. No sense in showing I'm shaking inside. If I'm being honest, I'm worried for Sam, not me. Ray's the type of guy to use Sam to hurt me if I get out of line.

Ray is sitting at the table next to his shiny red toolbox. The black Aston Martin sits on display like he hasn't moved the expensive ride since I first met him.

"About time you showed up," Ray says, eyeballing me with intent. He's sporting his New York Yankees ball cap tonight, and his bling is shinier than ever as though he polished it for me. Ray studies my face. "What happened to you? Your opponent bash your face in on the field?" He grins like a bastard. "Pathetic playing. You went from great to bad in a matter of seconds." He moves his head back and forth as if he's a fucking expert all of a sudden.

"Fuck you, Ray," I say. "I'm done. There's your phone." I set the burner cell down on the table. Then I pull out my wallet. "Here's five hundred bucks. This should make us even." I throw the bills on the table.

He gives me a half-grin. "You got balls, quarterback. Five bills won't cover what you owe me. I told you I'd have a word with Coach, and you still owe me time."

"Tell Coach. I don't give a fuck."

Ray gnaws on the inside of his cheek, appraising me with dark eyes as he stands. Then he circles the table. "I had high hopes for you, Miller. I see your boyfriend knows what you do now." He smirks, and I grind my teeth to my molars.

Sam sticks out his chin. "Adam made a mistake, and he's dealing with it."

"Is that so," Ray says, grinning as though he's got a secret of his own. He steps closer to me. "How's that beautiful strawberry blonde of yours? Doesn't Emily love Molly?" He nods a few times, his grin expanding. "Yeah, she does." He glances past me. "José, what's that dude's name she fucks."

"Some prissy name like Zeek or Zach," Jose says with a chuckle.

I'm opening and closing my fists. "Bring her up again, and I'll—"

Ray gets in my face. "You'll what?"

I don't even take a breath when I ram my elbow into his jaw. His head bounces back then forward, and before my reflexes kick in, Ray's fist comes out of nowhere and connects with my nose. The damn thing bleeds for the second time today, and it's a miracle if it isn't broken. But at the moment, I don't feel a thing as the adrenaline rushes through me.

Lunging, I tackle him to the pristine painted floor and pin him down. Ray might come off as one scary motherfucker, but he doesn't have the weight I have or the strength. Plus, I wrestled one year in high school, and I've got a few moves.

"As of tonight." I dig my knee into his gut while holding his hands together in front of him. "I no longer work for you. Come near me, my friends, my family, or my girl and I won't hesitate to rat you out to the cops. Are we clear?" I doubt I scare him, but I seriously will call the cops even if doing so implicates me.

He laughs, glancing at something.

I toss a look over my shoulder and freeze.

Motherfucker.

José has a gun to Sam's head.

Standing, I lift my hands. "José, put the gun down."

Sam looks like a deer in the headlights.

"He will," Ray says, pulling himself to his feet. "When I tell him. Now just so we're clear." He sidles up to me. "Run to the cops and see what happens." Without warning, he punches me in the gut, winding me. "Touch me again, and you won't live to see how I fuck up all your loved ones."

I know it's not an idle threat. I know he's capable of just about anything, including murder as Sam pointed out.

I wipe the blood off my nose. "I no longer work for you. Accept that, and we have a deal."

He peers at me through hooded eyes for a few beats. "Agreed, but you still owe me, and I will call in a favor." Slowly, he nods to José, and he lowers his gun. Then Sam pivots on his heal and drives his fist into José's gut. "I might not carry a gun. But I'm not afraid to use my fists. Fucker."

I want to fist pump the air and shout hell yeah, but I'm not dumb enough to claim this as a victory. He let me go far too easily. I'm still indebted to Ray, and I know, without a shadow of doubt, that whatever favor he requests will be something dangerous and illegal.

José sneers at Sam. "Cute, nerd. But next time you try it, I'll put a bullet in your skull whether the boss man gives an order or not."

Nice of José to give Sam a backhanded compliment, but it's time we get the hell out of here before they decide to shoot us for real.

24

EMILY

I'm pacing outside Fleming Residence Hall, trying and failing to look inconspicuous. I've been here over an hour, and Adam is still a no-show. Sam isn't around either. I only know because I snuck into the building via the back entrance and listened with my ear pressed to their door for any signs of life. After ten minutes, it was clear no one was home, so I came back outside to wait for them.

Adam has ignored the ten calls I've made since I hung up on him earlier, so I'm guessing he's still pissed at me.

But I'm confident I can sweet-talk him around.

I'm not opposed to using my body if I have to.

But I'm fucked if I'm leaving here without Molly.

With every passing hour, I'm sinking deeper and deeper into a black hole, and my nerves are stretched tight.

Dusk is descending, and I fall back into the shadows, removing the silver flask from the pocket of Adam's oversized hoodie. I'd refused to give it back to him one time, and it's become a comfort blanket of sorts this past weekend. His scent lingers on the fibers, and I inhale deeply, wishing he was here. I lift the flask to my lips, taking a healthy glug of alcohol. I drained the vodka last night, so

I've moved onto gin now. It's Mom's special edition Tanqueray 10. She'll blow a gasket when she discovers it's missing, but right now, that's the least of my worries. My hand shakes as I screw the cap back on, pocketing the flask when a familiar truck pulls up to the curb.

Licking my lips, I tug the hood down and smooth a hand over my hair to tame the wild strands. With more confidence than I feel, I stride toward Adam's truck, ignoring the pulse beating wildly in my neck.

Sam spots me first, his brows climbing to his hairline. He nudges Adam, and his head swivels in my direction.

I suck in a shocked gasp. His nose is swollen and encrusted with dried blood.

"What happened?" I ask when I step in front of them. I lift my hand to cup Adam's face, but he steps back, out of my reach.

Rejection is swift and painful, and I swallow over the lump clogging my throat.

"Your father is what happened," Adam spits out. I've never heard or seen him so mad.

"My father did that?" My voice betrays my incredulity. *How the hell did my dad find out about us?*

"What did you think would happen when you outed me to him?"

"Adam." Sam's tone is cautionary.

"This is between Emily and me," Adam replies, eyeballing his friend as he levels a silent communication.

"Maybe you should take this conversation someplace else," Sam suggests, glancing all around him.

"Let me worry about that," Adam curtly replies.

Sam bobs his head, glancing at me briefly before walking off.

"Why are you here?" Adam asks, reminding me I have a goal.

"I need Molly," I whisper under my breath, risking a step closer to him again. He sidesteps me, and hurt batters me from all angles. But I battle on because I'm desperate and that's all that counts in this moment.

"You're a piece of work, Emily." He shakes his head, disgust washing over his face. "Did I mean anything to you at all, or was it convenient to date me for the drugs?"

"Why would you say that? You know that's not true! You know how I feel about you." A familiar fluttering feeling invades my chest, alongside the accompanying pressure, as anxiety runs rampant inside me.

"Save it for someone who buys your lies." He moves to brush past me, and I grab hold of his elbow.

"What the hell has gotten into you? Why are you being so hostile?"

He shakes my arm off. "I could ask you the same thing except I know why you've done it. You threw me under the bus for your precious Molly." His lips curl into a sneer, and it's not a good look on him.

"What the fuck are you talking about?" I yell, throwing my hands in the air.

He frowns. "Your breath reeks of alcohol, and you're a mess."

"I won't be a mess if you give me what I need!"

"Why the fuck should I help you after what you've done." His nostrils flare. "Thanks to you, I'm off the team. And I've blown it with the scout. My NFL career is over before it even began."

"You're off the team?" I inquire, curious but not as much about that as whether he's going to give me what I need.

A muscle clenches in his jaw as he drills a look straight through me. "I should never have gotten involved with you. I knew it was a disaster in the making, but I ignored my gut."

"Fine," I snap as acute pain punctures my heart. "I got the memo. You hate me and you're through with me. But you're still a dealer, and you have to sell to me."

He snorts out a bitter laugh. "I don't *have* to do anything, and I'm done with drugs. I'm out."

"What do you mean?" My voice borders on hysteria. Zach won't give me the time of day, and Adam was our only supplier. They are my only hope of scoring some pills. "You can't quit." My voice trembles, and my hand shakes as I contemplate what this means. "And you must have some pills left over? I'll take anything. Whatever you have. Just give me something." I grab hold of his sweater, pleading with my eyes. "Please, Adam. If I ever meant anything to you, you'll do this one last thing for me."

"If I ever meant anything to you, you wouldn't have sold me out like you did."

I have no idea what the hell he's talking about, but I don't care right now. I need Molly or something mind-altering to eradicate the memories torturing me.

"C'mon, Adam." I drop my hand down the gap between us, palming his crotch. "I'm sure we can come to some arrangement."

His jaw locks tight, and anger blazes in his eyes. "You're offering to fuck me for drugs?" He takes a step back, and a myriad of different emotions washes over his face. "Jesus Christ." He scrubs his hands down the front of his face. "What the hell happened to the woman I fell in love with? Was she ever real?"

"I tried, Adam. I really did, but I can't do it. I can't let reality in. I need something." I drop to my knees, uncaring if we have an audience as my fingers creep up his thighs toward the zipper on his jeans. I look up at him with my best puppy-dog-eyed expression. "I'm begging you, Adam. Please." My desperate tone matches the desperation etched on my face. "Please just give me something."

"Jesus, Emily." He pries me off his legs, lifting me up under my arms. "What the fuck is going on with you?"

"I told you, I just need a hit," I say through gritted teeth, losing my patience. "So, stop acting all fucking sanctimonious, and give me what you've got."

He shakes his head. "I don't understand how we got here. What did I ever do to deserve this?"

I'm clear out of patience now. "Are you going to fucking give me some pills, or do I have to go elsewhere?"

Steel replaces the emotion in his eyes. "You mean your one-time fuck buddy."

"Zach isn't the only one," I semi-lie.

He squeezes his eyes shut, shoving his balled-up fists into his pockets. "Just go, Emily. I don't have anything, and even if I did, I wouldn't give it to you so you're wasting your breath."

"Well, thanks for fucking nothing." I pin him with an ice-cold glare as I back away. "I'm glad I found out everything was a lie before I invested any more time in you."

"Right back at ya, baby"

I flip him the bird. "Screw you, Adam. I don't need you anyway."

I take off running before he can respond, uncaring what he has to say. My brain is churning, going a hundred miles a minute as I consider all my options.

Reluctantly, I trudge home a few hours later, still empty-handed and pissed beyond belief. My entire body shakes as my withdrawal symptoms crank up a notch. I dropped by Scar's place, but she wasn't there, and I've been blowing up her cell and Zach's, but both of them are giving me the cold shoulder. Zach I expect after his reaction last night. But Scar's siding with him rubs me the wrong way. *What about the fucking girl code? And our friendship?* And I'm still pissed at Zach for his treatment last night. I thought I was more than a fuck buddy to him, but he made it obvious that it was all about the sex. I thought he cared about me, but if he did, he wouldn't leave me suffering like this.

Asshole.

Bitch.

They can both go to hell.

I was stupid not to get Ray Diaz's number from Zach or sneak a peek at Adam's burner cell when he wasn't looking. If I had his number now, I wouldn't be in this dilemma.

It's dark as I navigate through campus, mumbling obscenities under my breath and vowing to make all my so-called friends pay.

A man emerges from Randolph Hall, the building on my left, instantly catching my attention. My heart rate speeds up as I recognize him.

Oh, God, no!

Goose bumps the size of melons sprout on my arms as I watch him descend the steps from Mom's office building, heading toward me. My feet are rooted to the ground, and I want to move, but I'm frozen. The overhead light illuminates his features in perfect clarity, and nausea swirls in my gut. His jet-black hair is threaded with strands of silver now, and his face is more lined than I remember, but the evil glimmer in his eye is still there.

Pain spears me on all sides, and a whimper flies out of my mouth. Tears cascade down my face, yet I'm still rooted to the spot.

The large watch on his wrist sends me traveling back in time, and my silent tears transform to sobs as I relive it again.

The breeze on my legs as he shoved my dress up.

My wide-eyed panic as he clamped a hand over my mouth so I couldn't scream.

The ripping sound as he tore my panties off me.

His rough fingers as they plundered my most intimate parts, untouched up to that point.

The creepy chills dancing up my spine when he called me sweeheart as if it was an act of intimacy between two loving partners.

The searing-hot pain tearing my insides to shreds as he forced his way inside me, taking what he had no right to.

I double over, clutching my stomach as the worst pain imaginable grips my insides.

It takes a moment to realize he's staring at me, his eyes shimmering in excitement, as he changes course, diverting from the parking lot toward this very spot.

Impending danger snaps me out of it, forcing my limbs to move, and I'm running, pushing my legs harder and harder as I desperately try to put distance between me and the monster who stole my innocence when I was just fifteen.

At the time, I thought it was a random attack.

That my rapist was a stranger and I happened to be in the wrong place at the wrong time.

But he was around the corner from my house when he attacked me.

And I see now what I didn't know back then.

This was no random attack.

He was no stranger.

My rapist was my mother's lover.

He was only there that night because he'd been with her.

If she hadn't been cheating on my father, if she hadn't brought her lover into our house, he would not have been in the neighborhood that night, and he wouldn't have violated me, and ruined me, the way he did.

Another whimper leaves my mouth at the sound of footsteps chasing me, and I push my limbs even further. "You can't outrun me, swee-heart," he hollers, his voice sounding way too close for comfort, and I almost have a coronary. Adrenaline courses through my body at an alarming rate, and sweat glues my shirt to my back. I want to look behind me. To see exactly how close he is to me, but I'm afraid of falling, so I keep running, praying someone appears before he catches me.

Because if he gets to me again, I understand this time I won't come out of it alive.

25

ADAM

I toss and turn, pounding my fist into my pillow while Sam sleeps soundly. Kicking the covers off, I pluck my phone from the desk near my bed, squinting at it with sleep-deprived eyes.

Three a.m.

Can't sleep.

Can't shake off Emily and our epic fight earlier. I'm still pissed. She thought she could flash her big blue eyes and bat her long lashes at me and I would give her Molly, especially after her old man went for me. We've never traded such harsh words, but I was livid, and the fact she only wanted drugs fueled the anger flowing through my veins. Don't get me wrong. A part of me wanted to bundle her into my arms and protect her from her demons, but the anger won out. I don't know what made her fall off the wagon, and it's driving me insane. For hours, I've been replaying the times we spent together, searching for clues.

Nothing weird, odd, or out of the ordinary jumps out at me. One day, she's flying high and we're confessing our love for each other, and the next, she's nowhere to be found.

I just don't understand it.

I let out an audible breath as I open the screen on my phone. Phoebe's picture greets me, and some of the tension in my shoulders loosens. I don't care how bad my day gets; I can always count on my sister to put a smile on my face. Even now looking at her pic. Her brown hair is up in a ponytail, and she's beaming from ear to ear, holding the very first jewelry kit Mom bought for her.

I swallow thickly. Mom won't be happy when she finds out I was kicked off the team, which means my scholarship is toast. Somehow, I have to plead with Coach and get back in his good graces. I might have fucked up my NFL dream, but I have to find a way to stay in school, and without the money to pay the expensive tuition, I need to do everything I can to keep my scholarship. The amount I made working for Ray won't even put a dent in the tuition. Besides, I need to keep that for Phoebe.

Sam is snoring steadily when a soft knock sounds on our door.

I pinch my eyebrows together. The only person I can think of who would be here at this hour of the night is Emily. Anger and frustration bubbles to the surface. She's relentless.

I crawl out of bed and quietly open the door a crack. The last time I answered, Coach shoved his fist in my face. As desperate as Emily is for Molly, I'm sure she'll try anything to get what she wants. Like kneeing me in the balls.

"Adam," Coach whispers, and I detect the panic in his tone.

I give him a wide berth as he steps in, searching the room as though he knew Emily would be here. When he doesn't find her, it's not relief but straight-up fear that shows on his face.

Suddenly, my radar is up, and stress cords the muscles in my shoulders into tight knots. "She's not here." I rub the back of my neck. "What's wrong?"

Bowing his head, he drags his fingers through his reddish-brown hair as he sits on my bed. Defeat oozes off him. "Emily didn't come home tonight. I thought she'd be with you."

I flick the switch, and the overhead light comes on. I squint for a moment as my eyes adjust.

Coach glances at Sam, but the dude isn't even stirring. He sleeps like the dead anyway.

I cross my arms over my chest. "We broke up. I'm sure Emily is with her friend Scarlett or Zach." Ten to one, she's passed out with them. My muscles tense further at the thought she's anywhere near Zach. I can't contemplate what they might be doing if they are together. My fingers dig into my palms.

"They're next on my list." He scrubs a hand over his jaw, worry etched across his face. "I'm worried. As much as I don't want her near you, I was praying she was asleep here. It's why I came to your dorm first." His Adam's apple bobs in his throat. "I need to find her before she does something stupid."

He just sucker punched me with his words.

He emits a tired sigh. "I didn't even get a chance to speak to her earlier. After I overheard her talking to you on the phone, I saw red. I should've stayed and talked to her. Instead, I charged over here to confront you. When I returned to the house, she was gone. And I haven't seen her since. What happened, Adam? She seemed to be doing so well."

He eavesdropped on our phone conversation? *Fuck.*

I feel like a legit piece of shit. I didn't even consider the possibility Emily hadn't blabbed to her father. I jumped to conclusions, and now, I feel like a complete bastard. And, because I was so angry, I didn't stop to consider she's in trouble. *Why else would she go off the rails?* Something happened to send her spiraling. Instead of coaxing it from her, I pushed her away.

I couldn't hate myself more in this moment if I tried.

Self-loathing is a bitter pill, but I force it aside, needing to keep calm in the face of her absence.

"Sir, you tell me. She wasn't high once when she was with me. Then a few days before our away game, something changed. I've been wracking my brain like a crazy man." I rub a tense spot between my brows. "I have no clue what happened to her." It can't be Weston Blakely because he's in jail. "Did something happen at home?" I know her mother doesn't care about her. Maybe, they got into a fight and her mom drove her over the edge.

"Not that I'm aware of, but I was gone all weekend. Her mother is usually busy with work, but I can't seem to get ahold of her either." His brow furrows deeper.

As frustrated as I am at Emily, I'm starting to freak out. We had our fight hours ago. "Let me put some clothes on. I know a place she might be."

He jerks his head up, and a small amount of relief shines in his eyes.

After I leave Sam a note, Coach and I drive to the warehouse where I first met Emily.

"Where are we going?" Coach asks from the passenger seat.

I wanted to take my truck. As distraught as he seems, I didn't want him driving although I'm a little on edge too. I feel like a schmuck, accusing Emily of ratting me out to her old man.

"A rave." It's early Monday morning. I'm not sure if the party has broken up. I was usually there at around one in the morning, not three, when I was selling drugs. For all I know, the place is shut down.

"Is this rave where you sold drugs?" he asks in an even tone.

I zip through the deserted streets, stopping at lights and passing homeless sifting through the city's trashcans.

"It's one of the places," I tell him. "Coach, I'm so sorry."

"Sorry isn't going to help Emily, son." He doesn't yell, but he sounds like he's already lost his daughter.

And my stomach knots into one big ball.

"Why did you do it, Miller?"

"I needed the money."

"If you needed money, why didn't you come to me?"

"I can't burden you with my problems. They're *my* problems. Not yours."

"I'm assuming you met Emily through the drug scene. How long has she been doing drugs?"

I puff out my cheeks, releasing some nervous energy. Honestly, I can't give him a straight answer. When I met her, she was using. Still, it isn't my place to tell him.

"Coach, I want you to know you've been like a father to me. I don't think I've ever told you that." I pause to collect my thoughts, glancing briefly at him.

His lips are pinched, and his focus is on the road like he's the one driving.

"I fucked up. I know you're upset with me more about drugs than losing the football game. But please hear me out." I don't want to open up if he isn't going to listen.

"I'm all ears."

I launch into the same story I told Sam about my past and what led me to return to selling drugs again. By the time we're a block from the warehouse, Coach is up to speed on my entire life.

"I get you want to support your family," Coach says. "But the drug business isn't the way to do that."

I did what I had to do for Mom and Phoebe, but I'm not about to argue the point. "One more thing."

"There's more?" His eyes open wide.

My pulse quickens. "I love your daughter, sir. From the moment I laid eyes on her, she stole my breath away. I did everything I could to get her to stop. And she did. She was happy." I bite down on my lip as we approach the warehouse. "We both were."

I park across the street, watching a couple stumbling out of the warehouse, but it's not Emily or Zach or even Scarlett.

Coach climbs out of the truck, stalking over to the couple. I rush to catch up with him. I doubt he wants to see the scene inside even if Emily isn't here.

I cover my nose as we enter, almost heaving up the contents of my stomach. The place reeks of sweat, sex, and piss.

Coach's head swivels around in slow motion. "For fuck's sake." He scowls as he drinks in the scene.

A couple to our right is on a dirty couch fucking like dogs in heat, panting and moaning, uncaring who sees. The girl has her head thrown back, and her black sweaty hair is stuck to her face.

Coach stiffens, shaking his head sadly as he looks around. "I've failed my daughter."

It hurts me to see the pain on Coach's face.

He walks around, with that same sad look on his face, pushing people out of the way, as he searches for Emily. It isn't hard either. Everyone is strung out and too wasted to care.

The lights flash on and off, a sign that it's time to stop fucking and groping and go home.

"Surely, no one is driving," Coach says under his breath.

Not sure how these people get home. And right now, I'm not concerned about them. I catch a glimpse of a girl with hair like Emily's in the far corner where I know Zach likes to hang out.

"Coach, I'll be right back." I don't wait for him to answer as I rush in that direction.

If Emily is here and she's fucking Zach, it will gut my insides out. But my bigger worry is I don't want Coach to find Emily in that kind of situation.

It's clear he's about to lose his shit. Not only that, I want to be the first to throttle Zach if I catch him fucking her. I might just throttle him anyway.

But Zach's hangout is empty, and the girl with the strawberry-blonde hair isn't Emily.

Coach meets me in the middle of the warehouse, shaking his head. Relief floods my veins that we didn't find Emily anywhere in the joint. But it's short-lived, because it means she's out there somewhere, and we're running out of options.

Fear as bright as the runway lights on an airport landing strip glistens in his eyes, and his helplessness is palpable. His phone rings, and we trade worried looks.

I hold my breath as he answers.

"What?" he snaps at his caller. "Where are you? Is Emily home?" There's a pregnant pause. "Then check her room," he shouts.

I flick my head at the exit. We should get out of here.

"Fuck," Coach barks in the phone. "She's missing. Well, if you weren't so busy with work shit, then you might notice your daughter is under a lot of stress. Did you piss her off?"

I can't hear anything President Parker is saying, but that fear on Coach morphs into rage.

"Give me Zach McCartney's address." Coach's jaw is stone.

By the time we get to my truck, he's punching in Zach's address on his navigation app. "Let's try Zach's next." He squirms uncomfortably on the seat. "They seem close, or they were at one time."

Nausea swims up my throat, but at this stage, I'd be happy if she was there. Once she's okay. I can deal with my emotions after. All that matters now is finding her.

We're halfway to Zach's when Coach's phone rings again. "Did she come home? Is she okay?" he immediately demands. "What?!" He roars. "Oh, fuck, no." Tears sting his eyes, and I damn near stop breathing. "Is she…" His shoulders collapse in relief. "Thank God." He lets a shuddering breath loose. "Okay. I'll be there as fast as I can." Coach throws his phone on the dash, the sound exploding in the small space.

He casts a pained look at me, and I stop breathing again. My foot slips off the pedal, and the truck swerves a little. Coach urges me to get a grip with his eyes, and I swallow back bile, clutching the wheel tight as I straighten the truck and beg my errant pulse to calm down. I don't know anything yet and I'm already panicking.

"Where to?" I choke out.

"Cypress Memorial, son, and step on it."

I whip my head at him, not seeing the stop sign up ahead.

"Adam! Pay attention."

I slam on the brakes, and the truck screeches to a painful halt. We're both thrown forward, but our seat belts do their job.

"What happened?" I'm trying like a motherfucker to stay calm. But my heart has other ideas, attempting to break free of my body. "Is Emily okay?"

"She overdosed." Coach's tone is crestfallen. "But she's still alive."

Motherfucker.

I gun the gas since the streets are desolate, but I'm barely holding it together. If she doesn't pull through, I will never forgive myself for how I handled things with her last night. There are so many different ways it could've gone down. I should've done more to help her instead of pushing her into Molly's arms.

The lights in the emergency room are burning my eyes as I storm in behind Coach fifteen minutes later or maybe it was five. Time has escaped me. How I got us here in one piece is beyond me.

And I'd been worried about Coach driving.

Coach rushes up to the information counter while I pace near the double doors. I squeeze my eyes shut and grab the back of my head with both hands.

Please. Please. Let Emily be okay.

Heels click on the tile floor, drawing my eyes up and down the hall.

President Parker surveys me as she approaches, her brows knitting together. "What are you doing here, Mr. Miller?" she asks in her usual professional-slash-condescending tone. "Shouldn't you be in bed?"

I refrain from an eye roll. Word on campus is she's a bitch to deal with. I haven't had the pleasure to be summoned to her office, but two guys in my dorm have. Both got their asses chewed. She threatened to revoke their scholarships if they got out of line again and pulled any other pranks on the admin building. Apparently, they TP'd the trees in front of her office, and she was not a happy camper.

"How's Emily?" I ask as Coach sidles up to me.

She regards me with ice-blue eyes. "She's none of your business."

"Cut the crap, Carole," Coach says. "Adam is her boyfriend. He's every right to be here."

My jaw hangs in a similar fashion to President Parker, but this isn't the time to decode Coach's feelings on my relationship. If we still have one, because we basically broke up last night.

"Now tell me about my daughter," Coach adds. "How is she?"

She loses her scowl for a split second. "She's in a coma."

Her voice is flat, and her tone contains no feeling whatsoever. Emily was right. She is a cold bitch. I would never hurt a lady, but every fiber in me wants to strangle President Parker until she's turned blue. The woman needs to be committed. "Do you not give a shit about your daughter?" I know the answer. I want to hear her say it though. "How can you stand there like a robot and tell us that?" I grab fistfuls of my hair. "What the fuck is wrong with you?!" I shout.

"Get some air, son," Coach suggests, clamping a hand on my shoulder.

Gladly. I walk away, seething, unable to breathe. But I don't go outside, because I want to stay close in case anything happens, so I head to the waiting room. The minute I drop down in a chair in the almost deserted room, my hands start to shake. I hang my head. Going over it all again. Beating myself up like I deserve. I could've helped her. I could've convinced her to tell me what was bothering her. I handled her and the situation all wrong.

I don't know how long I sit there, arguing with myself and praying for Emily, but by the time Coach appears, I'm stiff, tense, and distraught. I've chewed my nails down to nubs.

He takes a seat in the chair next to me, placing his hand on my back. "She's in a coma, but her vitals are stable," he says as though he didn't believe his wife when she told us.

Tears prick my eyes. "I shouldn't have pushed her away."

"Son," Coach's voice is calming, a stark contrast to his earlier demeanor. "I can see you love my daughter. And as much as I want to blame you, I can't. Emily has always had a self-destruct button."

"She was getting better," I mumble.

"I had noticed," he says.

"I should have done more."

"You tried, which is more than can be said for me and my wife."

Shock splays across my face.

"It's the truth. We failed her again." He closes his eyes momentarily. "Look, we've a lot to discuss. I'm not saying you're out of the woods with me yet, but I misjudged you last night." He sighs heavily.

"Emily needs you. Hell, I need you. I don't want to lose my QB. We still have games to play, and the team needs you on that field. For now, let's just hope and pray Emily comes out of this."

I appreciate his words, but football doesn't matter.

Emily does.

26

EMILY

My mouth is parched as I slowly come to. I blink my eyes open, wincing as a bright light hits my retinas like a punch to the face. My eyes close, and my body is like a dead weight as I attempt to move my arms.

"Emily!" Dad's gruff voice tickles my eardrums, and I force my heavy eyelids to open.

A warm hand envelops mine as my eyesight slowly adjusts to my surroundings. The white walls, regular beeping of a machine some-place behind me, and the elevated cot I'm resting on confirms I'm in the hospital. "Dad," I try to say, but something is obstructing my airwaves. Panic sets in, and my eyes pop wide as I try to move around in the bed.

Dad stands, pressing a button by my bed as he leans in close. "Relax, Emily. You're in the hospital. You're hooked up to a ventilator, and you have a tube in your mouth and a feeding tube in your nose." He runs his hand back and forth over my hair. "Don't panic, princess. I've buzzed the medical staff, and they'll come remove them."

The door swings open, and a man wearing a white coat over dark gray pants walks into the room, followed by a woman wearing a blue, cotton dress uniform. "Ms. Parker. It's good to see you're awake," the doctor says, smiling as he approaches my bed. "We're going to run a few tests, and then we'll remove both tubes. Try to stay calm."

A half hour later, I'm free of all tubes with the exception of the one in my hand, which is hooked up to a drip. Dad stayed with me the entire time, and it's the only reason I didn't fully freak out. "What happened?" I rasp. My throat is sore, and my voice sounds hoarse.

"Here, honey." Dad lifts a glass with a straw, holding it up to my mouth. "Remember what the nurse said. You need to take tiny sips."

I take small sips before pushing his hand away. Dad places the glass on the bedside table, pulls a chair in closer to my bed and sits down. He threads his fingers through mine. "I thought I lost you," he says, and I'm shocked to see tears pool in his eyes. "You overdosed, Emily, and you've been in a coma for three days."

It all returns to me in a flash, and my heart speeds up. The monitor behind me starts beeping wildly.

Dad smooths a hand over my clammy brow. "You're safe now, honey. And you need to stay nice and calm. I only just got you back."

Pain slices across my chest as everything jumbles in my brain.

"Why, Emily? Why did you do this? I thought we were rebuilding our relationship. That you knew you could talk to me about anything? If you were struggling again, you should've come to me. I told you no judgment, and I meant it."

Tears spill out of the corners of my eyes. "I'm in so much pain, Daddy," I finally ₁admit, because I can't shoulder this alone any longer. My lower lip wobbles, and big, fat tears plop onto my cheeks. "He… He…" Tears continue to pump out of my eyes as I struggle to draw enough air into my lungs.

Dad lets loose a string of expletives, and if I wasn't currently fighting to breathe, I'd find it funny. He presses the button, hollering for the nurse, and she comes racing into the room like her butt's on fire.

Ten minutes later, my breathing has returned to normal, but I feel sleepy. Which sounds crazy. Because I've just spent the last three days sleeping, but I can't keep my eyes open, and I drift into slumber.

When I wake again, Dad isn't alone.

Beautiful emerald eyes peer into my face, and my heart thumps eagerly in my chest. "Adam," I whisper.

"Hey, baby." He brushes his thumb along my cheek, staring at me with so much love I could cry. I'm shocked when his shoulders shake, his lip wobbles, and tears build in his eyes. He cups my face, examining every inch of my features as if he thought he'd never get to look at me again, clearly struggling to keep his emotions in check.

Dad rises. "I'll grab some coffees." It's his way of giving us privacy.

The door closes after him, and silence descends on the room. Adam moves his chair in closer to the bed, his eyes never leaving mine. The air is thick with tension, and I don't know where to start. His face is an open book. His distressed emotional state clear to see.

"I'm sorry," we both blurt at the same time, and it helps to break the awkward tension. Our light laughter echoes in the otherwise quiet room.

Adam laces his fingers in mine, and I curl my fingers around his, clinging to him. Delicious tingles emanate from our conjoined hands, shooting up my arm, and I drag my lower lip between my teeth to stop from moaning. Seriously, one tiny touch, and I'm melting into a puddle of goo.

His mouth pulls into a beautiful smile, and it brings tears to my eyes.

"Let me go first," he says, and his rich, deep voice sends shivers skating all over my body. He bends down, pressing a feather-soft kiss to my cheek, and it's everything. "I'm so sorry for letting you down, Emily."

I open my mouth to speak, but he places one long finger against my lips, silencing me. "I need to get this out."

I nod, and he continues.

"I was so angry at you because I thought you'd told your dad about us. About me dealing. I thought you cared about Molly more than me and you'd ratted me out when I refused to give you any. I know the truth now. That Coach overheard us arguing about it over the phone. That you didn't betray my confidence."

Shock settles on my face as the dots join in my head. I'd been too strung out when we last spoke to call him out on his accusation, but now, it makes sense.

"I would never have told him, Adam. I wouldn't mess with your future like that." My eyes go wide. "Oh my God. If he knows, does that mean..."

"It's all okay." He squeezes my hand. "I've told him why I did it, and he's giving me a second chance."

"What about the NFL scout?"

He shakes his head. "It doesn't matter. And we should be focusing on you." Air expels from his mouth in a loud rush. "You were clearly in a desperate way the night you came to me, and I should've helped you instead of pushing you away. I'm so sorry, babe. I've been beating myself up over it ever since. If I had only—"

"Stop." I grab hold of his muscular arm. "There is nothing you could've done to stop me. I needed to get out of my head, and if you didn't give me pills, I would still have left. I wouldn't have told you the truth either. I—" An invisible hand breaches my rib cage, wrapping imaginary fingers around my heart, squeezing. "It's not your fault, Adam." I grapple with my emotions, taking deep breaths to avoid a repeat of earlier. "It's not my parents' fault either. It's all on me."

For the first time, I see clearly. This overdose has opened my eyes. Shocked me into facing reality. Or maybe it's an epiphany. I see now what I've always denied. I've pointed the finger of blame at everyone. Especially my rapist. And my parents.

But the only person to blame is me.

No one forced me to take drugs. I did that by myself. I chose to bury the pain of my violation instead of opening up. I never even gave my parents a chance to help me. I doubt Mom would have helped.

Especially knowing her lover was the one who raped me. But Dad would have.

I know that now.

But I denied him the chance to help me.

I denied *myself* the chance to help me.

Choosing to hide from reality instead.

"I wanted to die," I whisper, looking Adam directly in the face. I'm not holding back anymore. I want him to understand everything going through my head. "I went back to that bar, Randaddys, and I sought out the same dealer, knowing what'd happened the last time would most likely happen again. I also knocked back several vodka shots. I needed to forget. To blank it all from my mind." I sniffle, but I push through the fresh bout of tears waiting in the wings. "I knew there was a chance someone would call an ambulance like last time, but a part of me hoped no one did." A messy ball of emotion clogs my throat. "I just wanted it to end, Adam. I just wanted the pain to go away." My voice wobbles.

The door opens, and my father steps into the room with impeccable timing. "Help me sit up," I implore Adam as Dad walks over to the bed with two paper cups in his hand.

Adam lifts me gently, propping my back against a heap of pillows. I clutch onto his strong forearms and press my lips to his. "I love you." I want him to know that before I unburden myself because there's a strong possibility he'll want nothing more to do with me.

"I love you too," he instantly replies, and I love that he's not afraid to admit it in front of my father. "And you're still my girl. We will get through this, and you can count on me."

I kiss him again, hoping he still feels the same after I tell him what I've decided to do.

"Ahem." Dad loudly clears his throat, and we break apart. When my gaze swings his way, he's smiling broadly. "As much as I hate to break this up, I believe you were about to explain, and I think it's long overdue, don't you?" He hands Adam a coffee, before sitting in the chair. Adam perches on the edge of my bed, sipping his drink.

I steel my spine, ignoring the tight chest in my pain. Admitting this is going to kill my father. And Adam too.

I don't know if there's any good way to tell them the truth, so I just rip the Band-Aid straight off. "I was raped when I was fifteen," I admit, watching all the color drain from Adam's and my father's faces. "I was coming home late after dance class. You were away at some football thing, and Mom told me to walk home because she was running late."

Bile collects in my mouth, and I gulp over the pain of that admittance.

She lied to me.

She let me walk home in the dark alone so she could fuck her lover in her marital bed.

And it hasn't gone unnoticed that she isn't here either.

She really doesn't care.

She would rather go to work than wait by her daughter's bed.

Whatever.

I've washed my hands of her now.

"A man jumped me around the corner from our house," I continue. "He dragged me behind the Marsden's abandoned property, injected me with something which I now believe to be GHB, and proceeded to rape me."

I'll spare them the gory details. Over the years, I've been in two minds over the fact he doped me up. I don't know whether it's a good or bad thing that I can't remember much of his assault because my mind was spinning. I remember his face as he loomed over me doing unspeakable things to me, but I don't actually remember much of the assault. Sometimes, my mind goes into overdrive imagining all the things he could've done to my body, and I wish I remembered so I could stop torturing myself over that aspect of it.

I've often wondered if that first taste of mind-altering drugs is the reason why I turned to them, mainly, to forget my pain.

"Why didn't you tell me?" Dad's anguished cry pulls me out of my inner thoughts. "I can't believe that happened and I didn't know!" He completely falls apart, his broad shoulders shaking as tears rock his body. "I'm so sorry, Emily," he cries. "I'm so fucking sorry I failed you."

There is something so heart-wrenching about a grown man sobbing so painfully. I pull back the covers, needing to comfort him. Adam slides his arms underneath me, carrying me over and positioning me in my father's lap.

We cry together, clinging to one another, and it's therapeutic.

When our tears finally dry, I let Dad put me back in bed, locking eyes with Adam as he carefully pulls the covers up over me. His eyes are damp and red-rimmed too.

Dad flops into his chair, scrubbing his hands down his face, and he seems to have aged in the last hour. I hate to add to his pain, but there's no point in telling him half the truth.

"He's back," I blurt out. "The man who attacked me."

"What the fuck?" Adam shouts, his spine locking up.

"I thought he was a stranger, Dad. All this time, I thought it was random, but it wasn't."

A frown creases his brow. "What do you mean?"

"I'm sorry you have to find out like this, but Mom's cheating on you."

He scoffs. "Your mother has cheated on me for years. That isn't news. We are married in name only."

"He's her lover, Dad. He must've been coming from our house the night he raped me, but I only just figured it out because he's back. Or maybe he never left. Maybe they have always been together," I add as the thought occurs to me. Just because I haven't seen him since the rape doesn't mean he hasn't been around. They could've been together all this time. A shudder works its way through me, and I'm cold all over.

"I've seen them together, and Sunday night he saw me," I continue explaining. "I was walking through campus, and he was coming out of Mom's office building. He chased me, and I was sure this time he wouldn't just rape me. Not now I know who he is, but I managed to lose him because a bunch of coeds came out of the dorms just before he caught up to me, and he took off."

Dad's chair slams to the ground as he jumps up all of a sudden. Adam and I turn to the door at the same time. Mom is standing in the doorway staring at me in shock. It's clear she's heard enough to know what we were discussing. Adam wraps his arms around me as he shoots daggers at my mother.

Dad grabs her into the room, shutting the door behind her. "Start talking, Carole. Who is this man, and where can I find him?"

"Where can *we* find him," Adam says. "Because there's no way you're going there alone. I've as much right to kill the bastard as you do." His jaw is wired tight, his words clipped as he speaks. I've no idea if Adam is speaking metaphorically or he actually wants to murder him. I wouldn't have any issue with that except I don't want to see my father or my boyfriend behind bars. I'd much rather that bastard rots in a jail cell than my loved ones.

Mom recovers fast. "No one is killing anyone. We all know Emily is prone to fanciful notions. This is another pathetic attention-seeking attempt on her part."

Dad grabs Mom around the throat, pushing her up against the wall.

"Dad!" I scream, not wanting him up on any murder charge. "Stop!" I get out of bed or try to, but Adam stops me, shaking his head while he clutches onto my hand. "Daddy, please. You're no use to me in jail, and, besides, we need her to tell us who he is."

Dad reluctantly releases her. "Start talking, Carole, or I swear to God I will fucking kill you!" His voice rattles with rage. "That bastard you're sleeping with drugged and raped our daughter! You've never been a mother to Emily, but you will do the right thing now, Carole. You will tell us who he is. You brought him into her life. You're the reason she was raped when she was fifteen!" His voice cracks, and I fear he's going to lose it again.

Mom glares at me. "Quit with your lies. How dare you cast doubt on his character! Richard is the most incredible man I've ever met, and he isn't capable of the things you're accusing him of." The vein in her neck visibly throbs. "He isn't a rapist! Why would he rape anyone when I give him whatever he wants in bed?!"

She's even more delusional than I thought. For an educated, intelligent woman, she sure is acting dumb.

Her eyes narrow as she redirects her glare in Dad's direction. "Besides, Richard would never be interested in her! I mean, look at her!" She waves her hands around. "She's a mess! She never dresses appropriately, hardly ever wears makeup, and she loves flaunting her boobs like a cheap whore. She has no class." She tilts her shoulders back, tipping her chin up. "And she's only a kid. He would never go for her. Especially not when he loves me!"

This time, Adam loses his cool. "You are batshit crazy, woman. He raped your daughter, and you see it as some kind of sick competition? And now you're, what, defending him? Protecting him?" His body trembles, and I hold onto his arm, keeping him by my side, so he can't do anything that'll get him arrested.

"What is his last name, Carole, and where can I find him?" Dad asks, folding his arms.

She pushes off the wall, smoothing a hand down the front of her skirt suit. Her usual mask goes on. "I'm not telling you. If you want to believe our daughter's lies, that's up to you. But I'm not listening to another word of this, this…sick fantasy of hers."

Un-fucking-believable. You know, I think my mother might be clinically insane.

She strides toward the door.

"If you walk out of here, you are dead to me," I call out, surprised at how calm I sound when I'm seething inside. "And I'm going to the cops. I'm making a formal complaint. He is not getting away with what he did to me." I should have reported it four years ago, but I was afraid to tell anyone. But not now. Now I want to ensure he pays for his crime and that he's locked up so he can't do this to any other girl or woman.

She stumbles momentarily, but she doesn't respond, and she doesn't look back as she exits the room.

Stunned silence rings out for a few beats. I slump against Adam, but he keeps me upright.

Dad turns to me. "We're better off without her."

I don't disagree.

"What do you want me to do?" he asks.

Murder the pair of them in cold blood? The thought pings in my mind but I don't articulate it. Seeing him brought to justice is what I want and *need* to draw closure.

I pin him with determined eyes. "Call the cops, Dad. I want them both arrested, and we've no time to waste."

27

ADAM

I pace outside Emily's house as Coach leans against his car. The front door is wide open, and I can see into the hallway. Packing boxes line the wall on one side. While Em's in rehab, Coach will be moving all their stuff back to their old home. The college is in the process of appointing a new president to replace Mrs. Parker, and whoever that is will be moving in here in due course.

"Adam," Coach says. "Calm down."

I throw my head back, glancing up at the clear blue sky. "I'm trying to." The warm morning sun feels good on my face. I inhale deeply, and the scent of fresh-cut grass tickles my nostrils. "I know she needs this, but I want to be there for her." I return my gaze to Coach who is placid as the fall air. "What if she feels alone and can't cope? Who will be there for her?"

Coach pops off his car and grips the sides of my arms. "Son, rehab is the best place for her. And she wants this." His hazel eyes are pleading as though I have a say on whether she goes or not. "The last time she went to rehab, her mother and I forced her to go. She wasn't ready then." He lets go of me. "This time, it's her decision. She's facing her demons head-on, and we need to fully support her."

I nod. And I'm proud of my girl even if I'll miss her like crazy.

"She has you and me," Coach continues. "And she'll be fine. You will too."

I'm not so sure about me. I'm just getting her back, and now, she'll be gone until at least Christmas, depending on her progress. *Man up* chants through me. He's right. Rehab is best for her. When she returns, I know she'll be that strong woman I've come to love.

I exhale heavily. "I'm cool," I lie. The time without her will be hard, but I have to be strong for Emily. Just like I do with Phoebe and Mom. And I can keep myself busy with football and my studies.

Coach chuckles as though he's been in my shoes. Maybe he has been although I can't imagine how he could love a woman like President Parker. She doesn't have a caring bone in her body. Hell, she doesn't have a soul or the nerve to stick around for her daughter. Two days after word broke about a rapist on campus, President Parker came under fire. The media descended in droves. If she hadn't already gone into hiding, there's no doubt she would've been removed from her position. A rapist on campus is ugly enough, but when you add the Wes Blakely scandal to the mix, her removal as president was inevitable.

Her lover fled with her, and there are international warrants out for their arrest. We learned from the cops when they questioned Emily in the hospital that Richard Bennett, the man who President Parker is in love with, is a serial rapist, and law enforcement in several states have been looking for him for years.

Coach rolls back his shoulders. "We've got football games to play. I need you focused on that."

I will do everything in my power not to let Coach or the team down again. I'm grateful he's given me a second chance, and I'll do my best to make him proud of me.

"You got it, sir," I say before sucking in a sharp breath when my eyes land on Emily.

My heart sputters. My body warms, and my mouth is suddenly bone dry.

She's more beautiful than I remember. Her strawberry-blonde hair is twisted up on her head in a messy bun. Her blue eyes are as bright and clear as the sky above.

She sashays down the porch steps with a suitcase in one hand and her purse in the other, locking eyes with me. Her lips feather into a ball-busting smile, and fuck if my dick doesn't notice her too. If that isn't enough, her look says *I want to fuck you but it will have to wait.* As tough as it's going to be, I'll wait for her forever.

Coach walks over and grabs her suitcase. "I'll give you two a minute." He puts her things in the trunk then runs into the house.

In two strides, we're standing toe to toe. "Hey," I say. The urge to touch her is strong, but I'm afraid if I do I won't let her leave. I'm even afraid to kiss her. The minute I do, I'll be a blubbering mess. I know this isn't a permanent goodbye. But my heart doesn't agree because it's beating out of my chest.

She peers up at me seductively, sliding her small hands up my abs. "Will you wait for me?" Her tone belies the smile she gives me.

I rear back. "Baby, of course, I'll wait for you. I'm not going anywhere." I have a feeling she's asking if I'll date other women while she's gone. I wrap my arms around her. "You're the only woman for me, Emily Parker. I don't want anyone else."

She trembles in my arms. "I'm a little scared and not about rehab. I want that. I'm scared things will be different when I get back."

I tip her chin up to look at me. "It will be. But it'll be a better life, Em. A new beginning. For you. For me. For your dad." I press my forehead to hers. "I love you, and I'm holding on to you forever."

A tear slips down her cheek as she lifts up on her toes and brushes her lips over mine. "My heart is yours, Adam Miller. And I'm going to miss you so much."

I crash my mouth to hers, my resolve shattering. I need one last good kiss to commit to memory so I can replay it over and over for the next several weeks while she's away. I will need that kiss to keep me going until she's back in my arms again.

The kiss is emotional and wild, both of us taking, tasting, and teasing until her dad clears his throat.

"We need to get on the road," he says. "We have a long drive ahead of us." Emily's rehab facility is in Florida. It's one of the best in the South with world-renowned doctors and support staff.

Reluctantly, I pull away. This is the hardest thing I've had to do. I've never had to say goodbye to someone I love.

As if she's in my head, she says, "This is harder than I thought." A tear slides down her cheek.

I swipe it away with the pad of my thumb and swallow thickly. "I know. But this isn't goodbye, and we'll see each other at Christmas." She fiddles with the green and yellow bracelet on her wrist, and my heart warms at the sight of my girl wearing the gift my sister made her. If I needed reminding of how special Emily is, that just proves it. I kiss her lips one final time before inching backward, distancing myself from her. Otherwise, I won't let her leave.

Coach guides her into the passenger seat. Once she's inside and the door is closed, he turns to me. "I'll be back in two days. Coach Price will whip you guys into shape." He smirks, as if he knows something I don't about his right-hand man.

As of late, Coach Parker and Coach Price have been getting along better than ever. At the beginning of the season, they argued a lot. But in the last few weeks, something has changed. I'm not sure what, but I like that they're not fighting. The guys on the team agree too. It's just awkward to be in the middle of their fights over plays.

Coach opens the driver's door as Emily jumps out of the car. "Em," he says, fighting a smile.

But Em has one thing on her mind—me. She jumps in my arms, her hands locking around my neck as she squeezes me tightly. "I love you more than you know." She presses her lips to mine. "And I'll be counting down the days until we're reunited."

* * *

THANKSGIVING COMES AND GOES, AND LIFE WITHOUT EMILY IS BRUTAL on my psyche. The first week she was gone, I couldn't sleep. I tried to keep my mind occupied with football, working out, classes, and Mom and Phoebe. Thank God for Mom and Phoebe although Mom wasn't thrilled when I told her what happened when Coach found out I was selling drugs. But she's glad it was Coach and not the cops. And she's thrilled I'm no longer selling that shit.

I'd like to say the second week, or third week, was better without my girl, but it wasn't. As each day passes, I get more and more antsy to see her. I often think about her comment how things will be different when she gets back. I know they'll be better, but as time presses on and she's not here, doubt niggles in the back of my mind. *Emily was worried I might not be here for her, but what if she changes so much she doesn't want me?*

I shove the question aside as Phoebe runs toward me, pulling myself back into the moment. She's dressed in Cypress's school colors, and she's so excited to see me play today.

"Hey, love bug." I lift her in my arms. She's been in and out of the doctor's office for the last month, battling colds left and right. But in the last few days, she's taken a turn for the better, which is the only reason why Mom brought her to my home game.

"Win big, Adam." She pecks me on the lips.

"Only for you," I say.

She shakes her head. "And for Emily too."

I roll my eyes. "For sure. Emily will be right here." I point to my heart.

"I'm wearing Emily's new bracelet I made for her." She waves it in my face. The beads have strawberries on them.

"What's with the strawberries?" I ask.

It's her turn to roll her eyes. "You always brag about her strawberry-blonde hair."

I let out a belly laugh as Mom touches Phoebe's arm. "Okay, let Adam go. He needs to get inside."

I snuck out of the locker room when Mom texted to let me know she was here. But I do need to go. We always have a team pow-wow before the game.

I kiss Phoebe on the cheek as I set her on two feet. Then I do the same to Mom. "I'll see both of you later. Sam should be inside." He also texted to let me know he's here.

Mom and Phoebe head to the entrance while I make my way back to the locker room.

I'm in my head, thinking of the game, the plays, trying to focus. I've given one hundred and ten percent since Coach let me back on the team. I poured my blood, sweat, and tears into every play, practice, and game for the last month, and my efforts have paid off. We've won every game since my pathetic play at Greenville when the Bears' scout was in the stands.

Nothing can stop me now.

"Adam Miller." A familiar voice makes the hairs on my arm stand to attention.

Motherfucker.

I let go of the handle on the door into the sports complex and pivot on my heel.

Ray Diaz is standing at the corner of the building with his hands in his pockets and a grin that sends bile to settle in my throat.

Ignore him. Go inside. Play the game.

As much as my subconscious orders me around, I'm rooted in place, unable to move, because he wants something, and even if I run, he'll find me.

His long legs eat up the space until I can smell his garlic breath. "I've come to collect."

Those words he spat at me that night in his shop blare in my head. *You still owe me, and I will call in a favor.*

I jut out my chin. "I don't have time for your shit."

He whips out his phone and taps the screen twice before shoving it in my face. I have to move away to get a clear view of what I'm looking at.

When I blink, my stomach lurches. It's a picture of Emily sitting outside in a courtyard with others around her.

Son of a bitch. The fucker is stalking her at rehab.

The blood drains from my system, and my tongue won't move as fear, pure and strong, consumes me.

My gaze drifts from the phone to Ray. "What do you want?" It's the only thing I can ask. Because getting riled up or punching him isn't going to do a damn thing.

Ray Diaz is like a cockroach who is hard to kill.

A slow grin emerges. "After this, we're square."

I cross my arms over my chest. "Well?"

He's enjoying seeing me sweat.

He glances around to be sure no one is listening. "I need you to throw the game today."

My jaw comes unhinged. "What?" Shock splays across my face. "No fucking way."

He pulls up another pic. This one is of Phoebe and Mom leaving the medical complex where Phoebe's doctor is located.

Suddenly, Ray, the cars in the lot, and the building start to spin. I stretch my arm out, holding onto the wall. "Are you threatening my family?" I know he is, but for some strange reason, I want to hear him say it.

"Throw it, Miller. Or else, they'll get hurt." I believe him too. After all, he's been accused of murder.

I angle my head. "So, you bet on the other team winning? But how do you know I'll comply?"

He shows me Phoebe's picture then Emily's. "It's simple. Play like you did against Greenville. That shouldn't be a problem for you."

Fucker.

"Oh, and I'll be sitting next to your mom and sister." He winks at me, whistling under his breath as he leaves without looking back.

I walk into the building with my hands shaking. My mind scrambles for a solution where I don't throw the game. The closer I get to the locker room, the more I debate my options. I promised Coach I would make him proud. If I play like I did in the Greenville game, Coach will know something is up. But I can't tell him either. He'll have Ray removed from the stadium, and doing so would only serve to anger Ray more, and he'll be sitting next to my family.

I squeeze my temples. I can't call the cops. It would be Ray's word against mine. Although Sam has some dirt on him, it's not enough to bury him with. Otherwise, I would've already taken action. Ray is smart. I'll give him that. He waited until the last minute to dump this on me so I wouldn't have time to involve the cops or Coach or anyone.

I could tell Coach to bench me. But then he'll ask questions, which will escalate into pissing off Ray. I can't risk Phoebe's or Mom's or Emily's life.

I can make it look like I'm having a bad day. After all, fans have seen me play like shit before.

* * *

THE TEAM IS BUZZING WITH CHATTER AS WE PILE INTO THE LOCKER room at halftime.

I plant myself on the bench, my mind stuck on what to do. Throw the game or not throw the game. I know Ray means what he says, but I'm still struggling with my decision.

Carter drops down beside me, his blond hair stuck to his head thanks to his helmet. "Nice job out there," he says. "We should win this too."

We're up by six points, and we still have the second half to play. But six points is nothing in football. One touchdown and our opponents are right back in the game.

"You've been quiet," Carter says. "What's on your mind?"

I shrug. "I'm good."

"Pfft." He knocks into me with his shoulder. "The last time I saw that brooding look on your ugly mug was in Greenville."

I have to hand it to Carter for being perceptive.

The chatter is so loud I don't hear when Sam comes into the locker room.

I jump to my feet. "How did you get past security?"

He rolls his blue eyes. "I've got connections." He points to the door. "Can I talk to you for a minute outside?"

The coaches are busy talking strategy and Coach Parker won't give us a speech for a few minutes. So I follow Sam into the hall and around a corner.

Once we're safely away from prying ears, lines dent his forehead. "Ray Diaz is sitting next to your mom."

I mash my lips together, grinding my back teeth. "I heard. You should go. Make sure they're okay." He can't do much, but I feel better if he's with them.

"Why is he here?" Sam asks, narrowing his eyes.

"Don't ask me to tell you, because the less you know, the better."

I can almost see the wheels churning in Sam's head. Then his eyes pop wide. "Ray wants you to throw the game? That's the favor he's collecting?" His voice is low. I'm not surprised Sam has jumped to the right conclusion. He's smart as a tack.

I nod.

"Don't, man. You've come so far with Coach. Don't screw this up."

"He's threatened to hurt Phoebe and Emily."

He lets out a frustrated sigh, wringing his hands together.

"I have to do this. I'm not risking their lives." I would die before I let anyone hurt them. I don't care if I go to jail. I don't care about football. They are what matter most.

He reaches out and grips my shoulder. "Play your game. Throw a bad pass. Make it look like you're trying, but *don't* throw it away."

I feel the deep crease form in between my eyebrows.

"I have an idea," Sam says with confidence.

"Sam," I warn. "Don't do something stupid to risk your life."

"Adam, when are you going to understand that I have your back? I will never let anyone hurt you or your family."

I gulp over the lump in my throat. I know Sam has that file on Ray. But I'm not sure that'll keep Ray from hurting Phoebe and Emily.

"Do *not* throw the game." He repeats, drilling a look at me. "Promise me." I slowly nod, and his eyes warn me to trust him, but he jogs off before I can probe him further.

I want to stop him from doing something reckless. But Sam never does anything without thinking through every detail and the consequences. Even when put on the spot like this. I hope I don't regret it, but I'm going to trust my buddy.

Since the second half started, I've been a ball of nerves. I can't say I've played well, but I haven't played like crap like I did during the Greenville game.

Coach takes a timeout. "Adam, what is wrong with you?! Did you not see Carter wide open for the pass?"

"Sorry, I'm not feeling well." Not a lie. The nausea has been eating at my stomach lining since Ray threatened me and my family. "I'll get it together."

"You better." Coach glares at me. "Two minutes left in the game. We're up by a field goal, and we have the ball. So, the game is ours to lose."

What he means is don't throw an interception or fumble the ball.

"Get your asses out there, and show me how proud I am of all of you," Coach shouts.

He won't be proud of me anymore when he finds out why I'm so distracted. I plan on telling him at some point after I know Ray isn't going to follow through on his threat.

I steal a look in the stands behind our benches. Phoebe waves excitedly. Mom smiles, and I notice Sam and Mom have switched seats. Sam is sitting next to Ray now.

Sam bows his head, his lips moving, as Ray listens to him.

"Miller," Coach barks.

I snap to and jog onto the field. The crowd is electric, clapping and whistling and shouting and stomping their feet.

I feel their energy as we get into position. Unless I deliberately screw up, we'll win. *Then what?* Ray has full reign to do his worst on my family. *I want to trust Sam, but what can he do?* He can't stop Ray. Sam's a computer genius. Ray's a thug. And in this situation, Ray has more power and strength over Sam.

I call out, "Set. Red twenty. Red twenty. Hike."

Once the ball is snapped, I seek out Carter who's ready to receive the pass on this play, and he's wide-open. I'm ready to release the ball when one of the linebackers rushes me, knocking me to the ground, and the ball falls out of my hand.

The linebacker picks up the ball and starts running for the end zone.

I want him to score that touchdown. And silently I egg him on. The play was clean, and I did nothing deliberate to fuck it up. If we lose, and I've done nothing illegal, then Ray gets what he wants and he'll leave my loved ones alone.

But my relief is short-lived when one of our guys tackles the linebacker.

One minute to go with the ball on the forty-yard line. Our opponents can run the play or attempt a field goal, which is three points, to tie the game.

I leave the field as our defensive line goes in.

Coach sends me a glare, but I ignore him as I drop down on the bench. All I can do now is wait. If our opponents score a touchdown and win the game, then I'm off the hook, knowing I didn't get sacked intentionally. Still, I feel like a loser.

But the minute proves to be nail-biting when the team decides to go for the touchdown, and just as the clock ticks down to zero, the quarterback launches the ball.

The entire stadium is on pins and needles, watching, waiting, and not breathing.

Our bench of guys is on their feet as the quarterback throws, the ball spiraling down toward the end zone where their wide receiver is open.

As the ball starts to drop, one of our guys comes out of nowhere and dives for the wide receiver and tackles him before he can catch the ball.

The crowd lets out an audible sigh before the Cypress U fans start cheering and shouting.

I drop my head in my hands, and it's the first time in my life I'm gutted we won a game.

28

EMILY

I keep my smile plastered on my face as I watch my father cross the visitor's room toward me, hiding my disappointment. We are only allowed one monthly visit, and as this is my first one, I was hoping Adam would come too. But Dad is alone, and I'm trying not to read too much into that.

Shutting off the outside world is part of my recovery plan, so my cell was taken the minute I stepped foot in the facility, and I haven't spoken to Adam since the day I left. I have no clue what's going on with him. *He promised me he'd wait, but what if he's already decided I'm too much trouble? What if he's already found someone else?* Thoughts of his strong arms around me is the only thing keeping me going some days, and the notion I might lose him eats away at me on lonely nights.

"Hey, princess." Dad bundles me into his arms. "How are you?" He holds me at arm's length, examining me closely.

"I'm okay," I admit, tugging on his arm and bringing him out to the sunroom. We claim seats in the far corner where it's quieter and more private. "It was really rough the first couple weeks but it's getting better." Going cold turkey is never easy, but this isn't my first rodeo. Besides, I can handle the physical symptoms.

The emotional ones are harder to deal with.

Especially now I'm openly talking about the rape and how it made me feel. My relationship with my parents, in particular Mom, is also a hot topic of discussion as it's all tied up together. Not that I'm blaming them, but if they'd been more present in my life, I might have told them about the rape when it happened. The fact I felt I couldn't only added to my pain, and I'm trying to work through all my feelings retrospectively.

I've lost count of how many times I've cried myself to sleep or woken up in a cold sweat after hideous nightmares.

"Your psychologist called me. She wants me to attend a therapy session with you next week."

I nod, knotting my hands in my lap. "She wanted a family session, but I explained about Mom." I peer into his hazel eyes. "I assume she's still missing."

Dad nods, crossing one leg over the other. "They were spotted in Europe, and Interpol went after them, but they managed to escape before they caught up to them. But, it's only a matter of time. They can't run forever."

"I can't believe she chose him over me," I admit, hating that a small part of me hurts. You'd think I'd be used to her rejection by now.

"Your mother has always been a vain, self-obsessed, selfish bitch. I thought I was doing the right thing marrying her when she got pregnant, but I would've been better taking full custody of you and raising you myself."

I lean forward, taking his large hands in mine. "Don't do that, Dad. It's not your fault. And I'm learning that there's no point continuously looking back except to examine any important lessons. To ensure we don't make the same mistakes."

A wide smile graces his mouth as he tweaks my nose. "There she is. My smart, insightful, compassionate, beautiful daughter."

I wrap my arms around him in a hug. Just because I feel like it and I can.

He clears his throat after a bit, straightening up, and I sit back in my chair, quirking a brow in silent question.

"Your psychologist said it was okay to talk to you about this. That it's better to be open than to continue to keep secrets. She believes you are strong enough to handle what I have to say."

Now, I'm curious. "Okay. Let's hear it."

He runs a finger along the collar of his shirt, looking decidedly uncomfortable.

"Dad." I place my hand on his knee. "No judgment. Just support. Remember?" I pat his knee. "It works both ways, so spit it out."

"I'm gay," he blurts, and I almost fall off my chair.

"Uh, I wasn't expecting that," I truthfully admit. "But it's cool." It's not a lie. I mean, I'm shocked as shit, but I've always been a firm believer you should stay true to yourself. "Have you always known?"

"Yes, but it took me a long time to accept it. I spent a lot of years in denial."

"So how did you end up with Mom?"

He sighs, rubbing a spot between his brows. "I dated a lot of women while I was in denial. Your mom was like no other woman I'd met, and she intrigued me. Of course, I didn't realize she was a cold, calculating bitch until it was far too late." He leans forward a little. "But I don't regret it, because she gave me you, and you're the most precious thing in my life."

"I love you too, Dad," I choke out. "And I want you to be happy. You've spent years miserable with Carole. You deserve some love in your life. And I don't care if that's with a man. I honestly don't."

Tears well in his eyes. "You mean that, honey?"

I pat his knee again. "One hundred percent, Dad." I wet my dry lips. "So, eh, is there someone you love?"

He nods, and his eyes light up. "It's Tom. Tom Price."

"Coach Price?" I squeak.

"Yes." He shuffles nervously on his seat. "Your mother wasn't the only cheater in our relationship." At least he has the decency to look ashamed. "I've been involved with Tom, on and off, for the last two years. It's one of the reasons I've been so distracted. Why I didn't notice what was going on with you." Remorse is etched upon his face. "But I promise that's not going to happen again." He cups my face. "You come first, Emily. You will *always* come first."

"It's okay, Dad. I can share you." Tears prick my eyes as a giggle travels up my throat.

"You're genuinely okay with it?" His hopeful expression warms my heart.

"Absolutely, and I look forward to getting to know him better." Tom attended a couple of my mother's stuffy dinner parties the last couple years, and he always went out of his way to talk with me. Guess now I understand the interest. "He's pretty hot," I add, grinning. "Way to go, Dad."

"Okay, *now,* I'm uncomfortable." He says it, but he's grinning too, so I don't think he's *that* uncomfortable.

"Where's Adam?" I ask, unable to hold the question in any longer. "I hoped he'd be with you."

"He had planned to come, but there's been some developments with Ray Diaz, and he's helping the cops with their investigation."

My jaw drops to the floor. "Come again?"

He scrubs a hand along his smooth jaw. "Ray tried to blackmail Adam into throwing the game last weekend, and he almost succeeded." His jaw tenses. "He threatened you and Phoebe and Adam's mom."

A shocked gasp leaves my mouth, and my stomach churns unpleasantly.

"But Sam rode to the rescue. He trapped Ray into admitting his plan, and he recorded it on his cell. Turns out, he'd already hacked into Ray's computers and was building a case file. Sam wanted to wait until he had enough to destroy him." Dad laces his fingers in mine. "But Adam couldn't wait any longer. Not after Ray threatened the lives of his loved ones, so he took the evidence Sam had collected and went to the cops, making a full confession."

"Oh my God." I pull my hand to my mouth, and terror has a vise grip on my heart. "But they'll arrest him for selling drugs!"

Dad shakes his head. "Honey, relax. It's not like that. Although they've asked him not to leave town while they investigate, they aren't going to arrest him. He'll get off with a warning in exchange for testifying against Ray."

Tears spill down my cheeks. "I can't believe he turned himself in like that. What about football? And school? He'll lose everything."

Dad cocks his head to the side. "Not necessarily. He's suspended from the team, which may or may not be permanent. I've put in a good word for him, and we'll just have to wait and see what happens. But even if he loses his place on the team and his scholarship, he still has the things that are most important." He cups my face again. "His health. And you and his mom and sister." He presses his forehead to mine. "It took me a long time to realize that the people in your life are the only things that matter in this world." He smooths a hand down the back of my hair. "Adam is smarter, because he's already figured that out."

A sob bubbles up my throat.

"Everything will work out, Emily. I have one of the best attorneys working with Adam, and I'll do everything in my power to help him. For now, you concentrate on *you*, because he's going to need you to support him, and I know you want to be there for him."

"I do, Dad." I sit back. "I love him, and I'm not going to let him down."

* * *

It's two days before Christmas, and I'm going home. The doctors are delighted with my progress, and they've agreed to release me provided I continue the program on an outpatient basis at a treatment center closer to home. I'm standing in the lobby, waiting for Dad to arrive, when the most beautiful sight appears in my line of vision.

Tears immediately sting the backs of my retinas, and I drop my bag, blinking repeatedly, wondering if my eyes are deceiving me.

His happy smile sends a rush of butterflies racing around my chest, and my legs are on the move before I've even registered the motion. Adam runs toward me, and we collide in a tangle of arms and lips and tongues, and I could happily die in his arms and not regret a single thing.

We kiss and kiss, over and over, and I'm sure we're drawing attention, but I have zero fucks to give. Since Dad's last visit, two weeks ago, when he came for the family therapy session, I've been on edge, worrying obsessively about my boyfriend. Dad told me his attorney was negotiating a deal, but I've had no word since, and I didn't know if it was successful.

"I love you," I rasp when we finally pull our mouths apart. "And I've been so worried." I clutch onto his beefy arms, loving the feel of his muscles under my fingertips. "What happened?"

He reels me into a mammoth hug. "I love you too, and I'll tell you in the car. Just let me hug you. I've missed holding you."

We hug it out for ages, and I relish every single, delicious second of being back in his loving embrace.

When we break apart this time, he takes my hand, walking over to where I left my bag and my case, lifting them one-handed as if they weigh nothing. "You need to sign anything or say goodbye to anyone?" he asks.

I snuggle into his side. "Nope. I'm all done."

"Let's get the hell out of here then."

"So, tell me what's going on?" I ask, a few minutes later when we're situated in Adam's truck en route home.

"Tell me about you first," he says, reaching across the console to brush my cheek. He hasn't stopped touching me, and I love it. "Are you doing okay? You sure you're ready to come home now? I don't want you rushing the decision because of me."

I lean up on my knees, tracing my fingers over the velvety-soft hair at the nape of his neck. "I'm doing really good." I smile at him. "I've still a long way to go, and I'm going to need regular therapy, probably for the rest of my life, but for the first time in years, I feel hopeful for the future. Hopeful that I've turned a corner and put the past in the past."

I rest my head on his shoulder. "You're a big part of that, but I've got to do this for myself, so the answer to your question is yes, I'm ready, and no, I'm not rushing it on your behalf." I lift my head, pressing my lips to the underside of his neck, closing my eyes and inhaling his masculine scent. "I can't believe you turned yourself in," I admit. "Why did you do it?"

He chews on his lip for a second, and I watch absently out the window as we join the line of traffic in the left lane of the highway.

"I did it to protect everyone I love," he finally admits, pressing a kiss to the top of my head when I turn around to face him. The traffic is at a standstill, so he puts the truck in park. "Even if I had thrown the game, Ray would never have stopped. He would've always been a threat."

"And?" Because I'm sensing there's more.

"You were dealing with your demons, so it was time I dealt with mine."

"But football and your scholarship…"

He shrugs. "It's all still up in the air, but they don't matter in the bigger picture. Maybe I was never meant for the NFL." He kicks the engine into gear as the traffic starts moving. "The choices I've made have led me here so I can't blame anyone but myself."

"I'm sorry." I lift my head, palming one side of his face. I'm having a hard time not touching him too.

"Don't be, babe. It's all good. Ray is going down, and I won't have to do any time." He kisses my temple. "As long as Phoebe is healthy, Mom isn't stressing out, and I've got you by my side, I can conquer mountains."

I beam at him, reaching around to peck his lips quickly. "You have me, Adam. You're stuck with me now." I laugh, and he grins. "Nothing or no one is taking me away from you again."

29

ADAM - EPILOGUE

Breathing in the salt air, I stand on the balcony of our condo and watch the waves crash along the shore. The sun is barely up, but I love this time of morning when the world is still asleep and it's peaceful and quiet. I often get up before Em and come out here and let my mind wander.

It's been a year since I lost my scholarship and left Cypress University behind. Mom was proud I did the right thing in turning myself in, but I scared her out of her mind at the same time. Since I cooperated with the police and testified against Ray, I didn't do any jail time. Ray Diaz wasn't so lucky. Sam had compiled a bunch of evidence on him, and the cops dug up a ton more, so he's now serving twenty-five years for trafficking Molly.

I take in another dose of salt air when soft hands come around me from behind as Emily presses her body flush with mine.

"Mornin'," she says in a sleepy voice. "You're up early again."

I cover my hands over hers. "You know I love it out here."

Emily and I now live together in a small beach town on the Gulf Coast of Florida with the ocean outside our building. After the scandal involving President Parker and then the news about my arrest, we were the main topic of conversation around campus. It was clear we couldn't stay there, and we both wanted a new start.

"You know what I love in the morning." Her hand slides down to grab hold of my cock. "I want the pleasure machine." She starts rubbing her hand up and down my growing erection.

"You just had *the pleasure machine* a few hours ago." I tease, remembering our marathon session last night when we fell into bed. I'm certainly not complaining. I can stay in bed with Emily all day or all week and not come up for air.

She lets go of me, and I spin around and freeze.

She's shimmying out of her thong with a sultry grin as her big blue eyes hold me prisoner. When her thong is on the floor, she peels off her tank top until her beautiful naked body is on full display. No one can see her. We own a corner unit, and a tall stone wall separates our balcony from our neighbor's.

I drink her in inch by inch as my cock becomes painfully hard behind my board shorts.

Holding her bottom lip hostage between her teeth, she crooks her finger. "It's time you kissed me good morning." Her hand slips down to cup her pussy. "Here." She dashes inside, giggling.

Fuck me.

I chase after her to find her sprawled out on the bed with her legs open and her finger circling her clit.

I shake my head, pouting. "That's mine." I growl, crawling onto the bed and hovering over her.

She giggles again. "Well, take what you own then."

I chuckle. When Emily wants something, she wants it now. *Who am I to disappoint her?*

Flicking her hand out of the way, I trail my tongue along her inner thigh, licking a path along her slit before my mouth closes over her swollen clit.

She moans loudly, a sound that sends an electrical charge to grip my balls. I will never get tired of hearing her moan or seeing her squirm or listening to her screaming my name.

She buries her hands in my hair, tugging me closer as though she can't get enough. I flatten my tongue, licking then sucking, and settle into a rhythm.

Her breathing grows shallow, her moans louder, and her hold on my hair tightens until the muscles in her legs spasm, and she comes apart, her body quaking.

I move over her until my hands are on either side of her head, and I pepper kisses along her neck, jaw, and then her mouth. "Good morning, gorgeous."

She answers by grabbing my dick, pinning me with a sultry smirk as she guides me inside her.

I hiss and my eyes roll back in my head. She's tight and wet and gripping my cock like we were made for each other. "Holy fuck." Every time with Em is even better than the last, and I don't think I'll ever grow tired of fucking her.

Grinning, she wraps her silky legs around me, digging her heels into my ass. "Ready, big guy?"

"I was ready the day I met you." No fucking lie. I lower my head and capture a nipple between my teeth as I thrust in and out of her hot pussy. Slow at first, wanting this to last forever, but forever is right around the corner when Emily squeezes my cock so snugly I swear I see a bright light flash before my eyes.

I become a man on a mission, rolling us over until she's on top, and what a vision she is. Her hair is messy around her face, her cheeks are flush, and her tits. Fuck me. Her nipples are as hard as rocks, jutting proudly, silently beckoning me. I jerk upright, sucking on them one at a time, before she pushes me flat on the mattress. Planting her hands on my chest, she pivots her hips, rocking into me with a seductive smile that's almost enough to send me over the edge.

I shape her hips with my hands, guiding her as she grinds her hips back and forth, squeezing my cock, trying to suck the life right out of me.

And it feels so fucking good.

Like always.

No woman could ever excite me as much as Emily.

She's my addiction.

A craving I experience every minute of every day, and I can't get enough.

In a flash, she's on her back and I'm on top, and I'm not going to last. I reach down between us, frantically rubbing her clit until I feel tension building inside her again. Her pussy hugs my cock, jerking a little, and I know she's close. "Come with me, baby," I demand, pinching her clit hard. She screams, thrashing underneath me, and my balls tighten as lightning zips along my spine. One last thrust and my release hits, bringing me to new, dizzy heights. I groan so fucking loud I'm sure I woke the nice old lady next door.

I hold my hips still, my cock throbbing inside her, as she says, "Good morning, stud."

And what a morning it is.

We spoon for a few minutes, until both our heart rates have returned to normal, and then I climb off the bed, pulling her with me. "Shower." I have to be at work in an hour.

She pouts. "My dad won't be mad if you're late."

I arch a brow. "Fuck if he won't. Your dad cracks the whip."

Coach Parker and Coach Price opened up a private coaching business for kids in middle and high schools, shortly after we all moved here, and I'm one of their employees. We work with kids to teach them basic skills or help the advanced kids refine their skills for most sports, but we concentrate a lot on football and baseball.

I amble into the en suite bathroom and turn on the shower.

Emily follows me in. "I'm taking Phoebe shopping after I get out of class this afternoon."

I smile at my sister's name on her lips. I love how close they've become, and it only makes me cherish Emily more. When we decided to move, I wanted Mom and Phoebe to come with us. At first, Mom didn't want to intrude on Emily and me, but we both convinced her it would be better, especially when we found a place that is conducive to Phoebe's CF. Apparently, salt air is good for people with cystic fibrosis. So, we found a quaint beach town on the Gulf Coast of Florida. And Phoebe loves living here. She has good days and bad days, but the good ones far outweigh the bad.

As for Mom, she now manages a swanky hotel on the beach, and she's making more money than she ever has. Plus, she has top-notch medical insurance to take care of Phoebe's medical expenses.

In a funny way, everything turned out for the best. Although, it was hard to see it like that at the time everything went down. I knew going to the cops and fessing up was the right thing to do, but it doesn't mean it was easy. I was pretty depressed when the university decided not to reinstate me to the football program and took away my scholarship.

But I've been talking to the football coach at the local university in town—the one Em attends—about trying out next year. It's too late now, since they're three-quarters of the way through their season, but he seems eager to explore options. It's a lower division team, but if I could continue my degree program, play ball, and get to see more of my girl during the day, it's a win-win. It means I would have to amend my plans vis-à-vis my job, but Em's dad is flexible, and I know he wouldn't stand in my way. As far as the NFL, I haven't counted them out. As Mom tells me, "Anything is possible."

And I know that's true because the beautiful woman before me is proof dreams do come true.

I snake a hand around my girl and tug her to me. "Thank you."

She pinches her eyebrows. "For what?"

"For loving me. For loving Phoebe and my mom."

She places a hand on my face. "Adam, you're my world. And so is your family." Her tone is full of love and devotion. "And you are all so easy to love."

"You are my forever, Emily Parker." I press my lips to hers.

I don't know how I got so lucky, but I believe the challenges we faced in the last year have shaped our lives for the better, and in looking back, I wouldn't change a thing.

30

EMILY - EPILOGUE

I scan the online article to see if it offers any new insight, but it's just a rehash of the now-familiar story. Mom and Richard Bennett were finally apprehended in Italy a month ago, and they were extradited to the US, where they now await trial. Dad and I will both have to testify, but I want my day in court. The police investigation was thorough, and they uncovered victims across three different states spanning twenty years. That bastard won't ever see the light of day again, and I want to ensure I play my part in his conviction.

It will be tough, but I'll have Adam and our families and friends there to support me, so I know I'll do it. My therapist believes it's important to help me move forward with my treatment, and I know she's right.

"Whatcha reading?" Adam asks, slipping onto the bench beside me and handing me a homemade gin cocktail. Tom, aka Coach Price, is a bit of a cocktail connoisseur and anytime they invite us here to their beautiful house for dinner, we sample a variety of delicious drinks. Although, I always stick to one, two, tops, because alcohol is a slippery slope to drugs for me, and I like to avoid temptation.

"Just another article, but it doesn't mention anything about the

Weston blackmail." The cops found some interesting material on Mom's computer. It seems Weston had discovered Mom's affair, and he had photos of her and Richard in intimate poses. He was blackmailing her into supporting his efforts to date me, and she was also lodging considerable sums into his bank account every month. If Sam had kept digging, he most likely would've discovered this before the cops, and it all would've made sense earlier.

I couldn't understand why until the cops divulged the Blakelys are virtually bankrupt. It seems Weston wanted to marry me purely to gain access to my trust fund. But my grandfather was a shrewd man and I won't get the cool million he left me until I turn thirty. Either Weston didn't do his due diligence correctly, or he was hoping Mom would continue bankrolling him.

At least it went some way toward explaining why Mom was always defending him and pushing him on me.

"I'm sure it'll come out in court," Adam says, draping his arm around my shoulder. I lean into him, inhaling his comforting masculine scent that always reminds me of home.

I shut the feed down and switch off my cell, taking a sip of my drink. "Man, this is so good." I peer into the glass. "Is that cucumber?" I inquire, quirking a brow.

"It is." Tom sits down on the bench across from us, smiling warmly. "Serving Hendricks gin with anything but cucumber would be sacrilegious!"

The door pings, echoing faintly throughout the house. "Adam!" Dad hollers, lifting his sweaty head from the outdoor grill. "Will you get that?"

"Sure. It's probably Mom and Phoebe." Adam kisses my cheek before walking across the large well-maintained back yard and disappearing into the house.

"You've got a good one there," Tom says.

"I know. So do you," I add with a cheeky wink.

He raises his drink to mine, and we chink glasses. "Touché, pretty lady."

I grab hold of his hand and squeeze. "I'm so happy you and Dad decided to move here with us."

"It was a no-brainer," Tom admits, tilting his face up to the sky. Although it's December, the weather is always warm here. "CU was pressuring your father to resign after the scandal with your mom and then Adam, and we both wanted a clean slate to start a proper relation-ship where no one knew us and would judge us." He squeezes my fingers. "Besides, your dad could never be apart from you. You're his little girl and the center of his universe."

"He means the world to me too. You both do." And it's the truth. Tom has been easy to get to know and even easier to love. He makes my dad happy and he's gone out of his way to form a relationship with me. For the first time ever, I know what it's like to have two loving parents, because that's what our family is now.

"Emily!!" Phoebe's adorable voice resonates from behind, and I get up, turning around and opening my arms as she flings herself at me.

I hug her tight, loving her as if she was my own flesh and blood. I've always wanted a sibling, and now I have one in Adam's sister, and I couldn't be happier. She is the sweetest girl, with the biggest heart. She's a teenager now, having turned thirteen recently, and I know Megan, Adam's mom, is happy she has someone else to confide in as she enters puberty.

"Don't hog our girl," Megan says, winking at me. "I need me some hugs too."

Phoebe lets go, rushing around the long picnic table to hug Tom.

"It's so good to see you," Megan says, enveloping me in her arms. "We have to start up a weekly dinner get-together again."

"I know," I agree, extracting myself from her embrace. "But it's difficult with the hours you work, and my studies, and Adam's job and classes."

I hated that Adam had to drop out of college. I was lucky I got to transfer to the local university and that I'm getting to complete my degree. Dad got a generous settlement in the divorce from Mom. Something she couldn't contest as she was AWOL with her fugitive lover, so the courts granted him a sizable sum in her absence. He paid my college fees and offered to cover Adam's fees too, but Adam refused to accept it.

Dad already bought us a condo. Something I was opposed to, but he wouldn't take no for an answer. And him and Tom offered Adam a job with a generous salary and benefits so I understand why Adam couldn't accept anything else.

He's a proud man, and I'll never criticize him for that.

He enrolled in a local community college, and he's taking some business classes, hoping he can assume running the business side of Dad and Tom's company, as they would much rather focus on the coaching and consultancy side of the business. Adam is up for the challenge and looking forward to it.

The door chimes again and this time Dad leaves his grilling station to welcome the last of our guests.

Sam and his new girlfriend Marie, and Carter and Rachel step outside with matching smiles. Phoebe rushes to Sam, jumping into his arms. He loves her every bit as much as Adam and I do, and she worships the ground he walks on. Honestly, he can do no wrong in her eyes.

"Hey, hoss." Carter slaps Adam on the back as Rachel leans in to hug me.

"How was the trip?" I ask.

"Not too bad," Rachel admits as Tom wanders off to rustle up more cocktails. "I thought the traffic would be crazier with the holidays approaching, but it wasn't."

Carter pulls her into his chest. "We left at the right time is all."

"I saw highlights from the game last weekend," Adam says to his buddy. "You fucking nailed it, dude."

Carter shrugs casually. "It's still not the same without you."

"I miss you guys too," Adam admits, "but I'm loving my job and classes, and I have the girl of my dreams sleeping in my arms every night, so I'm good. And I've been talking to the football coach at the local university about possibly joining the team next year. His son comes in for coaching."

Carter's eyes light up. "That's awesome."

"It's a lower division school, smaller program," Adam says. "But it's still football."

I snuggle into Adam's side, stretching up to kiss him. Honestly, he's the most romantic man I've ever met. Not a day goes by when he doesn't tell me he loves me or show me in some way. I constantly pinch myself because some days I can't believe this is my life.

It hasn't been all plain sailing. I've had some hard days. Stressful times when I've wanted to turn to drugs so badly, but I haven't succumbed because I have a great support system and a wonderful life that is not worth risking.

I hug Sam and Marie next. "Thanks for coming. We hate that we don't get to see that much of you anymore." Sam is in his senior year at CU, and Marie just started junior year, same as me. We're all busy so we don't get to meet up as much as we'd like.

"We're hanging around for a few days before heading to my parents' place for Christmas," Sam says, clapping Adam on the back.

"Cool," Adam says. "You can come to ours tomorrow night for dinner. Emily makes some mean ribs, and her shrimp salad is to die for."

"Food is just ready," Dad shouts. "Grab a seat."

Tom and Adam push the two picnic tables together while I help Dad put the grilled meats on two platters, carrying it over to the tables alongside the salads and breads we prepared earlier.

Conversation flows naturally around the table, and the cocktails are in plentiful supply. Hours pass, and we remain outside, chatting and laughing, even as daylight turns to nightfall. Megan and Phoebe leave first when Phoebe's eyelids grow droopy, and it's clear she needs her bed.

We wave Sam and Marie and Carter and Rachel off before helping Dad and Tom clear the dishes. They offer to let us stay, and I'm down with it, but Adam insists we leave, promising we'll stay over Christmas night instead.

When we return to our condo, Adam surprises me by tugging me out onto the beach instead of going inside. I don't fight him on it. I'm happy to follow him wherever he wants me to go.

The beach is deserted at this hour of night, and we plonk down on the sand on our favorite spot, wrapping our arms around one another as we stare out at the sea. The water is placid, lapping gently at the shore a few feet away. A balmy breeze tosses strands of my hair around my face as a contented sigh leaves my lips.

"Everything okay, baby?" Adam queries, tucking me in closer to his side.

"Everything is just peachy." I look up at him. "I love you, Adam."

He kisses the tip of my nose. "I love you too, Emily. So fucking much."

He delves into the pocket of his jeans, producing a small black box. My eyes startle in surprise. "It's not what you think it is," he says, popping the lid. I stare at the small emerald ring in awe. "And I didn't want to give this to you on Christmas Day and have everyone rush to assumptions." He removes the ring, sliding it on my index finger. It's a perfect fit, but that doesn't surprise me, because Adam is so thoughtful and I'm sure he grabbed one of my rings to get the right measurement.

He pulls me onto his lap. "Because the day I propose will be a very special day with no expense or thought spared."

"Propose?" I almost choke on my words.

Not going to lie.

I've thought about us getting married, and we've talked around it before, but Adam has never been this direct.

"I want to marry you, Emily. I want to tie myself to you in every way possible." He nuzzles his nose into the crook of my neck. "But I want to be worthy of you, and I want to be able to provide for you, and I'm not there yet."

I place my hands on his shoulders. "You know none of that matters to me. I would live in a shack and be blissfully happy as long as you were with me."

"I know that, babe, but I've watched my mom struggle my entire life, and I don't want that for you. For us." He pulls my hand to his mouth, pressing his lips against my new ring. "I want to give you the world. For our children not to want for anything." He kisses my lips and his tender devotion melts my insides. "But I want you to know how I feel. To know my future lies with you. So, this ring is a promise of what's to come, and a commitment of my devotion to you."

"I didn't think it was possible to love you any more than I already do, Adam Miller, but I've just discovered it is." I plant a feather-soft kiss on his lips. "Thank you for all the ways in which you love me. And I want you to know I'm committed to you too. I want to grow old and gray with you. There is no one else on this earth I love more than you."

And as we cling to one another, staring at the sea, with the promise of forever confirmed between us, I am happier than I have ever been, and I know this is only the start.

The end

IMPORTANT HOTLINES

If you need to talk to someone regarding sexual assault, please call the National Sexual Assault Hotline in the US at 800-656-4673

If you need to talk to someone regarding drug addiction, please call the SAMHSA National Helpline in the US at 1-800-662-HELP (4357) or check out this resource site for a list of national and local support services - https://addictionresource.com/addiction-and-rehab-hotlines/

If you need to talk to someone regarding suicide, please call the American Foundation for Suicide Prevention in the US at 1-888-333-AFSP (2377) or via email: info@afsp.org

If you need to talk to someone regarding any mental health related illness, including PTSD, please contact Mental Health America in the US at 1-800-273-TALK (8255) or visit: https://www.mhanational.org/get-involved/contact-us

If you live outside the US, please contact your local support services.

SIOBHAN DAVIS

USA Today bestselling author **Siobhan Davis** writes emotionally intense young adult and new adult fiction with swoon-worthy romance, complex characters, and tons of unexpected plot twists and turns that will have you flipping the pages beyond bedtime! She is the author of the bestselling *True Calling*, *Saven*, and *Kennedy Boys* series.

Siobhan's family will tell you she's a little bit obsessive when it comes to reading and writing, and they aren't wrong. She can rarely be found without her trusty Kindle, a paperback book, or her laptop somewhere close at hand.

Prior to becoming a full-time writer, Siobhan forged a successful corporate career in human resource management.

She resides in the Garden County of Ireland with her husband and two sons.

You can connect with Siobhan in the following ways:

facebook.com/AuthorSiobhanDavis

twitter.com/siobhandavis

instagram.com/siobhandavisauthor

amazon.com/author/siobhandavis

bookbub.com/authors/siobhan-davis

S.B. ALEXANDER

Bestselling author **S.B. Alexander** writes young adult and new adult romances that span the sub-categories of coming of age, sports, paranormal, suspense, and military fiction. Her writing is emotional, angsty, and character driven. She's best known for The Maxwell and The Maxwell Family Saga series.

S.B. or Susan as she likes to be called is a navy veteran, former high school teacher, and former corporate sales executive. She's a lover of sports, especially baseball, although nowadays you can find her glued to the TV during football season.

When she's not writing, she's a full-time caregiver to her soul mate of twenty-one years who got a bad deal in life when he was diagnosed with ALS. Her motto: "Life is too short to waste. So live every moment like it's your last."

You can connect with S.B. Alexander in the following ways:

facebook.com/sbalexander.authorpage

twitter.com/sbalex_author

instagram.com/sbalexanderauthor

amazon.com/author/sbalexander

bookbub.com/authors/s-b-alexander

goodreads.com/sbalexander

BOOKS BY SIOBHAN DAVIS

KENNEDY BOYS SERIES

Upper Young Adult/New Adult Contemporary Romance

Finding Kyler

Losing Kyler

Keeping Kyler

The Irish Getaway

Loving Kalvin

Saving Brad

Seducing Kaden

Forgiving Keven

Summer in Nantucket

Releasing Keanu^

Adoring Keaton*

Reforming Kent*

STANDALONES

New Adult Contemporary Romance

Inseparable

Incognito

When Forever Changes

Only Ever You

No Feelings Involved

Second Chances Box Set

Reverse Harem Contemporary Romance

Surviving Amber Springs

RYDEVILLE HIGH ELITE SERIES

Dark High School Romance

Cruel Intentions

Twisted Betrayal

Sweet Retribution^

Jackson*

Sawyer*

ALL OF ME DUET

Angsty New Adult Romance

Say I'm The One *

Let Me Love You*

ALINTHIA SERIES

Upper YA/NA Paranormal Romance/Reverse Harem

The Lost Savior

The Secret Heir

The Warrior Princess

The Chosen One

*The Rightful Queen**

TRUE CALLING SERIES

Young Adult Science Fiction/Dystopian Romance

True Calling

Lovestruck

Beyond Reach

Light of a Thousand Stars

Destiny Rising

Short Story Collection

True Calling Series Collection

SAVEN SERIES

Young Adult Science Fiction/Paranormal Romance

Saven Deception

Logan

Saven Disclosure

Saven Denial

Saven Defiance

Axton

Saven Deliverance

Saven: The Complete Series

^Releasing 2019

*Coming 2020.

Visit www.siobhandavis.com for all future release dates. Please note release dates are subject to change based on reader demand and the author's schedule. Subscribing to the author's newsletter or following her on Facebook is the best way to stay updated with planned new releases.

BOOKS BY S.B. ALEXANDER

THE MAXWELL SERIES

Upper Young Adult/New Adult Contemporary Romance

Dare to Kiss

Dare to Dream

Dare to Love

Dare to Dance

Dare to Live

Dare to Breathe

The Maxwell Series Boxed Set 1

The Maxwell Series Boxed Set 2

Dare to Kiss Coloring Book Companion

Dare to Embrace^

THE MAXWELL FAMILY SAGA SERIES

Young Adult Contemporary Romance

My Heart to Touch

My Heart to Hold

My Heart to Give

My Heart to Keep*

STANDALONES

New Adult Contemporary Romance

Unforgettable

Breaking Rules

Rescuing Riley

THE HART SERIES

New Adult Romantic Suspense

Hart of Darkness

Hart of Vengeance*

Hart of Redemption*

THE VAMPIRE SEAL SERIES

Young Adult Paranormal Romance

On the Edge of Humanity

On the Edge of Eternity

On the Edge of Destiny

On the Edge of Misery

On the Edge of Infinity

The Vampire SEAL Collection

^Releasing 2019

*Coming 2020.

Visit http://sbalexander.com for all future release dates. Please note release dates are subject to change based on reader demand and the author's schedule. Subscribing to the author's newsletter or following her on Facebook is the best way to stay updated with planned new releases.